I0612463

THE BLACK RIFT

MICHAEL G. THOMAS

First published in the United Kingdom in 2014 by Swordworks Books.

ISBN 978-1-911092-42-1

Typeset by Swordworks Books
Printed and bound in the UK & US
A catalogue record of this book is available from the British Library

Cover design by Swordworks Books
www.swordworks.co.uk

THE BLACK RIFT

MICHAEL G. THOMAS

PROLOGUE

The Interstellar Network has always been something of a misnomer. It reality it was neither just an interstellar system, nor even a network. After the discovery of the Anomaly that joined Alpha and Proxima Centauri, it became clear that the theory of the Einstein–Rosen Bridge could be turned into a reality. A generation later the truth of the Anomaly would be uncovered, as would the principle of using the bridge to connect stars together. This long-range network led to the exploration of the Orion Nebula. A lesser-known fact was that with the invention of the technology, an entire transport and communication network could be created between moons and planets. By the time of the Biomech War there were Rifts connecting planets, moons, and stars in more than a hundred locations.

A Concise Guide to Interstellar Travel

Kha'Dri, Taxxu, Uncharted Space

The cocoon opened up, its long metal tendrils pulling apart to reveal the machine within. It was large, pale in color, and smooth to the point of translucence. The space around the cocoon was bathed in a pale blue light that barely penetrated the mist floating around the shapes. The machine creaked from an eternity of stillness, limbs and plates groaning under the pressures of movement. Finally, it pulled itself out and in front of the waiting group of smaller Biomech warriors. It looked at them, as a tiger would look at its prey.

"You have woken me, why?"

Three of the small machines moved close and then knelt before it. The mist was still thick, but the other cocoons were now visible throughout the vast enclosure. One of the machines made a gesture with both arms. A dull grinding sound announced the movement of the walls around them. One by one, the dark walls fell away, and behind them was nothing but the blackness of space. The thick, transparent material gave the impression of glass, but from this angle it was impossible to detect. The great machine watched a planet off to the right. It was a dead, black husk of a world.

"Answer me."

The nearest Biomech beckoned in the other direction. The machine hissed as it looked at the shapes to its left. It began to speak and then stopped. The imagery of the Great Seal, partially active and surrounded by ships intrigued him.

"The rebels have been located, and the Great Seal has been breached. We are ready to awaken the ancestors. You will lead our return."

"And the enemy? Has the plan been successful? Are they smashed, weak, and terrified?"

The machine took a step back with its body low.

"They are scattered, weak, and their remaining warriors are fighting our lost kin."

The machines fell silent for almost a minute. The larger of them watched the Rift and its broken, swirling colors with fascination. Hundreds of ships waited nearby.

"Show me."

Shapes flickered and holographic models of planets and star systems flashed by. None stayed for more than a few seconds. Finally, the imagery stopped to show a single world.

"This is a new world, the capital of the race that defeated our efforts to split them. Who are they?"

"The humans. They are a violent but resourceful race. Their greatest warriors fought in a rebellion that defeated our Exiles' efforts."

The images appeared again and flickered past views of battles, spacecraft, and even people. Finally, it stopped to show a single human. His form was muscled and scarred. He was in a prison cell and in the process of escaping.

"This one? He is the one that brought them victory?"

The smaller Biomech lowered its form again.

"Yes. The Exiles captured many leaders of the ancient races. We have taken prisoners from the Byotai, Helions, and the…"

"No," said the machine in a firm tone that oozed venom, "This one can rally them, can inspire courage and imagination. Where is he?"

The Biomech made a clattering sound from in its chest and then rose to its full form.

"He is here, along with the other prisoners. We have completed the indoctrination started by the Exiles. He is ready to fight alongside our soldiers."

The ancient machine moved away from the cocoon. At first it was slow but quickly gained confidence. It twisted and flexed, getting used to its body for the first time in centuries.

"Our army, is it ready?"

"Yes. The factories finished production a long time ago."

It pointed to shapes nearby. They were black, still, and dormant.

"Eighty million of our manufactured warriors. We used all remaining biological material to create them. They are the last and the greatest of their kind. Each is the match for ten Thegns. They sleep and wait for their orders."

"And the Defeated?"

The machine shuddered at the name.

"The Ghost Warriors wait to redeem themselves."

The machine looked back to the images of the humans. Pages of information flashed by on each side. Finally, it looked to the smaller Biomechs.

"Fear will weaken our enemies, and they fear nothing more than the darkest parts of themselves."

It pointed to the image of the man.

"Use the prisoners, use all of them. Let the enemy feel true fear."

"And the human?"

"He has been tested. His skills are…unexpected. In our simulations he has matched or bettered our own commanders."

"That is not surprising, not to me. You failed last time, why would you expect to perform better this time?" said the ancient machine.

The smaller Biomech said nothing and remained low and silent.

"I want this human to lead your Ghost Warriors."

He said those words with an icy bitterness.

"You will sow terror, and behind them we will follow with our entire might."

The imagery changed to show the hundreds of dormant vessels orbiting the current position. They were almost impossible to see, their forms only showing as they blocked out the view of distant stars.

"So, do the indoctrinated know of our legions?"

"No," answered the shorter Biomech, "The Despoilers are ready with their legions on board just as ordered, and the Defeated wait with the last of their ships and warriors. We saw no need to tell the indoctrinated of our true strength."

"This is their chance for redemption. Send the signal."

The machine stretched its limbs and then looked about at the other cocoons. There were dozens of them.

"What of my brothers, the last of the great ones? Have they been woken before today?"

"No. They wait as ordered. We woke just you, the youngest of the Ancients."

Those words seemed to bite deeply. Of only six remaining, he was certainly the youngest, as well as the one with least seniority. The machine looked to the cocoons of its older kin. They were clearer now, as most of the mist had faded. There were only six and one lay empty, covered in dust.

"Good. Let them sleep. They cannot be woken from their long rest until we can guarantee them a new life."

It looked back to the vastness of space and to the crackling energy at the collapsed Rift.

"I am awake, and I can never return to the long sleep. This is our one chance to return our light to the galaxy."

The machine twisted to face the cocoons.

"We shall awaken them all once Helios burns, not a moment earlier."

CHAPTER ONE

The banishment of the Biomechs is one of the greatest events in the history of the Helions. Songs and stories had been extended and embellished so many times that the final struggle turned into something akin to averting the Apocalypse. With the Black Rift finally opened, even if just for a matter of hours, everything changed. What lay so many thousands of light years away? Were the old worlds of The Twelve now teeming with half biological and half mechanical life? Or would their planets be barren, stripped out husks, now populated by corpses and tombs? There were few in the Orion Nebula that truly wanted to find out, with the overwhelming majority wanting to keep the Spacebridge closed. What did the Biomechs want, and why were they so intent on the destruction of every populated planet they now encountered?

Evolution of the Biomechs

Prometheus Seven Outpost, Prometheus Sector

Prometheus was a unique place in the Alliance. Its fiery world was inhospitable to life, yet over the generations multiple structures and engineering sites had been built directly into its surface. Only since the Interstellar Network had been activated had the location started to settle. In the past, its dangerous world and the surrounding storms could cut a ship in half, making it best avoided. Location, environment, and difficulty to navigate had made Prometheus the most popular place to find criminals, pirates, and illegal traders in everything from narcotics to slaves. Today, Prometheus was a changed place, perhaps the most important location in the Alliance.

There was more to this sector than just the planet. In orbit around the burning red world was the massive Prometheus Seven space station. Like the planet, the station was one of those places that always seemed to be in the middle of great events. It had played a vital part in the Uprising, as well as being the source of so many Spacebridges. Though built long ago as a massive trading platform and habitation base, it had changed use over the years. Few could have imagined it would have been used to conduct arms fairs, acting as a floating hotel, and more recently, the control-system for the local Rifts leading back to Terra Nova; as well as the massive long-range Rift to T'Karan space and beyond. What had been constructed as a civilian trade station had now transformed, as had the entire Prometheus sector. The days of piracy, organized crime, and secret gangs were long gone; replaced by science, industry, and interstellar politics.

The station controlled the most important piece of real estate in the Alliance, the single long-range Rift built by man. Its position and capabilities meant the Prometheus Seven Outpost now controlled access to the Orion Nebula and the Alliance territories far off on the other side of the galaxy. All of this was possible because of its position alongside the Rift entrance, and being the single massive power supply that opened and maintained the bridge.

"Come on, people, I need data. Who are they?" Colonel Pierce asked.

He lifted himself up from his seat and shook his head angrily. Tensions were high in the Alliance, but today was different; made clear by what he had just seen outside. Something much more serious was going on than simple trade or exploration. Deep inside the station waited thousands of personnel, monitoring their stations and watching the multiple screens. At the same time, the low level sirens played their song in every nook and cranny of the monstrous facility.

"And for God's sake shut the damned sirens off. I am well aware that a fleet of unknown Alliance ships has just arrived right on our doorstep."

Two-dozen blue flashes marked the engines of three squadrons of fighters that had just launched. It was too little, too late, but none of them had expected this kind of hostile action, certainly not this soon.

"Colonel, none of the ships are on the official registry. The names are all from decommissioned vessels."

"Sir, they are charging their capacitors."

The Colonel raised an eyebrow at this news. Most ships constructed now were equipped with rapid firing coilguns for air defense, and particle beam weapons for their primary guns. These capacitors matched the configuration of weapons used decades earlier.

Railguns, this is some old tech.

"Very well. Open the gun ports and get us some air cover. Nobody threatens my station."

Little appeared to change, but on one of the screens he could see green lights activating as each of the station's many gun ports opened to reveal their weapons. He had never given this order before, and normally there would be at least two warships guarding the Rift.

Is it accident or design that these guys arrived just as our escort left?

Colonel Pierce rubbed his chin while looking at the imagery. He didn't believe in chance, and his current predicament was far from enviable. The station was large and well protected against incursions by pirates and the like. A concerted assault by the flotilla waiting nearby could be deadly and result in the deaths of hundreds of people. The six ships circled the station warily, like big cats circling a wounded beast. No two were alike, with each of them coming from different parts of the Alliance. The average age was forty-three years, yet each had made the journey between planets without an issue.

Of the six, only one seemed particularly equipped for offensive operations. The ship was flagged as ANS Amazonia, but the station computer identified its silhouette and signature as a private security transport. He could only assume it had been reequipped as a military cutter. The largest vessel was a former Marine Corps assault transport, the same kind of craft that had taken entire regiments of marines into action in the past. Her name had long been forgotten to all but her crew, but the new name that ran down her flank was ANS Terra. The ship was constructed of a number of rotating sections of various sizes, and each of the rings housed multiple batteries of railguns. It was hardly the grand fleet that was currently engaged in massive fleet actions in the Helion System, but it was still six ships commanded by a man keen to prove himself.

"I need information. Their transmissions keep saying they are Alliance, but you're telling me they are not on the computer?"

He looked back at the mainscreen and pointed at the antiquated assault transport.

"Zoom in on that one."

The display shuddered from the optical lenses altering focus and angle until the ship came into view. The first thing that was clear to the Colonel was the coloring and markings. Each of the ships was different, but the red stripes of the Alliance designated them all as friendly. Without the mark, they might have just as easily been traders or pirates. He was looking for more than that, though.

"The paintwork is standard gray. The font is right, but where are the escorts? Why no more recent ships?"

The question was more to himself than to his officers. As he watched, he noticed a series of hatches opening up along the ship, and his stomach groaned in anticipation.

"Colonel, they're opening their gun ports."

Colonel Pierce shook his head angrily.

"Get our birds into position, and send out a mayday. This is getting out of hand."

He then looked toward where the pulsing Rift was normally positioned. Right now it was down, for fears the enemy might try and use it to sneak forces between star systems.

I need help.

"Get the Rift open, and send the prerecorded emergency transmission to the Admiral Jarvis Naval Station."

* * *

ANS Terra, Prometheus

The military ships changed their erratic courses and drew

themselves up into a static column. In this new position, each ship was able to place its entire flank alongside the station at a fixed distance of just eleven kilometers. Although this increased their target area, it also allowed each of them to target the maximum number of weapons. One by one, the guns and missile systems locked onto their targets and waited for orders. A pair of shells flew past the nose of ANS Terra at a distance of no more than a hundred meters and vanished off into the darkness. It was clearly a warning shot, followed up by squadrons of fighters screaming in and out of the ships' formations in an intimidating pattern.

"Get me a videostream with their captain, right now!" demanded Captain Jerome.

The young man was fresh from the Naval Academy on Terra Nova. His accent was sharp and crisp, and easily betrayed his wealthy upbringing on the capital world. He was short, thin, and pale faced, but his expression was of utmost calm and control. The effect on the crew following the gunnery was electric. As soon as the weapons had been detected, the mood had shifted from excitement to anger.

"Captain, their commander is already connected. He wishes to speak with you," said the communications officer.

Captain Jerome watched the mainscreen with a growing scowl showing on his face. He reached for the intercom and pulled it close to his mouth. The louder his voice became, the more saliva seemed to drip from the corner of his mouth. The image of Colonel Pierce appeared on the screen.

"This is sovereign Alliance territory under the control of Admiral Churchill of the Alliance Navy. Close your gun ports and state your business. Failure to comply will result in your vessels being boarded and disarmed."

Captain Jerome's eyes tightened at the words. "Increase power, I want this message burned into their consciousness. Every single ship and facility in this sector will see and hear this message."

He looked over to his own officers and gave them a nod before returning to the mainscreen.

"I am Captain Jerome of the Alliance warship ANS Terra. By the order of Magister Populi Harrison and the legitimate government of Terra Nova, I order this station to deactivate its weapons. Admiral Churchill, Admiral Anderson, and previous Chairman of the Joint Chiefs, General Rivers are all wanted for war crimes. The purchase, training, and transfer of private security forces are tantamount to treason."

He then lifted a secpad and dragged a document from the display to the communication screen. The data automatically overlaid his image so that anybody listening could see.

"I have orders from Magister Populi Harrison to retake control of this station and to bring back these war criminals for trial. The Rift to T'Karan will be permanently deactivated until such time that President Harrison deems it safe to reopen, and all private security units will be stripped of their weapons and shipped to their colonies of origin."

He swallowed, enjoying every minute of his little speech.

"We are living in a critical time, and the actions of rogue commanders are putting the entire Alliance at risk. We have already intercepted two transports on their way to you from Hyperion. Each of these was carrying Biomech mercenaries, for what we can only assume is an attempt to subvert the authority of the Terra Novan government."

His lip quivered a little as he said the final lie. The Jötnar were unlike the Biomechs in so many ways, yet to him and many on Terra Nova, they were nothing more than animals. He looked to his communications officer and pointed at him.

"Put up the feed from Mars. Quickly!"

The officer fumbled before starting the videostream. It was a mixture of imagery that showed containers being unlocked on board starships around Mars. Several Alliance officers, including General Rivers were present, as was hundreds of Thegn soldiers. A Jötnar warrior marched alongside them while barking orders.

"Magister Populi Harrison has been shocked by this footage of collaboration between Alliance officers, Jötnar, and the Biomech monsters, and we can only assume that these officers were compromised during their illegal activity on Mars. Therefore, as of today, the Prometheus sector comes under the direct control of Terra Nova and its senior commanders. High Command has dispatched new officers for this station, as well as a research team for Prometheus."

Again, there was no response, and all it took was the shaking head of his junior officer to send him off into a rage. He pointed at his executive officer, as though it was his fault the station was refusing to cooperate.

"Either they close their gun ports and let us board, or by God, I will open fire!"

The officer lifted his hands in mock defense.

"I…the station, Captain. It's out of my control."

It was the face of the Colonel on the space station that seemed to be causing the most trouble for Captain Jerome. Even as he waited for a reply, he was sure he could see amusement in his opposite number's expression. He walked toward the console in front of the ship's tactical officer. The smaller screen showed a wide schematic of the space station as well as the small swarm of fighters.

"Are our weapons ready?"

The young man nodded nervously.

"Yes, Sir. Main guns are charged, and our secondary weapons are tracking their fighters."

"Good. Load Sanlav rounds into the guns, just in case."

He then looked back to the mainscreen.

"Captain Jerome, if that is your name, we have seen the imagery from Terra Nova. Alliance officers are being detained without charge throughout our military facilities and at training bases on a dozen colonies. We can only assume this is an ongoing coup by President Harrison and his allies, and until the situation is resolved on Terra Nova, we are declaring all orders from High Command as illegal. We will continue our actions to protect the Alliance until this crisis has been resolved."

"Captain!" said the tactical officer.

Both of them looked at the magnified footage of the station. A pair of large-caliber guns had rotated about and was now facing them both. As they looked, the sound of the station commander's voice continued.

"Once again, I respectfully ask that you close your gun ports. We don't want to see violence here today, but if you push me, you can expect a decisive response."

Captain Jerome was not a patient man. His orders had been clear. He was to visit Prometheus to ensure their loyalty to the regime. Even the slightest resistance to the leadership on Terra Nova would be classified as a treasonable offense, and he had seen the footage from Mars.

These traitors are in league with the enemy. If we do not act, they will let us be defeated from within, just as the machines did in the Uprising.

He looked to his nervous officers and nodded to himself. He didn't need their agreement, but he did need to see the look on their faces. Unlike the rest of the fleet, the crew of these six ships was all from Terra Nova and had been carefully vetted for their loyalty to the regime.

"Ready the boarding parties. We're going in!"

* * *

Grand Palace, Terra Nova

A squad of eighty heavily armored Colonial Guards marched in perfect synchronization across the great courtyard. They were preceded by a pair of soldiers wearing heavy armor that shared much in common with the Vanguards of the Marine Corps. These particular models carried no obvious firearms, and their armor was smooth and partially reflective. Bulges in the limbs betrayed their hidden weapons, yet they moved with the same poise and dexterity as the other soldiers.

Hundreds, perhaps thousands of the most important and well-connected citizens of Terra Nova watched them with pride. They were a mixture of businessmen and women, politicians, and even a few celebrities. The one thing they had in common was their support of the Terra Novan regime. There were no children in sight, and the youngest there must have been at least twenty years of age. Flags and pennants flew at every point, with designs dating back to the founding of the first colonies nearly four hundred years earlier. Most were of the new Alliance design though, along with a smattering of plain red banners of the President's ultra-socialist political party.

"Terra, Terra, Terra!"

The chant through the crowd was messy and sporadic, proving to be the exact opposite of the regimented perfection of the Terra Nova Colonial Guard. The location was the site of the Alliance Senate, Colonial Guard Barracks, and a dozen other vast structures, each built on a Neo-Classical style reminiscent of Ancient Earth. Arches and columns were the key features, every section lovingly crafted from great chunks of semi-reflective marble. Not one mark remained from the damage a generation earlier, during the Uprising. The warriors moved silently, only their boots betraying their progress as they reached the middle and passed by a raised plinth. Atop the great stone structure sat a new bronzed sculpture, rich in detail and scale, but hidden behind a thin layer of red silk. Many pointed, but until the cover was removed, the imagery was impossible to make out.

On marched the eighty men and women, each of them outfitted in the finest PDS Alpha armor available on Terra Nova. The dark gray normally used in the Marine Corps had been replaced by a glossy, almost translucent black plastic material. Lines ran across the muscled sections to give an impression of both wealth and strength to the unit. From the guards' shoulders hung the long flowing cloaks of the Royal Guards unit. The bright red material was lined in a hundred different threads while rich and exotic patterns filled the open space in shades of red, violet, and yellow.

"Eyes...right!"

The loud voice coming from the head of the formation was the single officer for the company. Though wearing an equally flamboyant uniform, he also carried a plumed helm that exaggerated his height to nearly a meter over the others. While the guards carried their rare LR52 long rifles, their commander carried a deadly looking glaive in both hands. Its head was shining steel, the edges gleaming with menace. Each of the soldiers turned their heads to the right and directly at the beautiful sculpture. They looked with emotionless eyes at both the sculpture and the flag that surrounded it. They continued to march while the protective covering was pulled down. A light breeze ruffled the material as it slid away from the metal. A pair of dignitaries assisted as the silky material floated down to reveal the figures. The detail was exposed to the bright light, and gasps of surprise and pleasure rippled through the assembled citizens. As one, they turned their attention back to their front and the approach to the grand steps.

At the top waited a small entourage of military and civilian officials. The newly promoted Chiefs of Staff were prominent, but it was the two older men at the center, both of whom wore smart business suits, that stuck out. The taller of the two was President Harrison, the elected leader of the Alliance. Facing him was a man who until today had never stepped on the alien world.

"What do you think, Governor Trelleck?"

The commander of Earthsec forces throughout Sol barely managed to lift a lip.

"The creatures, they are so..."

President Harrison looked back at the sculpture. It was almost three meters high and showed a creature that resembled a man's worst nightmare. Limbs, blades, and tentacles seemed to ooze from its very core. Around it were men in heavy armor, quite unlike the tight-fitting PDS armor used today. Two lay dead on the ground, but three more engaged the creature with their hands in a titanic struggle. A tattered flag of the Confederacy lay over one of the bodies.

"I know. The Biomechs lay waste to our world. But brave warriors like the Terra Nova Guards stood firm and resolved. Even now, there are those among us that would seek the end of these...things."

Governor Trelleck could quite easily see the symbolism on show, and even he was beginning to find it all a little hard to swallow. There were as many rumors of the Guards unit collaboration with the Biomechs in the Great Uprising. It was only a generation ago, and already the official history was being updated once more. The President nodded at the Guards as they moved past before his observant eyes shifted to the Governor.

"Why did you bring me to Terra Nova? Earthsec has no influence out here?"

President Harrison smiled and indicated for the man to look toward the approaching soldiers.

"The Alliance is stable, that is true. But we are scattered through the stars now and often slow to react, especially when faced with our non-human neighbors. Our democracy is based around planets and colonies, and they often block key decisions and make the creation of policy; well, let us say, it can be difficult."

Governor Trelleck smiled at this part.

"We learned a long time ago that colonies work best when under the guiding influence of a good leader. Let them have their democracy, but keep it local. Leave the big decisions to those who understand them."

The President nodded slowly.

"Exactly."

He rubbed his jaw and then looked directly into the eyes of the man. His gaze was so intense, so powerful that the older man from Earth nearly took a step back in surprise.

"I have a dream, Governor Trelleck, one where humanity will be the beacon of civilization. Our trade, technology, and culture will dominate this region, but that can only happen if we purge ourselves of our own weaknesses. We can be stronger than the Helions, the T'Kari, and even the Biomechs."

He reached out and placed a hand on the man's shoulder.

"You have shown me what one man and a dedicated following can do at Sol. Your worlds are irradiated and sterile; your colonies scattered and lost. Yet after all of this you survived, even after being abandoned by the new colonies out here."

The soldiers were ranging ever closer, and even the Governor was becoming nervous. Cries continued to howl from the audience, but he could finally make out that at the back of the formation were a number of people being pushed along. He tilted his head in a questioning manner, but the President was still busy speaking.

"The Alliance is changing, Governor. And I intend on making us the premier power in the known galaxy. The days of infighting, politics, and insurrection are over. The Alliance was created from the fires of the Uprising, and together we can make it burn brighter than any could have imagined."

On and on marched the soldiers behind their two monstrous machines. Large columns of marble protected their flanks as they came closer to the large flight of steps. In a matter of seconds the unit began its short climb to the top where the great arched entrance to the Royal Palace waited. The men and women marched with such perfection that their feet stuck the ground as one entity, the weight and power of their bodies sending a continuous thud through the ground. Military and civilian alike kept well out of the way of them advancing up the carpeted steps and toward their leader. Once on the steps, they fanned out on each side, turning inwards to create an honor guard of two columns.

"Arms!"

Each of the soldiers lowered their weapons so that the butts struck the ground in unison. The open space fell silent, and everybody looked down at the four men now waiting in chains at the bottom of the steps. No one kept them there, but the lines of soldiers watched them carefully, looking for any glimmer of movement. President Harrison gave Governor Trelleck one last smile before lifting his hands to the assembled citizens.

"Ladies and Gentlemen of this great Centauri Alliance. Today we unveil this magnificent sculpture, a work by our finest artists here on Terra Nova, the heart of the Alliance."

Even Governor Trelleck found it odd that the President failed to mention even a single name as he thanked the sculptors. The audience clapped politely, but it was hardly a rousing chorus.

"This wondrous piece of art reminds us of the terrible price our world paid when the enemy sacked our home."

He lowered his head in a somber gesture.

"The enemy had already made deals with our foes on Carthago decades earlier to perpetuate this terrible war crime. Not only did they murder and pillage this planet, but they also established their command facilities right here, under this palace."

He looked back at the tall, marble clad buildings that filled the skyline. He took a few seconds to let it all sink in.

"Our brave citizens won that war, but we also paid a terrible price in defeating both the monsters they created, and the enemy within our own colonies. You see; we never faced a single leader or nation in that war."

He lifted his hand and shook it as he spoke.

"No, Sir, in that war we fought a brutal campaign against an enemy that only wished to weaken us ready for this day. When the Biomech war machines burst out from their homeworlds, they will engulf all before them. No alien system will stand, not Helios, not even T'Karan, unless we stand with them."

Again came the clapping, but this time it was even more subdued and quickly stopped.

"Yet as we fight for our very lives, there are those within our ranks that seek to undermine the very democracy we fought for a generation ago. In the last hour, my security staff have uncovered an attempt at a coup on this very world, by those entrusted with our protection."

He nodded to the group of men in chains. The two machines turned about and gestured for them to move forward.

"These men are the Chiefs of Staff of our own military, and they are behind a military coup that intends on turning the Alliance into their personal domain."

Instead of clapping, the sound and mood quickly shifted into one of surprise and horror. There were few, if any, that might recognize the officers there before them, but to a man the audience were appalled at what they saw.

"I have detailed evidence and intercepts that have been handed over to our law courts, but the facts are incredible."

He lowered his head and wiped his face. It was simple theater, but it had the desired effect. He appeared humbled and distraught, a man fighting back against the betrayal of them all.

"Just hours ago, they were captured in a short battle above our glorious capital. These men were attempting to transfer ships and equipment from our old colonies at Sol through to Prometheus and beyond. We caught them right in the act of forming a treaty with the Biomech machines themselves. Even General Rivers, the great war leader of the Uprising has fallen under their control."

He clapped his hands, and three orbs of light appeared over the sculpture that flashed and then showed a model of the battle that had taken place. It showed several of the ancient Earth warbarges, as well as a mixture of Alliance ships. The imagery was confusing, but the explosions did at least confirm that some kind of battle had taken place.

With each flash came a gasp from the audience. There was no sign of a particular planet, not even Terra Nova. The audience, though, noticed none of this and seemed enthralled by what they were seeing.

"It is with great humility that I accepted the short term of tenure as Magister Populi. With this position, I took on the roll of protector of all our citizens. Even then, I assumed our struggle would be around the alien worlds of the Orion Nebula. Who could have imagined that these machines would have been able to subvert our own military leaders so quickly?"

He nodded in a grim, disappointed fashion as the audience murmured.

"I will ensure your safety against all threats, foreign and domestic. Whether they are Jötnar mercenaries, Biomech armies, or human traitors."

He looked down at the four men, each of whom still wore a black covering over his head. The only identifying feature was that they were wearing their Alliance military uniforms.

"Guards, these men have already had their testimony and evidence examined in our courts."

He reached to his pocket and pulled out a secpad. He lifted it high above his head.

"The verdict is treason, and their guilt is proven beyond doubt."

"Major Grant, carry out the sentence."

The officer with the gleaming glaive and tall plume stepped out in front of his men and began barking orders. Eight rushed out, grabbed the men, and dragged them over to the beautiful new sculpture. They were all shackled to the structure. As the sound of confusion and excitement continued throughout the vast open space, the Governor tapped President Harrison on the shoulder.

"I don't understand. I thought they broke through the blockade."

President Harrison looked at him and grimaced.

"So?"

"Well."

The Governor looked back down to the men being tied to the sculpture.

"Who are these men?"

President Harrison smiled and then shrugged as though he had absolutely no idea. Governor Trelleck looked back at them just as the gunshots rippled through the plaza. The gunfire lasted just a few seconds, but by the time they'd finished, the four bodies lay riddled with holes. Fresh blood had splattered all over the brand new sculpture. Shouts came from the audience; the majority condemning the men they had never even formally identified. The guards dragged away the bullet-ridden bodies, and President Harrison nodded as though agreeing with the justice that had been done.

"This, my friend, is the new order. We will build a

stronger Alliance, one where loyalty and trust are aided by fear and respect of our leaders. The alien threat will be purged from our world like poison from a body. Don't you agree?"

Governor Trelleck was far from comfortable. But as he waited at the right-hand of the President, he realized that he quite liked the warmth of Terra Nova, and even more, he liked the idea of a strong friend on this world, although he found his methods even less desirable than his.

"Ladies and Gentlemen, from today, our Alliance will see a new, vibrant democracy, one where every citizen will get to play an important part. Each star system of the Alliance will be ruled by its very own senate, and each will provide a single leader to offer leadership and strength."

He beckoned toward the Governor.

"Let me introduce to you a man whose support and experience knows no equal, Governor Trelleck, the elected leader of Sol and the old worlds of the Alliance. He is our link to our past and the world from which we all came from, Old Terra. The cradle of humanity and of civilization itself."

The Governor clapped along with the audience, taking his place in front of the President. He hadn't liked what he'd seen, but there was one thing he couldn't argue with. The alien threat from Helios and the Biomechs was clearly something that had to be resolved. If that meant Earthsec would be playing a prominent part, then how could he say no?

Earthsec will be stronger than ever, and this man Harrison needs a strong Earth. We will back him, for now.

He glanced at the man only for a second and nodded in agreement.

If he can lead this rabble, then maybe one day so can I.

CHAPTER TWO

The Jötnar Mutiny is something of a misnomer as it was not technically the Jötnar that revolted. The name stuck principally due to general distrust of their kind after the war and the assault on Terra Nova. The mutiny occurred less than a decade after the end of the Great Uprising. Though known to few, it took place in the center of a mercenary fleet heading for an unknown destination. Information is scarce, but the resulting battle left more than a dozen ships destroyed and thousands wounded or killed. Alliance Special Forces were beaten off, and only direct intervention by Commander Gun, the Jötnar leader was able to stop it from spreading.

The downfall of Hyperion

Taxxu, Uncharted Space

Spartan could tell something bad had happened. It was

one of those feelings he got when an enemy was behind him with a blade. He opened his eyes and found himself in complete darkness, with nothing but cool air all around. A faint, barely discernible flicker far off into the distance was all that allowed him to even orientate himself properly. He lifted himself up and immediately stuck his head on something hard.

"Dammit!"

He rubbed his eyes and then his face, before finally shaking his head to try and wake properly. His voice was odd, and he felt a little nauseous.

Okay, where am I?

He thought back to the last thing he remembered. Images of the massed Mauler assault on the Rift Engine came back, but this time only in short bursts, as if the memories themselves were heavily damaged. He could see their armored forms as they braved the volleys of defensive guns. Every explosion slowed down to show him the carnage in exquisite detail.

The light flickered again in the distance, and then he found his eyes began to adjust. For now it was nothing but subtle shades of gray, but every additional second seemed to improve things. He breathed slowly and found the air cool yet dry. He could see more lights running in a uniform position down a wide passageway.

"Spartan," whispered a voice off into the distance.

He lifted his hands to his face, and to his surprise found

there was no visor. The last thing he remembered was the bloody battle for the massive Rift Engine. He knew he'd been wearing armor in that attack.

What the hell?

"Spartan," said the voice again.

Keeping his hands out in front, much like a blind man trying to make his way along a road, he began to walk. That was the moment he realized he was now floating and that his feet were touching nothing.

Zero gravity, great!

He spun about until his arm caught on a bulkhead extension and he could pull himself down. Unsure whether he was now on the floor or walls, he began pulling himself carefully through the passageway. Each meter he covered brought him closer to the flickering lights, yet the voice had vanished. Seconds drifted by until he was halfway to the light. Something flashed, and then a shape drifted in front of him. For a moment the shape blocked out the light and left him hidden in the darkness.

Wait a minute.

The shape reminded him of something, and as it continued on its course, he noticed the form of a person. They tumbled off to one side, but from this far away it was impossible to tell if they were dead or alive.

"Hey, you there!" he growled.

His voice was muffled, as though he'd lost his voice. The person kept moving past, and it was then it occurred to him that the atmosphere in this place might be thin, perhaps leaking out into space. Spartan instinctively closed his mouth and squinted with his eyes, dreading the terrible problem that came from freezing temperatures in breached craft.

"Help us!" somebody called out. This time it was a woman's voice.

The shape of the passageway was clear now, and Spartan could make out the diamond shape that ran for at least a hundred meters. Small hatches were along the walls at different heights, instantly betraying the internal design.

Zero gravity facility, this place must be as old as me, maybe older.

He kept on moving and finally reached the first of the working lights. They were small, no bigger than a fingernail, and only lit an area of a few square meters. It was enough to show the marks and stains on the wall.

Blood?

Spartan extended his arms and was shocked to see both of his hands. It had been so long since he'd seen his missing forearm that he hadn't even noticed he'd wiped his own brow with both hands. He pulled back his hands and rubbed them together. His excitement was short lived on noticing the congealed blood now stuck to both of them.

This isn't right.

Turning back to the lit section of bulkhead, he pulled himself in closer. The blood showed up as black, but

Spartan was all too familiar with the sight of this kind of gore. He began to lose control and reached out, rubbing his hand on the side panel. His hand left a long streak until he twisted about to face a damaged panel. With his other hand, he grabbed on to it and stabilized himself.

Okay, concentrate. Let's get this thing working.

He pulled on the unit, and it flipped open and revealed green letters on a small, very primate console; to the right was a tiny keypad with lit up letters. He moved his hand closer and tapped the screen; nothing happened, so he tapped a key with what appeared to be a power symbol. It clicked like a micro switch, and then the screen lit up and burst into life. For a second, he lost his night vision before his eyes finally adjusted. A small schematic showed the internal layout of a vessel of some kind. The details marked it out as being a Galactic class transport. The details meant nothing to him at all. The text was tiny, and with no other strong light sources, the words began to blur. He pulled on the panel and drifted closer so that he could read it. He nearly crashed into the bulkhead but instinctively lifted his other arm to brace himself. Now he could make out the ship's specific details, its length, mass, and more importantly, its name.

Bright Horizon.

The other details showed it was an interplanetary transport with cargo, forty-six crew, and three hundred and one passengers. The green schematic showed the outline of the vessel, and he was surprised to see the configuration of conventional rocket engines and ion thrusters.

This ship is one of those that follow a continuous circuit, month after month.

The first ship he'd been sent to as a Marine cadet had traveled in a similar way, but this was something often done with ore haulers and the cheaper passenger transports. Instead of using massive amounts of fuel accelerating and decelerating, these craft followed a particular course that was carefully plotted to make use of planets and moons to move on a never-ending journey through a system. Separate shuttles would then accelerate up to dock to load and unload passengers.

Where have I heard that name before?

Something moved up ahead and then stopped. Spartan froze, but at this distance the panel bathed him in green light. It made him stand out like a neon target.

"Give me your food," said the hidden person out in the passageway.

He shook his head and automatically reached down for his firearm. Instead, he found a cloth or piece of material tied about his waist, but there was something else. He grabbed the object and lifted it in front of his face. It was a knife, but not something manufactured in a factory somewhere. This had been fashioned from a hatch or locker door. It was slightly curved and dented and marked along its edges.

MICHAEL G. THOMAS

"I said give me your food. I'm not asking again."

The shape moved closer, and now Spartan could see it was a man, not unlike himself. Most of his clothing was ragged, and he carried a pack strapped to his body. In his right hand was a blunt object, and Spartan could see it was slick with blood.

"Now!" screamed the man.

The man drifted closer and closer through the zero gravity of the ship. In seconds, the man was there and seemed twice the size of Spartan. He tried to push the man aside, but his foe twisted about and kicked and flailed. A hand or foot struck Spartan, and then he was smashed to the wall, next to the computer screen and panel. The man pushed up against him, his size and strength well beyond him. Spartan gripped his hand around the haft of his improvised weapon and stabbed it hard into the man's throat. The blade pushed in slowly, and the flesh seemed to swallow the blade up.

"Why?" muttered the man, as bubbles of blood burst from his mouth and drifted about the vessel. Several struck against Spartan's own face, but it was far from over. The man grabbed Spartan's throat and lifted his hand to punch him.

"No!" said a woman's voice.

Something resembling a metal club arced across and slammed hard into the man's head. The grip on Spartan loosened, and he didn't hesitate. This time he yanked the

41

blade from the man's throat, and stabbed twice, three times and then pushed away the convulsing body. He glanced to his right, and the woman moved closer but kept the metal object well away from him. The green light from the display gave her an odd, almost ethereal quality.

"Spartan. Your father's found a lifeboat. Come with me."

* * *

Alliance Forward Command,
The Bastion, Helios Prime

A pair of Hammerheads screamed overhead, their guns blazing away. A single Biomech fighter did its best to escape, but it was to no avail. The smaller enemy craft was able to spin about in ways that manned craft could never manage. Even so, the turrets fitted to the Alliance heavy fighters were easily able to track their prey, and the continuous stream of rounds tore off chunks of metal and machinery. One burst ripped into the engine mount, and another a chunk of the control surface before it finally the lost control and dropped downward in a never-ending spin. By the time the Biomech fighter struck the ground, the pair of Hammerheads was long gone.

"Another one down!" cried a Marine private.

A few others shouted out in excitement as the craft exploded in a bright flash. From the surface of Helios

Prime, it wasn't easy to see everything that was going on. The city ruins provided good cover for both sides, and also blocked off line of sight in so many directions. The marines scrambled around the debris to get a better view while trying to avoid being spotted by the myriad of enemy snipers and infiltrators. More fighters screamed overhead to head off the newly arrived squadrons of Biomechs. The Bastion's defense turrets added their own fire if any of them strayed a little closer. Teresa made a mental note for the ninth time that day that the enemy had lost another fighter.

I've been here more than a month, and we're no closer to ending this.

Teresa automatically checked the strategic map for the latest command information on the Helios System. It only provided a very basic overview, but it did give her information on fleets and armies as they engaged the Biomechs in so many different places. Her eyes only made it as far as the enemy ship positions around Spascia when a pair of video requests came in from the fleet. An image flickered, and then stabilized in the lower right corner of her visor.

"Admiral Lewis, good to see you."

"Colonel, I see you've got your hands busy down there."

Teresa grimaced.

"You could say that, Admiral. What can I help you with?"

The man's forehead tightened a little as he spoke.

"The Rift back home is still down, but the local Prime-Spascia Rift is partially operational."

Teresa felt a surge of adrenalin through her chest.

"Look, Teresa, we've got a window to ship troops to help with the siege. You know how it is going there; they need every single extra soldier we can get our hands on. We haven't got long, though."

His image vanished and changed to show the Rift that joined the two planets together.

"Within thirty minutes of getting the Rift online, they detected it. The Biomechs aren't stupid; they already have ships lining up on the Rift. Once they have a clear line of sight from Spascia, they'll open fire on the station and shut it down."

Teresa nodded quickly.

"Take what you have, Admiral. Get to Spascia and help them."

Admiral Lewis tried to smile, but instead his expression looked more like a grimace.

"We've loaded two regiments of marines and a few Khreenk volunteers from the reserve. That leaves you with no reserve out here. Can you hold down there?"

Teresa looked at the forward outpost and the scores of marines, navy crew, and machines. The fight was not easy, and the reserve was something she'd already taken into consideration for operations over the next ten days.

"I'll manage. Spascia is on its knees."

"Understood, Colonel. General Rivers has given me orders to leave for Spascia within eight hours to join the relief effort. I just thought you'd want to know. We will speak soon."

Teresa felt her chest tighten at the mention of Spascia. Normally, she was an expert at keeping her mind on what needed to be done, but the very idea of that world filled her subconscious with images of the siege. Though both Helios Prime and Spascia were the scenes of major land battles, they couldn't have been more different. Spascia was a long, drawn out siege, with both sides lacking enough ships to prove decisive. The fight had devolved into a perpetual battle for the few cities on the planet. It had earned a nickname, one she tried not to think of.

Spascia, the Seventh Circle of Hell.

It was a story she was all too familiar from her religious schooling. Dante had been a strange companion as a teenager, yet the idea of the area of hell reserved for the violent sent a shiver through her body. It was a thought she really wanted to avoid. While Spascia was bogged down, the fighting on Helios Prime had taken a completely different turn. Both sides had spread across the surface, and though the Helion and Alliance forces had now joined in, the fight was a long way from over. Both sides had chosen their ground well, and there were heavily fortified and defended zones in every direction.

Two of her captains moved their hands around the tactical projector to direct combat units while Teresa leaned back against the recently destroyed Eques walker. A lieutenant approached and handed her a metal cylinder. She nodded her thanks, opened up her visor, and took a quick swig of hot coffee. The liquid slid down her throat and instantly put a feeling of fire back into her blood. She twisted slightly and felt her body trying to resist. The aches and pains of years of service had taken their toll, yet as she observed their current position, she felt more alive than she had done in years. It was what she needed to dull the pain of what had happened in the last six weeks since she'd entered the Helios System.

"Colonel, seismic sensors are picking up movement in sector six."

Teresa took a short breath and then pointed to one of the unattached icons.

"Send in the Khreenk. They had two squads out on patrol two klicks west. They can deploy sentry units and a robotic control unit."

She looked away and then again at the display.

"Make sure they get out of the area. The Biomechs could be planting mines."

The two men and a newly arrived third were more than capable of running this part of the fight. She walked through the base and checked on the engineers and officers running the place. As she walked past, they stopped and nodded, nothing more before returning to their duties. One of Teresa's first orders had been to abandon saluting in the combat zone. It was a dangerous indication and had already cost them several officers. She made it halfway to the reinforced entrance where she was expecting her junior commanders when the warning came.

"Ten seconds!" announced the stronghold's officer of the watch.

Teresa moved her eyes a little to track the movement of four guns. These were large caliber low-velocity weapon systems that were mounted onto the wheeled chassis of special Bulldog vehicles. They fired rocket-assisted shells that once at their peak altitude would deploy small wings and loiter for up to four minutes. Ground troops could then call in the shells exactly where they were needed over the entire frontline. Each gun had been moved into position inside a special dugout and then surrounded in sandbags for extra protection. All four guns lifted up another twenty degrees and then stopped.

Somebody is about to have one hell of a bad day.

"Fire!"

They all blasted away in a violent ripple. Teresa imagined what it would be like when the shells landed and hoped the forward observers would make the most of them. There were another dozen emplacements with similar guns all around the Bastion. What had been a forward base had now become an artillery position and command center for the frontline. The Alliance forces were as well equipped as they could ever expect to be, and with each extra day their long-range firepower and knowledge of the area grew.

Teresa moved her eyes a little to check the time.

Another four minutes.

She was due to meet up with three of her junior officers to plan the next seventy-two hours of operations. It was a long, drawn out process that required constant reports, updates, and intelligence from a hundred different units.

"Incoming counter-battery fire."

It was a faceless warning, followed by a shrill siren that was sent out every few hours. It had happened now so many times that she didn't even check to see where the warning had come from. The only thing she did check was the Alliance authorization that came with the warning. It all came up as clear and official, yet something deep down made her nervous.

They're smart, those damned machines. One false alert to keep our heads down could give them a chance to do something unexpected.

It was a quick thought, but also an important reminder as to how the enemy could so easily work around their procedures. It was enough for her to check on the position and rank of the marine that had called out the order. It was a sergeant, newly arrived and stationed on the northern bunker.

Good. In that case I'll get my head down.

Teresa automatically moved from her position and

down into one of the hundreds of dugouts now littering the ruins of Helios Prime. Three other marines waited there and looked at her nervously.

"First bombardment?" she asked.

Two nodded, but a third shook his head. Teresa looked at him and noticed the scorch marks along the man's shoulder. She'd seen them before, and they were from a weapon unique to this part of the universe.

"You've fought against the Helions?"

The man nodded.

"Yes, Sir, we were here during the Zathee Uprising."

Teresa looked down at her leg. A similar mark ran from her thigh right down to her knee. It was an odd thing to bond over, but the shared damage seemed to draw far more interest than it should have.

"We were hit by the Animosh on more than a dozen occasions."

The man sighed in agreement.

"I saw three of my squad die from those things. When are we going to get some armor that's proof against them?"

Teresa almost laughed at that question.

"You've seen the damage those weapons can do against a Bulldog?"

The man nodded.

"Well, do you want to be walking around in that gear? Not even the Vanguards are safe against repeated hits from Animosh thermal weaponry. Fire and movement are better protection against them, not worrying about armor."

She looked away from him.

Even if we did have new weapons and equipment, how would it get here? The Rift is still shut down.

The sound of interceptor guns rattled loudly, the final indication that the attack was coming. The micro-radar trackers were so accurate they could identify and monitor projectiles down to 20mm cannon rounds. In seconds, the automated gun turrets opened fire, and the sky filled with trails of projectiles, just as had happened a hundred times before.

Here it comes.

The bombardment was much shorter than expected. The first salvo struck short and merely shattered already ruined structures, as the broken shells disintegrated overhead and then fell like metal rain. Nine more shots came in after them, each containing high-explosive ordnance, but only three made it past the interceptors in one piece. The first struck one of the recently installed inner blast walls, tearing through it a hole the size of a man.

There's more to come.

Two more shells came down and shook the ground. There was no immediate sign of danger; just the expected shaking and rumble from the impact. Within three seconds, the all-clear signal blasted out thorough the base.

"Up top, we've got a war to fight, Marines."

Teresa was out first and in the low cloud of dust. She looked about and was relieved to see no bodies or burning vehicles. More marines emerged from their hiding places, like rabbits appearing from a warren.

"Back to your posts, move it!" barked a sergeant.

The seasoned marine emerged from his own shelter with his carbine held in one hand. The marines didn't hesitate upon spotting him, and as quickly as they had dispersed, they were back into action. Teresa walked back to the recessed command bunker and went inside. As always, the two marines at the entrance ignored her.

About time, somebody remembered to stop saluting!

Once inside, she headed to the tactical unit and looked at the mapping information. The two captains were still busily running operations, and four more junior officers assisted with the air support and logistics. It was a small number of personnel for such an important role. Off to their right was a large control unit that extended up into a massive antenna. Every single order that was issued was dispersed via the digital communications network, as well as being repeated directly to Admiral Lewis and General Rivers.

We've got a lot of eggs down here in this basket.

It was only partially true, of course. In reality, combat command could be transferred to any part of the network.

It was the beauty of the system, in that redundancy was built in from the ground up. An atomic weapon could wipe out Colonel Morato and her entire staff, and in less than a minute ANS Ticonderoga could take over the same role.

"Finally, we're making progress."

A tracked vehicle trundled past her, pulling a large wheeled trailer full of dirt and debris. The marines and engineers had dug three or more meters down in places, creating a separate world that was hidden from direct line of sight. Many sections were completely covered while others dug down to join the myriad of underground tunnels, road and rail systems. The one saving grace for Helios Prime was that during their long war with the machines, they had been forced to dig down. Over months and years, the vast cities littering the surface began building both above and below the surface. There were now entire parts of Helios Prime known derisively as iceberg cities; unusual urban zones where more existed below the surface than above it. The ground began to shake, and Teresa lifted her armored arm to cover her face.

"It's Captain Devon, Sir. He's taking the next patrol out."

Teresa looked to her left and watched six Bulldogs move out. The first and last were the mobile gun variants, whereas the other four were standard troop carriers. She made a silent prayer for them, knowing full well that ambushes and improvised roadside bombs were more likely to maim or kill them than an actual standup fight. The young Lieutenant approached while checking both left and right as he closed the distance. He stopped, saluted, and then handed her a secpad. It was all very old fashioned; the man could just have easily sent it directly to his helmet. Instead, this man reverted to a system that was millennia old.

"Colonel, here are the latest arrival reports."

She looked up and down at the man. Teresa had no idea of his name, but he was definitely one of the few that had survived the original orbital bombardment. She moved her eyes a little to the right where the visor on her helmet began to put up information on the man. Even though the unit details said he was from logistics, she could also see that his armor bore the marks of months of combat. The reports often told just part of the story, and right now she was intrigued by the two long scars on his chest that looked suspiciously like the weapons swung about by Decurion war machines. Colonel Morato looked down and then spotted a familiar face from the corner of her eye.

"Captain Tycho, about time you got back. I assume your mission was successful?"

The Captain approached, along with a pair of protective guards. He stopped and saluted with much gusto. The man moved with an awkward gait that betrayed the horrendous injuries he'd sustained years earlier. It didn't stop him continuing his duties, however.

"Yes, Sir, we've done it. The last assault by the Vanguards broke through to the Helion landing zone and into their underground forward positions. We've made contact with the Zathee resistance."

He shook his head in amazement.

"They've been down there for months now. Almost no food, few weapons, and still they want to fight."

Teresa had heard the same in the other areas they had quickly liberated in the first week of operation.

"This has cleared the frontlines, at least for awhile. Now we have access to our landing sites and can redeploy our forces a little quicker."

Teresa smiled briefly and then looked back to the tactical projector. The imagery had already confirmed their current position, but information from the man that had already been there was much more valuable to her.

"So. We have control of these sites. That's good. What about maintaining the links between them, though? The machines have proven adept at slipping between our defenses and continually isolating and picking off fortifications and supply zones."

Captain Tycho nodded quickly in agreement.

"That's true. They are avoiding out strongest positions and then surrounding and overrunning wherever they find left. The 13th NHA battalion took control of seven blocks of the Northern zones. We all know what happened there."

Teresa's lip twitched a moment as she recalled the reports.

"Yes, the NHA commander in that sector assured us he could keep the entire front secure. We redeployed our forces, and then the machines tunneled up into his command post. We almost lost the entire quadrant on that day."

Teresa shook her head bitterly.

"Yeah."

With her left hand, she traced the positions her forces had been fighting over for weeks.

"NHA forces have finally linked up with our marines at all nine locations, and each of them is expanding our areas of control slowly. The General is sending down another two regiments to reinforce our forces here."

Teresa nodded.

"Good. We need a reserve, if anything else."

She indicated toward a table on which a tactical battlefield projector showed a large map of this part of the planet. Although the world was in theory a massive urban settlement, there were some parts more heavily populated than others. The capital and its outlying districts for more than fifty kilometers in all directions had become known as simply the City since they had arrived. There were eight other locations across the globe similar in scale, and Teresa pointed to each of them.

"We have strong points in the most important parts of this planet, apart from the site of the Planetary Defense Installation. We only control two major zones in the Southern districts."

"True," agreed the Captain, "and the enemy has given ground at most of our major sites. They are regrouping and concentrating their forces at the site of the Planetary Defense Installation and the city districts within twenty kilometers of the site."

She then pointed to another two positions above and below the same place.

"Drones show their machines are constructing major defenses along the location of the old perimeter skywalks. Give it another week, and the machines will have three zones surrounded by fortified defenses and underground chambers."

Captain Tycho sighed.

"This is our concern."

He indicated the areas already taken by the marines.

"Our strategy has been successful, and we have taken back substantial areas from the enemy. Even so, the best estimate of their strength is over two hundred thousand, but that could be way off. They are pulling back from our forces and hunkering down."

Teresa leaned back and stretched her back a little. She had been concentrating on the attritional grind for so long now. The first two weeks had been completely different, with both sides vying for control of the planet. They had been evenly matched, but the enemy had changed tack.

"It's as though they want to preserve their forces."

Captain Tycho looked back to her.

"Of course. It's a delaying tactic. They don't want to win this, not yet anyway. They have control of the Doomsday Weapon, even if it is currently non-functioning, and the Animosh have been providing technical and logistical support."

Teresa could have smiled, if it hadn't meant the war would go on for even longer.

"So they want to keep us pinned down, but why?"

There was little opportunity to continue the conversation. One of the lookouts had already spotted them and called out as Teresa could see black shapes off into the distance. From there, even the enhanced optics of the PDS Alpha armor was unable to show much. All she could tell was that the craft were relatively small and heading toward Alliance positions. They were immediately followed by sonic booms that indicated the craft were traveling at supersonic speeds. Teresa turned and called out to the watchtower off to her left.

"Sergeant, who is that?"

The marine swung around a double gun mount and tracked the objects. A second marine checked something on the computer and then looked back at her.

"Three Maulers coming down from orbit. They are IFF tagged from Ticonderoga."

Teresa smiled at her Captain.

General Rivers.

"Looks like the General can smell the change. Get ready for his arrival. He'll be here in less than a minute."

The Captain saluted and moved off to prepare the ground staff for the imminent arrival. At the same time a young lieutenant, a man clearly keen on making a good impression, was shouting to marines. In just a few seconds, a hastily assembled honor guard of marines moved out and lined up. All of them wore almost completely unblemished armor and carried their carbines on improvised slings on their shoulders. Teresa finished sending a set of orders to the local patrols via the tactical battlefield projector and then looked back.

"What the hell are you doing?" she yelled at them.

A corporal, the unit's leader, looked at them and then to her. Teresa shook her head in disbelief at the site of the heavily defended Bastion, with its mixture of dugouts, thick walls, and watchtowers. There were three reinforced landing platforms and waiting next to them a line of marines. The absurdity of the situation almost made her laugh.

"Uh, Sir?"

Their armor betrayed them as new arrivals from the fleet. It wasn't the marines' fault. Teresa could see they were uncomfortable being made to stand out in the open, with no consideration given to cover or protection. Teresa moved closer, but not too close.

"Are you trying to draw attention to the arrival of somebody important? Contrary to popular opinion, the machines aren't dumb. Are you looking to get one of our commanders assassinated?"

The man shook his head nervously.

"No, Colonel, my apologies. I just…"

Teresa lifted her hand.

"I don't want to hear it, Corporal. Get back to what you were doing."

The sound of the Maulers became louder as the formation moved overhead. Teresa walked off to the right and away from the landing pad that had been cleared specifically for craft up to Mauler size. The three Maulers traveled in a wide, rather loose formation as they came in low. Each of them began to fire off flares in arcing patterns around the landing site. These small devices were a simple defense against potential heat tracking weapons, but as the first Mauler came in, there appeared to be no signs of enemy action. By the time it was twenty meters off the ground, the other two had begun to accelerate away into a circular holding pattern directly overhead. Teresa's visor automatically activated, sensing the coming dust storm. Her vision was quickly obscured as the large landing craft came down, with its corner-mounted engines blasting the ground. The screaming sound of its descent stopped, and the cloud of dust slowly cleared to reveal the dark shape of the squat looking craft. A door opened up, and the bright interior light spilled out to highlight the silhouette of a single man in full battle attire.

"General Rivers, good to see you on the ground once more."

CHAPTER THREE

The Great Biomech War solidified the Alliance's presence in the Orion Nebula, or more specifically, around the Helion Nexus. This critical juncture that joined stars and worlds together would prove to be the most significant reason for the violent success of humanity. Not since the gold rush years of early colonization in Alpha Centauri was so much wealth created.

Orion – The future?

Prometheus Seven Outpost, Prometheus Sector

Colonel Pierce watched the screen like a hawk. The enlarged imagery of the forces waiting outside could be seen in a dozen different directions. Most of the images showed the large warships and their weapon systems, but it was the bank of nine screens on the one side, functioning as a mock window to the world, that caught his eye. From that particular vantage point, he had a perfect view of the undersides of the Alliance ships. In the last two minutes, the launch bays of the assault transport had deployed nine military shuttles. These craft, like much of what waited near the station was old equipment. That didn't mean it was antiquated, but they were certainly not Hammerheads or Maulers, and that gave him hope.

If the regime of Harrison is as powerful as he says it is, wouldn't they have full access to the entire military spectrum of war gear?

He could only hope it meant the support for this transitional movement was poor at best; because if the forces on Terra Nova had general support throughout both the military and civilians, they could expect things to get much worse. He had no doubt the station could defend itself against a small-scale assault, but nothing more. That was what the fleet was for, and right now they had much more important things to worry about in T'Karan and beyond. He looked back out and toward the ships. The shuttles had positioned themselves into two small groups ready to make the journey to the station, but not one of them was moving. He shook his head, looking over to his communications officer.

"Did the signal get through?"

The man nodded.

"Good. Send out a general distress call that we are under attack by renegade military forces. I want the news to get to every colony. Mars, Kerberos, Carthago, Prime…

all of them."

"Aye, Sir."

He then turned his attention to Lieutenant Young, his security chief who was already waiting in full tactical gear, alongside a single four-man fireteam.

"We've got a single platoon of marines on board, right?"

The man nodded quickly.

"Yes, Sir, thirty-six marines, each one a veteran of the Helion Uprising. They are skilled and experienced, Sir."

He tried to look reassuring, but it was far from that. Instead, he nodded to the others in the station, especially the technical staff and engineers.

"We might be down on numbers, Sir, but all personnel on this station have been trained in basic combat. They are ready to defend themselves if necessary. We have the basic weapons and gear in the combat lockers, and I've drilled them every week for the last nine months on this."

He pointed to the plan of the station.

"We use our own people to provide a limited perimeter defense, nothing major, just a screen. Further back, we have the regulars as a mobile reserve. We've drilled it, and I can have a squad to hold a sector in a maximum of six minutes."

Colonel Pierce had his moment of doubt as he looked at the marine, but he couldn't argue with his logic. The never-ending drills had become something of a minor issue on the station. He had a hundred jobs that needed doing, especially with the clandestine operations to bring additional ground troops through the Rift. Many of these were no more than thugs and criminals, but there were plenty of retired military in the mix as well as those looking to make a quick buck. The risk to security with these people was much greater than normal, especially when a number of their commanders had been brought on board for clearance.

This is much worse.

The idea of marines defending tunnels and passageways was worrying enough. But this idea of sending out engineers, scientists, and technicians with light weapons could result in only one thing, mass casualties for both sides.

I've got to defuse this thing. I've got to.

"What about the transport? Are they still on board?"

Lieutenant Young smiled.

"I sent the order for them to stay until we knew what was happening. They are waiting to hear if we need help. The main landing bay is secured, and they are not far from us."

That was the first bit of good news he'd heard all day. He looked to the mainscreen where the live stream from the enemy command ship continued to run. He'd seen the same model of ship many times. In fact, the more he thought about it, the more he was convinced that this particular vessel had been one of those waiting to be scrapped. There were a number of high-orbit decommissioning sites around Terra Nova where old ships went to die. Even this far into the future, and with so many planets, it was more cost effective to strip down old ships than to harvest new materials. Scores of ships from the Uprising a generation ago had been sent there as they were replaced with newer classes of ship.

Surely not? Is this where Harrison has been building up his base of support, with the old shipyards and scrappers?

The entire industry of scrappage had been a massive issue of the last five years, primarily due to involvement by gangs and criminals. The materials and equipment used on military ships, even the old models, were worth considerable amounts of money. He rubbed at his jaw and made a mental note to look into this further. Then he spotted movement near the shuttles.

The idiots! Are they trying to start a war?

"Captain. Do not make the mistake of trying to board this station. I am authorized to use lethal force against any intruder."

The man chuckled on the other side via the live videostream that was being sent out unencoded and on more than thirty different bands.

"There are no intruders here. These are Alliance Navy vessels, and I am sending teams over to assist in your security operations. I expect nothing less than professional courtesy and all the help you can offer me."

The Colonel was on the brink of resignation when he noticed the groan from two female officers. He looked to them and watched as one dropped to her knees and vomited uncontrollably.

"What's going on?"

More of the officers began talking, but he could see the communications officer waving at him furiously. As soon as they made eye contact, the man beckoned for him to come to his screen. Colonel Pierce walked the short distance, along with a handful of other officers.

"What is it?"

There was no need to answer, though. It was a live videostream by the Alliance News Network, the official voice of the government. It showed the Grand Palace on Terra Nova. Lines of civilians and soldiers filled the space while a speech continued. In the center was a beautiful sculpture of men fighting creatures and on the floor a number of still forms. It was the scrolling ticker that stunned every one of them. It simply read that a full-scale coup was underway by the forces of General Rivers and separatists amongst the Biomechs.

"Is it true?" asked a junior science officer.

Colonel Pierce brought his fist down onto the console.

"How can you even ask this? General Rivers is assisting with combat operations in the Helios System."

He looked at the image and then pointed at three points

on the screen.

"Magnify those."

It took seconds for each of the segments of video to be enlarged and enhanced on the bank of screens. Each showed the scene from a different vantage point. The first was of the bodies, their heads still covered. The second showed long lines of soldiers in a strange version of the Marine Corps armor. The final image was of President Harrison and his entourage.

"It says those bodies are generals taken from the fighting over Terra Nova."

He turned back to look at his own officers.

"Those generals are already in T'Karan, along with Admiral Churchill."

"So who are they?" asked the science officer.

There was still doubt in the young officer's voice.

"I have no idea. But based on the expression on Harrison's face, you can be sure it is somebody he fell out of favor with."

"Sir. There's more," said the communications officer.

This time he didn't bother checking and simply diverted the latest feed to the three screens on the right. It showed several ancient warbarges and a number of other unidentified ships engaging in a violent space battle. The text underneath described how loyal Alliance forces had beaten off rebel separatists over Terra Nova.

"No, this is nonsense," said Colonel Pierce, "There

is no evidence that any of our military forces have been engaged in hostile action."

The chief science officer twisted about excitedly.

"You're right, Sir. Look. The computer has matched the location of the celestial bodies in the background. This is clearly Mars. I suspect it's part of the fight between the Biomech ship and the defending Earthsec vessels from over a month ago."

The Colonel looked at the footage and watched until he lifted his hand.

"Freeze that!"

With the image now static, he moved his arms to zoom in. The detail blurred for a moment but quickly sharpened to show the flanks of an ancient war barge. It was the ship alongside it that he was most interested in.

"There. That is no warship of ours. Look, she bares the insignia of Earthsec. Check her configuration with our systems."

The station's chief tactical officer was already on it. In a few more seconds, he had detailed schematics up on the screen and alongside the frozen image of the ship. It was clear they were the same vessel, right down to the name emblazoned in black on her bow.

"It's ESS Dauntless, Sir, a four hundred-year old Commando Carrier. Her commander is a Captain Thomas Cobb. According to our information, the ship is still at Mars, along with the Captain."

Colonel Pierce smiled, a grim expression that betrayed no real pleasure. He spoke loudly so that all those present would hear him loud and clear.

"This footage confirms just one thing. The government on Terra Nova is going through a major crisis. I suspect this is a localized coup, with minor support from some of the planet's less favorable criminals. There has always been a degree of distrust between the capital and the other colonies, but this…it is too much."

"Your orders, Sir?"

They looked at each other only for a moment, but there was a clear understanding now.

"They are fabricating evidence based on random videostreams spliced together. If they are prepared to do that, well, they are prepared to do almost anything to achieve their own ends. This last report is a mixture of the fighting at the Mars Rift several months ago and the relief force from Earth. The whole thing is garbage."

He looked away from the footage and tried to look reassuring.

"None of us will raise a hand against our fellow citizens. We will, however, deny criminal forces from boarding our facility. We will not fire first, but I'll be damned if I'll roll over for another dictator. Understood?"

A reasonably loud chorus of agreement came back. He knew they would do what was needed, even though none of them had the stomach for the potential bloodbath that was to come.

"Good. Get units positioned at all airlocks, and prepare the medical bay for potential casualties. If they do try and force their way in, we can expect losses on both sides. We will be ready."

He then looked back to the communications officer.

"Combine all of our external and internal feeds into a single stream. I want this broadcast to every repeater station in the Alliance. If Harrison thinks he can start his own personal fiefdom, he can forget it. We've had our civil war, and we're not about to have another one. This will go out live."

He then walked to the Chief Engineer.

"Keep the Rift open for as long as you can, but keep a close eye on it. If those ships try and make a break for it, you know what to do."

"I can close it right now, Sir?"

Colonel Pierce shook his head.

"No, the Rift is our gateway to T'Karan and to the Admiral. That is the only direction we can expect help. Just watch them. They cannot be allowed to enter T'Kari space."

With a nod the man went back to his screen, and now all Colonel Pierce could do was watch and wait. He looked to the screen on his right where a flashing message simply read that his status had been received. What kept drawing his eye was the counter. It read seven minutes.

Come on! Hurry up.

Lieutenant Young still waited, but he twisted his head and looked back for a second. He spoke quietly into his intercom and then stepped closer to the Colonel.

"Sir. They're armored up and ready."

"Good. Don't use the comms. I need this kept quiet, and if they've got access to our records, they probably already known our communications procedures. Send a runner down there and bring them back."

Lieutenant Young saluted smartly and then moved off at a jog.

* * *

ANS Terra, Prometheus Sector

Captain Jerome scratched at his cheek and looked over his shoulder at his crew. He remained completely confident in his mission, but the sight of the vast station was hard to ignore. He recalled his orders from Terra Nova and looked at it again.

They know we're Alliance military, so why are they resisting?

He glanced down at the tactical schematic and overlay on a smaller screen. The armor and weapon systems were impressive, but he also knew the station's weak points. President Harrison had given him unlimited access to the Naval archives, at least the data that was still accessible. For some reason, large parts of it had been removed or destroyed. It wasn't something he'd given much thought of, mainly down to his joy at being given such an important role. In all of his years on the planet, he'd thought his chance at starship command had long gone. The Navy was not interested, even though his record and credentials were perfect.

Racist, self-righteous liberals!

His opinion of the multi-colonial fleet had diminished year by year, spurred on by his inability to penetrate its ranks. He wanted command more than anything, and now he had it. While he'd been struggling to be accepted, he'd seen cadets from the Biomech spawned warriors on Hyperion joining up. One of the youngest had even been placed in charge of a frigate.

All appeasement to these creatures and their masters; first they burned our world, and then they pretended to be our allies by burning it again. We will deal with all of them in time.

He'd studied the plans for the station on his way out here, and what appealed to him the most was that the Prometheus Seven Station had never been intended as a military installation. Modern stations were designed with small entry points with each one being protected by redundant systems. This station was a grand affair from days of old, with massive landing docks, grand entrances, and staircases. Many of the interior sections had been designed to look more like early twentieth-century ocean liners. The exotic and degenerate had all been part of its interior aesthetic, and every part of it sickened him.

He smiled to himself.

This place is nothing more that a decadent hotel for the collaborators and their friends floating over a hellhole of a planet. If only Terra Nova had been stronger in the last war, we could have ended it on our terms, not theirs.

He had no respect for the station, let alone the research and manufacturing plants on the planet below. The longer he was stationed there, the more he was beginning to like this assignment. It was almost enough to distract him from the latest problem with his own vessel. Unfortunately, the levels of stress and tension inside the ship had increased to an almost unbearable level, not helped by the fact that the internal climate control system had chosen that very moment to fail. Several of the engineers were already on it, but he had no doubt the age and condition of the ship was more likely to be the cause.

"Somebody sort this out. Of all the times for this kind of failure, it happens in the middle of this!" he snapped.

The temperature had risen ten degrees and was still rising, leading all of them to sweat profusely. It was more than just an irritation to him because he'd been forced to cut his live videostream. The embarrassment was something he had no intention of being reminded of by those sitting in the comfort of that orbital hotel.

"Well, still no response?"

All of his officers shook their heads.

"Very well."

He turned his attention instead to a man in Terra Novan Guards uniform. The warrior had said nothing since they had arrived. Instead, he had been waiting and watching. The odd black hue gave the impression the man's armor was plastic, and his well-trimmed mustache marked him out as one of the planet's elite. He was neither a soldier, nor a politician. This man was an odd amalgamation of the two. A kind of politically indoctrinated officer, with influence back home with the new regime as well as in his own combat unit.

"Your troops, are they ready to do what has to be done?"

Lieutenant Dobbs smiled, a thin, cruel look that mirrored the ship's captain.

"I have my two platoons of Interior Ministry soldiers, and every single one of them is ready to do his duty for the homeworld. We all saw the execution of the traitors. They are well motivated to end this crisis, decisively."

The phrasing was unlike anything you might expect to hear from a member of the Alliance armed forces.

"Good. Send them in, Lieutenant. I want you to lead them, personally. We cannot afford any mistakes. Terra Nova and the Alliance were once ruled by humanity alone. It is time for us to lead by example. We will ensure all civilian and military forces answer through the chain of command directly back to us, no questions asked."

"Understood, Sir. This is a crisis, and Biomech collaborators will play no part in our destiny. It's time to take back our colonies."

With a single smart salute, the man marched away, and Captain Jerome was left wondering quite who was the most serious here. He looked back to the screens and allowed himself a small smile.

The Biomechs, the Helions, and the rest, they all play their games; but it will be humanity that will come out on top. The more they fight, the weaker they become. Admiral Anderson and his puppets will rue the day they sided with the bastard creatures of the Biomechs.

To the surprise of those officers nearby, he spat onto the ground.

We shall never forget what they did to our home.

A warm bead of sweat dripped over his left eyebrow and ran into his eye, immediately causing him discomfort. It was a minor thing, but in this stress-filled environment it was the last straw.

"Target their bridge and communications systems. Prepare to fire!"

Only one of the technicians looked back to him. The young man's eyes betrayed fear, or nerves. At this distance Captain Jerome wasn't sure. He made a mental note to keep an eye on the crewman.

If any of them falters on this mission, they will pay the price.

Even as he considered the repercussions, he reached down and checked his sidearm was present. For a brief moment he felt a flutter of fear, but then his fingers found the reassuringly metal and plastic grip.

Good. We're ready to show our hand. Are they?

* * *

Prometheus Seven Outpost, Prometheus Sector

The alarms had started up once more, but this time it was different. The danger wasn't that unknown vessels had arrived. The risk to everybody on board was now directly related to the shuttles and their cargo of heavily armed soldiers. Small groups of people ran about the station with guns in their hands. Even fewer wore head protection or body armor. Even so, they moved quickly to the key vulnerable points on the station.

"Colonel, we've got three more military shuttles on the way. That's ten in total."

From such a long distance the shuttles looked tiny, but with the magnified view the guns fitted to their stubby wings betrayed their true purpose. Colonel Pierce watched the shuttles as they split off into pairs and made for different parts of the station.

"Colonel?" asked the station's tactical officer, "Our fighter pilots need a shooting order. Can they open fire?"

He wanted to say yes. In fact, he knew he needed to say yes.

"No, tell them to hold their fire. We cannot start a

shooting fight with them."

He rubbed his forehead and then checked the screens for what must have been the tenth time. The Alliance was an odd, disparate collection of colonies, but he found it incredible that there could be any stomach for continuing fighting after everything they had all been through.

"How long do we have?"

The officer looked back at his screen and checked the incoming trajectories.

"Sir, the first two groups will make contact within sixty seconds. The last two shuttles to leave are heading right here."

He pointed off to the right where low-level lighting marked the route to a series of emergency blast doors. The entrance was wide, but half had been welded shut in the last year, as access points through the station had been improved.

"I think they're heading for the command section escape hatches."

The thought of hatches being ripped open was a horrific idea.

If they blow the doors, they'll vent this entire part of the station.

"Very well. I need a single fireteam, in here. It's time to enter lockdown."

Other officers were now watching him, perhaps waiting for their own orders to draw firearms.

"All non-essential crew will return to the secure zones

in the spine. The rest of you will draw respirators and sidearms, and then return to your stations. Let's go to work, people."

There was no argument, not now. The spine of the station was the only part of the massive facility that lacked artificial gravity. By sending the non-combatants to this point, he was keeping them as far from danger as he could. The spine also housed a high-speed elevator system that ran to each end of the station and the massive escape decks. In seconds, the entire place was deserted, save for the handful that had moved to the computer systems at the furthest points from the outer airlock doors.

"On my signal, you will kiss the ground and stay there until you are told otherwise. Understood?"

* * *

The lights were dim inside the landing bay, but the bright beams from the landing lights of the transport easily cleared the glare. The single marine ran into the open space and stopped in front of the six large figures. He almost tumbled as he choked and coughed. The bright beams from behind the figures hid their features and marked them out as nothing more than vast black silhouettes.

"What is it?" asked the nearest in a gruff, stern tone.

"Lieutenant Young. He needs you to stop the weapons transfer and to come to the command center with all haste."

Again the taller figure spoke in that grating tone.

"Why? We have work to do here, and it will be another hour before all of this is unloaded for your defense teams."

"There isn't time. The intruders from Terra Nova have sent shuttles. They're about to breach."

The two nearest figures looked to each other and then bent down to a large metal container. One pulled out a multi-barreled gun that was almost the same size as the marine. "I don't think so, marine. We've checked their configuration, and they are not Alliance ships. Any illegal vessel attempting to board an Alliance facility can expect only one response. If they tried this on Prometheus, well, I would be authorized to do whatever was required."

With a loud clunk, the safety clicked off, and the barrels gave three quick spins. The weapon was intimidating enough by virtue of its size, but the clicks as the barrels spun about, was the final straw. The figure bent down so that their faces were of the same height. The young man did his best not to flinch, but the great size was simply too much. One of those at the back began a throaty laugh that echoed through the hangar.

"You're scaring the boy."

The tall one sighed impatiently.

"Take us to your Colonel, and fast. It sounds like we don't have much time."

* * *

Lieutenant Dobbs was out of the shuttle first and pushed himself away from the craft and toward the outer skin of the vast rotating space station. With all exterior doors and hatches closed, the only way into the station would be via violent means, and the constant repositioning of the shuttles made the transfer very difficult. He was beginning to wish the ships had opened fire on the rotational mechanisms of the station to ease their entry.

"Watch for traps," he said calmly.

Like all members of the Guards, he had been trained in counter-insurgency operations. A large part of the syllabus included dealing with asymmetric threats, improvised explosive devices, and other non-conventional situations. More of the men left the two shuttles and helped each other to reach the outer surface of the station. The gap from shuttle to station was only thirty meters, but that short distance could feel like a kilometer when you lacked the ability to change course or direction.

"Squad One in position," said a quiet voice over the radio.

Lieutenant Dobbs had already noted the position of the unit making its way further along the station. He moved his eyes a little to check that each of the five assault teams was in the right place.

Good, almost there.

The shuttles were all waiting a short distance away while the two platoons of heavily equipped soldiers anchored themselves to the skin. The Lieutenant pulled himself around the surface and to a long series of grab handles. Because of the vast size of the station, the rotation felt very slow. Even so, as he grabbed, he could feel the tug as it tried to pull away.

"With me."

The others moved in close and took up positions alongside him.

"Fit the breacher."

Two soldiers moved past in silence and positioned the breacher unit onto the outside of the station. The spot they chose was along the right-hand side of the outer door's release mechanism. The hatch itself was only a two-meter wide oval, but the Lieutenant had selected it specifically due to its proximity to the command center of the station.

"Sir, we've got company."

He looked over his shoulder and spotted the Alliance fighters. Some were pointing at the shuttles, the others directly at his soldiers.

They won't shoot. They don't have the guts to start this.

The nearest technician looked back and gave him the okay signal.

"Do it."

The breacher charge vanished in a puff of gas, and the

outer hatch spun off the outside of the station. There was no sound and surprisingly little in the way of emissions from the inside.

"Go, go, go!"

Lieutenant Dobbs yanked on the grab handle and spun himself around so that he slid inside the section feet first. He moved on past the breached entrance and hit metal. He shook his head and immediately went for his weapon. The L52 carbine was identical to the weapons carried by the Marine Corps, with little to differentiate them apart from a few subtle shades of color and a simplified skeleton stock. It was simply known as the Terra Pattern Coilgun in the Guards unit.

The other squads confirmed their success as they breached a series of outer doors. So far none had commented on traps or defenders.

Will they let this station fall, without even a struggle?

He felt almost offended that military personnel would give up so easily. He looked ahead and at the next set of doors. Additional welded plates protected the hatch to stop it blowing out into space. He'd expected this and merely indicated for the technicians to move forward. Again the two went around the hatch, but this time they fitted a piece of equipment over the control unit to the side.

"Thirty seconds to breach, Sir," said the senior of the two.

Both moved back and out of the way to await access. The rest of the unit now came in closer and lifted their weapons to their shoulders. In their black armor they looked sinister and threatening, exactly the intention behind the design.

"Seal behind us. Let's keep this a clean operation. We need the station operational and the crew alive."

One of the soldiers placed a frame around the breach entrance and hit a button. A thin layer of material expanded out and then hardened into a temporary wall. Thin ribs bulged out to make the thing look like a section of a flying reptile's wing.

"Ten seconds."

Lieutenant Dobbs looked back to the entrance and lifted his carbine. The sights communicated directly with his PDS armor, but so far there were no tagged targets.

"Five."

He took three quick, short breaths and then moved his finger to the trigger. The weapon was already on rapid-fire mode, but each of them had also twisted their barrels to activate the subsonic stealth mode. This wasn't because he wanted to eliminate the sound; it was simply to reduce the recoil inside the station, in case there was a loss of gravity.

"Now."

The door slid open as the computer system was overridden. Lieutenant Dobbs grabbed the sides and stepped through. He didn't stop and moved into the large computer suites that housed upward of fifty stations. The slightly curved ceiling was high, at least twenty meters above his head and also filled with screens of data. He noticed a few showing their ships outside.

"Spread out, watch for hostiles."

The rest of his team followed in close behind and then spread out into a crescent. Even as they moved, he could feel his heart pounding inside his chest. He'd expected to find the placed filled with people, but it was deserted.

"Put down your weapons!" came a voice from ahead.

A shape moved perhaps twenty or twenty-five meters directly in front of him. As soon as one of his men spotted the shape, it was tagged and the data sent to the rest of the team. More and more shapes appeared from behind the final row of computer stations until he counted twelve of them.

"I am Lieutenant Dobbs, Terra Nova Guards. By order of the President, you will lay down your weapons and surrender this station."

The shape ahead was much clearer now. The man was in Alliance clothing and in the thinner PDS gear worn by some crews. It was proof against heat and pressure, but from memory he knew it offered almost no ballistic protection. The man's head was protected by a dark, tight-fitting pilot's helmet with a raised visor.

Colonel Pierce, it has to be.

His cheek tightened as he looked at the man. Though

of similar positions in the military, they had followed completely different paths. Dobbs had spent his entire career on Terra Nova, while this man had been living the high-life on ships and stations. Lieutenant Dobbs had no doubt it was this kind of exposure to alien creatures and attitudes that had left them so weak to start with.

"I am Colonel Pierce. This is my station. Put down your weapons."

Dobbs took aim directly at the man's chest.

"My forces are already aboard your station. Your people have collaborated with the enemy. Drop your weapons and accept your fate…or face the consequences."

He tilted his head in amusement as he said the last line. The standoff continued only for another six seconds, but for both sides it felt like an eternity. They were well matched in numbers, with a dozen fighters on each side. Dobbs' force had the advantage though, with each of his men in full tactical armor and carrying assault weapons. Only one of the defenders carried a carbine, the rest held no more than sidearms or the odd thermal shotgun.

"Very well," said Lieutenant Dobbs.

He pulled the trigger, and at the same time the commander of the station dropped to the ground. One of the defenders was too slow and took the full brunt of the coilgun fire to the face. At this range, the subsonic rounds tore through flesh and bone with ease. The cadet was dead well before the blood even hit the wall.

"Open fire!" Colonel Pierce ordered.

With those few words, the battle for Prometheus Seven began, and with it the very fight for the soul of the Alliance. Shots rang out, but for every pistol shot or thermal shotgun round, there were a dozen coilgun bullets. The numerous interior cameras captured every weapon discharge. Colonel Pierce lifted his handgun up and emptied the clip in the direction of the intruders while simultaneously checking his secpad. He'd managed to drop the unit, and the screen was cracked, but luckily it still worked. There were five other breaches, but marine squads had reached them in time, and they were contained.

Look's like it will be decided here.

Another of his crew was hit, but this time the man dropped down in time to avoid being killed. The round hit his cheek and did little more than cause a flesh wound, albeit a bloody looking one. Still the defenders kept up their fire. It was sporadic and poorly aimed, designed to do little more than keep the enemy busy. The secpad beeped quietly, and he nodded with satisfaction upon seeing the transmission status.

That's it. You keep murdering our people. Every round you fire is another nail in your coffin. And who is going to come and save the day, live on videostream for the entire Alliance to see?

CHAPTER FOUR

Many of the first private sector industries were some of the oldest. Piracy, crime, and prostitution spread through the new colonies and trading routes. As ships arrived at refineries and shipyards, they brought with them so many vices that a new industry had to be invented from scratch, that of private security. It began with bodyguards and then moved up to escort ships. As with all arms races, as the private security increased, so did the means of the criminal. The first pirate attack craft rendered entire sectors deadly to travel and so came the first security squadron, the infamous, Crimson Squadron. This unit was based around an old converted freighter that was equipped as a Q Ship and marks the origins of the Private Security Sector.

Origins of Private Space Travel

Taxxu, Uncharted Space

Spartan opened his eyes and tried to focus on the shapes

ahead. He could see the three machines, but only one of them changed into the correct color. As he watched, the machine shifted to blue and then red before turning to look right at at him.

"Spartan, are you ready?"

He looked at the red machine. Without a face or flesh it looked more like a metal golem. Apart from the odd movement of its cogs and motors, the thing was entirely stationary. He looked into its face and tried to see the eyes. All he could identify was the light red tint where its eyes were supposed to be. Spartan opened his mouth to speak but found words coming out without him even trying.

"They are weak, ready for the invasion."

The machine turned to its comrade and then looked back at Spartan. It lifted one arm, but instead of a hand there was nothing but a thin spinning disk. It moved so fast it was impossible to tell if the edges were sharp or not. The machine leaned in closer.

"Then wake up!"

It swung the weapon across his neck, and his vision vanished in a waterfall of red. In its place was the vast open space he had been in before, hundreds of machines waiting in long ranks. It wasn't them, the columns, or the huge vaulted ceiling that caught his attention. It was the view from the massive windows. A view of thousands of capital ships, each of them waiting patiently like people visiting some great sporting event. In the distance was some black world lit by a hidden star, presumably on the other side of the ship.

The three machines moved in front of him, but as always, it was the red machine that took pride of place. It walked up to Spartan and pointed to his arm. Spartan looked down and immediately noticed the artificial arm that he'd been given on Earth had gone. The flesh had been covered with some form of dull linen. There were blotches of dark blood on the surface, and he could only imagine what might be there.

"What have you done to me?"

The machine ignored him and instead reached for the material. It caught the edge and yanked it away to reveal pale new flesh. Spartan stumbled back a step at seeing his arm once more, the forearm, muscle, bone, hand, and fingers. They were all there.

"What? How?"

"New flesh is the first of your gifts."

The machine then looked back to the lines of machines. They all waited in silence, and it would have been perfectly reasonable if every single one of them had been an empty shell.

"What are my other gifts?"

The machine indicated toward the waiting horde.

"You will advise and lead our warriors into this domain. Together, we shall have our revenge and our age of enlightenment."

Spartan lifted his hand up in front of his face. He could move the fingers just as before, even though there was a slight tingling sensation in his muscles and tendons. He thought back of the battle on board the Rift Engine and then to Helios and beyond.

"Yes, the worlds of the Helios. Tell us of your people. Where are they strongest?"

Spartan looked at his hand and then to them. He could feel his mind nagging and clawing as though there was something he could simply not remember.

"Terra Nova is their capital. Destroy it, and human resistance will crumble."

The machine turned to one of its comrades and then again to Spartan.

"What of the human military? What is their weakness?"

Spartan lifted the corner of his mouth in amusement.

"Compassion. Threaten civilian colonies, and they will risk everything. The humans will not willingly sacrifice themselves for victory."

"Good," said the machine, "We have been waiting for a champion to lead our soldiers into the new domains."

He pointed to other figures off in similar locations to himself. He noted that one was a Byotai and another a Helion. There were others, but they were too far away.

"Despair will follow as each of you returns home at the head of our legions. Lay waste to all, and prepare the ground for our arrival."

Spartan nodded slowly in agreement. He hadn't noticed until now, but this machine bore a mark, a black symbol in an unfamiliar script. He pointed at the imagery.

"What are these marks?"

The machine looked at him for a moment, assessing his posture and mannerism.

"They are the mark of Taxxu."

That meant nothing to Spartan, and even less when the machine opened up. He'd seen this before, the odd metal protective suit that housed the brain and surviving functions of these ancient creatures. As this one opened, he could see the innards of this machine were like those of an animal. As the metal peeled back, it revealed flesh, bone, and tissue. It was as if he were looking inside a beetle.

"I don't understand."

From the shadow came another machine, this one almost identical in design and also red in color. It moved alongside its comrade and turned to face Spartan.

"We are the nine-hundred and twelve. The last of the Ghost Warriors, our limitless bodies remain on our ships, each waiting for the chance to bring about the end of time to these creatures."

Spartan could feel the hate in the machine's voice.

"We are nine-hundred and twelve, and our souls remain hidden and safe, where they will be guarded until the ends of time. The nine-hundred and twelve will fight across the

Great Seal and beyond."

Spartan nodded as if understanding. It was the voice of Z'Kanthu though that he could hear deep inside his mind.

"Discover their weakness. Where is their heart?"

Spartan had always assumed the Biomechs would have a leader, a commander or lead ship. Now he knew little more than he had a month earlier. Z'Kanthu had explained on multiple occasions how the Biomechs had been unable or unwilling to create new offspring since the Great Biomech War. They trusted nobody, not even their servants, and a new generation would create another risk, perhaps one that could finally destroy them.

So, there are less than a thousand of you. I can live with those odds.

He looked at the machines and smiled in agreement while clenching his fists, both his normal hand and his new gift.

* * *

ANS Warlord, 3 Days from Micaya

Admiral Anderson rubbed his forehead and looked at the group of exhausted men and women. The officers' mess was normally a place for relaxation and discussing the day's events. Now it was simply a place to learn of the latest in terrible events. The long table was laid out with trays and a mixture of bland looking food, none of which the Admiral seemed particularly impressed with. Around the table sat an odd collection of officers, as well as representatives from the Helion, Byotai, and Khreenk. He should have been maintaining his interest in them, but it was the latest report on his secpad that kept his attention. For what seemed like an age, he examined the data before putting it down and resting his hands down onto the table. With a final, long breath he beckoned to the other end of the table. The others hushed, all expecting to hear some terrible news.

"Khan."

"Admiral?"

The warrior answered with a dulled, almost emotionless voice, but Anderson could feel the bitterness that lay just below the surface. Since the fighting at the Rift, he had been a changed man, perhaps made worse by his new and unwanted responsibility.

"How are your troops?"

Khan sighed for a moment.

"The medical crews have done their best. We still lost nearly twenty percent of them in the battle. Another five percent have died over the last five weeks since the attack. All of the Black Ships are functional but damaged."

The Admiral moved his head just a fraction in acknowledgement.

"And with our victory at the Rift, we lost Z'Kanthu and Spartan. That was not what I wanted. Are the others still loyal? I've been hearing rumors."

Khan almost seemed offended at the implication. Admiral Anderson could see the hurt, but he needed to know, one way or the other.

"Tell me."

Khan's brow tightened as he answered.

"The Biomech commanders pledged themselves to operate under the chain of command provided by Spartan. I was next in line, so as long as I am alive, they will follow me. After me, it follows on to Teresa."

A few of the other officers looked at him, as he explained the last point. One began to speak at the mention of Spartan's wife, but a three-dimensional model of a female officer appeared right in the center of the table and stopped him in mid-sentence.

"Captain Decker, what can I do for you?"

The older, stern looking woman barely moved a muscle in her face as she spoke.

"Admiral, you requested daily updates on the Black Rift. I have reports in from the Guardians."

"And?"

"Nothing has changed, Admiral. The Rift is still a mess. Nothing goes in or comes out. Our engineers have recovered what they can from the flotsam out there. There's not much worth spending time on."

She ran her hand over her chin.

"But here is one thing that might be of interest to you. It just came in over the wire from Admiral Churchill."

The Admiral raised an eyebrow, but that was the limit of his apparent interest. He suspected it was the same news he'd just seen on his secpad.

"The war barges from Sol, Admiral. I don't know how he did it, but Admiral Churchill has transferred two to Prometheus, and three more are coming through the T'Karan Rift in the next hour. He must have had teams on continuous shifts to get that done."

Anderson smiled ever so slightly.

"I'm more interested in knowing how he got ships from Mars and Earth out of Earthsec territory, past Terra Nova, and then on to Prometheus. That is something of a miracle."

"He'd also managed to rustle up another three transports of troops. This time they're volunteers from Carthago."

Just mentioning the name of that fearsome world had an odd effect on the group. Carthago was known for more than just its soldiers and fighting spirit. There were as many reasons to take help from that colony, as there were to avoid it.

"More mercs?"

The Captain nodded.

"Afraid so, Sir. With the negative press from Terra Nova, I'm surprised we're getting any volunteers for the front now."

"Good. Contact their commander and have them brought here. They will be a useful addition to the gate defenses."

It was a minor series of reinforcements, but it did confirm one thing to the other officers. The Rift to T'Karan was open, and that meant ships and troops could now be transported from the Alliance worlds through to the Helios System. Admiral Anderson lifted his glass and took a sip of the fine port. It ran down his throat and left a warm, comfortable fleeing as it continued down his body. He placed the glass back down and then crashed his fist onto the table. Everybody, apart from Khan, jumped at the interruption.

"The enemy has fully withdrawn over half of its naval strength from the fighting at Spascia and Helios Prime. They've got enough there to keep us busy, and the rest is on its way towards Micaya. The first wave will hit in a week. Our engineers say they will have the Spascia Planetary Defense system operational within the week, but as you can see, all of this is building up to a perfect storm."

A stunned murmur spread quickly through the group. The two Khreenk officers looked to each other and quietly talked. Finally, the taller one spoke through its translator.

"Our forces are not ready at Micaya. We were assured we had over a month to prepare.

"Yes, so were we all. Things change, and that is something every one of us should understand. It's time to get this fleet together, and we need to be ready before the next attack."

He looked at each of the officers, only some of which were actually from ANS Warlord. Most were from newly arrived ships, and two were even from the Byotai.

"The enemy will be at Micaya within the week, people, and you can guarantee that when we are fully engaged, they will try and reopen the Black Rift again. It is what they tried before, and the imagery taken by the boarding parties showed more of these Rift Engines. That is why we are going to go for broke."

He looked at each of them with no expression visible on his face.

"Every ship we can spare must be sent to Micaya. I do not want to fight them just to protect the planet. I want a decisive space battle that will give us room to maneuver. Helios Prime and Spascia will manage with what they have coming in the next five days. Everything else; and I mean everything else, will go to Micaya."

He tapped his hands, and the image in the center of the table changed to show the Helios System and its orbiting planets. He pointed at a cone that ran from Micaya back to the Black Rift.

"With the combined fleets from all of our races, we will smash their fleet decisively, and then redirect from Micaya directly back to the Black Rift. If they try and come in while we're busy, they will be in for one hell of a shock."

The door hissed open and in ran a sweaty looking officer. He wore the uniform of the Intelligence Division.

"Admiral, news just in from Director Johnson on Terra Nova."

Even the Admiral was surprised to see then man barge in, even more so that he felt it reasonable to mention such important and presumably classified information in front of an unknown audience. He moved closer and then finally stopped.

"It's on every public network. The President, he's gone insane."

Admiral Anderson raised an eyebrow, more in surprise that anybody might think otherwise.

"Show us."

The man nodded and then moved to the control system for the table based three-dimensional projector. It flashed white and changed to a live feed from the Alliance Network News.

"This is Chuck Harolds, ANN Reporter live from the Alliance Prometheus Seven space station. Forty minutes ago, a group of intruders surrounded the sovereign station and demanded its surrender."

The Admiral reached for his secpad and checked the validity of the source. Coded information from High Command was already just arriving, but there was also something from Director Johnson.

Trust the media to be there first.

The man on the videostream walked through the station, along with a small group of marines. Running toward them were technicians carrying sidearms and thermal shotguns. The reporter grabbed the first.

"What's going on?"

"Terra Novan interior ministry soldiers are on board. Their killing whoever they find."

The man pushed past but next was a grim looking marine. A single bullet must have struck his helmet because it left a crease along the left cheek.

"The Colonel gave them fair warning, so they opened fire. So far, they have taken three decks and killed eleven Alliance crew."

"Why are they here and on whose orders?"

The man lifted his visor and looked directly into the reporter's head-mounted camera.

"President Harrison ordered the illegal attack. He's killing Alliance citizens, that bastard."

The video shifted to one side and another appeared of the area of space outside the station. It showed six ships. Each one looked ancient, but they all bore the markings of the Alliance as well as Terra Nova insignia.

"Who are they?" Anderson asked under his breath.

A series of bright blue lights marked the movement of Alliance fighters streaking past the ships, and the two exploded in a bright explosion. The effect on those watching was electrifying. Anderson looked to the intelligence officer and beckoned him to come closer.

"I need to speak to Director Johnson, immediately.

Where is he?"

The man swallowed, but it wasn't fear, it was anger.

"We've lost contact with the entire division, Admiral. Rumor has it that he and three senior military commanders were executed in the public square in the last few hours. We've only just received the news."

Admiral Anderson looked down at the message that had only just decoded on his personal secpad. He nearly dropped it at seeing the few words.

Coup on the Capital. Harrison is going to shut down the Prometheus Rift. They are coming for me. Good luck, old friend.

He dropped his face into his hands. The news was nothing like he had expected. President Harrison was a power hungry politician, but he also knew there was no powerbase in the military for him. Only the politically motivated troops of Terra Nova could offer him much in the way of help.

"Get me Churchill. He's the closest to all of this."

He then looked to the others.

"None of this affects our operation. Micaya first, then the Black Rift."

* * *

Prometheus Seven Outpost, Prometheus Sector

Lieutenant Young ran down the corridor with his squad close by. A straggle of survivors came toward him, some with terrible wounds inflicted by coilguns. He'd been on the move for three minutes now after securing the third sector landing deck. Reports came in from across the station as infiltrators penetrated hidden shafts and vents to hide their movement.

"Lieutenant, the command center has fallen. We're withdrawing to the primary passageway," said the Colonel over the intercom.

"Understood, Sir. We're a few more seconds out. Hang in there!"

They kept going, each of them puffing and panting, but still the gunfire could be heard not so far away. They rounded the next bend, and the passageway ran straight into a much wider section. This was one of the old levels that provided access to the lavish apartments, now research labs. Doors ran along the sides, but it was the colored glass ceiling that made the place stand out. It was truly stunning and both wide and high. Two men in black armor stepped out and took aim.

"Drop 'em?"

The marines didn't even stop and simply lifted their weapons to their shoulders and fired while sidestepping to confused the return fire. Only three rounds came back before both of the Terran Novan soldiers were cut down. Right behind them came five technicians plus Colonel Pierce. He moved slowly while helping another carrying a wounded cadet. Gunshots took chunks out of the wall as they moved from the corner and headed in the direction of Lieutenant Young.

"Colonel, over here!"

The wide and beautifully detailed passageway could have accommodated three Maulers in a long column, and the tall, intricately carved columns on each side provided the only cover from the bullets traveling in both directions. A single man in black appeared, and then more, as the pursuers entered the corridor and fanned out.

"Marines, cover them!"

The squad broke formation and scattered to the sides. From the relative safety of the columns, they were able to put down a withering hail of fire. The Colonel used that moment of respite for one last spurt with his people. They made it just as the black armored soldiers took the other end of the corridor. One went forward and pushed a large hexagonal plate in front of him. As he moved, the plate made a grinding sound, and smaller sections expanded out to create a substantial shield. Another moved up and did the same, creating a wall of armor for the soldiers to advance behind.

"What the hell is that, some kind of pavise?" Lieutenant Young muttered.

Colonel Pierce dropped down next to the officer and looked back at the enemy.

"They came here well prepared. We were holding them off till they brought up stun grenades and shields. Looks like they brought the full set of riot gear for this one."

A loud bang caught their attention. Both looked back and watched a door blast out behind them; a small group of black armored troopers appeared. They didn't wait and quickly threw themselves at the few marines still fighting. Gunfire lashed between them, as well as fists and bayonets. The group quickly spread amongst the defenders, but one in particular made for Colonel Pierce. Two others followed him, swinging their carbines like clubs to smash their way through. They fought hard, but weight of numbers quickly overpowered the marines until just four remained standing against Lieutenant Dobbs and his entourage. They finally stopped and moved up around their commander, taking aim at the two officers and two wounded marines.

"It is over," said the Colonel in a hard, bitter tone.

"You will give the order for your people to surrender, or we will vent this station."

Colonel Pierce lowered his sidearm and looked to his security chief. With a quick movement of his head, he confirmed for him to also lower his weapon. A loud crashing sound came from further along the corridor, and part of the wall ripped apart. Chunks of masonry, glass, and metal fell about as six shapes emerged from the dust cloud. They were massive, easily the size of Marine Vanguards.

"Get down!" came a loud, booming voice.

Colonel Pierce knew that voice anywhere and found

himself smiling as he threw himself to the floor, narrowly avoiding a bayonet to the face.

"Do it!" he yelled.

The seven black armored soldiers from Terra Nova and their leader turned their guns on the new arrivals. Coilguns blasted, but then came the high-pitched scream of powerful multi-barreled guns. The streaks of flame filled the passageway, and shells tore holes the size of apples into the body of anybody that got in the way. As he lay on the ground, he looked up at six dark shapes and the massive muzzle flashes that obscured them. Finally, the noise stopped, and all that remained were the grunts and groans from the wounded marines. Colonel Pierce tried to stand but stumbled and began to fall back down.

"I've got you."

A thick muscled arm covered in crimson armor grabbed him so tightly it actually hurt a little. He found himself upright and on his feet, staring up into the friendly face of a mighty Jötnar warrior.

"Osk, it's damn good to see you."

The dust and smoke began to clear, and as it did, so did the shapes of the Jötnar begin to clear. They all wore the armor of the Red Watch, the dark crimson that each of them wore so proudly. All of the Jötnar carried the massive Gatling guns favored by their kind, either on their shoulders on special pintle mounts, or carried in both arms. Osk, the first female Jötnar and commander of the garrison on Prometheus, swung her arm and struck the Colonel hard on the shoulder.

"It looks like we were in the right place at the right time."

He winced at the strength of the strike.

"Yeah, I knew keeping you on board for a few more hours was a good idea."

He looked back into the corridor and the carnage the Jötnar had wrought. It was more than just the bodies. It was the damage caused by their immense firepower. Entire chunks of columns had been torn apart, and the Terra Novan soldiers had seen limbs and heads torn clean off. Not one of the intruders remained alive.

"Okay, Colonel, what next?" she asked.

The blood splattered and exhausted officer looked to Lieutenant Young, who just nodded at him. He then looked back to Osk.

"We clear this station, and then we will…"

Movement caught his eye. He followed the motion and spotted the mortally wounded figure of Lieutenant Dobbs. The soldier's right arm had been shot off above the elbow, and his chest contained no less than three major puncture wounds. He tried to speak, but blood bubbled and gushed from his mouth. Osk walked toward him and then knelt down alongside him.

"Why?" she asked.

The man coughed twice and struggled to speak.

"To…remove you…"

Osk opened up her visor and laughed. It was a bittersweet laugh, but she continued nonetheless. The other Jötnar joined in for a while before quieting down. She reached out with her right hand to touch the dying man. He looked up at her, his eyes burning hot, but though he wanted to speak, nothing but blood now came from his mouth. Osk nodded gently.

"It's okay. We will visit your homeworld and introduce ourselves."

Her smile tightened into a grimace.

"Your soldiers will be punished for this outrage, animal."

He yelled in pain and anger one last time and then slumped back, the black blood pooling around his mouth on the floor. Osk paced back and forth and then stopped in front of Colonel Pierce.

"I'll tell you what we're going to do. We will load up the transports on Prometheus and set course for Terra Nova. We will remove this usurper and remind the people of that place who we are and what we can do."

She then turned and stormed over to her comrades. Colonel Pierce looked down to the shattered body of the soldier and reached down to close his eyes.

You fools! What have you done? Never, ever bring upon the vengeance of the Jötnar.

* * *

ANS Warlord, 3 Days from Micaya

The massive mainscreen showed the latest live feed from the exterior of the Prometheus Seven Station. It wasn't an encrypted channel or even a military channel. The logo at the corner actually showed it was a live feed coming from the station, and the space battle had just become fiercer. Admiral Anderson shook his head when a flight of fighters ducked and dived past the mothballed marine assault transport. Turret fire blasted nearby, but the Alliance pilots expertly avoided the attack.

"Those ships are crewed by buffoons," he said angrily.

They were weeks away from the action, and there was absolutely nothing he could do, other than send messages directly to his regional commanders. He checked the tactical display for probably the tenth time and then wiped his brow.

This is going to be close.

The space station had used its turrets to beat off the shuttles as they took away their wounded. The videostreams showed at least half of those that had made it to the station were now either dead or captured. Station defenses were no longer holding back, and the small railguns and point-defense turrets caused substantial minor damage to any of the ships that strayed too close.

"There," said the ship's tactical officer.

Admiral Anderson could already see the problem. The flashes of light along the hull of ANS Terra showed where her railguns had just fired. The Sanlav rounds split apart upon reaching half of the target distance before sending chunks of debris deep into the station's decking.

"Thank the gods they don't have anything more than that."

While the railguns were powerful, they were insignificant next to the power of the particle beam weapons used in the final stages of the war. The explosive energy of these direct-energy weapons was capable of exploding entire ships with a single burst. The Sanlav rounds would ultimately do the same job, but it would take hours, perhaps even days against a station as massive as Prometheus Seven.

"Sir, he's arrived."

The Rift alongside the station flickered and then changed in form to look like mirrored steel. From inside the odd colored shape came one, two, and then seven ships. All of them were heavy Alliance warships, each bearing the markings and insignia of the fleet. A video image on the open channel appeared on the right of the mainscreen.

"This is Captain Takei of the Alliance Navy Ship Alexander. Cease fire immediately."

Several of the younger officers cheered excitedly at this new arrival. Admiral Anderson was silent. Unlike them, he had experience of the wills of men, and the people of

Terra Nova had a strange attitude to situations like this. He was hardly surprised when ANS Terra altered her course to face the ships, and then immediately opened fire on the smallest of the escorts in the force. The initial volley of railgun fire punched multiple holes into the space armor of the ship; luckily he was able to move out of the line of fire and behind one of the larger Liberty class destroyers. Admiral Anderson sighed at seeing this.

"He has no choice now, just end this quickly."

The other ships moved in close to ANS Terra, and they then advanced on the formation of Liberty ships. It was unusual to see such a large number of the new ships in formation without access to a full-size capital ship. Even so, they continued to put down a hail of fire, most of which was stopped by interceptor fire from the anti-air turrets on the destroyers. The Rift flickered one final time, and in came a heavily worn looking Crusader class warship. Without warning, the multiple gun turrets opened fire, each hitting ANS Terra with solid shot. The gunfire exchange was impressive, but the energy bloom showing on the screen was what caught all of their attention. Though invisible to the naked eye, the overlays simply placed the particle beam buildup onto the visuals so that the gunfire could be seen. With a single pulse, the emitters released a burst of energy so great that the front third of ANS Terra vanished in a bright blue explosion. Chunks of ship tore off, with at least one section piercing one of the nearby ships.

"This is Admiral Churchill. Cease fire immediately or face annihilation."

Even Admiral Anderson was impressed at the few short words from the old warhorse. As surrender indicators appeared on the imagery, he turned around to look at his comrades.

"That, people, is how you make an entrance."

He rubbed his lower lip.

"Now, let's get this show on the road. I'm sure the Admiral is capable of resolving any outstanding issues on Terra Nova without our help. In the meantime, I have a war to fight."

CHAPTER FIVE

How do our forces match up with those of our enemies? Since the inclusion of second-generation technology, our ships have gained direct-energy weapons and artificial gravity. This level of advancement puts us on parity with the vessels of races such as the Helions and T'Kari. Even the Biomechs appear no less advanced than us, apart from their use of biomechanical structure for some of their ships. This level of resilience gives them great staying power in prolonged space combat.
Naval Cadet's Handbook

Low-Orbit, Spascia, Helion Sector

There was no glimmer of emotion from Teresa as she watched the mainscreen. The Captain of the ship continued to bark orders to the crew, but for Teresa the only thing of interest was the ruined city. She had seen the images months earlier, but the sight of the ancient ruins was still a shock. Spascia had been the site of one of the many massacres in the old wars. Now whatever remained of the city was long gone.

"It's incredible, don't you think?" asked Commander Jameson, the ship's XO.

"How so?" Teresa replied in a monotone voice.

"Helios Prime was destroyed from space. The bombardment flattened entire blocks of the city. Spascia is something else entirely. This destruction is from artillery and infantry assault. It's like something from the twentieth century on old Earth."

Teresa didn't know what to say, so she said nothing. The Marine transport was actually one of the newly commandeered civilian transports that had been upgraded to military specification. That last part she might have found amusing on any other day. The reality was that the computer systems, wiring, and paint scheme had been changed. There were also bunks where the cargo holds had once been. To the right was another of the transports, her hull streaked with fire as they smashed through the upper atmosphere. There was a single Byotai transport, its semi-biological look in direct contrast to the hard edges of the human vessels.

"Colonel, are your marines ready?" asked the Captain.

Teresa looked at the man and his worried expression. She could understand why in the circumstances. They were flying a glorified civilian transport directly into the teeth of an ongoing siege.

They aren't my marines.

She watched them file aboard, had even spoken with all their officers. But this was no Marine regiment, battalion, or even a company. The fighting on Helios Prime had seen to that weeks ago. These were squads and platoons from a dozen different units. Some had only just arrived to replace those on the ground; others were in transit to different parts of the planet when the orders had arrived. Teresa closed her eyes for a second and recalled the imagery of the three ships; each filled with nearly five hundred marines apiece. There were more vessels following, but these carried an odd assortment of private security and ex-military forces.

"They are waiting, Captain."

"Good, because we are coming down hard and fast."

The Captain sounded nervous, and as the clouds of smoke began to separate, she could see why. They were flying along the path of the great chasm, and off into the distance was the mountain. The view to the left was of smaller mountain peaks and crags. It was the wasteland to the right that was the most stunning. Unlike the ruins of Helios Prime, this city had never been a tall one. The collapsed superstructures on the capital world were still huge, even in their destruction. Spascia was a graveyard for metal and masonry.

"There they are," said the XO.

He pointed off to the right where vast amounts of gunfire could be seen. Teresa checked her overlay in her helmet that showed the tactical position.

"Yes, that's the frontline. Last reports from General Gun said our troops had cleared an area two kilometers from the chasm. They are holding them as long as possible so we can get our ships down."

"No, you can't be serious. That's the landing platforms, next to the bridges?"

The Captain looked to Teresa, shaking his head.

"Show me," said Teresa.

The Captain gave his orders, and the helmsman changed the mainscreen to show a magnified view of the landing grounds. The platforms were wide and easily large enough for assault craft and Maulers to land. There were three in operation; the others appeared to be filled with wreckage. Teresa looked for a moment and then realized two of them were covered with the wreckage of a Khreenk heavy transport.

"Yes, that's the spot."

"Colonel, I can't put us down in a space that small."

He looked back to the screen.

"It's impossible."

Teresa looked at the details sent over by Gun and tried to hide her smile.

"Captain, the specifications are accurate. You will have a fifty percent margin of error for the landing. You will put this transport down on the pad, and I will get our forces out and into action in less than six minutes."

She spotted him looking to his XO, who shook his head in disagreement. Normally, she was very restrained, but this attitude was beginning to annoy her. They'd left the rest of the fleet to join Anderson, Lewis, and the others at the assembly point off Micaya. These were all the reinforcements that could be expected for Spascia for a month, perhaps longer.

"Captain. If we do not land, then this planet will fall. We will lose the weapon, the world, and every single man and woman we sent here."

It was common knowledge that her son was one of those fighting in the never-ending battle. Mostly assumed it was a fruitless fight, but there was nothing that could be done to quickly resolve the situation. There was no way to leave the planet, and the millions of Helion civilians that would have to be left behind. General Gun's forces had done the impossible, and still the enemy attacked from their heavily entrenched positions.

"Captain, an urgent message from General Gun."

He nodded and pointed to the mainscreen.

"Put it up."

The image from the inside of Gun's helmet appeared. The footage was slightly blurred, and bright light from nearby sent flashes and flares into the lens. Teresa stood in front of the massive screen.

"General."

"Colonel, good to see you."

The image flashed white. The wizened General grimaced, and the footage shook. It blurred so badly that it was barely possible to make out his face. Then it settled again, but not for long.

"The frontline is weak. My Vanguards and Jötnar have plugged what they can."

He moved his eyes, shouting off to somebody to his left.

"Send two squads to the barricade. You, get that gun into position, now!"

Again came the flashes of gunfire as he blasted an unseen enemy.

"We can hold but not for much longer. How long till you land?"

Teresa looked to the Captain. He shook his head once more.

"I told you, Colonel, we can't do it."

Gun must have heard because his eyes moved to the center of his visor. It was as though he was looking right at those in the ship.

"What did I just hear?" he growled.

The Captain swallowed nervously, but Gun continued, giving him no time to reply.

"I have Marines, Jötnar, Vanguards, Khreenk, machines, and even Helion civilians fighting on this frontline. Every minute is costing us lives. You will land that ship, Captain, or I promise you, I will get to you and tear your damn throat out!"

His eyes widened as he opened fire once more, and this time it was possible to see the reflection on his visor. It was blurred and difficult to see, but Teresa was sure she could see a Thegn move right in front of him before Gun smashed it down with his arm.

"Colonel, get your people here fast. We need the bridges secured and a reserve line ready. I'll hold for fifteen more minutes. Any longer, and we'll be overrun."

Teresa pushed the Captain out of her way and moved closer.

"Hang in there, Gun. We're coming."

Gun nodded, and the image vanished. Teresa turned around to face the Captain. Her hand slid down to her thigh and perilously close to her sidearm.

"I don't care how you get us down. You can land with cheerleaders waving on both sides, or you can crash-land into the middle of the pad. Either way, we are not leaving this planet until every one of my marines is on the ground."

She leaned in a few centimeters so he could see her eyes.

"Do you understand me, Captain?"

The man took in a slow breath.

"Very well, I will do what I can."

Teresa feigned a smile.

"I can't expect you to do any more, can I?"

The vast starship shuddered at it continued down toward the thicker atmosphere. At their speed, the thermal energy was vast, so much so, that only a vessel designed for this kind of re-entry could ever hope to survive. A few low-level alerts triggered, but nothing too serious. The XO spoke briefly with the tactical officer and then moved toward the Captain. He ignored Teresa, but she waited and listened while watching the imagery of their descent.

"Sir, the frontline has been ruptured in four places. Heavy walkers supported by infantry are inside our lines. We have two groups making a run for the chasm."

Teresa pointed at the shapes overlaid on the mainscreen.

"Yes, in the next hour, possibly less, the Biomechs will have surrounded this strongpoint. They need to fall back to the chasm, now."

Commander Jameson looked at her as if Teresa had just spoken in a foreign language.

"Are you serious, Colonel? If they fall back now, the Biomechs will be able to reach the chasm in half the time."

Teresa walked to the nearest computer and spoke quickly to the junior officer. The young, nervous looking man pulled an intercom from its holder and handed it to her. She glared at the Captain and pointed to the screen.

"Get this ship down, and fast!"

He moved away, and she was left to speak on the

intercom.

"General, it's Teresa. Your frontline is broken. The enemy is heading for the chasm. You need to pull back, right now."

The audio was much poorer quality than before, but it was enough for her to make out the voice and exertions of Gun. He was clearly right in the middle of a fight for his life, yet still he spoke.

"Understood. It's about time one of you got here. Get a move on."

It was short, but even Teresa couldn't hide the smile on her face. Gun was as reliable as any man you could find. He would happily stay there and fight for the next week, or until he was physically unable to do so any longer. That was no help to her though.

I've got a battle to win, and somewhere out there is Jack.

The audio crackled, and then Gun spoke once more.

"Your boy, he's here. I'll make sure he gets out."

It wasn't much, but those few words from the Jötnar meant more to her than news that a thousand marines might have just landed. Just the mention of her son's name filled her soul with a hunger for the fight. She handed back the intercom and walked to the Captain and his XO. They both looked at her as she approached, but the Captain spoke first.

"We'll be on the ground in less than four minutes. I suggest you…"

Teresa lifted her hand to silence him.

"No suggestions, Captain. Get my people on the ground, and then prepare your ship to leave. You have the rendezvous point at Micaya. You will take whatever casualties are waiting, and then get the hell out of Dodge."

Teresa considered grabbing his collar but did her best to stay calm and collected. There was little point in insulting the man and belittling him in front of his own crew. She still needed his help, and it was critical he understood that his job didn't end when they hit the ground.

"Remember, this is just one battle. Anderson needs every ship he can get to fight at Micaya. Even this old bucket has plenty of fight in her, don't you think?"

She might have been smiling, but neither of the two Navy officers found her words particularly endearing. The ship was large and carried a substantial crew, but not one of them believed for a second their modified civilian transport would stand up to much in a major space battle. Teresa could see their confusion, and she started to walk away to join her fellow marines deep inside the vessel.

"Captain. Even an unarmed ship with no armor can make a difference. Admiral Anderson is a tactical mastermind. If you get the ship to him, he will find a use for you, even if it's just to make the fleet look larger than it really is. Good luck, Gentlemen."

Teresa walked out through the door and left them staring at her in surprise.

"Is she mad?" asked the XO.

The Captain shook his head and sighed.

"No, but she is the wife of Spartan. Would you expect any less?"

* * *

The Three Sisters, Spascia, Helion Sector

Jack reached into the ammunition pouch on his utility belt and opened the lid. It wasn't easy to feel inside with his armored gauntlet, but there was no way he was going to remove even a single piece of his protection. Finally, he pulled out the small metal container and tapped the button. The top opened up to reveal a small number of pills. He lifted it to his visor and activated the servos. The front flipped up, and in one carefully practiced movement, he popped two of them into his mouth.

"Jack, come on, we need to move," said Jana.

He looked across to his friend, who even now was busy tightening a bandage on the arm of a wounded Zathee fighter. This one was older than normal, perhaps forty or even fifty years of age. His clothing was burned, but the thick long-coat he'd used had at least kept the worst of the fire away from him. Jack swallowed and felt the tablets immediately stick to his throat. In a single short movement, he twisted his neck and placed his mouth around the small, rubberized tube. A quick sip pulled tepid water into his mouth and helped wash them down into his stomach.

"I'm ready."

A pair or shells came down just ahead of their position, and a Vanguard vanished in a bright yellow explosion. Two marines ran; both wreathed in flame, and with a dozen or more Thegns leaping at them with guns and blades. Part of the inner wall collapsed, and a trio of Jötnar crashed into the Thegns. The largest swung his arms and cast two Thegns to the ground before opening fire with a massive multi-barreled gun. Body parts flew in all directions as the three Jötnar blocked the route with their own bodies.

"Fall back!" yelled the largest of them.

"Gun," Jack said quietly under his breath.

Another rocket whooshed by overhead but landed somewhere between the last Marine position and the bridges. A hundred, perhaps a thousand weapons fired up into the sky at six or seven large transports moving overhead. They were easy to hit at this distance, though few amongst the enemy would have the kind of firepower required to dent, let alone damage something so massive. Jack took aim at the crowd of approaching enemy soldiers, but Sergeant Stone leapt over the bodies of two fallen marines and landed alongside him.

"Son, we're falling back. Move it!"

The Sergeant didn't wait to see if he did and moved further into the shattered defenses to pass on the order.

Bullets slammed into the ground all around him, but no matter where he moved, he seemed to avoid them. Jack shook his head in amazement as another marine; just a meter from the Sergeant, took three rounds to the chest while Sergeant Stone spoke to another.

"I wish I had his luck."

Something struck the side of his face, and he twisted back to look right back into the face of Private Jenkell. Corporal Frewyn and Private Hardman had both survived the last assault and were dragging one of the emplaced heavy machine guns. Another rocket flew overhead and exploded off into the distance.

"Leave it, now go!"

Jack looked up at Gun and his entourage of Jötnar. They both recognized each other, but there was no time for conversation or any other niceties. Bullets clanged off his armor as he looked down to them.

"I said leave it!"

Corporal Frewyn released the gun and signaled for Jack, Jana, and Hardman to follow. They wasted no time in moving past the collapsed walls and the last remaining of the three towers of the fortification. Jack glanced at it and shook his head.

I thought those towers would never fall.

He looked over his shoulder and watched with a mixture of shock and awe, as all that remained behind the marines was Gun and his comrades. A handful of

Vanguards had joined the synthetic warriors, and together they had formed a thin line of metal and flesh. Hundreds of rounds smashed into them, yet their return fire was devastating. Even the Thegns were forced to fall back and take cover or risk being cut apart.

"Eight o'clock!" called out somebody in front.

Jack spun about and lifted his carbine, just as a Thegn appeared from out of the dust. His visor had hundreds of other targets tagged, and no matter where he looked, there seemed to be enemy troops all around him.

They've broken through. We're surrounded!

Jack pulled the trigger, and the gun spat out the last half of the magazine. He continued to hold down the trigger even though nothing came from the barrel. One Thegn jumped in front of him and swung a short, curved blade that struck him under the arm with a thud. Jana spotted the attack and put a round into its temple. As it dropped down, another two replaced it and put two rounds into her chest. Both bounced from the curved plates, but the impact was enough to knock her from her feet. She hit the ground hard, and then more of the Thegns were on them. Jack tried to lift his arm, but the blade had pushed in so deeply that it had wedged on the articulation point. An arm grabbed him and pulled him from the fight.

"Get up! You have to keep moving."

More blades flashed about, but now there were a smattering of Helions with their improvised explosive weapons and even some Khreenk. Jack could feel his nerves returning and images of the last bloodbath spilled over to the front of his mind. He couldn't see the bridges. There were just warriors of all types, and every one of them was fighting for their very lives. He reached down to the blade, grasped it in both hands, and yanked hard. Jack screamed in pain as the blade pulled from his armor, with dark red, almost black blood dripping from its serrated edge.

"Jack, what are you doing?" Jana complained.

The Private lowered her weapon and took the weight of Jack's side on her shoulder. He moaned as she took some of his body weight, and then they were off. Marines ran by in front of them, but neither paid much attention. Jack couldn't have used his carbine even if he'd wanted to, and so went straight for his sidearm. As he lifted it up, another Thegn rushed past him. He fired, but it was fast and disappeared over a ruined Bulldog armored vehicle. As soon as it vanished behind the burned metal, a triple burst from artillery fire completely destroyed the entire area.

"Look, the tower," said Jana.

Jack lifted his eyes and watched the structure fall in on itself a short distance behind them. It quickly vanished into a massive cloud of dust. Then he heard a terrifying scream. He looked toward their destination and the vast chasm with its waiting bridges. He saw panicked groups of marines and Helions running for cover from the shape of five Eques walkers. It was like a massive pincer movement, and they had moved from the flanks to completely cut them off from relief.

We're done.

Jack shook his head, angry at them and himself. He looked to his pistol and the ammunition indicator.

Six more bullets, is that how it all ends?

Two Jötnar pushed past him, almost knocking him to the floor and right into the path of the machines. As one the alien war machines opened fire, a withering rain of fire hit both Jötnar that slowed them to a standstill. One slumped to its knees and dropped forward onto its stomach; the second staggered, fell, and then lifted its arm to fire a rocket. The missile screeched ahead and caught the nearest walker between its front legs. With a great blast, it dropped to its haunches and collapsed. A hand grabbed Jack and pulled him forward. It was Sergeant Stone again.

"Son, what did I tell you? You have to keep moving!"

Jack tried to focus his eyes, but the mixture of painkillers and loss of blood was beginning to affect him adversely. He lifted his handgun and emptied it at the shape of the machine. Helion civilians surged forward like a great clan of rats. One by one, they were shot down, but a few made it close enough to stab their explosive-tipped spears into the machines. Jötnar followed them and even a few Vanguards.

"Take this," said a Khreenk soldier.

Jack didn't see exactly what it was, but the device was heavy, and he was forced to use both arms to take the weight. It was longer than a coilgun, and thick bulbous cylinders ran sideways along its length. He lifted it to his visor, but the sight showed an odd mixture of symbols and indicators.

What the hell?

Jack blinked twice and then took a number of quick breaths. His vision cleared a little, partially helped by the extra boost of painkillers and adrenalin. Jana opened the monitor panel on his arm and checked his vitals.

"You need sealing and a cycle of boosters. Hold on."

She pressed a few buttons, and the suit felt as if it were inflating. In reality, it was quite the opposite. First of all, a special non-toxic sealant was spreading through the limbs and torso. As soon as it met the cool air from outside, it created a temporary, semi-elastic seal. Jana reached to her medical pack and took out a small metal cylinder. She pulled on a hatch and pushed in the device onto Jack's thigh.

"This will help."

Jack looked at it and nodded. It was no miracle cure, but a small drip containing a well-developed series of fluids designed to keep a marine in the field in just this kind of situation. He could feel some of the pain slipping away even though his arm felt partially numb.

"Get on the firing line and put these bastards down!" Sergeant Stone called out.

The invulnerable Sergeant was now in front of the marines and signaled them to rally around his position. They were just a hundred meters from the first and largest of the bridges, surrounded by wrecked vehicles from three different races. Two SAAR robots moved past him and then deployed in front of the marines.

"Come on, we have work to do," said Corporal Frewyn.

The two marines helped walk Jack toward their sergeant. By the time they were halfway there, Jack was able to move under his own power. More and more marines appeared, the survivors of the fall of the Three Sisters. He counted at least a full platoon, perhaps more, with a smattering of Vanguards and Khreenk. They deployed into a loose line, using any cover they could find.

"Put them down!" repeated the Sergeant.

Of all of them, he was the only one standing up straight. Two gunshots struck his right leg, and both ricocheted off into a burned out Helion truck. Two Eques machines moved to face him, and a dozen turrets twisted about to take aim. The Sergeant ignored them and lifted his carbine. It flashed one, and then again as he discharged high-power rounds right into the front of the machines.

"Fire!" said a familiar voice.

Gun and his blood-splattered entourage staggered into view and unleashed every weapon they carried. More and more marines opened fire, and the two nearest Eques walkers were covered in sparks and flashes. The carbines blew off chunks the size of a hand, while the larger guns smashed guns and fractured the legs joints.

Here goes nothing.

Jack lifted the Khreenk weapon up and pointed at the head of the machine. He reached for the trigger and found two levers instead. He looked to Jana, but both she and the other marines were down on the ground and blasting anything they could see. The two Khreenk were too far away, and both were lifting a heavy double-barreled weapon onto a third's shoulder.

"Screw this, let's do it!"

He pulled the first lever and braced himself. Instead of a blast, the weapon began to hum. Lights in the sight flashed. At first, it was just one and then two in an increasing pattern inside. He gripped tightly but could feel a slight hum and vibration building even through the protection of his suit.

"Huh?"

There were now five flashing lights inside, and the vibration was becoming intolerable. He fumbled for the other lever and accidentally lowered the weapon as he found it. The front vanished in a bright green blast, and he tipped over backwards. Luckily, he was able to put out his hand to avoid impaling himself on a broken machine. Jana went to help him, but the drugs were working well.

He lifted himself back and then looked at the Khreenk weapon.

"Holy crap, that was good."

A green residue had formed around the muzzle, and the dirt hissed and bubbled where he'd left it on the ground for just a few seconds. He lifted it back up as one of the Khreenk warriors approached. Behind him, the one with the shoulder-mounted weapon, fired and a double streak of blue matter hit the Eques walker. It began burning its way through its torso. Marines cheered in excitement, but their joy was short lived as more and more Thegns blocked the route with their own bodies. The Khreenk spoke through its emotionless translator.

"Powerful weapon, no more than level three. Or risk death."

The warrior tapped him on the shoulder and then moved back to the others.

"Level three? What does he mean?"

Jack looked at the weapon and then laughed.

"I think I might have just nearly killed myself. This thing is some crazy gear."

Jana pulled another magazine from her armor and slid it into her coilgun.

"What level did you get to?"

"Uh, five or six I think."

"You idiot."

She raised her carbine and fired in short bursts. After

the fifth, she threw him a withering look. It was one he wasn't particular familiar with, but he could tell she wasn't impressed.

"What?" he asked.

"I didn't patch you up to stand there gawping. Use the damned weapon!"

Jack looked back at it.

Yeah, good point.

He twisted about and kneeled down to both help with the recoil and also to avoid the massed volleys from the hundreds of Thegns now right in front of them. The sides looked about evenly matched, but the short patch of open ground to the bridge was impossible to reach. Jack pulled the first lever and began searching for targets. Half of the Eques walkers were down, but more had arrived, and around their feet moved a sea of Thegns. Though they had blocked the route, they also lacked the cover now being used by the marines.

"Let's clear a path."

The lights had reached a level of four, and when he pulled the trigger, it slammed hard into his body. This time he was ready and watched the short two-second pulse-burst blast out from the muzzle. It was unlike any weapon he'd used before, and to his surprise noticed the spread of impacts was wide.

"That is one inaccurate bit of gear."

Everywhere it touched flickered and imploded in a

spectacular fashion. The first five Thegns almost turned to dust before his eyes and exploded in a cloud. The parts of the Eques walker struck splintered and tore off as though the machines were casting off defective plating, weapons, and limbs. He pulled the lever again, and a new tone and flashing light started up. He looked over to the Khreenk and one spotted him. It lifted up his hand to show one finger, and then went back to his own work.

"One what?" Jack shouted.

The Khreenk had their own troubles though, and he looked back, took aim, and fired at the center of an Eques. A pair of Decurion walkers jumped up and took the impact instead. Both exploded in spectacular fashion, but at the same time, the weapon's lights flickered and then died.

"What the hell?"

Sergeant Stone moved from his position at the front and along the line of dug in marines and Khreenk. A squad of Helions tried to break out and run forward, but he forced them to stay down.

"Not yet, wait for my command."

Another squad of marines arrived and pushed on to the left. They moved in pairs, with a single Vanguard advancing in the middle. Gunfire clattered about them, but by either luck or good timing, they made it through. Jack looked at the weapon and began to shake it.

"Come on, you worthless piece of junk."

A single light flashed, and then the sight lit up as it had

done earlier. He lifted it to his shoulder and pulled the first lever. Nothing happened. He continued depressing the level while a separate green bar began to fill. As soon as it reached a marker, the other light came on; one, two, and then three before he pulled the second trigger. This time there was the kick and blast as it unleashed another burst of green energy. His aim was too low, and half the power was wasted on the metal and debris. Even so, at least six Thegns were hit, and parts of their bodies blown off in clouds of dust.

"That's it, advance!" Sergeant Stone shouted out.

The marines raised themselves from their hiding places and moved a step at a time. Jack pulled the level until it reach just one indicator and fired. The energy blast was much smaller, but he noted how the first bar had only just dropped below the marker and had already surpassed what must have been a ready marker.

I get it. The first one is the charge, like a generator. It takes time to refuel the gun. The second one is a capacitor for that shot. The first one holds energy for a long time, the second one is temporary.

He fired again, once more killing a handful of Thegns.

The lower the power setting, the less time it takes to recharge the gun.

He turned to the right and put a green blast of energy into the torso of a Decurion. The machine was busily ripping apart a Helion, and both vanished in the fireball.

"Hell, yes, I love this gun!"

He turned back around to fire, but Jana lifted her hand to block his target.

"Not there, Jack. That's the bridge."

He squinted and tried to look past the machines and their foot soldiers. The bridge was barely visible, but he could see large black shapes of transports coming down on the other side. He looked at her.

"So?"

She leaned in and struck him on the top of his helmet.

"Because if you miss, the energy from that thing will move over the bridge and toward the landing pads. Do you want to bring down our transports?"

Jack looked back to the bridges and quickly understood what she meant. Unfortunately, while he had been speaking, he'd completely forgotten about the weapon and its lever that he'd held down. Part of the stonework tore apart in front of him, and from the very ground beneath them came a trio of Decurions. They surged out behind what looked like an unlimited horde of Thegns. Three marines were cut down instantly before they could shoot back.

"Kill them all!" shouted an officer right behind the frontline.

Jack took aim and pulled the second trigger, not even noticing that it had reached seven flashing lights. The green energy blast was massive and hit the unit of Decurions and Thegns with more firepower than even an entire platoon of Vanguards could manage. Dozens were torn apart by the blast, and other marines hurled themselves into the fray. It was savage and brutal, but somehow the energy blast and the counterattack held back the machines. The Khreenk weapon simultaneously exploded as Jack fired, and it sent a plume of energy back toward his helmet and torso. Jack fell to the ground, knocked unconscious by the blast.

"Jack!" Jana screamed.

She ran to him and knelt beside his fallen shape. His PDS Alpha armor hissed as though it was a block of fat on a fire.

"I need help!"

CHAPTER SIX

The combat of the Great Biomech War proved to be a continuation of combat for many Alliance units. Some were involved in combat operations on Helios Prime against insurgents when the Biomechs arrived. Tech Sergeant Carsten became something of a legend after having been involved in fighting on Hades, Eos, Helios Prime, and then at the Black Rift. The fact that he survived made him the youngest man in the Marine Corps to have seen action on four worlds, as well as in two ship boarding actions.

Great Heroes of the Alliance

Taxxu, Uncharted Space

Spartan walked back and forth in front of the line of machines. So far, he'd counted over a hundred different models, and by his reckoning, there were probably ten times as many still waiting in the vast halls and barrack rooms of the ship. Each of the machines was about two-thirds the size of Z'Kanthu and his kin. Apart from the size, they had much in common, with all of them standing on two legs. None of these machines seemed to carry weapons, and their arms hung down with empty sockets where their human-sized hands should be. He stopped at one and looked directly at it.

"Who are you?"

Even as Spartan spoke, he realized his voice was different, as though he were speaking in some odd tongue. The accent and tone were new to him even though he understood exactly what he was saying.

"I am One-Zero-One of the Ghost Warriors. I have died seven times in the service of my people."

Spartan looked at the machine and then to the left at the lines of other machines. Every single one of them was of a similar height and build, yet the subtle differences from shades of color to the changes in shoulder armor and torso shape, marked them out as individuals. There were a few that were marginally taller, but the one he spoke with appeared to be fairly average among them.

"One-zero-one. What will happen if you die?"

The machine's torso twisted slightly and faced Spartan, as if looking at him. This machine, like many of the others, had no discernible face. The torso was in reality just a single large chest area, curved and well armored. The arms hung down from the corners like a great ape.

"Well?"

The machine continued to bend down and touched its handless arms to the floor. Motors whirred, and metal plates shifted to release six small, articulated grabbers. Metal components moved out from the floor and attached to the limbs. In a few seconds the machine was standing upright, with a small, four-barreled weapon on each arm. A high-pitched motor noise started up, and a light appeared at the tip of each barrel.

"This," it said stoically.

Spartan took two steps back and braced himself, expecting the worse. Both of machine's the arms twisted about at an impossible angle from the elbow and pointed the weapons at its own chest. The arm motors whirred almost silently until finally stopping. Spartan was unsure what was happening until the glow appeared to grow brighter and brighter at the muzzles of each arm.

"No!" Spartan shouted.

He began to move forward, but it was too late. There was a flash along the upper portion of the machine, and it vanished in a fireball. Chunks of metal and burned flesh scattered about the floor, some even striking other machines. One large section flipped about toward Spartan, and he was forced to lift him arms to defend himself. To his surprise and relief, it bounced off and fell to the ground. Not one of the other machines moved even an inch as their comrade died pointlessly on the ground.

Spartan lowered his arms and looked around for signs of guards, or at least somebody that might show some degree of interest.

"What? Why the hell did you do that?" he asked, walking about the ruins of the machine. There were scattered pieces of metal as well as chunks of unidentifiable organic matter.

"You said there were less than a thousand of you, and you do this."

He bent down to touch the shattered metal, but a familiar voice spoke from behind.

"I would not touch that if I were you. The weapon capacitors retain charge for many hours."

He turned about to find an identical machine to the one that had just been destroyed. Apart from the gleaming metal armor, this could easily have been the exact same machine. The most obvious and telling difference, apart from that fact that the other was destroyed was that this one had been polished and gleamed like it was fresh from a factory. Even so, Spartan was sure he could see marks and deep gouges under the layer of semi-translucent paint.

"Who are you?"

"I am One-Zero-One of the Ghost Warriors. I have died eight times in the service of my people."

Spartan walked about the machine, shaking his head. The words were all but identical to the first time they had spoken, all apart from the number of times he said he had died.

Is it a he? Who knows?

He reached the halfway point and stopped, noting the lack of weapons just as in the previous model. The metalwork was impressive and much better finished than even the Alliance Vanguards. The seams between sections were barely visible, and there were no obvious external signs of gears or moving parts. It was to all intents and purposes a perfect machine and an example of a mechanical creature. He finished a complete circuit and then stopped in front of it.

"Okay, so you're a copy of the same machine? So what? We have drones and combat robotics in the Alliance military. Are my new masters just copies of computer code? If they are, then we have a problem. I do not serve a machine."

The machine lifted its left arm and shook it.

"No. Only this body is a copy, just as your clothing is something to be made and used. These bodies allow the last of us to participate in your reality."

It tapped its torso with the arm.

"Inside I am One-Zero-One. If my mind dies, so will my name."

Spartan scratched at an itch on his forehead, but he looked far from convinced.

"I don't understand."

The machine looked away and moved to its fallen kin. It

pushed away the wreckage with its massive metal feet and then repositioned itself so that it was exactly where the previous version of it had been. Spartan blinked, realizing he could easily have gone back five minutes and would never have been any the wiser, save for the wreckage lying about them.

"Spartan, destroyer of men and machines. Are you ready for the tests?" asked another voice off into the distance.

Spartan looked around and then spotted it. This machine was colorless, its armor simple, plain steel. Though Spartan very much doubted that this machine was made of this. From everything he had seen, there was little chance they would be constructed from common metal. The machine and four others walked in the same direction as the one he had arrived from and formed up in a loose line. As they moved closer, he could see they were much bigger, with more complex armor, thicker legs, and multiple limbs. They kept going until reaching Spartan.

"You have seen our warriors; these represent the last of our people. They will continue the struggle to protect our existence, as they have done for more than ten thousands years. We were once millions, now less than a thousand."

Spartan knew the stories from the T'Kari, and to a lesser extent from the Helions, but Z'Kanthu had told him the most. He thought back to the machine but again, the harder he thought about it, the more the memories began to fade from his mind.

Learn, and discover their weakness.

He couldn't even remember who had said that.

"The others, the rebels. They were different to you."

The machine moved as though nodding, but with its entire upper body.

"Yes, The Twelve were no different to any of us, to begin with. The great tragedy occurred when they intermixed with lesser species."

It pointed with a single arm toward a single archway. It was massive, easily big enough to allow a small starship to enter through. Even so, the space was filled with a mist that made it impossible for him to see inside.

"The tests, we must ensure that you and the others are ready for the challenge."

Spartan nodded in agreement and began walking to the vast entrance, flanked on either side by the great machines. There were much smaller windows looking out to the countless armada of ships waiting. He recognized some of the shapes from the encounters he'd already been involved in, but there were just as many new to him. The machine noticed he was looking at them.

"Since our exile behind the Great Seal, we have been busily working to create a new army. An army that the chosen Warlords will take through the Seal."

Spartan could still see the ripples from the collapsed Rift.

"How can we go back through? Are the ships on the other side now gone?"

The machine showed no recognition of his question as they continued.

"The Rift, as you call it, has not collapsed. It is merely unstable. Our brothers opened it from the other side and kept the alien traitors busy, long enough for us to move in our machines. Soon, we will send in the next engine to reopen the Great Seal and beginning the process of a permanent bridge."

That was the first mention of any kind of strategic goal, and even Spartan was surprised to hear it. Two of the machines trailed behind, and he was convinced they were watching him with suspicion.

"How are The Twelve different to you? Aren't they Ghost Warriors as well?"

The machine kept moving, but it was another of the tall, colorless machines that answered. This one's voice was higher pitched, almost musical in tone.

"The traitors took their souls from…"

The first machine stopped and placed its arm in front of its comrade. Neither said a word, but Spartan had picked up on the body language, even though it was coming from machines.

"They transferred themselves into their final ghost bodies, permanently. By removing their souls from our domain, they left our sight. Leaving our society was a great betrayal; that is why we show them no mercy."

One of the other machines spoke; its tone was much harsher.

"Spartan. The traitors turned their backs on all of us by doing this. They started a war that decimated our way of life. We were forced to send many of our kin into battle in the same way, by making them take their souls, flesh, and armor out into the darkness. It was the only way outside of our influence this far away."

The first machine continued speaking.

"This tragedy almost destroyed us. We will never allow it to happen again."

There was warmth, perhaps even a little sadness at what the machine was describing.

"Most of our kin never made it back, and those of us that did have been forced to live with the shame in the lands of the enemy and their allies. Our losses were almost total. We will never again cross the Great Seal until we are assured of our safety."

Spartan listened, but he had no way of knowing how much truth there was in this story. The rebels of The Twelve were clearly of the same species, but for some reason they carried their own physical bodies inside their armor. At least that was how Spartan saw it. The stories from both sides were contradictory, but it was clear there were distinctive differences between the machines of both sides of the Great Seal. He assumed this referred to what was known as the Black Rift.

So these machines, they are like biomechanical husks, controlled from the actual body somewhere else.

"You are all drones?"

The first machine hissed. There were no words, but it still sounded angry to Spartan.

"We are the Ghost Warriors, the last and the greatest of our people. Come with us."

The machine and its companions continued on, and Spartan walked with them. Next to him they looked like metal giants, even bigger than creatures like Khan and Gun. Images of his old friends fluttered about in his mind, but no matter how hard he tried, as the imagery formed, it then vanished again.

Khan?

Spartan found he had no tangible memory other than the fact that his friend was big, strong, and violent. He focused his attention on the large archway as they neared it. The mist was unlike anything he'd seen before. Instead of it lingering over an area, it formed a curtain no more than five or six meters in depth. As they passed through, he could feel the coolness of the cloud about him. It was both cool and hot to the touch and left him tingling all over.

"What is this?"

The machines did not stop and simply continued through the mist and into a vast circular hall. Great curved columns arced out from the ground and met at the ceiling where they merged into a form that looked very familiar.

"Echidna."

The shape was not exactly the same as the imagery he'd seen before, bit it was a fusion of flesh and machine with limbs, bone, muscle, and tail all forming part of the strange shape. Spartan looked about the great hall and the many pedestals upon which stood machines of all configurations. One thing they had in common; they were ancient, perhaps nonfunctioning.

"Spartan, this is the hall of warriors. Our greatest commanders and heroes are placed here after their deaths, to remind us of what we have lost."

Spartan turned about on the spot and looked at each of them in turn. The first and best preserved were little different to the machines talking to him. The more he walked about the group, the more he could see a change. The larger machine moved alongside him with its faceless body pointing right at him.

"We have constructed many biomechanical creatures to fight for us, even created new minds to serve us inside bodies similar to our own. There has not been a new Ghost Warrior in millennia, though. We cannot trust even our own creations inside our realm. We were torn apart by our own kin, so how could we ever trust a single soul outside of those remaining?"

Spartan shrugged. He had no idea what to say.

"Those that were trapped outside of our realm were given the final plan; to sow destruction, doubt, and war in the half-century before our coming. They were to weaken and damage our foes in preparation for the coming of the comet. They have done well, Spartan, better than we could have imagined."

The machine held out its arms, and a projected image of many stars appeared.

"When we opened the Great Seal, we received word from our remaining kin. The old enemys' worlds lie in ruins, their fleets scattered, and the other races fight among themselves."

The stars moved until a new cluster at the end of a long tunnel appeared.

"Your own worlds, Spartan. They have avoided our grasp, even through our best efforts to assist. But with your help, we will change that."

Spartan nodded in agreement.

"You need me to help defeat the Alliance?"

The machine shook its body.

"No, you will help us craft this species as our servants. Your flesh is easily molded and repaired. Humanity will provide the resources we require for our rebirth throughout the stars."

A clanking sound off into the distance caught his eye. He looked at the movement, and then spotted a number of chains lifting a vast metallic structure, much like a pierced gateway. As it lifted, a large number of Thegns approached. These were as different as they were similar to those he had seen before. Each was the size of a man and armored in the same fleshly outer layer as the others. Their faces were featureless, save for a single eye right in the middle of their foreheads. In their arms, they carried reflective blades. They seemed to catch and bend the light as they moved, almost making the blades invisible to the eye.

"Who are these?"

The machine extended its arm and pointed at them.

"They are for your test."

The machine then looked off to the right where others had been brought in by machines of much the same design. Spartan could see a variety of alien races, and like him, they were all unarmored and unarmed. A shape fell from the ceiling beneath the statue of Echidna and crashed to the floor. The container split open to reveal a cache of blades, spears, and all other kinds of weapons. The machine lifted its arms above its head.

"You have sixty seconds to prepare. Those that pass the test will stand at the head of our legions. You will rain fire on a thousand worlds and bring our race into the light!"

With that simple command, the hundred or so Thegns spread out from the gated entrance and formed up in a massed formation of nearly thirty wide. They raised their blades and then waited. Some made noises, but not one moved from the formation.

"What about…"

He stopped his question at the mid-point upon seeing the machines withdrawing back to a series of barricades. Metal shutters came down behind them, and then Spartan realized where he was.

After all of this, years of training, combat and war, where do I end up? In a goddamned arena!

Spartan looked to his right and spotted a T'Kari warrior rushing to the center of the hall. A few of the others were doing the same, but at least two were waiting and watching.

Wait a second; is this all a trick?

He looked up to the sides of the arena where the bright light made it almost impossible to see. He was convinced he could see hundreds of machines watching, but his eyes could just as easily been deceiving him.

Screw this. Trick or not, if I'm going to die it will be with a blade in my hands.

He took a few paces and then noticed the other two doing the same. In seconds, all eight of them were sprinting from different points to the center. The T'Kari reached the scattered weapons first and quickly grabbed the longest, and most substantial looking rifle. Spartan kept moving and found himself amongst a handful of dull iron blades. He ignored them and moved on to where the T'Kari was loading in a magazine. It spoke to him in its alien tongue, and to Spartan's surprise, he understood every word.

"Arm yourself."

Spartan bent down and picked up a simple looking double-barreled weapon, only slightly longer than a large pistol. It was relatively light and attached to a bandolier. He cast the leather like material over his shoulder and pulled out the weapon. There was a trigger and a lever. He pointed it away and pulled the lever. The back of the barrels popped open to reveal two smoothbore chambers.

"Great, I find the short-ass shotgun."

Three more of the aliens were now there and rummaging through the gear. Each ignored the others until they were suitably equipped. None of the firearms seemed particularly advanced, and Spartan noticed one weapon in particular was being ignored. It was a long rod, perhaps two meters long and tipped with a razor sharp point. He bent down and grabbed it. Though it was long and didn't flex at all, it still felt no more than two kilograms in weight.

"Not bad."

An alien of a race he'd not seen before looked at him and laughed. It looked much like the Khreenk, but smaller and closer in height to a human teenager.

"What's so funny?" Spartan asked.

"A spear? Against them?"

It pointed off to the line of Thegns. The Byotai saw the weapon and went to pick up something that looked more like a medieval maul. The other six concentrated on collecting the most advanced looking firearms they could find. Even as they continued to rummage about, a loud horn sounded.

"The test begins," said an unseen voice.

Spartan spotted one other item and quickly grabbed it, pushing the weapon into the utility belt around his waist. He hadn't even noticed his semi-armored pants until now. They were skin tight, gray, and moved like a second skin.

Interesting.

"What is that?" asked the Byotai.

Spartan pulled the weapon from the belt and held it up with his left hand.

"Looks similar to the ancient Indian Katar, don't you think?"

The Byotai laughed in answer.

"It's a type of metal punch-dagger. I've never used one, but they are popular as pieces of art on my worlds. It's a push dagger with this unusual H-shaped handgrip."

He held out his hand with his fingers, grasping the grip and the blade extending above his knuckles.

"A curious idea," said the alien.

As one, the first of Thegns advanced. Spartan did a quick count and confirmed that it was indeed thirty warriors. They set off at a walking pace, and then increased to a jog. Each of the others took aim with whatever ranged weapons they'd found. Only Spartan bothered to look at them, rather than the Thegns. He moved amongst them and didn't even bother to pull out the weapon he'd taken. A modest volley of fire killed perhaps five or six. Then they were out of ammunition and moving back to keep away from the advancing warriors.

"To me!" Spartan called out.

The Byotai threw away the five-shot repeating rifle he'd been using, lifted his mace like a club, and moved to Spartan's flank.

"On my world we avoid this kind of fighting. Have you done this before?"

Spartan grinned.

"Once or twice."

"I will fight alongside you. The only way we can help the Ghost Warriors of the machines to achieve paradise is to work as one. What do you propose?"

Spartan edged closer to the alien.

"These Thegns are powerful and tough, but look at them. What do you see?"

Both looked out at the remaining twenty twenty-four Thegns. They were scattered now and approaching in a loose grouping. Some ran, others jogged, and a few even walked straight at them.

"I do not understand," said the Byotai.

Spartan was surprised at his lack of understanding.

"They brought you here for a reason. Who are you?"

"I am Vilusk, commander of the homeworld militant order. I commanded fifty ships and our flagship."

"And you don't know about this kind of fighting?"

The creature swung his mace over his head.

"Oh, I know about fighting, but out there in Space, not in here. Skirmishing is not part of that. I have commanded fleets for more than two generations. I am an expert in three-dimensional maneuvers and advanced weaponry."

He looked to his mace and laughed.

"How can I help in their victory if I am given just this?"

The Thegns were just seconds away now, and the others had spread out in a wide arc ready to fight them. Clearly, the others distrusted each other as much as the Thegns and were ensuring they could fight without being interrupted. The Helion and T'Kari had adopted similar stances, with the weapons lifted high and their bodies poised in a fighting stance. A few more gunshots tore into them, and two more fell.

"That's it. Now it's all hand-to-hand."

The lack of firearms was clearly designed to limit the amount of damage they would be able to do from afar. Spartan also suspected this might have just as much to do with keeping his new masters safe, as it did to the horde of Thegns. Spartan braced himself and positioned his spear with the head lowered and almost touching the ground.

"Point it at them," said Vilusk.

Spartan laughed and shook his head.

"No way. The point is the first thing they will try and grab or beat aside. Keep it out of their way, leave them open, and drive to the openings as you find them."

Vilusk seemed a little confused and looked to those coming at them. Spartan smiled to himself and watched the enemy carefully. The use of the spear was something he'd learned back in his time as a pit fighter on Prometheus. The memories of that time were faint, and the harder he tried to remember the more the memories seemed to fade.

What's going on with my memories?

As he waited, he noticed that Vilusk was looking away from him. He threw a quick glance at the large alien.

"Hey, Vilusk! These Thegns are advancing as individuals. If we fight together, we will multiply our effectiveness. One on one, and we will lose."

The alien nodded quickly and moved to just a meter from Spartan.

"Yes, I understand. Ship combat is no different."

He pointed to the space around them with his maul.

"If ten attack five, but the five use their superior training, to fight with larger numbers against smaller groups using distance and timing. Well, they will always have the advantage."

"Exactly," said Spartan, "We have a law back home called Lanchester's Law. It means we square the number of combatant to work out a ratio."

Vilusk was no fool and quickly added the numbers in his head.

"Yes. Even with just one different, just five against four

would actually give a ratio of twenty-five to sixteen. We call this the third law of numbers in our naval academy."

"Well, it is a universal truth," said Spartan, "so we need to make sure the odds are in our favor in every encounter."

The first five Thegns ran at the group, one attacking at a time. The Helion and T'Kari engaged their own foes in a furious and reasonably balanced fight. Spartan had time to watch the first few blows before the first one reached Vilusk.

They are faster and better trained than the Thegns we've seen before. They've been preparing a long time for this.

The Thegn ran up to Vilusk and began a complex series of whirring strikes. Vilusk beat them off but like the T'Kari, he was being hard pressed. Spartan waited until they were both fully committed and then moved close to Vilusk's left flank. Before the Thegn knew what had happened the spear tip embedded in its throat. It twisted about and howled at Spartan.

"Now!"

Vilusk stepped in close, right between the Thegn's two blades and brought the maul down onto its head. The alien's muscles were tough, but force of the weapon was so hard it smashed its way down to the thing's shoulder blades. It tipped over backward, already dead.

"That's how we bring them down."

Two more Thegns rushed toward them, one for Spartan and the other heading to the Byotai.

"Step back!" Spartan said.

Vilusk moved, and that brought his own foe directly alongside Spartan who struck it across the back of the head with the staff of the spear. The warrior stumbled, and Vilusk finished it off. The second Thegn was now onto Spartan and pushed him hard. The blades whirred and took chunks out of the spear before it snapped in two.

"Crap!"

Spartan reached down for the double-barreled pistol and pulled the trigger. Both barrels discharged and punched orange holes through the thing's chest. It staggered and then collapsed to the ground. The other six aliens continued their individual fights, and in less than ten seconds all of the Thegns were dead. Spartan bent down to the fallen warriors and pulled the curved blades from the hands of the first.

"What are you doing?" Vilusk asked.

Spartan rose to his feet and threw one of the weapons to his new ally. Vilusk caught the blade and swung it a little clumsily in his right hand. Spartan clenched the Katar loosely in his left and began to practice a rapid series of cuts with the Thegn's curved blade. It moved quickly and made a gentle hissing sound. Finally, he stopped and found the T'Kari and Helion were also there watching him.

"What?" Spartan asked.

The T'Kari looked at him and then the Byotai. Then Spartan spotted the cuts to the alien's left arm and leg. It was the same for the Helion.

"These warriors are better than the old models."

The sound of scores of feet caught all of their attention. The wall of Thegns advanced, but this time it was every single one of them. They all lifted their blades high and yelled in unison. The Helion moved to one of the many fallen warriors and took both of the blades. With a flick of his wrist, he cast the second to his T'Kari friend. Both looked incredibly similar, though like Spartan and the Byotai they also wore the gray armored pants and chest armor. Spartan pointed his punch dagger at the approaching Thegns.

"Now, space apart and watch your flanks. One moves, the other protects and looks for openings. No heroes, or we lose this fight."

They raised their blades and waited in the position Spartan had called, each standing in complete silence and looking at the great horde of warriors. The Thegns let out another howl, and then the first dozen swamped the defenders. Two of the aliens off to the right vanished under a mound of attackers. Spartan shook his head and then focused his attention on his own problems.

"Kill them!" Vilusk yelled.

He swung his blade out in front and caught a Thegn in the throat. It stumbled and fell forward so that two more tripped over the dying warrior. As they floundered, the T'Kari slashed at them and finished them off.

"Three down," said Spartan.

More moved around their flanks, and Spartan was forced to beat off multiple attacks with his stolen blade. Another came in at his left, but he displaced it with the punch dagger. The Thegns pushed in and struck the Helion so hard that he stumbled and fell onto his back. Through the gap came two more Thegns, but Vilusk stepped out in front of the fallen Helion and held them off long enough for the other to stab and hack at them.

"Keep them busy!" Vilusk said.

The Thegns presented an impenetrable wall of sharp blades. As each of the defenders cut or stabbed, a group of those with mirrored weapons would beat them back. Then for no apparent reason, three of them moved apart and created a channel in the center of the horde. Standing amongst them, and spinning two blades over her head, was a tall woman. At first Spartan thought she was human, but she was taller, slightly thinner, and her skin as pale as alabaster. Her eyes were a piercing black, the exact opposite of her skin, as was her long hair that ran down past her shoulder to the middle of her back.

"Attack!" she hissed.

Vilusk looked to Spartan who gave him the nod. Both of them pushed ahead, and the other two did the same. One by one, they pushed into the breach where the alien female continued to whir about almost like the blades of some ancient helicopter. Heads and limbs flew in all directions until just thirteen Thegns remained. One rushed Spartan and smashed the hilt of its sword like weapon into his face. The strike was hard, and for a second Spartan was completely disorientated. He spun about and then found the weapon arcing about and coming down to his head.

Defend!

He brought up his right arm and parried with his own sword in the nick of time. The blades ran down each other until the thick part near the hilts pushed together. Sparks ran down the blades as the material screamed like fingernails on a blackboard.

"Now you're mine!"

The warrior took a step back, but it was too little, too late. With an uppercut motion, Spartan stabbed the punch dagger up into its ribs. One strike, two strikes, and then with the third he stabbed it hard into the throat. The Katar was a deadly weapon at this distance and easily punched through the armor, flesh, and bone. He yanked out the weapon and foul looking goo pumped from the wound. It dropped to the floor while Spartan remained on his feet.

"Who's next?"

Three more Thegns stepped out to block his path, and Spartan simply shook his head and laughed. At the same time, he flicked the Katar so that the congealed blood splattered against their armor. He had no idea if that would annoy or upset them, but it felt like the right thing to do. A loud horn sounded, and the warriors withdrew immediately. Even the nearest that had already lifted its weapon to strike decided to back off. They moved back, each watching the small band of defenders, as they abandoned their dead and dying comrades in pitiful clumps about the floor.

"What now?" asked Vilusk.

All five of them move closer together to form a tight circle. They kept their weapons ready, ever watchful of the Thegns coming back in with their final assault. Then Spartan remembered the weapon. He pulled the lever, snapped out the rounds, and took two more from the bandolier. With a click it snapped back together, and he thrust it back, loaded and ready for the fight. Lights flickered in the distance, and then the machine appeared. It was only one, though Spartan did recognize the model. It was smaller than the rest of the warriors, but still a substantial machine. He estimated it was about half a meter taller than Vanguard armor, but unlike the tech used by the Alliance, this was clearly a fast, agile combat robot of sorts.

"What do you want of us?"

The machine moved to within twenty meters and stopped. It lifted its arms, and this time Spartan could see it was carrying short, squat looking blades of the same material used by the Thegns.

"This is the final test. Survive and lead our legions to victory."

All of them were now watching the machine, but Spartan was busy looking about the arena. To his amazement there was one other creature. It was shorter than him, squat, and its arms hung down almost to its knees. There were at least a dozen dead Thegns all around it, yet still it refused to come over and join the other five.

What about the others?

He moved his eyes quickly about the great arena, but no matter how hard he looked, he was unable to find anything resembling the others he had seen. None of it really mattered now though, the machine was stomping toward them.

"Now!" it hissed.

Spartan had nearly forgotten them and twisted about just in time to see the Thegns rushing back into the fray. He watched as they approached and lowered his stance, bracing for the coming fight.

What the hell? This is hundreds of years after the invention of brass cartridges rifles, and we're using swords. What in the name of hell is going on here?

The Thegns threw themselves at them with such abandon that three were killed in the charge. This time they were not fencing or fighting with tactics or skill. This was something else. As Vilusk dropped to the floor with two bodies on top of him, Spartan realized what they were doing.

"Spread out!" he screamed.

One after the other, the Thegns threw their bodies at the defenders, each doing its best to engage or occupy them long enough to force them down. Both Vilusk and the Helion fighter were down and pinned when the shapes began to fall from the ceiling. One hit the ground and lifted up to reveal another Thegn; this one carrying long spears and shields.

"This is nonsense!"

The new arrivals were not quite close enough to be an issue, though. They had the first group to finish off, and several were already close to him. Spartan sidestepped the first and then cut to its face. Halfway through the cut, he redirected the blade over his head and cut upward on his left side. Caught by surprise, the blade hacked through its right and up into its ribs.

"Not quite…finished."

Spartan yanked the blade from the flesh and spun it over his head before delivering the coup-de-grace to the Thegn. It slumped to its knees as its head dropped from its shoulders. Another ran in, and Spartan dropped to his knees and hacked low into its stomach. It doubled over in pain and provided the perfect angle for a vertical decapitation strike. It too dropped to the ground, leaving Spartan alone among their bodies and with blood pooling around his feet. His new gray armor was covered in splotches of blood while his unarmored face was covered in dirt, blood, and grime.

How are the others doing?

He looked about and found each of them busily fighting or wrestling with the last of the original group. In the center of the arena there were now twenty, perhaps twenty-five of the new arrivals, and every few seconds another dropped from the ceiling. He looked up and shielded his eyes from the bright lights. There were entry points in the ceiling, and shapes were moving around them. Spartan lifted both of his weapons and shouted out with all his might.

"What kind of a test is this?"

There was no reply, just the cries of dying warriors and the sounds of more and more Thegns landing on the ground. Spartan looked to his new comrades who had regrouped and helped the two on the ground. The Biomech machine remained where it had been, unmoving and to all intents dead to the world.

I wonder, thought Spartan.

He ran toward the machine, much to the surprise of his comrades.

"Stay with us. That thing will kill you," said the T'Kari warrior.

Spartan ignored it and reached the machine just as the battle cry from the Thegns began again. He looked at the machine and noticed the lower torso was partially open. He reached out and pulled hard. The hinged plating lifted up, revealing a completely empty interior.

No flesh, no AI Core, nothing.

He looked at it in complete surprise. There was more than enough space to fit something in there, perhaps even a person. Spartan looked at the sockets and joints in the machine and then to his own arms. He hadn't noticed before, but there were tiny fingernail sized studs at different points on the new skin like armor.

Really?

He looked back and watched as the first Thegns reached the T'Kari and Helion. Blades flashed and swung about, but it was clear from the never-ending numbers falling from the ceiling that it couldn't go on forever. He looked back at the machine and then grabbed onto then metal framing.

"Screw this!"

With a tug, he pulled himself into the machine and twisted about to place his feet on the rubberized plates. As he leaned back, the studs on his back and lower legs clunked into place with the seals in the armor. He pushed his shoulders into place and with a loud click the hinged plates began to close toward him.

This had better work!

The plates clamped down tightly, and for a fraction of a second he panicked. The idea of being quickly crushed to death inside a Biomech war machine was the last thing he would have wanted. Something hissed near his head, and then he could see as clearly as if he was bareheaded again. He lifted his hands but instead of seeing his, there were massive metal gauntlets with the short, gleaming blades attached. He took a few test swings and found the movement and speed to be comparable to his own.

"Now this is more like it!"

He moved on the spot and found his group of comrades busy hacking away at the Thegns. From his raised position, he could see over a hundred of them now, and more continued to arrive. Spartan flexed his muscles, clicked his shoulder, and moved off at a quick jog. With each step, the very ground seemed to shake. He charged directly at Vilusk who turned about and raised his weapon s to defend himself.

"Stay back!" he yelled.

Spartan jumped once, and the legs crumpled down under the impact. He then pushed again and leapt fully over those fighting, right into the middle of the Thegns. Four or five were immediately crushed by the weight of the armor. He then proceeded to swing and hack with the blades until scores lay trampled, cut and torn apart by his ferocity.

Cuts, stab, slash! he said, moving through them like some ancient demon.

The others watched with a mixture of awe and horror as he tore the entire unit of Thegns limb from limb. After ninety seconds of blood and gore, there was not a single Thegn left standing. Spartan walked back to them and activated the armor to open at the front. The plates moved apart to reveal him to them.

"What are you doing in there?" Vilusk asked.

CHAPTER SEVEN

The Proxima Emergency caused much calamity to the worlds of the Confederacy. Millions died and countless numbers of ships were crippled. Though the conflict was derided as an internal war that pitted brother against brother, it was also praised as being an engine for the development of vessels and technology. Everything from habitation, to engines and weapons were improved, as was the infrastructure of the entire Confederacy. The ground and space forces of the Biomech War were vastly different from those that fought against the Echidna Union.

Reports of the Proxima Emergency

The Bridges, Old Spascia City, Helion Sector

The doors and hatches spun or flipped open before the transport even hit the ground. Teresa and Captain Tycho waited at the first ramp. The screaming from the engines was loud enough to hide the impact as they landed. Teresa held on tightly to the magclamps near the doorframe as the vessel lurched and then came to a stop.

"Everybody out, now!"

She jumped the meter drop and hit the dusty surface with a thud. Captain Tycho was next, and then came squad after squad of marines. All around them were great clouds of dust and smoke that merged together to create an almost impenetrable wall. She activated the overlay mode to combine thermal and infrared to see through the dust. She looked to the Captain.

"You know the plan. You will take the lot and dig in on this side of the chasm."

He nodded in agreement.

"Good luck, Colonel."

Teresa pulled out her carbine, flipped off the safety, and glanced back at her motley collection of marines, Khreenk, and volunteer fighters.

"Okay, 1st Company with me. Let's take this damn bridge!"

She moved off and the rest chased after her. They were on the largest bridge in less than a minute and surging across when she saw the battle with her own eyes for the first time. A strong gust of wind had pushed much of the smoke away, and the remains of three fortified towers burned fiercely in the distance. Tracer fire, rockets, and explosions filled the horizon, as both sides fought a desperate last action for that tiny sliver of territory along the chasm. Teresa checked the status of the first squad that was running with her. She barely knew their names, but every one of them knew of her reputation.

"Gun, are you there?"

Her intercom crackled, but the interference on the ground was massive. She heard something, but streaks of green energy overhead crashed amongst the landing pads and incredibly managed to find nothing other than rock to hit. The explosions and noise were massive, however, and for a second completely drowned out any chance she might have of hearing.

"Colonel, you've arrived?"

"You bet your ass I've arrived."

She tried to sound confident, but as she moved ahead, it was clear her single company of marines would be unable to turn the tide. A quick glance to the tactical overlay showed that Captain Tycho had established strongpoints at the end of each bridge, and was already moving heavy weapons and SAAR robots into position.

Good work, Captain. That's exactly what we need.

A single squad managed to outrun her and moved nearly twenty meters ahead. They made it almost to the end of the bridge when a vast burst of gunfire ripped into the ground around them.

"Take cover!" cried their sergeant.

The man didn't even have time to duck as the turrets

from a single Eques walker spun about and blasted him apart. Teresa slid behind a stone barricade, lifted her carbine, and took aim.

"Volley fire, center mass!"

She tagged the spot she wanted hit and opened fire. More carbines joined in, each adding to the damage. No one weapon brought down the machine. It was simple weight of numbers from each coilgun blasting holes into it. As the machine settled down on its haunches with smoke belching from a hundred holes, Teresa lifted herself to her feet.

"Onwards!"

Another squad of twelve marines rushed past with one carrying a large flag showing the Alliance colors. Teresa shook her head in amusement at such an anachronism. It served little purpose, but incredibly managed to get them across the bridge in half the time they might have expected.

"Colonel, I have artillery in position. Khreenk and Marine volunteers are heading for the mountain. Just send us your targets."

Teresa slipped in another magazine and continued forward until finally reaching the end of the bridge. The destruction wrought in just this one square kilometer amazed even her.

"Understood, Captain."

She then tagged all her platoon commanders.

"This is Colonel Morato. Artillery and air cover is being coordinated via mountain command. Tag your targets and send in your requests. We've got the big guns. Make sure we use them!"

Teresa lifted her head and watched squad after squad of marines fan out and edge forward through the cover. The unit carrying the battle standard was right in the center, exactly where the greatest concentration of enemy fire was.

The crazy fools.

Teresa could sense General Gun was near, but more importantly to her, she was convinced Jack couldn't be far away. From their current position, there were large Biomech ground units moving on both flanks. Teresa tagged four platoons of her marines and gave them their deployment orders. All of them left, using the cover as best they could. She looked back and checked that the second company that had just landed was also crossing the bridges.

"Captain Tycho, send engineer teams to the bridges. We're going to need them brought down within the hour."

There was a short pause.

"Colonel? You want the bridges rigged? Correct?"

"That's right, Captain. The Biomechs are massing on this side, and I estimate we have a matter of an hour, probably less until they smash this bridgehead."

"Understood. Anything else?"

Teresa again looked off into the distance, trying to find any sight of the trapped marines and others as they fought their breakout from the Three Sisters fortification.

"Yes, one last thing. I need a Broken Arrow fire plan prepared. When I give the order, I need a single coordinated bombardment of this entire sector. Get them organized, and fast, Captain."

"Yes, Colonel."

Two lieutenants moved up alongside her, as well as a Marine corporal with battered and burned armor. The difference between the relief force and those that had been there for months was easy to see.

"Colonel, this is Private Forgeng. He one of those that broke out before the encirclement."

Teresa nodded and then ducked as a triple rocket volley whistled past them and exploded against the wrecked carcass of an Eques walker.

"Private. I can't reach our forces back there. They are being blocked. How many are there?"

The man opened his visor and began to speak loudly.

"Hundreds. General Gun and the others are stuck in a bottleneck three hundred meters back. The machines have dug in on both sides, and there are more of them blocking their route this way."

"Okay, how many made it out?"

"Over nine hundred, Sir. We wanted to go back, but the General's last orders were to get over the bridges. He said he would keep them busy for us."

Teresa shook her head.

Typical Gun, never one to back down in a fight!

"Very well. Stay here, Private, and tell my officers everything you know."

"Will you help them?" he asked, a pleading tone to his voice.

Teresa did her best to look reassuring.

"Son, we're here to turn this fight around. We'll get them out of here if it takes a year."

He looked to the other two officers, but neither said a word. Teresa nodded to the nearest of them and pointed off in the direction the Private had described.

"They won't have long. I need assault units, Vanguards, and any Jötnar you can rustle up."

"What's the plan, Colonel?"

Teresa lifted her weapon and checked the horizon once more. The crackle of gunfire had now increased, and reports came back from the four platoons. All of them had now reached the enemy and were heavily engaged.

"Colonel, we've got a single Vanguard squad en route. They only hit the ground three minutes ago. There's also a platoon of Combat Engineers at the bridges. Captain Tycho says they are available if we need them."

The CES teams were something Teresa had almost forgotten about. In the years since the Great Uprising, their use had dropped as the Vanguards took over.

Though the latter were substantially more advanced, they had also changed in capabilities. Whereas the Vanguards were a hybrid war machine driven by a single marine, the CES units were heavily armed engineering machines. The CES marines were able to construct defenses and attack position that even a Vanguard would find difficult. She looked at the officers and grinned.

"CES units are exactly what we need. Get them to this position, fast. Here's the plan."

* * *

Taxxu, Uncharted Space

The arena was supposed to have been a test, but as Spartan looked out at the carnage, he failed to see quite what the point was. The Thegns had long since stopped in their bizarre release from the rafters, and the group had now been left on their own for more than ten minutes.

"What now?" he asked.

The alien female with the pale alabaster skin walked around him, examining the machine in great detail. She stopped and looked the blood-covered blades with equal interest before reaching out and touching them. She pulled back her finger, now coated in the blood, and placed it in her mouth. All of them watched her, but not one understood why she was doing it. Finally, she pulled out her finger and licked her lips. The Helion muttered something and then turned away from her.

"The test is over," said the voice from before.

The light subdued and low-level lighting lit the outer levels of the massive enclosed space. Shapes moved, and dozens of machines shifted for a better view while one in particular approached. The little group retained their weapons and turned to face the new threat while Spartan closed up his suit and moved to face it. On came the machine until it stopped before them all.

"One-Zero-One," said Spartan in amusement, "what was this test for?"

The Helion and T'Kari walked around the machine, both still carrying their weapons. They moved closer, but the machine simply ignored them and continued speaking to Spartan.

"This test was a simple one."

That was when the two aliens struck. The Helion slammed its blade into the leg of the machine while the T'Kari thrust some kind of pulsing firearm into a crevice on the flank of the machine. Both rolled back and took cover from the expected retribution. The Byotai warrior, the one that Spartan had fought so hard alongside, also lifted his weapons.

"No, step back!" Spartan snapped.

The firearm the T'Kari had attached flashed and then exploded. The hole it created burned through the armor and left it still standing, but an empty, ruined husk. Spartan looked back at the wreckage and then to the others.

"Why did you do that? They are our allies, our kin. We are to lead them to victory over the traitors."

Vilusk laughed and then swung his weapon over his head.

"No, Spartan. We are not their puppets. We will fight, and we will destroy them. Now step aside."

He moved one step closer, but the pale female leapt to the side and brought down her blades to sever Vilusk's arm. He howled in pain; the limb dropped to the floor quivering as though still alive with a mind of its own. She looked up to Spartan with her head twisted slightly to one side.

"No, we are both here to serve them. You have betrayed their trust, and for that you will be destroyed."

Vilusk, the T'Kari, and the Helion backed off and moved carefully to the abandoned cache of weapons. With the threat of the Thegns now gone, they were able to rummage through the items to find something different to fight with.

"Put your weapons down!" Spartan ordered.

His voice boomed through the armor with greatly increased volume and a throbbing bass. The very ground seemed to shake as he gave his orders. Vilusk used something in the heap of weapons to cauterize the wound and then yelled out in pain. Something else moved off into the distance. The Helion pointed at it and pulled out a long, curved hacking blade from the heap.

"What is it?" he asked.

The shape emerged from beneath a pile of Thegn bodies. Spartan's enhanced vision via the armor allowed him to see it clearly, and it made his stomach lurch a little.

"A Jötnar?"

He took a step to his right and looked at it in surprise. There had been eight of them in the arena, but those on the other side had been hard to see. He didn't recall seeing this monster of a warrior, but it was clearly not another Thegn. The shape moved closer and stopped to look at each of them. Now Spartan could see what it was. Although technically the same synthetic machine as his kin, this was actually one of the models used by the Helions.

"To me!" the thing growled.

Spartan had not actually faced one of these before, but he'd seen reports and videostreams of their capabilities. As far as he knew, the Helions had betrayed and killed most, if not all of them. He failed to see why this one would therefore turn on him. The pale female drew closer to Spartan, watching the other three and the Biomech monster with care.

"The machines created me and wiped out my race. I seek vengeance, or death!"

The Biomech roared once more and then ran at Spartan.

"Oh, great!"

The thing was big, perhaps two and a half meters tall and muscled. Like the rest of them, it was encased to the neck in the same kind of protective skin as the Thegns. Spartan automatically dropped into a fighting stance, his left leg forward and his hands out in front of his torso.

"Okay, let's do this!"

Vilusk had found some kind of long tube, and the end flashed in Spartan's direction. With a quick twist of the torso, he moved out of its path, and the missile whooshed past and struck something near the wall. Spartan was surprised to see a blue flicker and then it vanished.

An energy shield of some kind?

He'd almost forgotten about the charging Biomech. Looking back, it was barely ten meters away.

"Oh, no!"

Spartan lifted his arms to protect himself, and then it was on him. They were evenly matched in size, and although Spartan's strength had been greatly augmented, it was still a fair matchup. As they wrestled with each other, the others rushed in to attack the female warrior. Sensing danger, she used her footwork and distance to keep away while striking at any opening.

"Destroy it!" she cried out while evading a blow.

Spartan tipped over and landed hard on his side while the Helion synthetic battered at him like a troll of ancient myth. Each impact struck like a hammer on an anvil, yet Spartan was still able to move. He pushed down and then rolled before coming back up on his feet. Still the thing was holding on tightly.

"I am getting tired…of this!"

In a classic self-defense move, he grabbed its right arm, twisted it around, and then locked it straight and behind the warrior. It yelled out in pain, but that wasn't enough for Spartan. With a brutal snap, he cracked the limb right at the joint. With its arm useless, Spartan took a step back, panted, and lifted his hands ready to continue the fight. The creature roared and began to laugh. It pulled the arm with its left hand, and with a sickening crunch it locked back into place.

"What the hell?" he muttered in surprise.

The synthetic looked about the ground and leaned down to rip two of the unusual blades from the fallen Thegns. Spartan felt a knot in his chest when he saw the gleaming blades. He had no idea what kind of material they were made from, but they were clearly something very different to normal metals. The armor of the Thegns was proof against light firearms, and there was no chance he should have been able to strike with the punch dagger so effectively.

Some kind of monofilament edge, maybe?

He shook his head and laughed.

It doesn't matter, just fight!

The Helion synthetic seemed preoccupied with selecting weapons, and Spartan saw that as an opportunity. He glanced to his left and spotted the female warrior moving back with all three of the others in pursuit. Spartan rolled his shoulders and called out to her.

"Keep back, I'm coming!"

With five long strides, he covered the distance and kicked the T'Kari in the side of the torso. The impact from the large metal leg sent him flying nearly two meters before he crashed to the ground. Spartan then delivered two savage uppercuts with each arm as he attempted to strike the remaining two. Both parried his blades, and the Helion even managed to strike against his left arm with one of the swords. To Spartan's surprise, it tore open a gash the length of his forearm in the plating.

What are those things?

He swung his left arm out to cover the damage, but the Helion was still busily hacking away, desperate to fight his way inside the armor. Spartan parried repeatedly, but he became more and more frustrated at his foe. The Helion tried to cut again, but this time Spartan brought down the blade of his left arm so hard it beat through his defense and pushed down into his shoulder blade. Spartan didn't stop and continued to push until making it down to the chest. Blood gushed like a fountain as he slumped down dead.

"This is over. There is no need to keep fighting."

That reminded him of the synthetic. He looked over and watched as it stood upright, almost bored and resting the blades across its body with the back edges against his shoulders.

Strange.

Spartan turned his attention back to what remained of his previous allies. Only Vilusk was left. He was standing with just his maul and his cauterized stump. He looked pitiful. Blood covered his body and a dozen cuts on the armor where Thegns had managed to get through the thick hide. They faced off against each other, but Spartan felt nothing but irritation by him. After their betrayal, he had zero tolerance for any of them.

"Why?" Vilusk asked, "We could have fought back. We could have defeated them from inside. You are a traitor to your species, human!"

Spartan just looked at him and shook his head.

"They are the only way there can be peace. You've seen how we manage on our own, war, repression, and genocide. They will bring order and stability, but only once we have defeated their armies."

The Byotai sighed with a single long breath.

"It didn't have to be like this."

He lifted his mace, let out a strange howl, and then charged at Spartan. There was no need for him to even prepare to fight. It would be the female warrior that finished off the wounded Byotai, not him. He stayed in the same position, much like a statue and watched her do her beautiful work before him. Where Spartan was powerful and brutal, she was fast and elegant. The warrior spun behind Vilusk and delivered a horizontal cut that arced on a perfectly flat plane. This was no heavy cut or hacking attack. No, the cut that struck him in the back of the neck was a work of artistic perfection, and the decapitation was flawless. Head and body struck the ground at the same time while she dropped to her knees and then looked up to him.

"Spartan, are you ready to lead?"

He looked at her and to the synthetic now approaching.

"I was always ready," he said calmly.

The synthetic stopped, and dozens of machines moved out from the sidelines. As before, a red armored machine stepped forward and pulled out ahead of the others. It walked toward Spartan until reaching a distance of just a few meters. Finally, it stopped and twisted about to look at the other two. Spartan looked carefully at the armor.

"Who are you?" he asked, already knowing the answer.

"I am One-Zero-One of the Ghost Warriors. I have died nine times in the service of my people."

"Of course you are," said Spartan quietly.

The two machines squared off, but apart from the fact the new arrival was unarmed, there was little to tell them apart. Spartan tapped his chest and then pointed to the machine.

"Is this you?"

The machine moved its torso a few degrees as though

looking inquisitively.

"No, this armor is new. It was built for a new warrior."

Spartan suspected he knew the answer, but he wanted to hear it from the machine.

"What new warrior?"

There was a pause, not a long one but enough to make even him doubt what the answer might be. Finally, it spoke, the words flowing with a subtle echo that gave the impression of a dreamlike state.

"It is yours."

Spartan sunk back a little into the armor. With the mount points on his outer skin, it clipped together and moved as though it were part of him. He rocked his shoulders a little, finally feeling a little cramp from staying still after such exertion. Even as he did this, the sound of another machine came from further away. This one was colorless, much like the Thegns, but taller than One-Zero-One. Its designed was lithe and scrawny, the exact opposite of the armored simian of his own suit. The aesthetic reminded Spartan of the T'Kari and their agile warriors and equipment. One-Zero-One gave a hand gesture to the synthetic. He then bowed and turned away to leave the area.

"Wait," said Spartan.

The creature looked back over his shoulder. There was a cut on its cheek that ran right down to its neck. Congealed blood had already formed along the wound, and the bleeding had stopped after just a few seconds.

"Why are you leaving? We have unfinished business here."

Spartan moved to face off against the creature properly. He lowered his arms and bent his legs ready to fight. The synthetic creature shook its head and spoke in a low, guttural voice.

"No, Spartan is warlord, not enemy."

He then turned back and continued to walk away. Spartan glanced over to the female warrior who still knelt before him, her blades resting on the ground, both dripping the blood of the fallen Vilusk.

"What about you?"

She moved her eyes to stare at him but said nothing.

"The test is complete, and both of you have passed," said the machine.

Spartan could feel sweat dripping from his brow and lifted his left arm before realizing he was still in the armor. With just a thought, the armor hissed and the shell sections around the torso opened up slowly. One by one, the petal shaped sections moved apart until he was completely exposed. He pulled his arm hard, and it detached from the armor.

"Why?" asked Spartan, "Because we survived?"

The machine didn't move, but the voice continued.

"No, this was a test of leadership and commitment. Both of you are ready to serve. We take no risks with our servants. Each of you has been physically and mentally tested, and each of you has been prepared for us."

Spartan found the idea of being prepared a fascinating one. He tried to remember when this might have been but came up short. His oldest memories were the hard times before he'd ended up as a pit fighter. That was hardly his most hated time, and he had enjoyed the victories and the glory, as well as the money that had been building in his personal account. There was no preparation by people or machines back then, not as far as he remembered. Since then, he'd met Teresa, been married, and had a long career in the military as well as running his own security outfit.

"I don't understand. You said I was prepared? When? How?"

The machine walked around him, looking at the armor as though it was the first ever time he'd seen it. Spartan felt he were on show, yet the machine continued on its course.

"You were rescued by our agents during your own crisis in the alien worlds. We examined your thoughts, your background, and memories. There are markers left by our people to show the work they have done."

It used one arm to point at Spartan's arm. He looked down and recalled the missing body part.

"Do you remember how this happened?"

He thought back hard. Images of the red machine immediately appeared, and he felt anger. Those images vanished like dust and again he was confused.

"My memories, they are fading."

"No," said the machine, "The lies are being withdrawn from your mind by your own subconscious. Our kin found you and your friends in the wilderness. They helped repair you. Healed your own body, repaired your bones, and helped you escape that prison."

Spartan tightened his brow and did his best to remember, but the images were gone.

"You are one of the few humans that have the ambition, skill, and ferocity to fight. You are more than that, Spartan. We have seen the Bright Horizon. You will do whatever it takes to survive. My people number less than one ship's complement. We also need to survive."

He continued his circuit and then stopped between the two of them.

"Humans have proven unique and shown us great tactical awareness and resilience. Information from our kin in your own star system shows you have managed to avoid our advances, even when given access to our cloning and warrior construction facilities."

The machine then pointed at the female warrior. She still remained in the same place but did lift her head to look straight into the torso of the metal machine. Her eyes were piercing in their blackness, like obsidian marbles.

"The Anicinàbe show great skill in arms and cunning. Rise, Thayara."

The female Anicinàbe rose to her feet, and Spartan

found himself staring at her form. He'd seem relatively few of her species before, and never quite this close. The close-fitting gray outer skin they both wore proved perfect for the examination of others, and he was especially interested in how the Anicinàbe's limbs appeared longer and thinner than should be normal for their bodies. Thayara saw him watching and looked at the machine for a short while before turning her attention back to One-Zero-One."

"Your people are independent and unable to work together. Individually, you are greater pilots, engineers and, warriors than even the humans, but you squander this on war and tribal conflict. With us at your side, you will unite both the Anicinàbe and the humans into a force we can use to restore order. "

The machine looked at them both and pointed at the newly arrived machine. It waited much like the earlier model, and its shell opened up to reveal an empty interior. Thayara swallowed, either in excitement or nerves at what she had just heard.

"This machine has been waiting for a warrior of speed and skill for many of your years. Together, you will lead the legions into your domain and bring our vengeance. Are you ready?"

Thayara was already halfway into the armor as the machine continued to speak. She pushed herself inside as she had seen Spartan do and clunked her shoulder into position. The armored shell pulled in around her, and then flesh and machine were as one.

"Yes, I am ready," said Thayara.

She took a step and stumbled before righting herself. Then came a few muscle stretches, and she was moving about and swinging her arms. Finally, she stopped when noticing the other two were waiting. The three machines were in a triangular formation in the center of the arena. Spartan nodded even though there was no way for any of them to be able to see his head.

"Yeah, it's time to fix this, once and for all."

"Good," said One-Zero-One, "Come with me. I will show you your forces. You will join the assault in ten hours."

Spartan reached out to touch the machine and immediately found a metal arm from another blocking his path. He pulled back his hand and waited for the machine to give him its attention.

"What do you mean, join the assault? I thought we were leading it?"

The machine made an odd noise before the words became clear. One-Zero-One had been relatively calm, but that one question seemed to trouble it in a way Spartan couldn't understand.

"Every one of our souls is worth an entire star system."

Those words came out much louder than even the machine seemed to have intended. It stopped, made a venting sound, and then continued in a much lower tone.

"Your skills are in ground combat, something we have been less successful at. The sight of humanity's greatest hero leading our forces will strike terror into their hearts."

Spartan understood at least that part of the plan.

"Even so, we will not conduct this war with just our armies of machines and creatures at your command. Three of my kin will lead our forces through the Great Seal. Each will command an armada. One for the Helions, one for humanity, and the third in reserve."

It pointed to both Thayara and Spartan.

"Both of you will command our armies that will take the fight to the enemy. You will bathe in the blood of those that betrayed you, as they did us."

"So we will not command the fleets?" Thayara asked.

Two of the machines made that odd noise, and it sounded suspiciously like complaining, perhaps even laughter.

"No, we will never relinquish the fleet. We retain control of the ships. You will control the soldiers that we give you and offer advice to them when requested."

Spartan nodded.

"Very well."

The three walked out through the mist. As they passed through, Spartan looked back. He wasn't entirely sure but felt certain that as they made it halfway, every single body inside flickered and then vanished, leaving nothing but an empty hall or training arena.

That's not weird, not weird at all.

He looked back and moved on after the machines.

So, they will give me soldiers but no ships. So I can fight and die for them, but I will be unable to choose where. How can I help them in this victory if they hold me back like this?

He sighed and recalled several of the great battles in his life. He'd often been able to control the smaller thing, but there was always somebody else above him, a superior that had overall control of a battle or campaign. He'd watched so many die because of somebody else's great idea.

Just like old times.

One-Zero-One spoke in almost hushed tones.

"Spartan. Every victory you achieve with us will bring you a step closer to your own enlightenment. The warrior that brings us final victory will be offered a place alongside our greatest people."

He carried on, but a voice continued to nag at him. It was distant and felt like an old memory. There was more to it though; it seemed to be speaking directly to him in a voice he'd almost forgotten.

"Every creature has a home, Spartan, a nest, a ship, or safe place. Remember the plan, Spartan."

He stopped and looked back; convinced the sound was coming from behind him. There were the other machines, but nothing from their body language suggested it was one of them.

"Where is the weakness?" continued the voice.

Spartan turned back around and continued to walk ahead. One-Zero-One noticed his confusion and called out to him.

"Spartan, what is wrong?"

Spartan moved one foot in front of the other, maintaining the pace even though his mind was on something completely different. The voice was still there, like a pain in the base of his skull and throbbing. He tried to avoid it, tried to not listen, but the words followed him wherever he went.

"Where can they be made to suffer? Find it, Spartan, find the weakness."

CHAPTER EIGHT

Space-based fighter combat shares very little with that of atmospheric combat. Maneuvers that seem second nature when spiraling through the air prove impossible in a vacuum. Scissors and Immelmann turns are replaced by long-range sensor combat and advanced strafing techniques. These movements are critical when used against capital ships but also allow a fighter to take full advantage of its arsenal, no matter the craft's heading. The first time a pilot spins on the spot and fires on his pursuer is usually the first stage of understanding to new-generation pilots.

Fighter Combat for Beginners

ANS Warlord, 1 Day from Micaya

The mighty warship had been decelerating for days now. The great bulk of the ship had been spun about and her engines firing as though she was accelerating off to another destination. In one of the many peculiarities of space travel, only half of the trip was spent accelerating toward the target. In the past, when ships hadn't carried enough fuel for long burns, the middle phase would consist simply of drifting. The vessels of the last few centuries had changed that with efficient engines and power systems. These new breeds of ships had allowed large warships to travel between planets while continually under power. It was a costly way to travel, but the fastest known way to move ships from A to B without using a local Spacebridge.

At this distance, the assembled fleet of ships waiting around the Helion world looked nothing more than grains of sand. Admiral Anderson looked at them with interest via the tactical display, counting up the squadrons one by one in his head. The numbers were pleasantly surprising, especially the timely arrival of forces from the Khreenk and the Byotai. Even more surprising to him was the small group of fifteen Klithi heavy traveler ships. He'd seen reports on these highly advanced vessels but never been this close to them before. The data alongside the formation showed they had some form of surface shielding, as well as substantial numbers of defensive weapons known as 'territorial blockers'.

I'd like to have seen them in action, thought Anderson. *The last time they went up against Biomechs they destroyed the lot, for the loss of not a single ship.*

Admiral Anderson and his staff were not the only ones looking at the disposition of the ships. Alongside him were Admiral Lewis and the Byotai commander, General Makos. The two of them commanded the two largest contingents of ships currently waiting at Micaya. General Makos was a large figure, much larger than any human about the flagship. His reptilian form and thick body armor betrayed a general lack of interest in war and battle for these people. Admiral Anderson looked at the figure and shook his head a few centimeters.

The Byotai are tough for sure, but they have no interest in a long war. Who would have known this from the way they look?

The creature spoke, and it took until he reached the third word before the translators on his armor kicked in.

"Admiral, every hour our numbers grow. Are you sure you want to keep back our forces? Homeworld is busy with the Anicinàbe, but they have still furnished me with fifty-two ships, the pride of the fleet."

He opened his mouth and said nothing for five or six seconds. It was a bizarre movement, and Captain Louise Decker was forced to lean in to explain in his ear.

"According to our files, the Byotai do this when they have absorbed too much heat. They can use their suit coolers, but it is considered rude in the company of others."

Admiral Anderson smiled. He recalled owning several small desert dwelling lizards as a child. One image in particular rushed back of the small animal sitting on a rock with its mouth wide open.

"I understand."

She stepped back and watched quietly as the rest of the senior commanders spoke. They discussed numbers and vessel configurations, and very soon there was a disagreement between T'Kron, the aged looking T'Kari commander and General Makos. They spoke in a mixture of their own tongues, and it quickly became heated. Admiral Lewis tried to intercede, and the General pushed him away.

"Enough!" Admiral Anderson snapped.

Both of the aliens turned to look at him.

"I don't care who has the most ships or who has lost the most. History means nothing right now. This fight with the Biomechs is just one of war now, not politics, science, or the stories of old. If we survive this one, we can all argue about the details later. We can expect the combined efforts of their space forces within one day. We have to be ready for whatever they throw at us."

Admiral Lewis was quickly losing his patience with them. It was part of his character that had changed in the last months as the situation out here had deteriorated. He'd lost weight in that time, too, and his face seemed much grayer than before. His usual good humor had also vanished, instead replaced by bitterness at having the bulk of his forces pulled from the line that was barely concealed. He looked to Admiral Anderson and finally decided to say what he'd wanted to say for hours.

"Admiral, I've had to move out all my combat vessels from Helios Prime for this. General Rivers could finish that fight in a month, but only with my help. Now he's stuck fighting a long, attritional war with an entrenched enemy."

"I know this, Admiral. General Rivers sends me full details of the campaign daily. The Biomechs are regrouping around the defense installation and digging in. He has orders to contain them, but not to assault."

He looked to General Makos and then to the others.

"If they come through that Rift, as I suspect they will, well, we will have fought for nothing. These ground battles are not to win territory. They are not even about controlling the Rifts as I originally suspected."

The General nodded quickly.

"My assessment as well. Look at our dispositions."

He pointed his large left hand at the tactical display. There were taskforces and armies spread throughout the Helios System. There were obvious and significant numbers at specific points.

"First, they hit Eos and then moved onto full-scale invasions on Helios Prime and Spascia, and now the enemy forces have arrived at Libuscha."

"Yes," interrupted Anderson, "but they have begun the exact same process at Spascia. Their ships began an immediate assault on the planet against entrenched positions."

He moved his hands and imagery of the planet appeared.

"Colonel Horst Brünner has had plenty of time to prepare. With the intelligence gleamed from our fighting at Eos, Prime, and Spascia we have a good idea as to their procedures. He kept the 4th Heavy Battalion and the primary Helion forces hidden in bunkers, and left turrets and SAAR robots on the perimeter."

General Makos grinned as he listened.

"I saw the videostreams. His defense has been very... interesting."

"Quite," replied Anderson with a raised eyebrow.

"It isn't ideal. But after they landed, Colonel Brünner has been fighting a hit and run battle, leaving robots to fight the static battles. By using distance and timing, he has managed to outmaneuver them after their initial landings. The four cities are in ruins, but this battle of agility is playing to our strengths. He is trading territory for time, and so far it is working."

"But what about their air cover? He can't keep running about in convoys of Bulldogs and dropping in marines via Maulers, if they are hit from the air."

"That's just it, Admiral. They have pulled all their attack vessels and sent them here, to Micaya."

He took in a long breath as though that was what

he needed to continue speaking. Each of them waited for him to carry on. The ship still smelled a little of oil and fresh paint, a strange mixture at the best of times. It was a reminder of quite how new this massive vessel was. Another even more important reminder was the single shattered computer display on the right wall. It had malfunctioned during the last engagement at the Black Rift, and no replacement had been found. So it sat there, broken and useless. After what seemed like an eternity, Admiral Anderson finally pointed to all the formations of ships.

"We have a vast armada, the greatest in history, I suspect. If we survive this, you will be able to pass this story on to your grandchildren. It was the day that people from a hundred worlds joined together to fight a common enemy."

Both of the aliens looked at each other but said nothing more.

"There are one hundred and sixty-three Alliance ships. This includes many of our newest Crusader, Conqueror, and Liberty class vessels that we've pulled from other assignments. Three of every four ships we have are out here today. That is the level of our commitment to victory."

He pointed to the icons on the right that showed the stars of Alpha and Proxima Centauri.

"We have our own problems at home, right now. Most of that is because our forces are spread thin. Even so, anything that happens on the home front pales to insignificance to what will happen if the machines win."

He turned and nodded to Makos.

"The Byotai have provided fifty-two of their best warships and most experienced officers, a major commitment, especially when you have internal problems with your neighbors. Like us, you have been forced between your own self-interest and the long-term. I am pleased to see your commanders have joined with us to end this, today."

He pointed to the smaller groups of ships.

"With the destruction of most of the Helion forces at the Black Rift and Helios Prime, they have been left weakened. In the last three days, they launched continuous waves of ships against those Biomech ships still over Helios Prime, against my express wishes. The last flagship, the Starlance, she was destroyed eight hours ago."

General Makos sighed in irritation.

"The stupid fools. We cannot afford battles like this."

Admiral Lewis appeared to be in agreement with this point.

"True. Casualties are heavy on both sides, but they've lost every single experienced commander because of this. The Starlance rammed a Biomech Cephalon command ship, and both were lost. The Helions are getting desperate, and they are resorting to suicide tactics."

Admiral Anderson walked between them and pointed

to Helios Prime.

"Suicide attacks will lead to one conclusion...defeat."

He then turned to T'Kron.

"I understand your own forces have not fared much better, have they?"

T'Kron lowered his head as though he had just been greatly dishonored.

"We have just six ships remaining, and only one with a stable Rift deformer. My people are assisting aboard your own ships, where possible. The T'Kari are not what they were."

Admiral Lewis could see the hurt in his face and wondered quite what point his superior was trying to make.

"But your contributions outweigh your numbers. It was your own ship that finally collapsed the Black Rift, was it not?" said Admiral Lewis.

He pointed at a small group of escorts and focused in on three Liberty destroyers.

"All of these ships are commanded by T'Kari officers, and so far they have accounted for seven Biomech warships, for the loss of none of ours."

Even General Makos seemed intrigued at this. He spoke, and his translator took time to catch his guttural words.

"Perhaps your people work better on board others' ships?"

T'Kron either ignored or failed to see the insult and merely nodded passively. Admiral Anderson licked his lower lip and then turned away from the display.

"T'Kron. Without you and your ships, this war would have been lost years ago. I have another task for your experienced officers."

He changed the tactical display until a number of vast orbital structures appeared. They each went closer to examine the framework that extended out for kilometers in all directions.

"The Micayan Shipyards," said General Makos in hushed tones.

Admiral Anderson moved his hands and pointed to various parts on the model.

"These shipyards were once home to the Helion Fleet. Now most of the site is derelict, with just forty personnel managing the dismantling of the old ships."

He turned the model to the right and highlighted one section.

"Here we have another hundred and six Helion ships, all waiting their turn to be scrapped. Most of these are over a hundred years old and in a poor state of repair, but they are the last to arrive here."

He turned to face the T'Kari commander.

"T'Kron. I need you to take teams of your own people and mine. Get aboard the shipyard and run triage. You have twenty-four hours to mobilize whatever you can find."

"What about the Helions? Why would they listen to a T'Kari? Assuming I find any usable ships, they will need Helion crews," asked T'Kron.

Anderson smiled at this, but only he and Admiral Lewis seemed to understand what had happened. He looked back at the tactical display and pulled it back to show every inhabited star system from Sol to Taxxu on the other side of the Black Rift.

"Have you not heard? In the last six hours, the Helion League has collapsed. With no surviving system of government or control, each of the individual colonies will have to fend for themselves. Officials on Eos have already requested formal political, military, and humanitarian assistance from us."

Admiral Anderson paused and glanced at them, trying to gage their reactions. General Makos fidgeted but said nothing.

"We have offered them the full protection that the Alliance has to offer. The Helions have been crippled though, and they want more from us. That is why in a secret session deep underground on Helios Prime, the remaining politicians of Helios have voted to begin integration procedures with the Alliance with any Helion colony that chooses to do so."

Again he paused to let that sink in.

"It will take time, probably years, but if this goes the

way I think it will, this will mean a democratic system with colonies and races from Sol to Helios. Each of the Helion worlds will be able to choose to stay as they are, or to join the Alliance family."

He looked back to the tactical display.

"What better way to maintain peace could there be than as one family?"

Admiral Lewis leaned in to to him and spoke quietly.

"What about Terra Nova, Sir? How can we take on new colonies when we have a potential civil war brewing?"

Anderson smiled.

"You underestimate Admiral Churchill. He's already on the way."

* * *

The Bridges, Old Spascia City, Helion Sector

Teresa watched the battle just a short distance in front of them. The machines had dug in around the beleaguered remnants of General Gun and trapped him in an area no larger than four city blocks. The mixture of marines, soldiers, civilians, aliens, and robots had created a zone that even the Biomechs were unable to penetrate. Unfortunately, time was not on their side. While the battle raged, a ceaseless horde of Thegns moved around the trapped marines and on toward the bridges. Teresa's newly arrived troops had managed to hold them back, but now the entire stretch of ground was under attack.

"Colonel, we have movement on your left flank, two squadrons of Eques walkers with substantial Decurion support," said Captain Tycho.

"You should be back here. We need a commander at this position. The situation out there is becoming untenable."

From his position on the other side of the chasm, he was having a much calmer time. He was putting it to good use by using every spare minute to improve the defenses, as well as rigging the bridges for demolition.

"Forget it. You are more than capable of defending the mountain and the bridges, Captain. It is my responsibility to get Gun and the others out of there. We promised them help...I promised them help...and here it comes."

Teresa looked at the overhead view provided by the drones. Enemy positions had been tagged wherever found, and it was not looking good. A thin crescent of green was all that held back the Biomechs from the bridges. Everything else was colored red, all but one section, the part held by Gun's forces. Teresa shook her head at the stark reality of the battle.

"Give me the numbers, Captain. What's coming our way?"

"Twenty-four Eques walkers, plus upward of four hundred Decurions. These came out from the underground tunnel system. I suspect they hit rock, so that's the closest they could get."

A triple burst flashed overhead, and she looked up. Two Biomech fighters and a pair of Alliance Hammerheads had just moved into position over the battle. One for each was quickly shot down, and the others were chased away by thousands of rounds fires by the Eques walkers. Teresa was sure that the second Biomech fighter was even struck by its own side, but that didn't stop the guns from firing.

"Air cover isn't getting through, Captain. I need you to hold them back with the big guns."

Another squadron of fighters screamed overhead. This time it consisted of X57 Drones. Six of them came in low and fast, unleashing a bombardment of precision guided missiles. They struck targets that had been identified and tagged by the troops on the ground. As they moved overhead, the craft strafed the ground with their attached Gatling guns. There were multiple explosions but only four of the drones made it; two downed by the avalanche of turret fire.

"What about you, Colonel? I can buy you minutes, no more."

More explosions rippled along the horizon, and the shape of the first two Eques walkers came through the smoke and dust. Missiles raced across the open ground to greet them, but every one was shot down. Only the artillery and gunfire made it through their defensive cordon.

"That's enough time for me, Captain. I'm waiting for the CES teams, and then we're going in."

"Very well. Good luck, Sir."

She looked to her left and then to her right. There were scores of marines, all well equipped and waiting in whatever cover they'd been able to find. Each time one of them lifted up to fire, a dozen guns at once hit them. All the while the terrible bloodbath continued around Gun's last position.

We have to get through to them before it's too late.

She began to move, her mind desperate to do something, but her body trying to hold her back. With her armored head above the broken ground, she could see at least five wrecked Eques walkers. Hundreds of enemy troops filled the ground around the wreckage, and dozens of flickers marked the firing of guns. Behind them was a great cloud of dust and smoke, but even that wasn't enough to hide the silhouettes of fighting men. Right in the middle was the great black shape of a Jötnar. The figure was atop of some wreckage and twisting about, presumably engaging targets with his weapons.

Gun!

Her mind jumped back to Prometheus, that fiery world that seemed to be the pivotal location for so much of the calamity in her life. The series of flashbacks reminded her of a period that felt a lifetime ago. The enemy had created the monster creature she now called her friend in their secret labs on that world. Gun, in particular, carried a ridiculously oversized gun, and that had been the determining factor in his choice of name. Gun had been freed, and contrary to expectations, had been the catalyst for their escape.

I can't leave him, or any of the others out there. I have to help them.

Teresa tensed her muscles and then heard the approach of heavy machines from behind. She looked back, immediately sensing danger. It wasn't the enemy, though. It was Alliance reinforcement.

Finally.

Teresa smiled and looked at the advancing machines. They had the appearance large metal beetles. Another platoon of marines was with them to provide additional protection. She counted at least thirty of the CES engineers plus a handful of Vanguards out on the flanks. They moved at a fast walking pace, and the odd stray round that struck them simply bounced off their armor. The first of the group made it to within thirty meters when its commander spoke.

"Captain Ader, 25th Engineers. I hear you have something that needs dislodging?"

Teresa picked up on the sarcasm from his voice, but she could tell it wasn't directed at her. The battlefield looked more like a barren world filled with scrap than something worth fighting over. Yet she needed them and their special set of skills.

"Good to see you, Captain. You've arrived at just the

right time."

At the same moment, the defensive fire from the Thegns and Eques walkers sent yellow streaks out in every direction. It was the nearest thing to hell, but nothing stopped their advance. Their large cumbersome forms made slow progress on the rough ground, but not even shattered machines and broken masonry would hold them back.

This could work, she thought hopefully.

From here, Teresa could see these were the latest and heaviest CES units available. These machines were designed for creating defenses, or breaching them while under enemy fire. Now that Vanguards existed in numbers, the CES teams had seen their armor actually increased to create these new enhanced models. As well as the large digging blades that replaced their forearms, they were also fitted out with a myriad of improvements. Huge slabs of spaced armor pushed out from their torsos, and even their legs were covered in thick scales of plating. A pair of red flashing lights blinked as a warning to friend and foe that they were here.

Finally I have the right tool for the job.

It was a running joke in the Marine Corps that no matter what units or equipment a commander had, they never quite seemed to have the right one for the mission. They had air cover when they needed artillery, or squadrons of Bulldogs when they needed barricades and pillboxes. And when they had all the equipment they needed, the order would come through to disengage.

"I need a breach, and I need one fast."

Teresa pointed to the Biomech positions and tagged the area she wanted with her visor. There were many places they could try and break through, but she needed it to be done fast. The selected area consisted of a section thirty meters wide and heavily defended.

"The two broken Eques walkers. Sir, you want us to assault at that point?"

Teresa nodded.

"Yes. Tear a hole so I can get our people out. Smash your way through, and keep smashing until they are all out. We have a Broken Arrow fire mission ready upon completion of the job."

There was a short pause; the officer must have been considering the implications. A Broken Arrow call was something very rarely done. In fact, just the mention of the term must have been pretty shocking. By sending the call, Colonel Morato would be confirming that a position had been overrun and that organized resistance had failed. All available units from artillery to fighters would be redirected to that location. If any friendly forces remained in the area, they would be killed unless able to evacuate or hide. It was a desperate call, and it seemed to provide the right level of motivation.

"Understood, Sir. You want us to stir up this hornets'

nest. We're just what you need. We can create an opening into hell if you need it. Just give us the word before you call in the strike. I don't want to get burned!"

Teresa breathed a sigh of relief. Captain Ader was cocky, that much was certain, but she could live with that.

"Fair enough, Captain. You'll have a sixty-second window. I'll make sure you get it."

The Captain didn't waste time, and rather than stopping to check, he simply strode out past the marines and straight into the hail of defensive gunfire. The projectiles from the Thegns pattered off like rain, and even the larger caliber rounds from the Eques walkers proved unable to destroy them in one go. The thick bulldozer blades proved highly effective at beating off the armor piercing projectiles.

Good, we might have a chance at this rate.

Clearly, Captain Ader was as efficient as he was brave. No sooner had the first twelve moved into their attacking formation, and they were already halfway toward the enemy. They advanced in three groups, with each small squad raising their armored digger blades to create a protective wall in front of them. It was a wall of metal and flesh that moved one careful step at a time. A triple volley of missiles arced downward and headed right for the Captain's walker. A pulse of flashes rippled about the group as interceptor rounds launched and exploded around them, instantly destroying or damaging the missiles.

Keep going! Don't stop!

The first four disappeared under the bombardment for a few seconds. Then the cloud cleared, and on they went, covered in dust and burning material from the exploded warheads. Teresa looked back and made sure the rest were still coming. More were advancing, and a small, final group was only halfway to her position.

"Captain Ader, keep the last squad back to cover our retreat. They won't make it to you, anyway."

"Affirmative."

The machines kept going forward as he acknowledged the order. As well as the twelve walkers, the small group of Vanguards also walked alongside them, watching for signs of targets to shoot. As they moved ahead, they twisted at the hips, checking for potential signs of the enemy. These combat ready fighting machines were the next down in size and protection from the enhanced CES walkers.

"Marines!" Teresa called out.

Multiple heads twisted about to look to their commander. It was uncommon to find senior officers leading such attacks, but both Spartan and Teresa had something of a reputation in the Corps, even to the younger generation to whom this was probably their first engagement.

"I am Colonel Teresa Morato. I've fought these machines for most of my life, and I have never lost a battle."

She pointed her carbine off toward the enemy.

"General Gun, the hero of Terra Nova and one of

our greatest commanders is trapped inside there. The machines outnumber him ten to one, and still they cannot finish him off."

To emphasize the point, an Eques walker staggered about and collapsed under a massive volume of gunfire off into the distance.

"A direct assault on Gun will be a victory they cannot afford, right now. They have to reach the bridges and fast."

Teresa turned around and pointed to the direction they'd come from. A column of CES units and marines continued coming toward them.

"Their casualties will be too great in a direct assault. Instead, they are crushing the last of them with slow, attritional combat while their mobile forces secure this beachhead. Will we let Gun and his marines die slowly, like prey to some alien predator?"

"Hell, no!" shouted the nearest marine, a balding man in his early forties.

The response from the other marines was equally clear.

"Good. Stay behind the machines. We will rip open a hole to get them out of there. Keep moving, and don't get pinned down. Are you ready?"

A rousing chorus of "Yes, Sir!" ran along the thin line.

"Then let's move out, Marines!"

Teresa jumped up from cover, and two rounds immediately struck her. The first glanced off her visor and left a deep scar in the material. The second struck her carbine in the main feed, instantly rendering it useless. She cast it aside and pulled out her issue sidearm and continued on.

"Keep moving!"

Four marines stayed close to her, with two in front and scanning ahead with their carbines raised. Two more were on the right, both of them carrying the venerable L48 rifles. All of them fired almost constantly. Some of the rounds were at specific targets, but the majority fired to provide suppressing fire. Out in front moved the twelve engineers. They stomped ahead like great iron trolls. Every second something hit them, yet on they went until the first four reached the improvised barricades of stone, metal, and machine. As soon as they arrived, a wave of Thegns and Decurions fell upon them.

"Covering fire!" Teresa hollered.

The marines fired, even if they couldn't see an immediate target. It wasn't hard to find something to shoot at, though. Some Thegns even climbed on top of the machines to try and tear them apart. Teresa took aim with her pistol and squeezed. She expected at most a strike, but instead the head from a Thegn vanished and its lifeless corpse tumbled to the ground. Another roar almost blinded her as a Vanguard passed her and fired with its shoulder-mounted cannon. The weapon was the same unit as used on the mobile gun variants of the Bulldog.

"Keep going forward!"

The marines moved like ants around hornets as the wave continued on. In the middle of the formation was the squad with the unit standard. Teresa wondered why they bothered, especially as it had been hit at least twenty times now. It was riddled with bullet holes, and one of the corners now no more than a torn rag. One of the marines carrying it was struck in the face and dropped down into the dirt. As the standard fell with him, another marine picked it up just before the material hit the ground.

Insanity.

Two CES units lay burning, but the other ten were at the barricades, smashing and digging into the protective position. With each strike, a hole opened up, but that didn't stop them. Teresa was just ten meters from the first fallen Eques and now she could see inside. There were dozens, perhaps hundreds of bodies, but most were clearly Thegns. More of the marines reached the barricades and threw themselves against what cover it offered. The engineers still smashed at the metal and stone to open up a dozen lanes of entry.

Just a few more meters.

Teresa looked along the barricades and at the blood and dirt covered marines. They hugged the cover and put in a withering fire against the machines and Thegns on the other side. The fighting was now at a range of no more than fifteen meters. Rifles, carbines, and grenades moved back and forth.

"Captain Tycho, is the Broken Arrow fire mission ready?"

The officer replied almost immediately.

"Yes, Sir. I have rockets and artillery sighted and ready. You don't have long, though. The Eques walkers have penetrated the left flank and are moving in to cut you off."

Teresa felt her heart almost stop at the news. If their flank was broken, the machines could roll up their entire line and cut them off from the bridges. And if that happened, they would be in an even worse position than Gun.

"I've sent a Khreenk unit, a Helion squad of auxiliaries, plus eight SAAR robots over the bridge. They are heading to this position where they will pin the Biomechs down for as long as possible. Their commander has promised me ten minutes, twelve at the most."

"Understood. We won't need that long."

Teresa looked to the ground and found what she was looking for, a dead marine and his carbine. She reached down and took the weapon, doing her utmost to avoid looking at the broken body. Try as she might, she simply couldn't resist. The young man looked peaceful and might have been sleeping, were it not for the three metal spikes embedded in his chest from a Decurion. The machine lay alongside him, its body torn apart by one of the CES engineers. The carnage only spurred her on further.

"Follow me!"

Teresa pulled herself over the barricade, right into path of two Thegns. She didn't stop and simply pulled the trigger on the L52. The high rate of fire sawed through the first, and without removing her finger she spun about. The remainder of the clip cut into the second Thegn's face, and then it hit the ground. Teresa stepped over the bodies and slipped in another magazine. It was automatic; something she'd practiced so many times she didn't need to even look for the magazine or where to fit it. As soon as she raised the weapon, another group of Thegns advanced. She tapped the bayonet release, and the tactical bayonet spun about and extended out half a meter in front.

Just a few more meters!

CHAPTER NINE

SAAR robots were used in the early stages of the Biomech War and proved invaluable in the fighting on Spascia. This bitter and bloody engagement saw the combined might of the Alliance and Helions against a massive Biomech invasion fleet. The SAAR robots suffered ninety percent losses but fought in every possible situation. While designed for sentry duty and scouting, the SAAR robots soon found themselves working in groups to fight as rearguard formations. The combat success of these simple devices proved once and for all that the time of the robots had come.

Equipment of the Alliance Marine Corps

Grand Palace, Terra Nova

Director Johnson ducked back behind the column and looked at the two young operatives alongside him. From this position, they had a clear view of the wide plaza and the newly installed statue to the glory of Terra Nova. The executed bodies still lay on the ground, untouched for more than a day.

All three of them wore smart suits and long gray coats, much like trench coats. It was the standard clothing of the Intelligence Division and instantly marked them out as officials. One of the operatives moved his foot and then stopped at the sound of new arrivals.

"Do not move," said Director Johnson.

He looked in the direction they'd just come from. Two of his comrades lay slumped against the wall where they had bought them time to escape. Two soldiers lay dead just meters from them, but another was searching through their clothing.

"They'll want to identify them. They don't have a chance."

"Sir, shouldn't we ditch the clothing?" asked Agent Erryne Colee.

He was one of his most successful operatives and the man singlehandedly responsible for bringing down the Crux Cartel the year before. Director Johnson looked at him and then nodded.

"Ditch the coats. The suits look like every other person in this damned place."

They cast off the heavy coats and pushed them low on the ground. At the same time, a squad of heavily armed Terra Nova Guards moved past at a brisk pace. This was no parade drill, however. This was something very different. He was sure he could almost smell the nerves. Johnson looked to the other two.

"You've seen the protestors on the ANN channel. President Harrison's coup is failing, and we need to provide the push. The Marine Corps barracks has already barricaded itself in. They only have a few platoons of cadets, but that will be enough to get things moving here."

"The Colonial Guard are loyal, though, Sir, over eight thousand of them, and each loyal not to the Alliance but to the office of the President. We have to get out of here and try to..."

He made to move, but Johnson grabbed him.

"No, if we rush out, we'll be found and picked off like the rest of the unit. We've got to play the smart game. Is the transmission ready?"

The sound of a drone roared overhead and then it vanished well off to the south. A double gunshot rang out, and the device reappeared before spinning out of control. A long line of smoke ran from behind the craft before it struck a building and broke up into chunks of metal and plastic. Erryne Colee checked his own secpad and then nodded.

"Yes, Sir. The package is loaded, and the dishes are ready to activate. Just give me the word."

Director Johnson had watched a few segments of the material, and it was damning. Apart from the material leaked from the Alliance Network News, it also contained copies of private briefings with the President. They were sealed and not supposed to be opened for at least thirty years.

Sometimes there are more important things than the rules, he thought.

The two he'd included were to do with the proposed declarations of martial law on Hyperion, Hades, Prometheus, and Carthago, and even more concerning, the plan to eradicate the inhabitants of Hyperion, formally known as the Jötnar. There might be little love for them on Terra Nova, but few could argue that they had done more than their duty in the war. These two stories would spread fear and doubt about the new regime. The videostream containing the President's rants about the Jötnar would be enough to send the Alliance into a civil war.

This had better do just enough. Too much, and this will get a whole lot worse.

"Sir, we lost three operatives getting that data from the archives. The rest are ready, but they can't hold for much longer. We need to transmit now."

Johnson checked the data on his secpad once more.

"There is a fear here, fear that there's going to be a violent counter revolution. If that happens, what will happen to the Guards? I promise you, they will stand only for as long as they think it is viable."

He nodded to persuade as much the two of them, as

himself. He swallowed on saying the last words. A day earlier the soldiers had come to his office and demanded entrance. He'd sent as much data as he could find off world, especially to Anderson and General Rivers. His time was limited, though, and he'd been forced to rely upon his security doubles to buy him time to escape.

Their blood is on my hands.

It was a hard feeling knowing that dozens of his loyal staff had been butchered. He could have stayed there with them, but then it would have been his body out in the courtyard.

"We have to do our part to help this come about. Send the signal."

He watched the shapes of the soldiers moving further away, and then right to the bottom of the plaza. It was a spot usually avoided by most, as it was where the two memorial gardens had been planted. They marked the landing site of the Confederate forces in the Uprising, and several of the plants had already been uprooted. A wall of almost three meters blocked the plaza off from the rest of the capital. It wasn't a major fortification, but it was enough to keep all but the most determined people out.

"Sir, do they know you're still alive?"

Director Johnson shrugged.

"If they have half a brain, they will know that without a body they have no definite kill. Harrison has tried to get me out of the way on several occasions. The last one though, well. We have the footage of their assault on our facility as part of the package, don't we?"

He suspected they'd always known he would never ally himself to Harrison, or even provide him with basic intelligence. He could only hope that with the data getting out, he would have bigger fish to fry.

"True, Sir. It will take time for the information to get out there, and even longer for people to react. Assuming they even bother to do a thing."

Johnson looked at him with an odd look to his face.

"Son, don't ever think of underestimating the value of an enraged populace."

"Sir," said the other operative, who until now had remained silent.

The sound was faint from their current position, but if they listened carefully, it was possible to hear the chants and shouting from outside the palace. Occasionally, there was the crack of gunfire. That was the moment Director Johnson spotted the first column of black smoke.

"It's the city's citizens. They've seen the videostreams from the ANN, and they know they've been lied to. When they see the rest of this, they will go...well, you can imagine."

"The footage of Helios Prime might have helped, Sir."

Johnson nodded, his expression grim.

"True. The sight of the combat and sacrifice of our forces has been a rallying call during the live, unedited broadcasts from the Helios Sector."

Admiral Churchill had helped to maintain the transmission all the way through T'Karan, to Prometheus, and then repeated from mobile transmitters just inside the Terra Nova Rift.

Who wants to start a revolution while our people are fighting the real enemy?

There was one piece of footage more than any other that had changed things. In the last six hours, the news reports had started about the fighting at the Black Rift. Images of ships from different races, including those from the Alliance, had fought and been shattered by the Biomechs. Terra Nova citizens knew better than most what the Biomech threat was about. Many had seen their families butchered in the occupation. Somehow, the allies had heroically held back the machines, and support from President Harrison had somehow vanished, in an instant.

"Wait."

Two soldiers moved out of the shadows from the right, with a third being dragged between them. They all wore the standard armor and gear of the Terra Nova Guards. Johnson pulled out a modified secpad and checked the details once more. He had the full plans for the palace, as well as markers for every Terra Nova security unit. It was the aerial shots of the palace quarter that surprised him the most. He turned and showed the unit to them.

"Look, the citizens are tearing down the smaller

buildings on the periphery and building barricades."

He leaned a little further around the column and watched as the two pushed the man up against the wall. The man struggled and punched one right in the face. There was a scuffle, and finally the man was beaten with a rifle butt and pushed back against the wall.

"It's begun. Even their own ranks are turning on them."

The first raised his rifle and took aim.

"Sir, what are we going to do?"

Director Johnson closed his eyes while simultaneously taking out his X2000 series sidearm. It was far from standard issue, and actually a more advanced, but scaled down version of the prototype X2000 coilgun series being developed for the marines. This new family of 6mm coilguns would provide a standard platform for pistols, carbines, rifles, and machine guns. Few were in general use, but he had contacts like no other and had managed to procure one of the first production models, for evaluation.

"We light the fire, Gentlemen. We light the damned fire."

He looked to the holsters on the flanks of each of them.

"Draw your pistols."

Both slid their standard sidearms out and flicked off the safety toggles in one smooth motion. He looked back from the safety of their hiding place and took aim; a low-level light came on that could only be seen by looking through the sight of the pistol. Unlike the L52 carbine, this pistol was a single barrel affair. Even so, with a coilgun mechanism and a magazine that housed twenty rounds, it was a deadly and powerful weapon.

High-power.

A gentle tap on the side of the weapon selected the high-power mode. It would take longer between shots but would also expend the internal capacitor in one go. This in turn would accelerate the projectile to an incredible two thousand meters per second. That was twice the muzzle velocity of the standard conventional battle rifles, making a true hand cannon.

"Take the one on the right...wait for it."

He took in a slow breath and then began to let it out.

"Now," he hissed.

He fired the first shot, and the gun kicked back a little. The recoil was closer to that of a conventional kinetic target pistol, but still barely enough to throw off his aim. The other two fired two shots apiece, every round striking a target. The soldier to the left took the hit from the coilgun, and the effect was instant. The 6mm round tore through the PDS armor with ease, and what remained of the misshapen round tumbled into the man's flesh. Four more rounds hit the second, and then they were both on the ground.

"Move in!"

The three Intelligence operatives moved quickly and

carefully to the fallen men. The one to the right was already dead, with one round in the head and another in his chest. Two of the other rounds had deflected from his body-armor. The other soldier lay groaning on the ground. Director Johnson bent down to check the man who tipped over and landed on his back. As Johnson moved closer, he spotted the handgun come out of its holster. He could feel the adrenalin surging through his body, a mixture of raw excitement and fear.

A black hole appeared on the man's helmet, and then he was down, blood splattering the dust covered floor. Johnson turned around and found another soldier, a man in his fifties, slightly sweaty and clearly uncomfortable about the whole thing. In his hands, he held the still hot L52 long rifle, the primary weapon of the Guards.

"I can't do it. We've been ordered to secure the palace. The use of lethal force has been authorized. I didn't sign up for this. I've seen what's happening out there."

Director Johnson lowered his own weapon and nodded reassuringly.

"I know, this wasn't supposed to happen. What about the rest of your unit? Do they feel the same?"

The man shook his head.

"No. A few of the older ones are staying away, but the youngest. Hell, they won't stop killing until the President authorizes it."

"I see. How many feel the same as you? Five, ten, a

hundred?"

The man looked up as he counted.

"Most of my platoon, we're all from the same district. I can contact..."

Johnson lifted his hand.

"No. Communications are being monitored. Have you seen the footage? The killings?"

Again the man nodded yes.

"We've all seen the material. Last night we saw the latest report from Helios Prime. There were some big arguments, and one guy was dragged out. I haven't seen him since."

"Okay, so you know what's happening? The President is in the middle of a violent coup, but the military are not going to help. The only reason this could happen is because our troops are off fighting at Helios. Any other time they would have stepped in and kicked him to the ground. Now it's up to us. Will you help end this?"

The man looked at the bodies on the ground and back to Johnson.

"Who are you, Sir?"

Johnson straightened himself, doing his best to look the part.

"I'm Intelligence Director Johnson, head of Alliance Intelligence."

The man tried to smile, but no matter how hard he tried, it just wouldn't happen.

"We were told you were executed, along with the traitors."

Johnson laughed.

"Do I look dead? No, none of those bodies is mine, and I'll tell you something else. They are not Alliance generals because right now, all of our senior commanders are in their bases on ships or engaged in battle."

"So who are they?"

Johnson shrugged and began moving across the open ground. He walked without bothering to hide himself and simply stood up tall and straight, as if he owned the entire place.

"Is he mad?" asked the soldier.

Agent Colee shook his head.

"Often the best place to hide is right in plain sight. Does he look out of place?"

The Director walked for nearly half a minute until reaching the statue dedicated to the glorious dead of the Uprising. He paused, looked at the detail, and tried not to laugh; or even worse, to attack the piece of so-called art. The monstrous creature with its tentacles reaching out resembled nothing he'd seen in the war.

And who are these, the brave soldiers of the Confederacy fighting to save the city?

He looked down at their armored forms and tried to imagine who of them had actually fought the creatures.

Perhaps the reality of collaboration would have made a lesser statue.

He then looked at the bodies that had been unceremoniously dumped on the ground. A quick look confirmed there was nobody watching. He bent down and pulled back a cover. The pale, puffy flesh made it hard to make out, but one thing he instantly noticed was a tattoo on the neck. He leaned in closer and then worked out the unusual shape. It looked like an antenna with the round shape of a planet underneath it.

The War Correspondence Unit for the ANN?

He pulled back the covers to check the others and found the same markings on them all. He closed his eyes upon the realization that these were another group of people that had died, essentially due to his own orders. He pulled his secpad from his side, held it over them, and recorded a video sequence. Using the secpad was his first mistake. Three bullets hit the sculpture, and one struck his ankle, instantly felling him.

Crap!

Johnson rolled and kept on rolling until he was to the side of the great piece of art. Gunfire ripped into his position, but he was now in big trouble.

You idiot, now what?

He looked down at the equipment he had to hand, a secpad and a pistol. With one in each hand, he looked between them while at the same time a flurry of shells hit above him. Chunks of stone ripped from the plinth, and slivers of metal smashed off to clatter on the ground. One of the creature's tentacles seemed to explode above him.

Secpad, get the information out there.

He ignored the gunfire and sent the data packets directly to the public reception point at the Alliance News Network. It was the standard way to send unsolicited data. In less than ten seconds, he'd finished and lifted himself up to take a look.

What the hell?

Two groups of soldiers from the Colonial Guard were spread out and engaged in a violent gun battle. He estimated there were at least twenty on each side. It was the one on the right where he had just left that seemed to be doing best. They used cover and spread out while the other group moved headlong in a desperate attempt to overrun their position.

Young hotheads versus experience, always the damn same.

The gun battle was short, and he was forced to watch from the exposed position at the sculpture. Finally, the last of the soldiers was sent running, and a pair pursued them a short distance before falling back. The soldier that had helped him before came over to him but kept low in case he was shot at.

"Director, the President is trying to escape."

That surprised even him. He stood up, and the man positioned himself in the way of any stray soldiers.

"My entire squad, bar two, has refused their illegal

orders. There's a message from our Colonel to begin a crackdown."

"But it's not working, right?"

The man nodded slowly.

"Less than nine hundred turned up for duty today, out of eight thousand. With this order, only one company has stayed back. They are right there."

He pointed off to the domed structure at the side of the palace.

"The Senate building?"

The soldier nodded.

"Yes, Sir. They are fortifying it as we speak."

The two operatives signaled to him, but for now he stayed where he was. Even so, he lifted himself up and looked carefully at the man.

"We have to end this today. If Harrison escapes, he will carry on this little insurrection of his."

The man sniffed, opened his visor, and rubbed at his nose.

"What are you thinking?"

Johnson was without access to his normal data sources, but he did know the city and the people. He considered the options for a few more seconds, and then a small, slightly crooked smile formed on his face.

"Get your men and meet me at the entrance to the Senate building in five minutes."

The man nodded and went to leave, but he stopped and

looked back.

"I can get sixty, maybe seventy guys. That won't be enough to break in. Harrison has a picked company of man and carefully chosen ground."

Johnson's expression implied he completely agreed.

"Sergeant," he said for the first time using the man's rank, "What's your unit's designation?"

"Pegasus Company, Sir."

"Well, Sergeant. I'll get your winged horses back up in a matter of minutes. President Harrison will stay and fight, but only for so long as he think he can win."

"Very well."

With that, the man was gone, and Director Johnson was left on his own. He didn't waste time and ran to cover the ground to his two comrades. Both were still hunkered down behind the column.

"Sir, that was a little…"

"A little what?"

"Uh…a little crazy, Sir."

Johnson couldn't argue with that. Instead, he looked back and pointed at the opposite end of the palace. The columns of smoke had increased from one to three, and visibility was already decreasing. He'd seen footage of this kind of thing before. The first time had been during the popular uprising on Kerberos. More recently, he'd seen just the same on Helios, amongst the Zathee who had turned to violence against their Animosh oppressors.

"We need manpower, and outside the palace we have untold thousands."

Agent Colee checked his pistol and looked in the same direction.

"How do we know they won't turn on us?"

Director Johnson tapped his temple. Agent Colee leaned in and stared intently at the Director's eye.

"You're wearing a Retina?

He blinked with just the one eye.

"Since we were attacked in our offices."

He pulled out his secpad.

"I've been transmitting since we left. ANN have been getting this via the emergency transponder."

Agent Colee looked less confused already.

"I see. That would explain why they are already out there protesting."

"So let's find a way for to them help us. Follow me."

He ran from their current position and down one of the narrower paths through the public gardens. There were large stretches of open ground all around them, but line of sight to most of the buildings was interrupted by shrubs, bushes, trees, and columns. Agent Bowyer spotted movement to the right and ducked down just as gunshots blasted out at them

"Get down!"

Director Johnson ducked but refused to stop. A pair of bullets struck the ground, and Agent Colee joined Agent

Bowyer as they took aim. Both fired precise shots, but at this distance, the soldiers with their rifles had a substantial advantage. They succeeded in suppressing them for a few seconds.

"I've got this," said Agent Bowyer.

He looked to his superior.

"Keep going. I'll buy you time."

More shots hit near their position, and Johnson placed his hand on his agent's shoulder.

"Thank you."

He ran as fast as he could and ignored the shots coming in. Agent Bowyer moved one step at a time toward the gunfire. As all of the agents had been trained, he made use of careful shooting, never wasting the chance to hit a target if it presented itself. Something moved overhead, but he was far too busy to take his eye off the three, perhaps four targets ahead. He took aim at another moving shape.

"Sir, we've got air cover in the area, be advised."

It seemed to take an age, but after another minute of running, Director Johnson and Agent Colee were at the wall and the bottom end of the palace. The memorial site was overgrown and the sections of ships and war machines covered in graffiti. The old path ran to a large square door that was blocked with a thick and heavily rusted chain. Two small pillboxes protected each side, with sentry turrets tracking back and forth.

"Look, they've activated the sentry guns. No wonder

they are building barricades."

Agent Colee reached for his secpad.

"Sir, I can do this."

He moved off to the panel at the side of the door and entered his security details. The override unit flipped out, and he placed his secpad nearby. Electronics and security overrides were a standard part of the Intelligence Division training. Director Johnson waited patiently while his agent deactivated the guns. He looked back and could see Agent Bowyer taking cover alongside the wreckage of a CES engineer suit. The armor had been stripped of weapons, and it had been placed to look as though it was standing as a sentinel against an invader. The agent might not know, but Director Johnson knew too well that the only CES units involved in the fighting on Terra Nova were those that had been on the Confederate side. The attackers led by General Rivers, Spartan, and the rest.

"Almost there, just a few more seconds."

The sound of turbofans increased in volume, as did the amount of dust being kicked up around the open space. Every second the level increased so much that he was forced to move nearer to the wall.

"Almost there," said Agent Colee.

The only way to tell that the weapon system was armed was by the color of the light at the back of each pillbox tower. It was currently green. Agent Colee looked back and gave the okay signal. At the same time, the lights flashed once and then turned red.

"Good. Now the door."

He looked back to the unit and began pressing buttons.

"Get away from the panel!" said a high-pitched, heavily amplified voice.

Agent Colee ignored the words and continued to press buttons. The craft, a small civilian Cobra shuttle twisted about to give the passenger a clear view of the large locked door. A light flashed, and a round struck Agent Colee in the arm. It must have been high-velocity because it slammed him hard into the wall. He dropped to the ground unconscious.

"Bastards!" Director Johnson shouted.

He turned around and took aim with his own pistol. Another round fired and missed him by mere centimeters. He took his time and aimed at the armored glass cockpit. With a single squeeze, he sent one high-power round straight through the glass and into the goggles of the pilot. The craft spun about lazily, and to Johnson's satisfaction, the shooter tumbled out and fell the short distance to the ground. Even as the man struggled to move, he took aim and put another right into the man's chest.

"Stay down," he muttered.

As the craft continued to spin out of control, he moved back to the control panel. The code sequence had been bypassed, and all that remained was to select 'deactivate' on the screen. With one tap, there was a loud clunk, and the chain dropped to the floor. Nothing else happened, and for one terrible moment he doubted his plan. Then centimeter-by-centimeter the door opened. A hand pushed inside and then all kinds of pandemonium ensued. Dozens of men and women wearing improvised riot gear ran inside. Some wore sports armor, others looted security gear, but every one of them wanted to get inside the palace grounds.

"That way!" Director Johnson shouted, pointing into the grounds.

There was no real need for directions, though. Based on the amount of people with secpads and other communication devices, it was clear they knew what had been going on. He even noticed two Bulldogs with local police units dismounting and joining them. There must have been at least a dozen of them, and all were armed with shotguns, rifles, and current issue armor.

Good, that's more like it.

A woman in a long gray coat was with the police and waved to get his attention. As the scores of people pushed inside, the squad of riot police moved closer; the woman in the coat was leading them. They came through the doorway and into the memorial gardens.

"Director," said the woman politely.

"Agent Nuttall."

He hadn't expected to see the agent, especially after the chaotic scenes at the Agency. In fact, she had been one of the volunteers to hold the entrance while the senior agents attempted an escape.

"Sitrep?" he asked in his usual no-nonsense style.

"Guards units are standing down. There's just the one you showed on your transmission. We have police units and agents surrounding the place, right now."

"Good, very good. I have a platoon of soldiers in the same area."

She nodded.

"Yes, we ran into them. They are preparing for the assault. If it comes to that."

"Come on, then. We don't have much time."

The agent waved him off and beckoned for him to move aside.

"We can do one better than that, Sir."

With a simple hand signal, one of the Bulldogs moved to face the gateway, and with a loud rev of the engine it began to accelerate. In just a few seconds, it crashed headlong into the opening and straight through. Chunks of old masonry ripped off but did little more than dent and scratch the armor. It skidded to a stop, and the side hatch opened up.

"This might be a little quicker."

The journey through the grounds took a fraction of the time it had taken to go the other way. They took both of the agents with them, and Johnson was pleased to find his comrade was still alive, though still stunned from his impact with the wall. They bumped and jostled over the terrain until finally skidding to a halt among three other similar vehicles. Scores of police, agents, and even Colonial soldiers had surrounded the round building. The odd gunshot rang out from the upper floors, but it was mainly quiet. Director Johnson stepped out in time to watch, but one of the police units had already begun a full-breach.

"What's going on here?" he demanded.

A young police commander leaned over a large display unit as he coordinated the attack. Director Johnson approached and grabbed the man by the shoulder.

"The President is a desperate man. We have to de-escalate this, and fast!"

The man looked at him and shook his head, simultaneously pushing his arm away.

"It's too late for that, Sir. He'd taken senators hostage and threatened to blow up the entire building if we do not fall back."

"Then what the hell are..."

A bright white flash filled every single windows of the vast domed structure. It was immediately followed by the blasting of the windows, and a great roar as the very ground shook. The explosion was massive, perhaps the largest any of them, including Johnson had ever seen. It began at the lower levels and then spread throughout the large dome. A single squad of riot police was moving to assist the breaching team, and the shockwave sent them all flying through the air. Everybody else threw themselves behind whatever cover they could find.

"Keep your heads down!" Director Johnson called out.

He pulled himself behind the police Bulldog just as the first chunks of dirt and broken rock began to fall about them. The worst part for many was the dust cloud. It began at the base of the dome and then accelerated out to engulf them all. In thirty seconds, the cloud had reached the open plaza and the bullet-ridden sculpture. On the cloud went like some massive ethereal beast that consumed all. The cloud sent soldiers and civilians running for cover. Others tried desperately to avoid the choking powder.

Wait a second! This took some serious planning, thought Johnson.

He climbed into the back of the Bulldog and to the small driver's cupola. He slid into position and activated the external feeds. At first, he only saw the dust, but a quick flick of the toggle to the right moved through the observation modes. Infrared was first, and that did little more than turn to a monochrome image of dust. The thermal imaging was something else entirely. The equipment easily saw through the cloud and into the heart of the dome. There were scores of shapes as people staggered about. He suspected some would be wounded, but the majority was trying to get away from the dust.

Wait, what's that?

Off to the right was an oval heat bloom. It changed shape and then began to rise. He focused in on it and waited as the servo mount altered its position and zoomed in to the target. The thermal imaging gave a fuzzy image, but as it stabilized, he immediately picked out the shape.

"A goddamned passenger liner."

He jumped out of the seat and immediately struck his head on the top of the vehicle. Luckily for him, the innards of the Bulldog were lined with a thin layer of absorbent, rubber like material. He lifted his hand and rubbed his head. It hurt, but there was no sign of blood.

We need air support and fast.

He looked about but could see nothing. The Bulldog configuration was different to the military specification, and the Agency didn't make use of armor. He went to the rear of the vehicle and looked at the computer system. A shape emerged at the hatch.

"Director, do you need help?"

It was Agent Nuttall. She climbed in alongside him.

"I've been on the conversion course with the riot unit. I know the tech."

"Good," he answered calmly.

"I need to get an open distress signal sent out."

She nodded and pulled herself into the nearest seat. Once in position, a motor drive held her in tight to the side along the computer.

"Who should we contact?"

The screen flashed blue, and a map of the capital with active units appeared. There were police vehicles and squads throughout the city, but it was the metro command right in the heart of the city that he pointed to.

"Metro command, then Naval command, and finally the Marine Corps barracks."

Agent Nuttall quickly established a communication network with all three of them. Even Director Johnson was impressed with her speed at reaching them all.

"Online, Sir, what do you want to send them?"

He looked up and pointed.

"There's a liner moving out from here. It's got to have Harrison on board."

Agent Nuttall began transmitting, and at the same time opened three tracking windows.

"Each of these is slaved to the external feeds."

Johnson pointed to the second. It was marked 'driver'. There was no need to say anything as she quickly took control of the mount and moved it a few degrees until reaching the heat bloom. A green rectangle appeared over the shape, and the computer began a series of comparisons to the police database. It took six seconds to find the exact model.

"It's an interplanetary liner from Galactic Excursions. The company was grounded last week, and all of its vessels placed under observation by Colonial Guard troops. One craft is missing, GE Adventurer."

"Yeah, I wonder why that might be."

"Wait, Sir, there's something else."

She adjusted several of the windows aside and went back to the wide area tactical screen. The current distance showed the city, but with a few taps it changed to show the curvature of this part of the planet. Off to the side were icons for the Spacebridge to Prometheus, as well as a myriad of other objects, including orbital defense platforms and freighters.

"Well?"

Agent Nuttall moved two more sliders and then focused on the area around the Spacebridge. A single green rectangle marked the shape of a ship.

"It's the Meteor."

CHAPTER TEN

358CC was the golden age for private security companies, but before then there were small outfits from one-man bodyguards to entire businesses. Cemgil Kurt was one of those one-man outfits and became something of a legend in the inter-war years. The attempt on the life of Kerberos Ambassador Robert Perkins left him hospitalized for three weeks. Cemgil Kurt had only been hired three days earlier and single handedly protected the Ambassador for thirty-six hours until relieved by Security Personnel of the ATU. When they cleared the building, they found thirteen bodies plus the mortally wounded Cemgil Kurt. The ambassador took two bullets, all to the left leg. Ever since, the deeds of Cemgil have become something of a gunslinger legend.

Private Security Directory

Military Outpost, Rintau, Eos.

The forward position was silent, just as it had been for

three days now. The walls were low, and the towers modest in their size. They must have been constructed generations earlier and had the look of ancient monuments or relics. Even the New Helion Army garrison was modest, and numbered just fifteen soldiers. These volunteers protected the perimeter, while in the center a single landing pad with the damaged Mauler still sitting there. Wictred leaned against the Northern tower and breathed in the cool air. He looked around him and at the refinery complex far into the distance and the partially damaged town of Rintau where their outpost was located.

"What are you so happy about?" Captain Carter asked.

Wictred looked out to the hills ringing their position.

"I thought we had something important back there. That Bioray should have been our ticket off this rock."

He sighed and Captain Carter laughed.

"And then we find the fleet has already taken five in the battles of the last month. It happens. In any case, our experience has proven useful. Our numbers are low on Eos, but so are the machines. What we lack in strength, we make up for in experience. Do you know anybody that has more combat time against them than us?"

Wictred shrugged and then pointed to a single heavily modified Marine Bulldog. Large parts of the armor had been removed and a metal mount welded onto the back. On top of the contraption sat one of the turrets from the captured ship.

"At least we got our new guns," laughed Wictred.

A flash far off into the distance caught their attention.

"We've not seen action in weeks. There can only be a few hundred, perhaps a thousand of them left."

The Captain shook his head.

"And you think finding them is going to improve your day?"

He pointed off into the distance where the low hills surrounded their position. The odd puff of smoke marked NHA artillery hitting the remnants of the Biomech forces.

"We have a damaged transport, and we supposedly crashed in this ancient archeological site. It must be the most exposed and poorly protected site on the whole of this rock. Are you sure your plan will work?" Wictred asked.

Captain Carter laughed.

"We've been hunting the last of them for weeks now, and whatever we do they keep slipping away. We need to finish them, and the best way is to act like a hunter. We draw them in with something too irresistible, even for the machines."

Wictred nodded and tried not to laugh.

"True. I just hope the plan works. This outpost is weak, very weak."

Captain Carter pulled off his helmet and wiped his brow.

"True, but if it was any other way, would they risk the

last of their forces? We are weak enough to beat, but not too weak to look like bait."

Vadi, the synthetic warrior approached them. On his back he carried one of the looted guns they'd taken from the crashed vessel.

"They come?"

Wictred nodded in reply.

"Yes, very soon."

Captain Carter pulled the ruggedized secpad from his thigh and checked the latest drone scans. The information was current but also lacking in clarity for their immediate area.

"Looks like they shot down the last one. As far as the machines are concerned, we've got no surveillance and no help within a hundred and fifty klicks."

He looked back at the Mauler.

"That's what caught their eye. They must have tracked our so-called emergency landing."

He licked his lips for the third time in the last few minutes.

"It can go one of two ways, and the outcome is dependent on them."

A light rose up high into the sky and then arced back down toward their outpost. It struck just outside the wall and exploded. Another two followed it, and at the same time the black shapes on the hills began to move.

"Yeah, here it comes," said the Captain.

He looked toward the scrawny looking NHA soldiers running out to man the walls. A warning siren wailed, but the response seemed modest, especially compared to the size of the threat.

"Just pray this doesn't become another Dien Bien Phu."

He pulled on his helmet and used the stabilized optical mount to examine the troops moving in on them. He tagged each of them as he turned his head. Finally, he stopped and looked back to Wictred.

"Okay, maybe the plan was a little too optimistic."

"How many?" Wictred asked.

The Captain took in a long breath. Just over twelve..."

Wictred raised an eyebrow.

"...hundred."

Vadi climbed up onto the wall and looked as far as he could see. Without the optics he was forced to rely on his eyes.

"Where?"

Wictred tapped the warrior on the shoulder and indicated for him to climb back down.

"Don't worry, friend. They will be here soon enough."

He then looked to Captain Carter.

"Might be an idea to send out the distress call to command. They had better be ready for this one."

The officer was already speaking into his helmet. He stopped, and the visor flipped open.

"Not quite according to plan. They've jammed the

area."

He looked up to sky.

"We'll have line of sight for orbital communications in about thirty minutes."

The first volleys of rockets came down in front of the wall and then the first direct hit. The blast was impressive and blew a hole big enough to drive a Bulldog through. Captain Carter and Wictred looked to each other at the same time.

"Get them ready, Corporal. It's time."

* * *

GE Adventurer, Over Terra Nova

The liner was the newest of the Traveler class and bore a surprising similarity to the supersonic jetliners of the twentieth century. The hull was long and cylindrical, with a pointed nose and eight massive engines fitted above and below the delta wing design. The engines themselves were installed in special banks of four and were capable of sending the craft both into space and through a planet's atmosphere. The new and highly advanced air-breathing rocket engines were a special hybrid design that could function in a jet or rocket engine, depending on the configuration. It twisted about as it left low orbit and activated its rocket mode to continue on to escape velocity. Streams of flames gushed from the eight engines so that from a distance it looked almost like a comet.

The paint scheme of the liner was absolutely pristine, and it could easily have been a craft fresh from the factory. The exterior had once carried the stripes and insignia of the GE company, but in the last few days there had been major changes. The color had been altered, and the crest of the position of President emblazoned along the flank. There was nothing other than the name Adventurer to mark it out as anything less than an official Alliance vessel.

"We are out of Terra Nova controlled airspace and into orbit. Please leave your magclamps on until we reach our cruising speed," said the pilot over the vessel's intercom.

The liner wasn't the only craft making its way from Terra Nova. A group of four Lightning fighters, each in the color scheme of the Presidential escort unit moved close by. They all matched the liner beautifully in terms of colors and insignia. They had been waiting aboard one of the many orbiting defense platforms placed at different heights around the planet. Each of the fighters was configured for space travel and combat only, and they would lack the fuel or power to continue with the liner on its journey, if it intended on traveling to another planet in the Alpha Centauri System. Instead, they followed as escort, making sure the craft made it safely out of reach of the planet.

"Fighter escort is in formation and watching us out. ETA to the Sol Rift is three hours, seven minutes."

The mood aboard the small liner was far from a happy one even though they had escaped completely unscathed. Governor Trelleck sat in one of the many large lounge chairs and directly opposite President Harrison. Unlike Trelleck, President Harrison was nervous and checked the large windows for signs of trouble. The Governor, on the other hand, simply paged through something on his secpad as though this was a day like any other. At one point, he stopped and looked up to the ceiling.

"I like your ship, Mr. President. Can I assume the Senate voted for it? It was a very wise move on their part."

President Harrison tightened his brow and looked back to the man.

"What? What did you say?"

Governor Trelleck smiled, that officious, polite smile that he knew was actually anything but polite.

"I asked about your ship. I understand you have designated this as your official Presidential transport. Did the Senate vote for it? Also, why not change the name?"

The President shook his head.

"What? No, of course not. There is no need for them to vote. It is not necessary."

The Governor smiled again.

"Why, of course."

He looked back to his secpad and left the President fuming from within the comfort of his own mobile palace. Unlike military ships, this vessel had been constructed specifically for executive travel and short to medium distance excursions. Comfort and views were much more important than any other concerns. Governor Trelleck looked out of the window as the craft began a slow spiral. The view of the planet shifted to show the stars, the Spacebridge, and even the odd freighter moving through orbit.

"Impressive, very impressive."

The President turned about and brought his fist down hard on the small oak table. If there had been anything on it, the objects might have moved, but the only thing in sight was the Governor's secpad, and even that device was resting in his hands, not on the beautifully stained wood.

"Are you all right, Mr. President?" he asked, with a special emphasis on his title, "You seem a little, well, a little agitated?"

The President looked at him as a small globule of fluid dripped from the corner of his mouth. Normally, it would have fallen down, but now it just sat there until he moved his head. The small ball drifted off to the side and vanished inside the spacecraft.

"The traitors. I thought you said Johnson and the others had been dealt with?"

Sitting next to Governor Trelleck was Major Grant, the commander of the President's security detail, and he looked almost as comfortable as the Earthsec Governor, much to President Harrison's annoyance.

"We were lied to by several of the ministers within the government, Sir. I told you that a group of the Senators were plotting something."

President Harrison pointed at him and shook his head.

"Yes, and I had each of them arrested and brought before our military tribunal. The ringleaders paid the price out on the palace lawns, to the cheers of the crowds."

Major Grant raised an eyebrow to this.

"Well, Sir, they were the men behind the attempt to get your term as Magister Populi removed. There were others, though."

"Who?"

"Senator Yatsenyuk, Minster for Science and Education. She has been speaking with the Biomechs from Prometheus and Hyperion over the last three months. You recall her attempts to get them to send their own senators to Terra Nova."

President Harrison shook his head.

"No, I don't remember. This Senator Yatsenyuk is a traitor to her own blood. None of these Biomechs has any place in our domain. Terra for Terrans, that is what I have always believed."

Governor Trelleck curled his lip a fraction, forming the barest glimmer of a smile.

"I can assure you, Sir, that on Old Terra, we do not have this problem."

President Harrison was in no mood to be lectured by

the old man, not today.

"Really, Old Terra, the radiated wasteland that was abandoned centuries ago? There is a reason so many fled for the new worlds, Governor. It is a hole not worthy of the effluence I flush down my toilet."

There were a handful of others inside the craft, most coming from various departments in the government that answered directly to the new office of Magister Populi. Right at the back was a single unit of eight Colonial Guards, still dressed in their full battle attire. There was one strange omission, though, and it had taken this long before even President Harrison noticed.

"Wait a minute. Where the hell is Trajchevski? He was supposed to be with us."

He twisted around and found the harness stopped him from fully turning. He went to reach for the maglock clamp, but Major Grant lifted his hand to warn him.

"Mr. President, we are still in the acceleration phase. You don't want to take off your harness until we're clear. Zero gravity will occur once the engines deactivate at cruising speed."

The two men looked at each other, but no more words were said. Governor Trelleck looked out of the window and to the sight of the ever so slow, shrinking world. Terra Nova looked much like Earth had once been; lush green and filled with life. It was something he'd never seen, though, and Terra Nova just reminded him of the weakness and corruption he'd come to expect.

"So, how do you intend on spending your exile from the almighty Terra Nova?" he finally asked.

The sarcasm in the Governor's voice was plain to hear, especially the odd way he said the word 'Terra'. President Harrison looked at him and then to the Major.

"I want to know where the hell Kocho Trajchevski is?"

The man swallowed as if there was something uncomfortable in his throat.

"He took a shuttle twelve minutes before we left the Senate building."

"What? And only now you are telling me this?"

The President's face was already beginning to change color.

"Are you telling me that Trajchevski, my most senior officer, chose to leave before us? Why? Was he forced to go, or did he deliberately leave us behind?"

Major Grant raised his shoulders in confusion but said no more. The President began muttering before stopping and then moving data about on the screen in front of him. He quickly came to the latest reports from the Alliance News Network. There were multiple stories coming in from many parts of the Alliance. The most prominent was the buildup at Micaya. His attention was focused on that for a moment, and he might have even forgotten about his own dilemma, if only for a minute or two.

"So Anderson's great plan is to cut me out of the loop

and send everything to Micaya. And he announces it to everybody. I thought he knew what he was doing. So why do this?"

He was talking to himself, and neither of the other two bothered to answer. He then went through other stories, with one in particular describing the fighting of the allied forces throughout Helios. The videostream was from a reporter embedded in a mountain on Spascia. The camera spun around and pointed to lines of marines, machines, and aliens. They were dug into trenches while more machines moved about carrying ammunition.

"Aliens. We have no business getting involved in their war."

He struck the unit, and this time the story was much closer to home. The first feed showed the burning Senate building."

"Good, so we got it in the end."

Governor Trelleck and Major Grant watched the President as he savored the moments of his opponents' death or mutilation. Neither man seemed to like what they were seeing. As he watched, his expression turned from childish glee.

"What, they say I have fled the city, and my supporters have been captured and imprisoned?"

He looked up, but something even more significant caught his eye. He watched the videostream of the plaza, presumably recorded in the last few hours. It showed the site of the sculpture, as well as the bodies on the ground. The camera moved in closer, and he could make out the voice of the man talking.

"Intelligence Director Johnson, I knew he would be the death of me."

The image vanished, pulsing white before being replaced by one of a man wearing a flight suit and helmet. The man looked nervous, like many of those on board the space liner.

"Mr. President, we're receiving a message from a nearby ship."

"What ship?"

The pilot looked away and checked something. The colored shapes reflected on his visor, but it was too blurred for him to make out any specifics.

"It is the recently reactivated ANS Meteor. She's one of the retired frigates that fought in the Uprising."

"Meteor?" said the President.

He thought long and hard but couldn't place the ship. There was something about it that gnawed at him.

"Sir, it's Mr. Trajchevski. He says it is urgent."

The mention of his recently promoted advisor quickly snapped him out of it.

"Put him on."

The pilot's face vanished and was replaced by the smartly dressed man.

"Mr. Harrison," he said in a stern tone, "I didn't expect

to see you off-world."

"President Harrison," corrected the President.

Both men looked at each other for what felt like an eternity. In the last few days, there had been nothing but pleasantries between the two of them. Everything had changed, and the President was beginning to feel cornered and even a little claustrophobic. It was Mr. Trajchevski that spoke first.

"Have you seen the news reports from below?"

He shook his head as though scolding a naughty child.

"Quite frankly, I am stunned at what I am seeing. They are showing footage of your troops storming government buildings, killing agents, and attacking senators. These are yours, are they not? The Colonial Guard?"

For a few seconds, his face moved away to show footage of the violence below.

"Senator Yatsenyuk has called for your impeachment, and I have already been in touch with her to offer my full support. I fear your term as President is over."

The President shook his head angrily.

"No, I have a term of office that cannot, and will not, be halted. I have work to do, and your attempt to undermine my powerbase has already failed."

It was then that he noticed the other civilians around Mr. Trajchevski. He recognized at least one of the senators from the planet. There was even a press crew with him, as well as a camera that seemed to be pointing right back at him.

"I managed to get some of the senators out of there, prior to your assault on our citizens. I just wish I could have been there quicker to try and halt these excesses. I had no idea how far you were willing to go to achieve total control."

He rubbed at his forehead.

"I will, of course, hand myself in as soon as this crisis is over, but I have already offered my resignation. I had no interest in this power grab of yours, only a chance to make the Alliance stronger and safer."

He pointed to the screen.

"As for you, well, I think we all know what is going to happen when…"

A bright flash from the window caused the photosensitive material to darken for a brief moment. All three of the men looked out toward the Rift as a small group of warships came though. The first to arrive was a battered looking Crusader. At this distance, they could make out the shapes of every one of them. The screen changed color and was quickly replaced by the image of an Alliance officer.

"This is Admiral Churchill, of the warship ANS Wolverine. By order of the emergency Senate Committee, under the control of Senator Yatsenyuk, I order all ships in this sector to power down and prepare to be boarded. The Terra Nova Sector is back under Alliance control."

The acceleration of the liner quickly stopped, and it proceeded to drift, giving its passengers a complete lack of gravity. As with all vessels of this type, not a single object in the craft was loose, and nothing could detach unless specifically removed beforehand. Governor Trelleck and Major Grant looked to the President, and then to each other.

"This is madness," said President Harrison. We cannot just let them come aboard and take us prisoner."

Throughout the craft there were men and women releasing their harnesses and pulling themselves toward the lifeboat points. One, an older woman in the uniform of the internal police unit from the capital, looked to the President; and then quickly away before following the others. President Harrison scowled as they left.

"Like rats, each of you, deserting the sinking ship."

"What are your intentions, Governor?" asked the Major.

The two men looked at each other suspiciously. On one hand they had both pledged to work with the President. Both were also perfectly well aware that the politic sphere had just shifted against all of them.

"I've had enough of all this intrigue. I will return to Earth, just as intended. It would appear that you have your own problems to resolve out here, and this is not a particular area of expertise to me."

The Major slid his hand down to his leg, but the Governor shook his head.

"No, keep your hands on the table."

Major Grant considered his words carefully. There was no way to see what the man had under the table even though they were sitting next to each other. The Governor had pushed one hand under his own tunic, but he could feel something metallic pressed against his thigh. The only assumption he could realistically make was that it was a weapon of some kind. There was also the chance that the man was doing nothing more than simply bluffing.

"What's going on here?"

President Harrison sighed and then nodded to his protector.

"I think we are seeing the Governor for the man that he truly is. Traitors surround us when what we need is to regroup and prepare for a new offensive. Our ships at Prometheus are just what we need."

The gunshot seemed to boom through the craft. Blood splattered against the wall and window, and then it was followed by three more. The body of Major Grant slumped about, but the magclamp kept him firmly in place. Governor Trelleck lifted his hands to the table and rested the pistol on the oak ledge.

"Now, I think it is time to discuss the future, don't you?"

The President looked at him, speechless for the first time. Governor Trelleck ran his finger along his cheek and then smiled. It was a short, intentionally fake smile, designed to annoy Harrison who tried to push forward.

"Ah, no, you can stay right there."

"We have an Alliance boarding party at the aft airlock. I am granting them access, now," said the pilot over the intercom.

There was a gentle vibration as the collar from the new arrival mated with that on the liner. All the while this continued, the pistol sat and waited on the table. President Harrison was already facing the airlock entrance from his grand looking seat, whereas the Governor was masked by his own seat. Another set of clunks shook the vessel, and then a loud hiss.

"Step aside, and lower and deactivate your weapons," said a stern voice.

Shapes moved through the airlock as four marines entered. They wore standard issue PDS armor and carried coilguns in their arms. The first two looked about and then spotted their target.

"Mr. President?" Governor Trelleck asked.

The man's eyes turned back to look at the man he had so recently called friend.

"Catch."

With a quick movement that was hidden from the marine, he pushed the pistol and released it. The weapon drifted across the table and up into the air. It was an old trick, the kind of thing one might expect from a child or some sibling's argument. In the heat of the moment, even an educated and experienced man such as President

Harrison could still be fooled by it. Seeing the weapon as his only way out, he reacted without thinking, as almost any person might. The gun was already at head height and moving away when the President reached for it.

"He's got a gun!" yelled the Governor.

The man ducked down just as Harrison grabbed the weapon and pointed it at him. From the angle of where he was sitting, and the position of the Governor, it looked as though he was aiming it toward the airlock. He quickly realized his mistake, but not before the rounds from the coilguns struck him. These were the low-power subsonic rounds designed for stealth operations or for working aboard ships. The first hit his neck, and two then struck his lead arm. The pistol fired and punched into the skin of the liner. On any other vessel, it might have penetrated, but the round somehow embedded in a layered bulkhead and did no more than dent the material.

"Get a medical team in here fast. We've got gunshots!" said the leader of the squad.

They moved through the vessel and toward the cowering Governor, who kept his head down and hands up."

"Are you hurt?" asked the marine.

The Governor looked up and shook his head.

"Good. Then put these on."

The man extended out a pair of cuffs connected to a magnetized rod.

"You are wanted for crimes of murder, insurrection,

and tyranny within the Centauri Alliance during a crisis and in times of war."

The Governor looked at the man and then tried to move. Unlike him, the marines were well trained in movement and combat in a zero gravity environment. As the first kept him busy, the second drifted overhead and placed a stub needle against his neck. It quickly punched the layer of skin and injected its serum.

"That will keep him quiet for now," said the man.

The unit leader looked about the craft and checked for other signs of potential trouble. Each of the security personnel had already laid down their weapons without a fight. Satisfied that the craft was safe, he made contact with his ship.

"The liner is secure. We have the Governor. The President is dead, though. He raised a weapon, so we were forced to take action."

* * *

Alliance Defenses, Old Spascia City, Helion Sector
The bayonet slid quickly into the Thegn as Teresa stabbed down. The first strike had glanced off, and she had nearly fallen over. The second one she delivered with more care, and this time it punched into the neck and down to the ground. Without thinking, she yanked on the gun and twisted it around. The tearing effect on the creature's

throat easily ripped it open, spilling bubbling blood over the ground and onto her boots. She looked up at the confusion that now completely surrounded her.

"Keep moving forward. Grab everybody you can find. Leave nobody behind."

She lifted the carbine back to her shoulder and stepped away from the body. A grenade exploded three meters away and showered her in dirt. It did nothing to slow her progress. Four other marines formed up alongside her, and they advanced one step at a time. All around them more marines fought tooth and nail for every meter, while at the same time the Vanguards and a handful of CES engineers ran amok amongst the defenders.

There they are.

Just ahead were black shapes and the continuous flashing of guns. She increased her speed and jumped atop the ruins of a shattered Eques walker. From this slightly elevated position, Teresa could see the remains of the four city blocks and the thousands of enemy bodies that littered the place.

"Teresa?" said a familiar voice.

She lowered her eyes and found a group of Jötnar standing in an oval with scores of marines around them. Gunfire flickered around them, but they had positioned dozens of Thegns into some kind of sandbag position. She dropped down and landed among them at the same time as the rest of her unit. Even as she approached the

Jötnar, the first of the Vanguards clambered over, pushing past the exhausted defenders. A single Decurion pushed up from the bodies and threw itself at the group.

"Colonel!" shouted one of the Vanguards.

Not even Gun was close enough to stop it, but it didn't matter. Teresa twisted just a fraction and pulled the trigger. Her carbine hammered into the machine, and it staggered and stumbled to one side, bringing it closer to the Jötnar. One of Gun's warriors grabbed it with his armored paw and yanked it nearer. One by one, the other Jötnar stamped and shot at it until the thing lay shattered and ruined.

"Damn good to see you," said Gun as he opened his visor.

Explosion after explosion lit up the background, and Teresa realized she'd forgotten to check the time. With a quick glance, she could see they still had minutes. Gun looked at the blasts and then at her.

"A creeping barrage, very nice. I assume it's time to go?"

Teresa nodded and then looked about the battlefield. Gun stepped toward her, his armor groaning from the damage it had taken.

"He's here."

He pointed off to the right where two Bulldogs and an artillery pieces formed a curious piece of cover. Inside the ruins were seven marines, each injured to various degrees. A female marine went from one to the other as she tried to stabilize the wounded. At the same time, a pair of Khreenk warriors fired from the top of the wreckage and off into the distance. The female marine spotted her and began to salute. Teresa shook her head.

"It's okay, don't. I'm Colonel Morato. I'm looking for…"

"Jack?" Private Jana Jenkell answered.

Teresa looked down to the bodies and the multiple wounded. Right in the center was a shape that was impossible to confuse. He lay there, his visor open, and his eyes closed. He armor was stained with a dull green mark and covered in corrosive burns. The sight of him lying there made her take a single stumble back. Her foot caught and then firm hands caught her.

"Teresa, he took a blast from a Khreenk weapon," Gun said as he held her.

A hundred tiny lights flashed in the distance, and the projectiles clattered among the defenders. Two marines were killed, but the rest of the gunfire rattled about the improvised defenses. Teresa moved toward her son, but Gun held her back.

"No, not yet. He's unconscious. Get us to the bridges."

Teresa continued to pull away, but Gun held firm.

"Colonel. If we stay, we all die. The only way to save him, or any of them, is to get back now."

Teresa turned around to face him, and for the first time, he could see a burning rage in her eyes. Her face was as olive tanned as ever, but her eyes burned in a similar way to his kin when in the middle of battle.

"To the bridges," he said one final time.

Artillery continued to strike off into the distance, right into the heart of the enemy positions. Even so, Teresa's visor showed multiple enemy formations inside the Three Sisters and advancing toward them.

The Khreenk!

A glance to the overhead view showed that small formation of gallant warriors and the robots. According to the mapping information, they were being hit with brigade strength numbers. It was an impossible defense.

"Marines, we have to leave, now! Leave gear behind, take the wounded, and fall back to the bridges!"

The fresh marines swept through the rubble and opened fire on the approaching enemy. At the same time, more of them surged throughout the small four-block enclave and grabbed whomever they could find. It started as dozens, then scores, and finally hundreds were moving back in a slow, bloodied column. A squad of medics loaded more wounded onto three mules. Teresa spotted Jack being loaded onto one, but Gun was already calling to her. She closed her eyes for a moment, tried to take a calming breath, and then followed him.

"There's an advance party of Decurions a hundred meters there."

He pointed in the direction of the artillery fire. Flashes

were at every point, but the closer ground continued to move. She altered her optics and nearly stumbled at seeing them.

"The Decurions are tough. Hard to spot in the broken ground, and the artillery barely touches them."

She could see the explosions and the fact that the machines simply ignored the blasts. Occasionally, one would be hit and might lose a limb, but not even that could stop them. Much further back, the newly arrived Thegns were sheltering in cover from the artillery bombardment coming down upon them. The Eques walkers continued their slow, methodical advance, but the gap between them and the Decurions was increasing by the second.

He looked back to her and grimaced.

"If we don't do something about them, they will overrun our column before we get halfway to the bridges."

Teresa nodded in agreement.

"So, what do you suggest?"

Gun looked at what forces remained. His troops were exhausted, low on ammunition, and more importantly, almost every one of them was wounded in some way.

"What are your troops like? Will they stand?"

Teresa mouth changed to a smile.

"Of course."

He nodded.

"Good. We'll set up a firing line with a single L56 there."

He pointed in the direction of the broken Eques

walkers that Teresa had climbed over.

"That will be our firing line."

He then turned about and faced the direction the enemy was coming from.

"Give me a single platoon and join me over there."

He pointed to a lower wall nearly thirty meters away, a terrible place where the marines had been defending from all out Biomech assault for hours now. It was around a meter high, and there were scores of bodies from both sides all round it. Two L56 machine guns lay broken to one side, along with a squad of marines killed where they stood. All that remained was a single SAAR robot that continued to blast any targets of opportunity. Whoever had been maintaining it had left two crates of ammunition connected to its hopper. The barrels hissed from the excess heat generated by near constant shooting.

Gun moved to the wall and proceeded to drag the bodies of Thegns out of the way before lowering himself down. The SAAR robot continued to shoot, uncaring about the fact that its primary weapon was seconds from failure. With one arm, Gun dragged a broken Decurion and pulled it over his torso.

"You're not serious?" she asked.

The requested platoon moved in around them, and their lieutenant approached Teresa. Gun watched in satisfaction as the man did not salute.

"Sir, where do you want us?"

Teresa looked down to Gun who nodded slowly back to her.

"I need you and your marines to hide among the dead. Wait until my command. Understood?"

"Yes, Sir."

The Lieutenant passed the orders on to his sergeant who was already barking like some angry dog. It didn't take long for each of them to find bodies and equipment to hide under. Finally, Teresa joined them, choosing to shelter under the remains of two broken Thegns.

CHAPTER ELEVEN

Even today there are those that argue about the effectiveness of edged weapons in the Proxima Emergency. Very few people that were there at the time would agree with the argument. Assessment after the conflict showed that almost a third of all Confederate casualties were caused in hand-to hand-combat. These injuries included cuts, stabs, and bites. It was this exposure to such ferocity that saw the development of weapons such as the advanced L52 carbine, a weapon capable of performing the same job as the venerable L48. More importantly, the weapon featured a high rate of fire mode that could shred multiple targets in seconds.

Edged weapons in the Emergency

Alliance Defenses, Old Spascia City, Helion Sector
The first sign the enemy was close was the crunching sound of the SAAR robot being torn apart. Teresa watched the

icon for the machine flash as a warning before deactivating as it was destroyed. That meant two things to her, first, the machine had gone, and second, the Decurions were about to overrun their position.

What if they detect our heat signatures?

Her pulse quickened as she realized the machines might simply move amongst them and stab and kill any one they found. It was too late to change now, and she was forced to remain under the bodies and wait for whatever was coming. She lay there for three minutes until finally she spotted movement. At first it looked like a slowly moving cloud, but then she spotted the legs. The machines scuttled over the bodies with speed and precision and then on toward the gun.

That's something at the very least.

She moved her finger very slowly around the grip of her carbine. She'd been still so long that cramp had begun to settle in. She could live with that, but with the numbness she'd started to doubt the gun was even still in her hand. Feeling the hard material was immediately reassuring. Teresa moved her eyes from left to right and identified six machines in her vicinity. They had gone six meters past her, and from what she could hear, even more were climbing overhead.

How many more?

The visor overlay wasn't particularly helpful. She could see that over half of those on this side of the battle were now at the bridges. The Khreenk were giving ground and withdrawing to one of the smaller bridges.

We don't have much more time.

Another group of Decurions passed overhead, but that appeared to be the last of them. The machine gun blasted at them, but most of the shots were too high and easily missed the targets. Teresa just hoped the gunners were protecting those hiding under the bodies, and not simply failing through fear or incompetence.

"Now!" Gun bellowed.

Teresa pushed hard and found herself stuck. Panic was settling in, and she kicked and struggled until the Thegn pulled off to the side. She lifted up to one knee, spun about, and took aim. The first burst struck the back of a Decurion, right in the center mass. It dropped to the ground, its internal functions shattered. More marines appeared, and the gunfire tore into machine after machine. Gun took the longest to emerge, and four Decurions immediately made for him. It was a futile gesture; the great warrior tore them limb from limb while shouting insults.

One marine was pinned by two of the machines, and they quickly dispatched him with stab after stab. The sharpened tips at the end of their limbs easily punched through the PDS armor as though it were no more than a thin sheet of plastic.

"Help him!" yelled the Lieutenant.

Another Decurion leapt from the outer wall and

decapitated the officer with a single slash. Two marines turned their guns on the machine, and with high-power rounds blew off chunks of metal and limbs until its remains lay quivering on the ground. Teresa ran over to the pinned marine and lowered her carbine to fire at point blank range. One blast was all she could muster before the one to the right twisted a limb about and smashed her carbine from her hands.

"Gun!"

She didn't bother looking for aid, and instead whipped out her handgun and emptied the clip into the machine. Her heart was pounding as she faced off against the horrific thing.

"Die!" she screamed.

Teresa knew only too well how ineffective a pistol would be. Yet she continued to shoot, and half of the rounds managed to cause damage to its torso. They tore into the metal plating, but the Decurion was still able to deliver a final stab to the poor marine before turning to face her. Gun stormed into view and kicked the machine against its comrade. As the two tried to untangle themselves, Teresa retrieved her carbine while Gun punched and kicked at them repeatedly. Only one continued to move, and a short burst from Teresa quickly finished it off. They looked back to their unit and found they'd suffered only modest casualties. The last three Decurions had been forced back to the outer defense and were easily picked off by careful carbine fire.

"Excellent work, marines," said Gun.

He watched with a wistful look as the machines' assault faltered and then completely failed. A squadron of Hammerheads swooped overhead in a low, high-speed pass. All of them opened fire at the advancing line of Thegns and Eques walkers before vanishing off into the distance. Incredibly, not one of them was destroyed.

"Good, that will buy us some time."

Teresa looked about their position. The wounded were already being carried past the machine gun position and on to the bridges. One of the sergeants continued barking his orders, and each squad fell back in good order. She looked about for signs of Jack and was relieved to see the group of injured had made it out of the maelstrom and was already at the main bridge.

"It's time to go."

They joined the others and climbed over the wreckage to leave with the rest of their forces. Teresa couldn't help but turn around and look back at the enemy. The sky above them was black and filled with clouds. Movement could be seen everywhere, and the bulk of their numbers couldn't have been more than a kilometer away.

"How the hell will we stop this?"

Gun looked back and laughed.

"The way we always do. With bullets, blood, and sweat."

* * *

Taxxu, Uncharted Space

Spartan kept his eyes closed and tried to recall what he'd just seen. The numbers, the pageantry, and the sheer amount of technology on display was staggering. Never before had he seen such advancements in one place. His memories of the Bright Horizon were clear now, and each time he thought back, the other memories began to fade. He could see the look on the face of his mother when they reached the lifeboat, the blood from where his father had been cornered and butchered, and even the empty escape hatch where the lifeboat had already been jettisoned. He thought back to the days and weeks that followed, and found some of the images too much to bear.

So much death and destruction, so that was my childhood?

The one image he could not shake was that of him being restrained by Confederate security troops. At some point, they had boarded the ship and found him. As they helped him out of the ship, he was almost blinded by the bright white lights of those waiting outside. Some were doctors, others the press. But the one thing he kept hearing over and over again was people asking how he had survived. The very last memory he could find was of him looking back at the vessel from a window aboard a station or other ship. The wide umbilical shaft connected them together, and teams of medical staff were bringing bodies out of the infamous ship. A man leaned in close to him and spoke in a soft, friendly voice.

"Son, how did you survive in there? You're the only one we found alive."

Spartan shook his head and cast the memory aside for now.

You can reminisce maybe when all this is over, and if you're still alive.

He opened his eyes and found himself staring into blackness. There was nothing out there, just the cool, dry feeling of the interior of the ship. His mind had drifted and for a little while he found it difficult to get his bearings. Images of ships, battles, and training all flashed about his eyes. He leaned forward, and the lights in the room flickered into life. He found himself looking right into the face of Thayara who sat on her own bunk opposite him.

"What is it?" she asked.

Spartan still found it odd that he could understand them all, even though his mind was telling them they were speaking in an alien tongue. As the light increased in brightness, he could see her skin lighten until she seemed to reflect the very light itself. Her cool, black eyes looked back at him inquisitively.

"You are concerned about the simulation?"

Spartan thought back and then shook his head.

"No. The simulation was fine, just like the last ten of them."

She moved nearer, leaning from her bed and under the ceiling mounted strip light. The harsh lighting cast long shadows down her lithe body, and only then did Spartan realize she was naked. He moved back a few centimeters.

"What is it?" she asked, following the gaze of Spartan as he looked at her from head to toe.

"Does my form offend you?" she asked.

Her tone wasn't coy or playful; it was anything but. As usual, Thayara was all about the work, and the looks she was receiving from Spartan were intriguing at best, but more likely annoying. Spartan cleared his throat.

"On my worlds, we do not present ourselves unclothed to each other."

Thayara sighed and then rose to her feet, exposing herself to him even more clearly. He could see her skin now under the light, the pale smoothness, and her long black hair that disappeared behind her back.

"Your people are primitive, Spartan. We were like you once, before we embraced passion. You hide behind clothes, rules, and bureaucracies. Is it no surprise your people are so angry all of the time?"

She turned away to the single washing area they had been provided with. It was completely open to the elements and consisted of a marked section that blasted the floor with moisture that evaporated after traveling just a few meters. She stepped onto the plate and was quickly surrounded in the cleansing mist. Spartan watched her as the fluids ran down her flesh before fading and vanishing before his eyes.

"If your people were so advanced, why do they spend so much time fighting each other?"

Thayara turned to face him, deliberately baring her full form to him. Spartan chose to accept it and looked at her face with a whimsical expression.

"I did not say we are perfect. But we do leave with our worlds in harmony. All of our colonies are self-sufficient and when we do fight, it is between the Anicinàbe only. I have seen reports on your wars. You will fight and leave nothing alive, plants, creatures, oceans, and forests. You will consume and destroy them in your violence and greed."

She shook her head, and her long black hair flicked from side to side. The fluid ran off and across the room. Spartan half expected it to strike him, but just before it could make contact, it vanished into a fine mist that did little more than cool him.

"Perhaps, but there's a reason I've been chosen from all of my people to help end the violence out here."

He lifted his arms and turned about, as though he could encompass the whole galaxy within his own arms.

"You remember the last simulation, do you not?"

She looked at him with an expression of wry amusement about her face. The strange fluid ran down her shoulders, over her chest, and then vanished just as it hit the ground.

The light played with the paleness of her skin and made flashes of reflection and color about her body.

"The assault on the Byotai flagship was a victory for both of us, that is true. Our numbers were even, and I suffered fewer losses than you. I don't see how you consider your attack more successful."

Spartan rose to his feet and moved close to her. He continued until he was standing just a meter from her naked body, deliberately moving into her personal space. He sensed a moment of hesitation in her, but then finally she settled.

"Thayara," he said, shaking his head, "you lost three Ghost Warriors and killed everybody on that ship. What did you achieve?"

He spotted something off to the right. At first he thought it was just a moving shadow, but then he noticed the subtle dome in the ceiling.

So, they like to watch. I thought as much.

He looked back her and waited for an answer.

"I achieved a victory. I wiped out our enemy for minimal losses. I destroyed their ship with precision strikes, as well as every soul on board."

She laughed, a short, irritating cackle. The sound was enough to drive any desire Spartan must have felt at looking upon her nakedness.

"You were responsible for badly wounding twenty-five Ghost Warriors in your own attack. How is that better?"

Spartan smiled.

"Because I only killed six Byotai, including their commander in an honorable fight in front of their warriors. I did not kill them from afar where they were unable to defend themselves. They fought and died with honor, and because of this, I was able to dictate terms. From the bridge of their own ship, I forced their second-in-command to surrendered the ship and their warriors to me, and left him in charge."

Thayara looked confused with his explanation.

"For my losses, I increased our fleet and added more than a hundred battle hardened Byotai ground troops. The Ghost Warriors could be repaired in less than six hours, while your combat losses would require fresh warriors, assuming there were any on hand."

Thayara ran her hands over her hair and then down her body, making sure that every drop of the fluid had soaked into her flesh.

"Under the command of their own officer. How does that help us?"

Spartan shook his head in irritation.

"You do not understand, do you? The Byotai are not a traditional fighting force. They are well equipped for war but try to avoid it. They are a society of citizens who will fight when called upon. They value leadership, strength, and honor; things that few of the other races give much consideration to."

He wiped his chin, considering his words carefully.

"It is not enough to just defeat our enemies. We must absorb them into ourselves, to somehow increase us, to better us. If we simply kill everything we find and destroy every ship, we will continue to shrink, and to eventually diminish until we are too weak to win. My strategy would make us stronger with every victory."

He closed his eyes and thought of the planets in each of the alien domains. The warm worlds of the Helions, the barren rocks of the remaining T'Kari, the lush green world of the Jötnar, and the lavish, rich planets of humanity.

"Every one of their worlds and races can help us. Their ships increase our fleets, their colonies give us resources, and their people will provide the material for foot soldiers. We do not want to fight them all. We do not need to fight them all."

She stepped away from the cleansing unit and brushed past him toward her Thegn clothing. He ignored the contact, pulled off his clothing, and stepped onto the unit. The odd fluids pumped out and soaked him from head to toe. He immediately felt the grime and warmth of his body being pounded, scrubbed, and replenished. He turned about and wiped at his face and eyes until he was facing back into the room. Thayara stared at him with a look of fascination showing clearly across her brow.

"You think that you alone can bend their will? The Helions will not simply lay down their weapons and stand alongside us. And what about your own people? Will they side with us to end this violence?"

Spartan wiped the water from his face, brushing it from his cheeks.

"This is where we differ, Thayara, and that is why you will be an excellent second-in-command."

She bared her teeth in mock annoyance and then hissed at him. A glowing sphere appeared in the center of the room and right where Thayara's right arm was. She moved off to the side, and both of them looked at it. It was distorted, with little in the way of detail or information.

"Our forces are ready for the final battle. It is time to formulate our strategy. Join us on the battle deck."

The sphere changed into an oval shape that looked closer to a face.

"You have both proven yourselves. You are ready to play the part you have been waiting all your lives for. Join us."

* * *

Battleship Retribution, Taxxu, Uncharted Space
Spartan moved alongside Thayara and looked at her, resplendent in her exotic Ghost Warrior armor. They paused in the great hallway of the battleship and looked at the machines. These were great sculptures made from the frozen remains of ancient warriors. There were some

that depicted creatures wearing plates of what looked like steel, and then others wore augmented sections and larger limbs. Above each of the figures hung long banners covered in imagery, runes, and text. No two were alike, yet all followed a similar set of standards, much like ancient human heraldry. After what seemed an age, a great thumping sound shook the very ground.

"I think they're ready for us," said Thayara.

The sounded repeated over and over as hundreds of objects struck the ground in a slow, rhythmic beat. On and on came the sound until even the banners and heraldry began to shudder from the impact.

"Yes, I think you're right. Let's go."

The two machines walked out from the corridor and out onto a narrow, obsidian colored platform that extended out from the wall. They moved toward the edge where one machine waited for them.

"One-Zero-One," said Spartan.

The machine turned to face them and then performed an odd movement with one arm that seemed to be a kind of honorific gesture. Spartan tried to do the same and failed badly. Thayara, on the other hand, managed a perfect mirror of the movement. One-Zero-One made a positive sound and then turned back to look out onto the vast battle deck of the warship.

"You have fought twelve simulated battles in space and on the ground. As we predicted, your solutions to the scenarios were imaginative, and truly unexpected. We have compared your results to our own simulation over the last seventy-one years. The results were most interesting.

"How so?" Thayara asked.

The machine let out a long, slow hiss, much like a sigh.

"We are powerful, technologically advanced, but long out of practice in the arts of this kind of struggle. That is why we left orders to find the strongest, the best, and those prepared to do whatever had to be done to win. There are some of us that believed you would not exist."

The machine pointed to parts of the battle deck.

"With all of this advancement, can you blame us? We have had generations to perfect our technology and our skills. Yet after all of this time, you have won your scenarios with less than a quarter of our projected casualties. In total, we expect our campaign to take between six and thirty years to complete, yet your victories in our scenarios suggest you could do the same in less than six months, and with fewer losses."

Thayara began to speak, but Spartan interrupted her with a raised hand and his palm outstretched toward her.

"This is not a measure of your weakness, just your isolation. We can fight better because we have been pushed, tested, and challenged. By entrusting your troops with our leadership, we can guarantee you a quick war, with minimal losses."

Spartan looked away from the machine and out to the

army with a strange mixture of surprise and awe. He'd seen the same many times before in the simulations. He and Thayara had fought alongside them in battles on human worlds, aboard alien ships, and even in the void. There was something very different at seeing them all arrayed before them, each waiting for its orders to enter battle.

The battle deck was an odd feature of the ship, much like a combined CIC from an Alliance ship and the hangar on a carrier. It contained tactical information, maps, the leadership, and all the warrior caste of the Biomechs. The ground level below them was actually a vast open space with long dividing walls nearly a meter tall. From the ceiling hung magclamps, and underneath these were hundreds and hundreds of machines. Each one was much like the machines he'd already seen, except they were all clearly awake and watching him. Spartan scanned from left to right before realizing that One-Zero-One and Thayara were both there with him. They each seemed as intrigued as the next at what they could see.

"The Grand Armada is ready to reclaim that which we lost so long ago. We have planned every possible outcome and selected the two of you to be the face of our assault. Our warriors and machines will do the work, but it will be your faces that they remember."

The center of the battle deck altered into a massed projection of the Black Rift. Hundreds of ships waited, along with dozens of the monstrous double-ended Rift

Engines.

"Our machines will open up the Rift on our command and begin the process of stabilization."

"What is that?" Spartan asked.

The machine remained stationary, but the view in the center of the battle deck shifted to show one of the Rift Engines.

"Our Engines are our greatest achievement, a piece of technology that surpasses anything we have ever constructed before."

"What do they do?" Thayara asked.

"The machines allow us to open an existing long-range Rift passageway or even to create new short-ranged ones. Once active, they can stabilize them over time. After the ship enters the Rift, it remains on both sides of the bridge and reconfigures it into a permanent passageway."

Spartan said nothing, but he could immediately see the implications. Once the Rift was secured, there would be no way to close it. He'd seen that already in the assault upon the Rift Engine in the last battle. While the machine existed, so did the Rift.

"It takes ten hours to fully prepare a Rift, and after fifteen hours the process is irreversible. We will never again be banished to this side of the Great Seal, nor will our enemies be able to hide. Finally, we can leave our banishment on the ancient worlds of our people."

Spartan listened intently and made a mental note of

any mention of the technology and the plan.

"This is your assault force, a mere handful from the great host you will lead. These seventy-five Ghost Warriors are to be your watchers and your bodyguard. They will ensure you maintain the path of glory and will fight, and if necessary, die for the cause."

The machine then looked to Thayara who was resplendent in her new armor.

"Thayara. As a superlative combatant, and an expert in the art of hand-to-hand combat, you will have an honor equal to mine and Spartan's to join our holy Triumvirate in the coming battle."

Thayara looked to Spartan, her suit of advanced armor creaking as she twisted about.

"You've already discussed this?"

Spartan nodded in agreement.

"Yes, of course."

In the last hour, he had spoken with the twelve senior commanders of the so-called Ghost Army, one of which was One-Zero-One. Until now he'd assumed that Thayara would have been given the same conversation and choices. He suspected this was some kind of power play.

"The three of us will provide everything that is needed to win this war."

He looked out and past her and the columns of warriors, and instead to the great floating sphere that functioned as a three-dimensional tactical display. It showed every one of the myriad of vessels waiting in the Taxxu System. He didn't bother counting ships and instead looked at the formations. There were clearly twelve subgroups, each one based around a gigantic vessel. He didn't recognize the design, but it was very similar to the Ravagers he'd encountered before.

"Our battleships will strike as spear points into the minds of the enemy," said One-Zero-One.

The machine then pointed one of its limbs to the floating display. The twelve largest vessels blinked three times. They were massive, at least three times bigger than anything else out there and almost half the size of the Rift Engines.

"Each of our battleships contains seventy-five Ghost Soldiers and one of the Defeated."

He said the word with obvious shame, tinged with reverence.

"They are the supreme commanders, the only of us entitled to a place among our ancestors."

"What?" Spartan asked, "A place now, or when you're dead?"

"Yes," said the machine, much to his annoyance.

Thanks, that makes no sense.

"Wait, are you one of them?"

One-Zero-One lowered his torso in a partial bow.

"I am one of the Defeated. We chose twelve of our number to lead us, until the…"

The machine stopped, made a clicking sound and then continued.

"Our reward is to live among our ancestors. We live with immortality and the reminder of our shame. One of us commands these battleships, the divine spirit of our people."

The machine twisted about, indicating toward the walls of the battle deck.

"Even this hallowed vessel, the battleship Retribution carries its own force of Ghost Warriors, of which I am one. When the Helions see Retribution, it will strike fear in them. It was this very ship that burned the ancient city of Spascia in the last war."

Even though there was no obvious emotion, Spartan was convinced he could hear it in the machine's words.

"Seventy-five? I thought this was an army?"

One-Zero-One faced Thayara and stayed silent for an uncomfortable moment.

"This ship, like our other battleships, contains the Ghost Warriors of my people, seventy-five of the most powerful warriors in history. One of these ships could take on and destroy an entire world if we deemed it necessary."

Spartan shook his head and found the armored suit merely moved a few centimeters. The idea of any seventy-five warriors subduing a world greatly amused him, but he had no interest in upsetting his new masters and allies. He faced off toward the machine.

"What happens if any of these warriors is killed in battle? You know from the simulations that we can still expect heavy losses, especially when we move closer to their homeworlds."

The machine again pointed to the large battleships. With a simple gesture, each of them flashed.

"Each of the battleships contains the souls, assembly machines, and armaments to put thousands more warriors into the battlefield. If a Ghost Warrior falls, it will simply move its soul to a new machine and continue the fight. In a matter of days, we can replace our losses. We are both all seeing and ever living."

"I see. And what about cannon fodder? I've seen Thegns in the thousands. We cannot win the coming battles with just these Ghost Warriors. I will need expendable forces to give me tactical flexibility and options."

"Of course. Our Triumvirate has been granted full control of half of our forces to engage the enemy. This force will comprise of three hundred ships, half of our Ghost Warriors and half of our infantry. This is a great honor for all of us."

The machine let that sink in for a moment.

"Between us we will be commanding five hundred bandon of our latest and most advanced warriors. Spartan will provide the tactical knowledge of the area and the strategy to finish them quickly. Thayara, you will command the Ghost Warriors under the direct command of Spartan."

She twisted her torso about to look to Spartan.

"You are giving me command of four hundred and fifty Ghost Warriors?"

Spartan said nothing and instead added up the number of troops in his head. The total of four hundred and fifty Ghost Warriors was a start, but it was the idea of five hundred bandon of soldiers that intrigued him the most. He'd seen Alliance reports on the Biomech formations on his way to Helios, but never in these numbers. It was a host design to truly end worlds.

"One hundred Thema have been assigned for the invasion. How many warriors is that?" Thayara asked.

"We will need enough to defeat their ground troops, but also enough to occupy their worlds. Occupation forces are large and time consuming."

Spartan smiled, though neither could see due to him being safely inside his armored form. He had no doubt that Thayara was a great fighter, perhaps faster and even stronger than him. It was her grasp of war that made him smile the most; her almost juvenile idea that they would need to invade and defeat the enemy in such a way. One-Zero-One twisted his hand to show a model of a ship. It opened apart to show lines of warriors.

"Bandon were our standard military strike force in the days of old. Since then, we have increased manufacturing capabilities and enlarged our warships. We now use the ancient system of our ancestors, the Thema."

The machine brought up a model of a vessel that looked like a small Ark, but much larger than any Alliance warship.

"These are our Despoilers, a heavy assault transport that carries a complete Thema of ten thousand. Warriors. This number is primarily Thegns but also eighty heavy walkers, and more than four hundred new generations assault machines. As part of your fleet, I give you a hundred of these to prepare the way for our factory ships and the second phase."

A million warriors, thought Spartan. *That is an impressive number. It is hardly going to take over the universe, though.*

"Is that it?" asked Spartan, "That is not enough to prosecute a war to its conclusion. Surely we have access to more warriors than this?"

One-Zero-One made a clicking sound and shifted about before answering.

"A million warriors is a full half of our entire active strength. We have spent many years stripping our worlds of all resources to create this force. Every single remaining biological source has been extracted to construct warriors and biomechanical machines to end this struggle."

The small model changed to show an unnamed planet. Around it moved thousands of ships, all of which looked dead and abandoned.

"These Tomb Ships contain the remains of more than

nineteen millions casualties recovered in the last war. Each of them succumbed to their wounds. Since then, they have been frozen and dormant, each waiting for the final components to restore them."

The image vanished.

"They cannot be woken until phase one is complete, and we have fresh materials and biological matter to bring them back."

Spartan looked to him as he considered the machine's words.

"Which casualties?"

The machine answered quickly, and as usual, with no emotion.

"They were the first of our Thegns, volunteers from within our own ranks to don our experimental flesh armor and weapons. When we were being driven back, we took as many with us as we could. Each of them fought and died fighting for us. Our promise to them all was that we would restore them with the flesh of our enemies."

The words should have repelled him, but instead Spartan found himself wondering how much flesh would be required to bring them all back into service. The dead bodies of recently killed Helions could be harvested to bring these ancient and frozen warriors back to life. Nineteen million souls was an army of undreamt power.

"Like on Prometheus. I saw this being done to create warriors."

One-Zero-One clicked again.

"Yes. The flesh can be used to create new life, but this will take time. We will need territory to install our machines and a source of material."

Thayara looked out at the lines of machines and walked right to the edge of the ledge. She lowered herself down to one knee and looked at the nearest one immediately below her. She spun around as though a miraculous thought had just occurred to her.

"Why not just cannibalize some of the bodies to restore the others? Turn nineteen million casualties into a million fresh warriors."

One-Zero-One took a step back in disgust.

"These Thegns were not the mindless slaves you have seen before. These were people of our blood. They volunteered for the process when we were unable to create machinery quickly enough. Over eighty million souls volunteered for the project before our defeat. The last survivors succumbed generations ago and joined those already frozen on our orbital Tomb Ships. All Taxxu flesh is sacred and cannot be reused. Our promise to each of them was that we would use our defeated enemies to maintain their bodies."

The machine straightened up and shook its shoulders. Spartan looked to Thayara, and then returned his gaze to the machine.

"It is time for us to agree on our final plan," it said, "We have seen you both perform in the simulations, and from what we have observed, we have created a strategy. Here it is."

One-Zero-One pointed to the model. This time it changed to show the Helios Star System and its multiple planets. There was no mention of the other alien races, not even the human worlds. Shapes moved in through the Black Rift and then on to the outlying planets in the Helios Sector. It was a long, drawn out plan, with sub units attacking small colonies and moons while other forces swept in again on the larger planets.

"This is not a good plan," said Spartan, forgetting where he was for a moment.

One-Zero-One made that long, slow hissing sound and pointed one hand at his two new allies.

"We had you sent here past the Great Seal at a great price to us. Our kin on the other side are slowly being exterminated while we ready ourselves. We have been trapped here for centuries waiting for the Great Seal to open once more. Now that it is, we will end this."

The machine faced Spartan, then Thayara, before resting on its haunches.

"How would you suggest we achieve our goals of a safe, compliant territory that we can dominate and mold to our will? A place where my people can one again move without fear of death and war?"

Spartan said nothing, waiting for Thayara to reveal

herself. She must have sensed his unease at speaking and saw it as an opportunity to take the initiative. Thayara moved in front of Spartan, her shoulders back, and her suit of armor standing tall and proud.

"Our plan is a simple one. The enemy is weak and already fighting each other. First, we defeat their forces at the Great Seal. Second, we establish a strongpoint to build up our forces. This will take months and allow us to reactive the first of the Tomb Ships. Third, we continue our systematic cleansing of every enemy world until victory is achieved."

Spartan sighed as he listened.

"That is one option, perhaps a good one. But this will cost lives and time, and it comes with a great risk. I have a way we can do the same, and keep the enemy as our servants. My plan will see victory in twenty-four hours."

Even One-Zero-One seemed surprised at his announcement. The machine froze as if its circuits had failed. The massive globe vanished and was replaced by eleven ethereal looking creatures. They were bipedal, like all other races Spartan had come across. Their build was similar, if not identical to Thayara. They talked, sometimes individually and other times in groups. Finally, they stopped and looked toward One-Zero-One.

"Tell us this plan, Spartan. What do you propose?"

Spartan walked closer to the massive projection and lifted his hands to manipulate the shape. The position of the worlds moved as though he'd always known how to use the technology. He moved the Great Seal to the side so they could all see the planets.

"Each of these people has been weakened by war. The Helions are crippled, weak beyond hope, the Khreenk assist, but only in small numbers. The Byotai and the Anicinàbe have been encouraged to fight each other."

He changed the display to show Helios Prime and the Spacebridge to T'Karan.

"This Rift takes us to the T'Kari and on to my worlds. They are rich in life and resources. If we take a systematic approach, my people will turn to industrial war."

He looked at one of the creatures in particular, the tallest, and noblest of them all.

"In the past, my people have fought these wars, wars where millions have died to take territory of just a few kilometers. There is a reason why your people failed to weaken us before."

"What is your plan, then, human?" said the taller creature.

"We do not fight a war of attrition. We fight one of terror and technology. I have already examined the fleet and the capabilities in our force. You can create short-range Spacebridges at will, and the six battleships you have given us; they carry what you call World Cleansers. On my world, we call these weapons neutron bombs. I will take this fleet and smash through the Great Seal."

"And then?"

"We will create local Spacebridges to each Helion world and give them the opportunity to surrender. When they refuse, I will irradiate the planets with World Cleansers. I will then lead a direct assault with all our ground forces on their capital world."

He lifted his right arm and pointed to the sphere representing Helios Prime.

"I promise you, after the nukes and my assault, they will beg for us to stop."

"And then?" said the machine in the exact same tone.

"Once Helios Prime falls, we will land factory machines on the surface and begin rebuilding our forces from the Tomb Ships. While this happens, I will turn on the homeworld of the humans, known as Terra Nova, and threaten the same. I will lead our troops to their homeworld while the rest of the ships threaten every inhabited planet with nuclear genocide. This single assault will burn in their hearts and break their resolve."

He looked to Thayara and back to the machines. The taller creature was already speaking in answer.

"What of the Byotai, Khreenk, Klithi, and the Anicinàbe? We tried to fight them before and were banished for our efforts, with billions of dead."

Spartan nodded, again forgetting the armor interfered with his expression. Before he spoke, he tried to deactivate the suit, but it let out a warning and refused to open the petals of armor to expose him to their gaze. He tried once more, sighed, and then looked back to the machines.

"That is why you fail, and that is why you look to me for help."

He extended his arms out to those machines assembled before him.

"Even with all this might, you cannot fight them all and expect to win. A million warriors is not enough to guarantee the defeat of a single world, let alone all of them. We have the ships, the Ghost Warriors, and the technology, but our numbers are still too small. Trapped beyond the Great Seal, there is no longer the life to support this war machine."

He pointed to the Great Seal, projected out before them all.

"Out there, beyond the Seal, is the greatest diversity of flesh and mind. Yes, we will reopen the Tomb Ships, but we can do more. We will mold our vanquished enemies to our will; create entire legions of creatures from the very races we defeat."

Even he was beginning to like what he was hearing.

"My plan is simple. We will crush the will of the two nearest enemies just as I have described. We will then use their people and resources to build a vast horde to take the fight to the others, one race at a time. We will offer the others the chance to join us in the fight, or suffer extermination. Either way, they will provide the resources for each phase of the war."

"You would use your own people in this way?" asked the creature.

Spartan didn't hesitate in his reply.

"You have given me a task, to make this galaxy a safe place where your people can travel and flourish in safety. I can crush their fleets and bring the capital of the Helions to their knees in one day. Helios Prime will serve as an example of my loyalty and the viability of my plan. All we need to do is take control of Helios Prime and Terra Nova, and the war will be all but won."

The creatures seemed dumbfounded at this. An argument quickly ensued between it and its comrades. Spartan looked at Thayara and shrugged, but she remained completely silent. Spartan turned back to One-Zero-One.

"I do not understand. What is the problem?"

The machine moved from watching them to face him.

"We fought for years against the Helions and their allies. You diminish us by suggesting you can do what we never did, in less than one day."

Spartan coughed and cleared his throat before addressing the ethereal creatures. He started speaking even as they conferred with each other. One-Zero-One attempted to stop him, but he stepped out of his reach.

"You brought me here because you know my skills and my reputation. If I achieve this victory, it will be because of you placing me here. Let me bring the Helions to their knees, and we will do the same to every race that gets in our way!"

Thayara looked to Spartan and lifted her hand in front of her face, in mock shock at what she was hearing. She took two steps to him and spoke quietly, in the vain hope that nobody else would hear.

"This plan, it might work. But what of your own people on Helios? They have already landed more soldiers there. Will you destroy them with nuclear weapons as well?"

Spartan smiled.

"We will demonstrate our power against all of their worlds. When we arrive at Helios Prime, they will beg us not to do the same. I doubt we will even need to fire a single shot."

He hadn't intended on letting the Biomech leadership hear him, but all of them had stopped speaking to listen to him speaking to Thayara. Spartan was so intent on getting his idea across that he continued, completely unaware of his great audience.

"Thayara, we can stop this fighting by sacrificing a small number. This will be better for every one of us, not just the Biomechs. Even the Helions will live better under our control. No more war and no more injustice. They will play their own part in this new order, and I know that if they help, as we have, they will be granted a place alongside the machines."

He then turned back to look at the creatures.

MICHAEL G. THOMAS

"We will change things for the better. I can start this war for you easily, but there is nobody else that can end it the way I can. I will be your sword, and not one soul will dare stand before me after I have razed Helios Prime."

The creatures all said something in unison, their voices spreading like a ghostly crowd. Then their images faded to leave only the models of the worlds and the position of fleets.

"What's happened?" Spartan asked.

One-Zero-One appeared stunned. Thayara asked the same question, and finally he answered.

"The great council of my people has spoken. You will put our enemies to the sword, just as you have promised. If you are both successful, you will be the first outsiders to be offered the chance to join our ranks."

"As a Ghost Warrior, like you?" Spartan asked.

The creature hissed just one word.

"Yes."

"On this ship?"

The machine answered without really considering the question.

"You would join us on homeworld. Until it is time for us to…"

The machine stopped and then looked back to him. It clearly had not intended to go any further with its explanation. There was a short pause, and Spartan immediately regretted asking the question. The machine hissed and continued to speak.

"First you must be victorious."

Spartan walked up to the ledge and looked down at the columns of Ghost Warriors. Dozens of armored machines twisted and shifted a little to look up at him. He lifted his hands up high, and they did the same, each joining him in a simple gesture of solidarity. Spartan found he was smiling as he watched them almost cheering him on.

Do not worry, my friend, I always am.

He turned around to face his two comrades.

"Prepare the Rift Engine. It's time to start this thing."

"And the fleet?"

Spartan looked up at the model of the Helios System.

"This is what we're going to do."

CHAPTER TWELVE

Spartan is a name none will ever forget. His name was taken from that ancient Laconian race now almost unknown. His family background was known to few, and the events of his childhood known to even fewer. The culmination of all these experiences was to create an independent warrior, a man that would do whatever it took to get the job done. No one could disagree that every decision Spartan made was for the greater good, the only question that remained was whether that included the people directly affected. Terra Nova is often cited as one example of his savagery, but this moved to an entirely higher level at the Black Rift.

The Rise of Spartan

ANS Warlord, Micaya Shipyards, Helios Sector

The Grand Alliance, as the media was now dubbing it, stretched out in a massed formation. This great fleet of

Byotai, Khreenk, and Alliance vessels watched and waited, their gun ports open and fighter squadrons flying patrols. They were less than eighty thousand kilometres from the great Helion shipyards that had supplied the fleet for centuries. The main Micaya Shipyards were actually a massive artificial series of structures positioned over a million kilometres from Micaya, and a hundred times that distance from the Helion primary star. This position was known to humans as a Lagrangian point, an area in space where combined gravitational pull of two large bodies such as Micaya and its star provide exactly the centripetal force required to orbit with them.

Impressive, very impressive, thought Admiral Anderson.

In reality, the site might easily have been mistaken for an artificial moon by anybody unfamiliar with the sector, but the Helions had chosen well for its use. The orbital configuration made transportation and communication easy while keeping dangerous supplies and potentially faulty vessels out of harm's way. Even if a ship were to suffer a catastrophic reactor breach and exploded, there would be little chance of the debris coming anywhere near the planet. It was as useful as it was elegant.

Admiral Anderson's officers had returned to their own contingents, with General Makos returning to his own fleet, while Admiral Lewis rejoined the battered remnants of the force that had relieved Helios Prime. There was a stark different between the ships that had been out here fighting bloody battles for weeks and months and his own. The fresh vessels that had come through the T'Karan Rift were a mixture of seasoned combatants from the fighting at Prometheus and newly launched ships from the shipyards of the Alliance. Unlike in previous battles, he was not spreading out his forces, or making any particularly complicated plans. He had just a single trump card, and he was keeping it at the shipyards.

This is going to be the simplest and the bloodiest battle in the history of our Navy.

He looked out at the mainscreen and the icons that signified the combined Biomech forces in the Helios Sector.

"Tactical, give me a full analysis of what's out there."

He already knew what was there, but that wasn't enough, he wanted to hear the words from somebody else.

"Admiral, the first wave will clear Micaya into our direct line of sight within seventeen minutes. Total strength is one Ark, codenamed Beelzebub and…"

The man swallowed and tried again.

"Just under three-hundred enemy capital ships in total, Sir. They must have sent everything here."

Anderson looked at the imagery, but none of it seemed to faze him.

"Tell me about their configurations and deployment."

The man swallowed again and then began to point out the various forces.

"They have one hundred and seventeen Biomanta warships plus seventy-one Ravager class vessels. They are surrounding this force with some kind of high-power jamming equipment that is stopping us performing deep scans."

He moved his hands as he made a few configuration changes.

"Their deployment is almost non-existent, Sir. The best way I can describe it is as a large box formation. The Ark is toward the rear and centered between a large formation of Biomantas."

"How about command ships?"

"Three Cephalon vessels, and they are moving directly behind the Ark."

"And the status of the Ark?"

He pressed on the screen, and the imagery shifted to concentrate on just the slightly blurred image of the Ark. It was truly massive, and even he felt a slight shudder in his stomach.

"The Ark has already opened up and released warships. They're learning, Sir."

Admiral Anderson raised an eyebrow to this suggestion.

Perhaps, but are they learning the right thing? This must look like a desperate last stand for Micaya.

He rubbed his hands together.

Good. That's exactly what I want them to think.

"And our disposition matches my plan?"

The man brought up a flattened two-dimensional view of the shipyards.

"We have deployed our lines at the eighty-thousand kilometer marker. At this position, they will see our ships ninety seconds before spotting the shipyards."

The overhead imagery confirmed that, although from the dispositions, it looked as though a large number of the ships were in queues to dock at the shipyard.

"Good, and T'Kron has activated the ships on the lower gantries of the shipyard?"

"Yes, Sir, I am detecting over a hundred powerplants active on the site."

"Excellent. So we are ready, then?"

"Yes, Sir."

"Thank you."

The tactical officer moved back to his duties, and Admiral Anderson looked to the mainscreen. It was a massive fleet, there was no doubt in his mind about that, but his own forces were equally impressive. By stripping ships from Helios Prime and Spascia, his own fleet had increased in just twenty-four hours to a size he had not thought possible. T'Kron had also managed more than he'd expected on this special mission. He looked at the figures and found a smile forming. The alien had somehow managed to bring an extra twenty-two Helion ships in various states of repair. There was something else that he'd done though, and even he had been surprised. T'Kron had activated more than a hundred wrecked, decommissioned, or partially scrapped ships.

That is one hell of a diversion.

He scanned through the myriad of vessels, and it took a moment to find the one operational ship anywhere near them. With so much debris, scrap, and wreckage at the place, he had to rely on the secret IFF signature. He'd done everything possible to ensure ANS Explorer would remain undetected amongst the pylons, gantries, habitation blocks, and hundreds of decommissioned ships.

"Get a message to Explorer. She needs to get her IFF switched off and fast."

The tactical officer confirmed and then sent the appropriate message. In seconds the transmission stopped, and the large Alliance vessel vanished into the clutter. Admiral Anderson looked at the large clock he'd had positioned above the tactical display. It now read just six minutes. He felt completely alone on board the ship, even though he was surrounded by some of the best men and women in the fleet. All the crew of his age and experience were off leading the other contingents. He leaned toward the tactical display and activated the command module. The hazed shapes of the Byotai and Alliance commanders moved into view.

"Admiral," they said at the same time.

"Your ships are ready?"

They nodded, but Admiral Lewis spoke first.

"I must apologize for our last meeting. I've seen the reports from Helios Prime. Our forces are holding and digging in. You and General Rivers were right. They are settling in and waiting this one out. There's no rush to finish that fight."

Anderson nodded quickly.

"Understood. We have just a few minutes remaining. Is there anything I need to know?"

General Makos grunted and then began to speak.

"We are powered down, and the empty cargo containers are in position. I will need ninety seconds to get my vessels into action."

He then looked to Admiral Lewis.

"And your own vessels?"

"At their moorings on the other side of the shipyards. It will take us less than a minute to power up. I've positioned the shipping containers as written in the plan."

"Understood," replied Admiral Anderson.

He looked back to the overview.

"The important thing is that we give the right impression. As far as the Biomechs are concerned, we know they're coming. They have accelerated though, and we need to let them think we are desperately short of men and ships."

Admiral Lewis nodded quickly in agreement.

"If I was approaching this, the first impression I would get is total pandemonium. We have two-thirds of our fleet around the shipyards undergoing repair and replenishment.

Then we have the rest of our ships arriving in groups from Micaya in convoys. The defense force is just the first division of my own vessels."

Admiral Lewis selected his own ships on the perimeter of the shipyards.

"So when they arrive, what will they do? Will they hit your ships, or the shipyards?"

Anderson shook his head.

"It won't matter. T'Kron has managed to activate a large Helion contingent along this section of the facility. We have more than a hundred ships in an area nearly five thousand cubic kilometers. A quick scan will show they are cold and powering up. That has to be the target."

He swallowed and then pointed to his own forces centered on his battleship.

"I will withdrawal from the field when they arrive. They will pursue, and if the plan works, they will hit the shipyards with everything they have. A partially powered ship is an easy kill."

He stopped speaking and looked to his two commanders.

"In less than an hour, the battle for Micaya will be over, and I intend on finishing them, completely. No weapon is off the table, so make sure the safeties are off on your atomics. It's time to take the gloves off, Gentlemen."

* * *

ANS Tempest, Micaya Shipyards, Helios Sector

Captain Garcia checked the display for what must have been the tenth time in the last hour. Every single indicator said the vessel was operating in top condition, but that wasn't enough for him.

"Sir, I think she's ready for the fight," said Lieutenant Takeda.

He looked to his pilot and shook his head.

"The ship might be, but not me."

He looked up to the narrow windows and out into the blackness of space. Indicators in front of them marked out the hundreds of allied vessels as well as the projected position for the enemy.

"Have you ever seen anything like it?"

Lieutenant Takeda shrugged.

"The last few fights have been pretty...well, pretty spectacular."

"No, I mean the fleet. Just look at them."

He nodded in the direction of the nearest vessels. There were entire formations of Crusaders, the first of the new generation of warship and now the standard ship of the line. Mixed between formations were multiple Liberty variants, with them easily outnumbering their larger cousins. Even bigger again were the seven battlecruisers, each one configured to a special task. ANS Ticonderoga had been General Rivers' command ship, and now it functioned as a fleet control and aviation vessel. Captain

Vetlaya's ship, ANS Dreadnought, on the other hand, had been fully outfitted as a heavy battleship.

"I never thought I would see so many battlecruisers in the same fleet; apart from a few transports, and those Anderson left at the Black Rift, they are all here. This is one of those moments we'll look back on."

He moved just a fraction so that he could look to the center of the fleet. This was out of the view of the front windows, and he was forced to swivel about to look through the smaller starboard window. Right there, in the middle was the heavily marked and damaged hull of ANS Conqueror. The tired looking ship had been the command vessel for the entire Helios Prime operation and now had an official tally of six enemy warship kills.

"Incredible," said Captain Garcia.

He was now looking above the large Battlecruiser and toward the massive hull of ANS Warlord. It was an ugly looking ship, one that made even the Crusaders looked attractive.

"That has to be one of the worst looking ships I've ever seen."

Both of them looked at the double-hulled battleship.

"I saw the specifications for her. It's like they grabbed two hulks and welded them together," said Takeda.

"Well, that's pretty much exactly what they did. From what I heard, there were three ships being outfitted in T'Karan when the Admiral arrived to supervise construction. Apparently, there were problems with the powerplants of two of them. They units had come directly from Terra Nova and were underperforming, but the real problem was crew. He had only enough to crew one of the ships."

Lieutenant Takeda shook her head in amazement.

"So he ordered that two of them be joined together?"

Captain Garcia shrugged.

"Hell, that's just what I heard. There was another rumor that he had the thing built as a terror weapon, one that he could use to get Terra Nova in line."

Neither was particularly sure which, if any of the stories were true. Instead, they simply looked on at the vast, dark shape of the bastardized vessel. Its ugliness only served to increase its intimidation factor.

"Beta Cruiser squadron. You are cleared for docking on arms six through fifteen. It's your turn for replenishment," said the voice from the shipyard's open channel.

Both of the officers looked at each other as though they had just heard the greatest ever secret. Exactly on cue, the squadron of six cruisers peeled away from the primary fleet and headed toward the designated points at the sprawling complex.

"I heard that when this place was built, there was enough space for over a million personnel and four thousand active military and civilian ships. It was said that you could see the facility from the surface of Micaya."

Captain Garcia rubbed his forehead.

"I doubt we'll ever see something like this again. Ships from multiple species, all working together against a common enemy."

He nodded in the direction of ANS Warlord.

"Drink in that view, Lieutenant. It will stay with you for the rest of your life."

To his surprise, his pilot almost laughed at his comment.

"Yeah, okay, Sir," said Lieutenant Takeda.

She noticed the confused look from her superior and regretted her automatic response. Even so, she could hardly leave it like that, and therefore felt obligated to say something more.

"You're making a big assumption there, Sir."

"Which is?"

She smiled at him. "Well, we have to live to be able to look back on this moment."

Captain Garcia laughed.

"Even in death, we can look back at this. It is still something we can look forward to."

The younger officer shook her head in disagreement.

"You don't believe that religious mumbo jumbo, do you, Sir?"

She tried to sound coy, but the offended look on her Captain's face confirmed that she had gone too far for him.

"Maybe I do. My family comes from a long line of

Neo-Christians from the Kerberos colonies. I assume you believe in nothing, Lieutenant?"

She was worried for a second, but there was a slightly playful look to his face. She just hoped it was all tongue in cheek, but Takeda could tell she'd managed to say the wrong thing, at the exact wrong moment. She didn't want to say anything, but then she remembered the number of times in the past when she'd let such comments slide. Even after hundreds of years living in a secular society, there were still as many religions on the colonies as before.

"On the contrary, Sir, I believe in far more than any religious person might."

The Captain appeared fascinated.

"Please do continue. I was under the assumption that the secular had no belief?"

She shook her head in irritation.

"Really, do we have time for this?"

He creased his brow in a mocking gesture.

"If you're an unbeliever, and this really is our last mission, then it's my duty to prepare you for what is to come. To make sure you're ready for life after death. How can you be ready for the end of your life if you believe there is nothing more when you go?"

She laughed, finally seeing he was doing no more than trying to goad her.

"I'm not interested in preparing for life after death, or as I like to call it, death. I am much more interested in planning for my life because I've only got one."

Now Captain Garcia appeared genuinely happy.

"Exactly. There is nothing I find more offensive than the idea that somebody without belief in a deity can have anything to die for. After all, they are saying they will have no afterlife. That must be terrifying."

"Yes, Sir, and that's why we have to do everything we can to enjoy what we have. Just like this enemy fleet coming for us. We have one chance, and if we fail, well, that will be it, Sir. You will never find a more motivated person than one that doesn't believe in fairy tales."

Captain Garcia looked at her, and his face finally relaxed.

"I know. And for the record, I might come from a long line of Neo-Christians, but that doesn't include me. There's no way you'll find me believing in talking snakes and rules and regulations going back to the bronze age."

He looked to the right and checked the weapon status. Takeda shook her head again as he did so.

"I know, I know," he said defensively.

"These torpedoes are burning a hole in my hull, and I want them off my ship ASAP. We're not equipped for this kind of operation."

Lieutenant Takeda pointed to the mainscreen.

"Look, the first part of their fleet is about to move from behind the planet."

Both of them took in long, slow breaths while watching the ships.

"The battle is about to begin."

A single red alert indicator flashed repeatedly.

"Here is comes."

Captain Garcia reached forward and tapped the icon. The audio from ANS Warlord came through loud and clear.

"Enemy warships have arrived. All vessels withdrawal to the secondary deployment area, launch fighters, and prepare for battle."

Captain Garcia nodded as though the Admiral could see him.

"So, we feign a withdrawal, but will the enemy fall for it?"

* * *

Battleship Retribution, Taxxu, Uncharted Space

Zero-One-Zero, Thayara, and Spartan watched the massive Rift Engine in complete silence; the floating model that sat suspended in the center of the battle deck and easily filled the vast open space. Like the last vessel, it was double-headed and truly gigantic. Behind it moved more ships of the same design plus scores of warships and escorts. Amongst them, like a shark around a shoal of fish, were the Biomech battleships, each unique in its shape and configuration, yet they dwarfed all but the Rift Engines.

"It is time," said Spartan.

"We agree," answered One-Zero-One.

The model changed to show the Rift and the ship, as they seemed to merge into one.

"How long will this take?" Thayara asked.

No sooner had the one end of the machine approached the Rift, and it began to spark and flash. Vast streams of energy crackled along its entire length, but it remained just out of reach of the collapsed entrance.

"The machine will take less than an hour to stabilize the entrance. Then we will create the bridge and send the engine through to maintain the connection. When this happens, the engine will maintain the bridge until it becomes fully stable."

"And nothing will be able to collapse it afterward?"

"Once the Spacebridge is constructed it will be as stable as any other astronomical body. We will use our machines to open the old Rifts and to create a permanent network suitable for our return."

Spartan looked back at the massive projection. Even he had to admit the mighty Rift Engines were unique. Their ability to build and support the Rifts was unlike anything he'd heard of before. In his mind he could see whole networks of Rifts, each allowing travel and trade between stars, but without traveling. He thought of Terra Nova and Hyperion, and of ships moving between them filled with traded goods.

What am I doing?

He looked to Thayara and almost panicked upon seeing so many of the machines around him. Even the female warrior was draped in the finery of the Ghost Warriors. He lifted his hand to wipe his brow, and once more found himself stunned. The mechanical arm was something he'd forgotten about in the last few minutes.

One of these days I'll do this, and the machine will be more me than the flesh.

He looked to the two of them and then pointed to the Rift.

"What about traveling in Helios? You said you could take care of that."

"Yes, we will," said the machine.

Spartan sighed.

"I need more than that. How long will this all take?"

The machine flashed white, and a hologram of the Helios System appeared once again.

"Our Rift Engines can create short tunnels for a few minutes at a time. Once we are through, we will build a tunnel directly to the enemy."

The machine then pointed to Spartan.

"This is where you will come in. Our simulations show that your first-strike strategies have a greater likelihood of success than ours. You, Spartan, you will have the honor of selecting the first targets, as we discussed."

"Then get this damned Great Seal open. I have a target

for you."

* * *

ANS Warlord, Micaya Shipyards, Helios Sector

Admiral Anderson watched the tactical screen as it filled with more and more ships. The icons showing his active vessels paled compared to the vast Biomech horde. Even so, he watched with no expression, as his own forces withdrew away from the shipyards and in the direction of the Micayan planet.

"Any change in their course?"

The tactical officer shook his head.

"No, Sir, the entire fleet is making directly for the shipyards."

"Good, let them come. There's plenty of scrap for them to shoot there.

He noticed eyes staring at his and twisted about to find Captain Louise Decker.

"Yes?"

"We're ready, Admiral. All of our crew at their stations, medical bays ready for casualties, and every gun is loaded and targeted."

"Excellent work, Captain, truly excellent."

"Admiral, the enemy vessels are launching missiles," said the tactical officer.

Admiral Anderson looked at his tactical display and

spotted the shapes moving from the enemy fleet. At this distance, the timers showed they would take nearly a minute to strike their targets. It was more than enough time to move, assuming they were ready to do that. Against a fleet unprepared for battle, it should give them no chance to escape. He tapped the icons for the commanders at the shipyards who were waiting aboard the operational ships to the rear.

"Activate defensive batteries, release four ships to the forward skirmish line."

They must have been waiting for such an order because in less than thirty seconds there were four ships accelerating away from the vast gantries.

This had better work!

Captain Decker and her XO moved alongside him, watching in silence as the missiles moved closer and closer to the vessels positioned at the shipyards.

"Why just the one volley?" asked the XO.

Captain Decker pointed to the structures.

"They are checking our defenses and trying to spring any traps that might be out here. It's a smart play."

"Admiral, here's the feed from Admiral Lewis."

The imagery from the mainscreen was of hundreds of derelict ships, all of them sitting out in the open and connected to gantries. Markers showed that large numbers of them were powering up their engines, but only those in the fleet knew they were a distraction. Admiral Anderson pointed at the area of space between the two sides.

"Launch fighters, put up a protective screen around the shipyards."

That was when the first missiles made impact. The largest derelict was a ship known to the Helions as the Aorvorr, apparently a name from an ancient hero. The vessel was close in size to an Alliance Battlecruiser, yet this one was a wreck. Her hull was holed and broken, and several large sections had been removed over the last generation. Even so, at least one powerplant was active in her hull, as were four point defense turrets. Streaks of gunfire opened up and were quickly joined by the small number of active defenses on this side of the gigantic facility.

"Great work, T'Kron, damned good work," said Admiral Anderson.

Over half of the missiles were exploded well out of range before they were through the perimeter. They then had to run the gauntlet of the fighters. Six missiles punched through the worn out armor of the Aorvorr. Explosions wracked her innards, and her powerplant immediately went offline. A second ship just behind her was hit, and then secondary explosions crippled two more.

"Sir, their fleet is breaking. They are moving in to the attack," said the tactical officer.

"Yes, but what are their targets?"

The display showed the vast group of Biomech

vessels, along with projected lines showing their targets. Every few seconds the lines changed to show the revised projections. They all waited a little while longer until the data conformed what they had all hoped. The XO said what they were all thinking.

"Looks like they've taken the bait. Eighty percent of their forces are heading for the shipyards. The Ark and its escorts are coming right here."

Admiral Anderson lowered both of his hands to his hips.

"Very well. This is it, then."

He reached for the intercom and pulled it to his mouth.

"It is time. Break and fall back."

With that single order, the entire fleet of Alliance and Helion ships broke formation and moved away from the potential battle site. ANS Warlord led the bulk of the Alliance ship on a direct path to Micaya while the others scattered in small groups. They moved slowly, and many ships changed course repeatedly as though trying to avoid being attacked. A handful of destroyers were the last to leave, and they took the full brunt of the Biomech assault, as the enemy fleet surged on to the shipyards. Admiral Anderson watched in silence as all six empty ships operated under full automation.

"Will this work, Admiral?" Captain Decker asked.

Two of the destroyers exploded with their innards exposed to the void. The other four scattered just as the advance wave of Biomech fighters and Biomantas screamed past. All four Alliance ships emptied a torrent of fire at their attackers, but they were quickly silenced, but not before destroying a pair of Biomanta warships.

"They were crippled, and I didn't have the crew to man them. This way they have done their job, and with no loss of life."

The shipyards were arrayed in a series of vast spokes, each connected to a massive hollow central structure the size of a moon. These spokes extended out hundreds of kilometers and from them came more sections, many of which were surrounded by ancient and mothballed ships. The first of the Biomechs were now at the closest tendrils and attacking the docks and gantries. The site was massive, and the ships barely visible at this distance. The site was so large that the entire Biomech fleet and their Ark could have hidden amongst the active and derelict ships on one of the vast spokes, let alone the huge central hub that would dwarf many small moons, and none would have been the wiser. It was only at that point he realized he hadn't answered the question.

"You wanted to know whether this would work, Captain?"

Both looked to the mainscreen where the footage from Admiral Lewis' own ship showed the advance party of Biomanta ships and scores of fighters darting aboard the shipyards. They blasted every target showing an energy signature. Alliance fighters were busily fighting them, but it was clearly a one-sided battle.

"We have to give the trap time to settle."

He looked about the command deck. The dozens of officers were all busily managing the vessel, leaving him clear to command the entire operation from the horizontal tactical display.

"Too early, and surprise will be lost, too slow though, and they will discover what we have waiting for them."

He rubbed at his chin.

"It's time to send in a little help. The Biomechs can't take the site too easily, and they aren't stupid. Let's spring the trap that they expect."

He moved his hands about the display and highlighted two squadrons of Liberty destroyers and a force of four Crusaders. He then selected two attack squadrons of mixed smaller craft with his left hand and merged them all together. With a quick gesture, he drew a set of curved trajectories to follow.

"Yes, that will do nicely."

One by one the ships moved from his fleet of slowly retreating starships and on an intercept course for the shipyards. The numbers above them stated they would be in range within four minutes.

"Launch all fighters at the shipyards. Let's turn this up a notch."

* * *

ANS Tempest, Micaya Shipyards, Helios Sector

The forward displays showed hundreds of ships now in action, and Captain Garcia was beginning to lose his patience. They had been trailing behind the fleet while at the same time a great battle raged throughout the shipyards. The twenty-two ships arrayed along the arms and gantries of the first of the great spokes had been completely destroyed. Even so, from the very wreckage came burst after burst of fire, and in death the old ships refused to go quietly.

"Look!" said Lieutenant Takeda.

They both looked at the display and the projected course just received.

"Finally," Captain Garcia muttered.

He tapped the transmit button on his control column.

"Bomber squadrons Alpha and Bravo with me. Follow course Charlie Six and prepare for mass-bombardment."

Both of them had been waiting for the orders, but now they were finally here it seemed there just wasn't time. With a deft bit of maneuvering, Lieutenant Takeda spun the ship around and hit the main engines. The two squadrons of craft did the same. There were eight Maulers in each group, and all had been loaded out with torpedoes taken from the crippled Liberty ships. The same number of X57 Avenger drones formed up around them in a defensive screen while Hammerheads pulled up in front. The wave of small craft totaled just fewer than forty, and Captain Garcia had the command of the entire force.

Not much further, he thought as they moved silently through space.

Captain Garcia counted the seconds and minutes as they drew in closer and closer to the raging battle. They could now make out the scores of burning ships and thousands of lines of tracer fire. Even though few ships had moved away from the monolithic structures, there were still a great many involved in the battle. He looked to Lieutenant Takeda.

"I don't know how the Admiral did it, but somehow he got over a hundred ships to do something out there. Last I heard they were all mothballed or half scrapped."

The Lieutenant nodded twice.

"Based on the fact that they haven't moved, I'd say somebody managed to get a few engines fired up. All you need is a powerplant and a few defense turrets running and you have a realistic looking target."

A ship exploded in a spectacular yellow flash right before their eyes. Lieutenant Takeda's goggles flashed in the reflected light.

"Just as well, because that kind of ship would have just meant the loss of upward of a thousand Helions."

One of the Maulers took a heavy hit to its left flank, and a great cloud of debris blew off and into the path of a following Avenger. The small craft vanished in a white light, and then the formation was down by one.

"Well, that's one reason to cut down on the pilot program!" Takeda muttered.

A few of the guns aboard the many Biomech ships started to change direction, and then as quick as they could be seen, the arcs of four ripped into the formation. At this distance, it wasn't easy to hit the fighters. The forward guns of the Hammerheads opened up and created a wide flak corridor for them to advance along. At the same time, the Avengers released medium-range interceptor missiles. These were special weapons that would intentionally explode and scatter razor-sharp metal debris into the path of approaching warheads.

"The enemy is working systematically through the shipyards. We will ignore the initial attack and hit the secondary wave of ships. Target the following craft and prepare to fire on my mark."

Using just his eyes, he tagged two Ravagers and a pair of escorting Biomantas. After so many battles, the Alliance had a good idea of the weaker areas of these ships. This information allowed the computers to automatically select the nest areas for the torpedoes.

"We hit them with a single bombing run and then turn on their forces currently engaging our ships."

Each of the craft sent in their acknowledgements, with the exception of the drones. These were the latest models with upgrade artificial intelligence nodes and the ability to function fully autonomously. On and on flew the Maulers until they reached their optimal firing range.

It was possible to make out the ship silhouettes and configurations from within the cockpit of the Mauler.

"Are we ready?" Captain Garcia asked.

Lieutenant Takeda didn't turn her head; she was transfixed on their current course and the long line of Biomech warship blocking their path. She began shaking her head at the prospect of having to face down and defeat such an overwhelming enemy.

"As ready as we'll ever be," she said stoically.

"I want our torpedoes heading right for the snout of that Ravager, understood?"

She nodded slowly.

"Yes, Sir, targeted and calibrated. We're ready to launch."

Captain Garcia selected his formation of fighters and Maulers and sent them the code all had been waiting for.

"Release your bomb door and launch. This is a free fire authorization. Let them burn!"

The Maulers opened up their cargo areas and lowered the massive torpedoes. Each craft was capable of carrying only two, and they unleashed the entire arsenal for this attack. Sixteen Maulers launched thirty-two hypersonic torpedoes between them. Each of the guided weapons had been configured with a mixture of dense penetrating slugs or high-explosive rounds. There were also four tactical atomic missiles that could devastate an entire ship, if they could get the device inside the armor. The warheads streamed forward, leaving no trail behind them as they moved faster and faster toward their intended targets.

"Break and attack, I repeat, break and attack!" Captain Garcia ordered.

The mixed formation of craft split apart like an arrow striking the end of a piece of bamboo. They fanned out as the massed volley of torpedoes tore into the flanks of the four ships. One of the Biomantas managed to turn away and blast apart all those heading for it, but the other three were hit hard. The second Biomanta spun to avoid the impact and merely managed to crash itself into the flank of a Ravager. At the same time, a mass of torpedoes hit them. The heavy density slugs ripped through the hull, and two even appeared on the other side, vanishing into the blackness. High-explosive rounds tore out chunks of metal, but it was the atomic warhead from ANS Tempest that achieved the greatest result. Captain Garcia watched it entered the bow of the nearest Ravager as they rushed away at full-speed.

"That was one hell of a hit," he exclaimed, as it crashed into the wrecked nose of the mighty capital ship.

Then came the explosion. It started as a blue and white flash, running down the entire length of the vessel like a cannon fuse. As the blasts hit the rear, the ship ripped open and explosions wracked through the hull. All of the

Maulers made it away safely, but each gave the damaged and ruined ships a parting volley of gunfire from their turrets as they passed them.

"Where now?" Lieutenant Takeda asked.

Captain Garcia looked ahead and at the wall of explosions that marked out the lowest tendril of the shipyard. The imagery reminded him of some of the Helion illustrations of the last Great War with the Biomechs. A time when vast fleets fought each other and entire worlds burned.

Yes, which one next?

There was little time to select a target though because they ran directly into a wall of fighters. They started off as a few dozen, and then there were hundreds all around them. The gun turrets on the Maulers were rapid tracking devices, but even they had a hard time pinning and destroying the enemy. It fell to the brave pilots of the Hammerheads and the soulless Avenger drones to try and beat them off.

"That one."

Lieutenant Takeda looked at the tagged target on her display and swallowed.

"The Cephalon command ship? How, Captain? We're out of missiles."

He looked out through the starboard viewport and at a group of four Avengers. The delta-winged drones were the same size as a conventional fighter and armed to the teeth.

"We don't always need missiles, Lieutenant."

He tagged all of his craft and then allocated them different parts of the command ship.

"We'll rake her from bow to stern with everything we have, and then move on to these."

The display shifted and changed to a group of eight Biomech Bioray assault transports. They were being unloaded from the Cephalon on the other side of the ship.

"What are they doing there?" Takeda asked.

"Probably a boarding party for this part of the shipyards. Right now they are a fat, juicy target for our fighters."

He targeted all of them for the drones and turned briefly to face his pilot.

"The Avengers are not just fighters. With the right orders, they become a guided missile."

CHAPTER THIRTEEN

Social underclasses existed on dozens of worlds, with few exceptions. During each crisis, these lower classes were always those that seemed to suffer the most. Even the privileged worlds of the Alliance found their civilian populations stripped down in times of war. There were always a few volunteers from certain classes, but the weight of combat generally fell upon those unable to support themselves or their families. The result of this was the lowest classes of all felt they had given the most in times of crisis, and it was this that led to so much of the social conflict that followed the deadliest of the wars.

History of Slave Labor

Alliance Defenses, Old Spascia City, Helion Sector
Three large black shapes dropped down from the sky and moved in on a direct course for the chasm. Even at a distance of thirty kilometers, they were easily identified

as Biomanta warships. Around them came the same number of Biorays with large amounts of escorting fighters. No sooner had the ships dropped through the gray sky and they opened fire. Gunfire and missiles rushed down to hit at the defenses all around the mountain. The overwhelming majority of the shots came down around the newly erected defenses all along the base. Some made it through, but Captain Tycho had done his job well. Interceptor batteries were now in position at fixed points all around the defenders. Counter-battery missiles arced up to reach the attackers while short-range rockets and guns attempted to shred the warheads just before they reached their targets.

"They come like this every single day," said Gun.

The battle-hardened General waited at the bridge like a mighty sentinel. Marines, Khreenk, and Helion alike streamed past and on to the safety of the newly erected defenses. From the west bank of the chasm came a deafening roar of gunfire. Hundreds of warriors with a vast arsenal of weapons continued to pour fire off into the distance. Gun took aim with his own weapon and released a single long burst while roaring in delight. His eyes moved up and tracked a group of missiles as they struck the flank of an approaching Bioray. The large assault transport was small compared to warships, but it was still substantially larger than an Alliance Mauler.

"Bring it down!" he yelled.

There was no need to issue additional orders. The Khreenk concentrated their advanced weapons on the Bioray while a flight of Hammerheads raked it from bow to stern. It tumbled out of the sky and vanished deep into the bowel of the wide chasm that split Old Spascia from the mountain stronghold.

"Gun, are you done?" Teresa asked.

He looked down to her and laughed.

"Almost, just a few more to get across. They keep trying to land troops on the other side. The chasm is filled with broken ships."

He glanced over to her.

"Jack and the other wounded are being taken to the infirmary inside the mountain. Our best people are there. You got here just in time. Another ten minutes, and we would have been Biomech breakfast."

He spotted movement, and with a quick twist he tracked the three Thegns and opened fire. They had been sneaking up on a pair of Helion volunteers who were still dragging a machine gun unit. The bullets cut the Thegns cleanly in half and stopped just short of hitting the two of them.

"Not bad," said Teresa in mock admiration.

Gun continued to check the horizon and added his fire where necessary to assist those retreating. He wasn't the only one, and at the end of each of the bridges was a small rearguard. They could hold back the machines for a time, but not indefinitely.

"Your timing was good, Teresa. Shame Spartan wasn't with you. It would have been just like old times."

Teresa swallowed, that hard uncomfortable feeling she knew meant something much worse was going on.

"He's vanished, Gun. He went through the Black Rift with Khan and the others. They collapsed the Rift, but he didn't get back in time."

A triple volley of missiles screamed past them from the enemy lines, but the majority were brought down by weapons fire from the mountain. Gun opened his mouth to speak and then looked at her.

"The Bastion to the south is being hit hard. They are completely surrounded."

Their eyes met, and Teresa could see there was no chance her friend would leave any of them to their deaths. She checked her carbine and moved to the side to let a squad of Khreenk march past.

"What's the plan?"

She could see that Gun wanted to personally involve himself in the rescue, but things had changed a great deal. He was no longer just a warrior in charge of a contingent. He was a general now, and it was his responsibility to maintain the war effort, even if that meant sacrificing his own warriors.

"It's Commodore Hampel. He was commanding our air cover when his ship was hit. He's coordinating the withdrawal."

He pointed to the right.

"Their firebase is strong, and they have a single functional landing pad. But the last shuttle to leave was shot down trying to land."

Gun shook his head angrily.

"They are not going to make it out of there."

She was convinced there was something in his eyes, a message that was hard to read. He looked past his shoulder and to the mountain and then back to her.

Yes, he wants me away from the mountain, for now.

It was understandable, though not ideal. Teresa was an experienced commander, perhaps one of the most experienced in the entire Alliance. But she had already concentrated more of her effort, and even her own person in the rescue of Gun and the others. Many would question her command ability so near to her badly wounded son. At least another hour would give them time to get him into the infirmary, and she could put her effort where it was properly needed to continue the siege.

I have a short window, and I can use that time better out here than managing troop dispositions and barricades.

"How many people are in there?"

"Less than thirty, barely a platoon in strength. There's an entire company of Eques walkers and troops between us and them."

Teresa placed a hand on his arm.

"Gun, you secure west bank and blow the primary

bridges. I'll get them out. Just leave me the small one to the south."

Gun looked at her and gave her a barely concealed grimace.

"I'll make sure you get artillery support. Just be precise, Teresa. Don't do a Spartan!"

Even Teresa couldn't fail to laugh at that little jibe. Spartan was many things, but calm and collected wasn't one of them. It was easy to send the wrong information when under great stress.

"Okay, Colonel, do it. I will rally our defenders and prepare them for the next stage of the battle. When you get back, you can give a speech, and tell us all how you're going to win this war."

He turned and moved across the bridge with his bodyguard following right beside him. Even as more gunfire ripped into the bridge, he kept going. Nothing was going to stop him, not fire, rocket, or bullet. At the same time, Teresa connected directly to Captain Tycho.

"How are the defenses?"

"Colonel. Everything is in position. I have the outer defenses operational, and the reserve is moving into the fortress. We have interceptor batteries running at full strength and pads are rigged to blow."

"Good work, Captain. I need you to keep at it. The defenses must hold, no matter what happens to the rest of Spascia," she replied.

"Understood, Sir. I have news on your son. His unit has already reached the mountain, and he's being taken to an intensive care unit."

Teresa almost choked at hearing that.

"How serious is it?"

There was a silence, and Teresa could tell it was bad news.

"He's in a coma, Colonel. The doctors will do what they can, but right now there's nothing you or I can do. The quicker we can get him to a proper medical facility, the better."

Teresa closed her eyes and ignored the sounds of explosions that never seemed to end on Spascia.

Gun was right. I need to focus. Jack and the others need me to end this, and fast. Spascia is not just about surviving.

She opened her eyes and looked up to the mountain. Flags of the Alliance, Khreenk, Helions, and a dozen other contingents ran up at different points. The largest was an old Helion flag with icons of their burning hot star. It was burned and riddled with holes, yet it still hung up high and proud.

"Sir, are you ready to cross?" asked the Sergeant.

Teresa turned back around to the man and found a ragged group of marines, along with their Lieutenant. One of the women, a tall, blonde haired firebrand carried the platoon's standard. The flag had been ripped and attached to the end of a broken Helion assault pike. Teresa looked to them and couldn't help but smile.

"You fought damned hard at the Three Sisters, but we have more work to do."

She could see all of them were from different units, and two were from the regiments originally sent to defend Spascia. The Lieutenant and one of his privates bore the same markings as the regiment that had arrived with her. A single Helion waited among them with a Khreenk rifle in his hands.

"You are an interesting squad. Will you come with me to the Bastion?"

She pointed off to the south.

"We have a platoon trapped in the defenses, but I need help."

One of the battered looking marines nodded quickly.

"Colonel, we know your reputation. My father fought with you on Euryale, back in the big one. I would be honored to fight with you."

Teresa looked over the chasm and to the landing pads. She'd completely forgotten about Captain Tycho.

"What about the mobile element?" she asked over the radio.

"The Bulldogs, Sir?"

"Yes."

There was a very short pause, and Teresa used it to scan about her position. Apart from the squad that currently protected her, she could see less than a dozen heading for the end of the bridge. There was a single mobile gun Bulldog parked thirty meters to the north. Every ten seconds or so, it would fire its primary gun off at targets in the distance.

"I've got eight APCs and one of the mobile guns waiting at the landing pads. Why?"

Teresa checked her overlay and tagged the Bastion position. It was a small stronghold further to the south and shrouded in smoke and dust. Its main job had been as a perimeter defense, and also to offer air defense against craft assaulting the chasm from the south.

"We have troops pinned down there. I plan on getting them out."

"Understood. Sending them to your position now. Colonel, you don't need to command that kind of mission. I can easily do that."

Teresa shook her head, not that the man could see her.

"No. You have the situation under control. This is something I can do. Send them to me now. I have my own platoon that can assist on this side of the chasm."

A single rocket arced up high and then began to drop down, heading right for the bridge.

"Take cover!" yelled the Sergeant.

Teresa joined the rest of the squad as they threw themselves behind whatever wreckage or rubble they could find. It came down with a terrifying screaming sound and then a bright yellow flash. The flash extended out for fifty meters and engulfed the debris field as well as the Bulldog. Right after the impact came a squeal and then a loud hiss. Teresa leaned around the rubble and watched a cloud of vapor appear around the Bulldog.

Typical. I seem to recall we used to own the patent on this bit of kit.

She climbed out, and the squad moved back around her. The Private that had mentioned Euryale spoke up.

"Colonel, I know the ground along the chasm. I can get a vehicle down the trail without being seen from the east."

Teresa nodded.

"Good. You can take the lead Bulldog with me. I intend on getting there in minutes."

The sound of vehicles was already beginning to match the sound of battle. Teresa looked back and found herself staring at the shape of a convoy weaving its way over the widest bridge.

"Get ready, marines. This is going to get interesting."

* * *

ANS Tempest, Micaya Shipyards, Helios Sector

The Mauler twisted about its entire length as it moved between the two Biorays. The Biomech vessels were easily twice the size of the Alliance ship, but that didn't tell the whole story. Whereas the Biomech vessel was large, tough, and filled with warriors, the Mauler was short, fat, maneuverable, and bristling with gun turrets. It vanished through the gap with only meters to spare and out the other side, just as the following Avengers crashed headlong into them both. Exactly as planned, the internal warheads exploded on impact, and both assault transports were torn apart by multiple explosions.

"Yes!" Lieutenant Takeda shouted.

Captain Garcia said nothing; he was more interested in holding onto the cockpit brace brackets as the craft spun about. The magclamps easily held him into position, but with all the buffeting and shaking, he felt much more comfortable using his hands to maintain some semblance of being in control.

"You know this thing was designed as a heavy landing craft, don't you?"

Two kinetic rounds punctured through the port side of the hull and clattered about inside the empty cargo area behind them. The breach alarms blared, but neither seemed particularly concerned. Takeda laughed, and she twisted about once more.

"Yeah, well maybe they shouldn't have fitted her out with thick armor, formidable weapons, and the most powerful engines this side of a frigate! At least we're not hauling passengers today."

It was true; being as they were operating as heavy torpedo bombers, there was no need to carry marines. If they had, then many of them would have just been killed, due to the breach in the hull.

"Get us in closer to the Ravager; I'll bring the others in a column behind us. Be ready to slide."

She nodded and altered the configuration of thrusters to bring them incredibly close to the flank of the nearby Ravager. This ship was massive, easily the size of a full Alliance ship of the line and bristling with weapons. They moved fast and close, doing their best to avoid as much of the enemy gunfire as possible. Two more Maulers fell in behind, and soon all of them were moving in a loose column down its length. A handful of Biomech fighters turned to attack, but every shot that missed simply crashed into their own ship. A number of rounds did manage to penetrate the armor of two, but the rest kept on. At the same time, the Maulers were able to combine their turret fire to create a wall of metal that destroyed seven more of the enemy.

"You ready? Captain Garcia asked.

Lieutenant Takeda nodded.

"Good."

He pressed the button to communicate with the Mauler squadrons.

"On my mark, slide strafe at my target."

Captain Garcia had already selected the key known weak spots of the Ravager into the computer. The targets appeared on the main display in front of them all.

"Mark!"

The Maulers continued on their present course but spun about so that they faced the flank of the ship. Each opened fire and continued slowly rotating so that they could continue to blast apart the storage tanks, gun systems, and personnel. At the same time, the Maulers maintained their existing course, so they looked like a long line of ice skaters spinning about their axis. They would be unable to destroy the ship, let alone even cripple it. By the time the squadrons cleared the capital ship, they'd left a trail of destruction and scores of turrets destroyed. The data was automatically passed on to the command ships that then sent the modified data to the targeting systems and commanders of the other ships.

"Where to now, Sir?" Lieutenant Takeda asked.

Captain Garcia had already selected the next waypoint. It flashed up bright and clear in the primary display in front of them.

"Are you sure, Sir?"

He nodded slowly.

"Oh, yes, it is time."

The formation of battered, but still operational Maulers pulled away from the damaged warship and made for the opposite side of the Micayan Shipyards. Every few seconds, a missile would streak toward them, but the defenses on the Maulers, as well as the nearby Liberty destroyers, made missiles all but useless. The navicomputer selected the best possible route through the hundreds of kilometers of shattered gantries, wrecked ships, and broken cargo units. Waypoint after waypoint appeared until there was a total of fifty-two of them.

"That's an interesting course, Sir."

The Captain nodded.

Green rectangles moved about in the display to show the projected route. Even Lieutenant Takeda was surprised at its complexity. She didn't complain, and in less than thirty seconds they were moving through the first of the markers. The vessel continued its bizarre corkscrew maneuver, and then they were back in the middle of the maelstrom. The entire section of the vast shipyard's complex was burning. Large structures were wreathed in flames that burned the compartments from within. It was the scores of ruined civilian and military vessels on this part of the facility that caught both officers' attention. Captain Garcia sighed.

"Incredible, and to think that all of those burning ships were already mothballed or partially scrapped."

More of the Maulers joined them through the wreckage and on toward where the fleet was waiting hidden and dormant nearby. Every single one of the ships had powered down and hidden deep within columns of ruined vessels. It was the cool, dark part of the massive facility, and so far it had been completely avoided by the ships of both sides. A light flashed on the console indicating a flash communication from High Command.

"This is Admiral Anderson. Commence Phoenix in

T-minus ten minutes. I repeat, T-minus ten minutes."

The two looked at each other at exactly the same time.

"How did you know?" Lieutenant Takeda asked.

Captain Garcia tilted his head a fraction and looked over to her.

"Look at the battle. The tide is turning in favor of the machines. They are heavily engaged, and our reinforcements with Anderson are already moving through the outer defenses. We look weak and desperate, and they know it."

Takeda wiped her brow and then pulled on the controls to perform a complex series of twists with the control thrusters. The g-forces as they slowed and then moved about were incredible and pushed both of them firmly into their seats. Then came a violent shudder as the main engines activated and blasted them off toward the next waypoints. Captain Garcia spotted the targets just as they moved out from cover.

"Three fighters at point five."

He moved his hands over the controls while tagging each of them via his retina. He selected them, and right away the vessel's turrets tracked and fired on them. Even when the fighters moved away from one, they would simply be hit again from another turret.

"All I know, Sir, is that they are inside the shipyards, and the Ark is leading its main force on a wide orbit that will take them right to the planet. All that stands in front of them is the last Helion line. Seven ships won't hold back an Ark. Are you sure we should be heading away from the fight?"

He smiled back at her.

"Trust me. They are going to want us there. The Biomechs want us kept busy, and right now they have a chance to strike a killing blow. What better way is there to keep us busy than by wiping out our fleet?"

* * *

ANS Conqueror, Micaya Shipyards, Helios Sector

Admiral Lewis lifted the glass of water to his mouth and took a sip. His hand shook slightly, and a drip of water fell from the side before he could catch it. He lowered the tumbler and placed it on the counter next to his seat and again found himself shaking. He'd refused to wear the newly issued PDS protective suits and instead wore his Naval dress uniform. That wasn't enough to keep him warm, so he'd pulled on an old and battered great coat. The effect was to make him look like a staff intelligence officer.

We can't stay shut down like this forever. What if the powerplants take too long to come back online?

He'd been watching and waiting for what felt like an age. Since he'd taken refuge on this remote spoke of the massive shipyards, he'd been forced to watch the destruction of dozens of ships. Now the Maulers and fighters of the Alliance were busy attacking the Biomech ships as both sides ran amok through the wreckage. There were so many burning ships it was hard to even find a vessel that hadn't already been smashed to pieces by guns and missiles.

"How long till Anderson and his ships get here? It's looking like a scene from Dante's Inferno out there."

Lieutenant Vitelli, the ship's tactical officer pointed to the IFF signatures on the tactical display. Each of the Alliance ships carried the important transponder to ensure there would be no cases of mistaken identity.

"At their current speed, they will pass through the outer docking clamps in three minutes."

The officer looked up at the mainscreen and altered the focus of one of the external long-range cameras to point directly at ANS Warlord.

"They are already under heavy fire. The Biomechs know Anderson is here."

The display confirmed what he was saying as they watched the vast fleet. At the heart of the force was the infamous ANS Warlord. Around this ship moved scores of other capital ships, and every single one of them was firing as they advanced through the shipyards. The older Crusader warships put down a hail of railgun fire in a constant barrage. Fiery streaks flickered out from them as point defense turrets operated as interceptors. Only the particle beam projectors appeared impotent as they released their invisible blasts of energy at the Biomech ships. As this great fleet surged into the fight, it was joined by squadron after squadron of Avenger, Lightning, and Hammerhead fighters.

"That is a lot of ships," said Captain Marcus.

Admiral Lewis shuddered from the cold and turned his attention back to the display. Moisture was already forming on the glass-like surfaces, and every few minutes a crewman would wipe off the excess with a cloth. Captain Marcus joined him and looked at the formations of ships.

"Apart from those in hiding, we're now fully committed. This is going to be very close."

Admiral Lewis nodded, but before he could speak, Lieutenant Vitelli spun around in his seat, his face transformed to something close to elation. He coughed as he spoke, cleared his throat, and then repeated himself.

"The Ark, it has changed course."

Admiral Lewis couldn't believe what he was hearing.

"To where?"

All three of them looked to the tactical display where the great battle was taking place. Long lines with subtle curves showed the projected course for the Ark and its escort; every second it altered and moved a fraction closer to the shipyards before finally settling just off to the side. The number indicated the huge vessel would be just over a hundred kilometers from the outer limit of the orbital facility. In orbital distances that was point-blank range.

"So, what are they doing, then?" Captain Marcus asked.

Admiral Lewis nodded as if he'd just worked it out. He put his hands over the display and concentrated on the route the Ark was taking.

"The Ark has changed course so that they can pass within gun-range of the shipyards. They can't risk a direct route, and there's no chance of major course changes, not now."

He then moved his hands to the lines of mothballed ships.

"They surely intend on hitting anything that is left as they move by and then on to the planet."

He straightened up and looked to his executive officer.

"You know what this means?"

Captain Marcus looked at their dispositions and back to the Ark.

"They will be close enough to tear out the guts of our fleet, for starters. You remember the firepower of the Ark over Helios Prime. We hit it time after time, and not once did we come close to destroying it."

"True, but this time we have twice the numbers and a few extra surprises."

Admiral Lewis pointed to their position inside the far off section of the shipyard. Icons showed the Alliance ships even though none were transmitting.

"Over half of our ships, plus the entire Byotai

contingent is waiting for the right moment. We will stay offline until the Ark is at this point."

He pointed and left a mark on the display. The computer had already assessed the timing required for the ships to hit their targets before they would be moving away, but not too early that they might be able to change their course. Captain Marcus and the tactical officer both looked at his projection with a growing level of apprehension.

"Very nice," said Captain Marcus, "So we hit them at their point of no return, and then what?"

"By the time they move away, we will finish off their fleet, right here."

He indicated the heart of the shipyards.

"What about the Ark?"

Admiral Lewis sighed.

"We will do whatever damage we can. They will head to Micaya and enter a low orbit. Once we're done here, we can regroup, and then hit them when it's convenient to us, not them."

"Uh, Admiral. At this range we might have a chance," said Lieutenant Vitelli.

The officer moved his tracking plans over to the display. They matched up with the projected course change for the Ark. Both of his senior officers looked at the data with interest.

"You think we can disable the Ark from here?"

The man nodded, the weight of his idea now beginning

to dawn on him. Admiral Lewis looked at the data and shook his head in surprise.

"That's a risky proposition. You're suggesting we hold fire until the Ark is already leaving and then hit from the rear, at this point?"

Lieutenant Vitelli nodded, but he was too nervous to speak. Captain Marcus appeared less convinced.

"Admiral, if we do this, the Ark will gain nearly eleven minutes worth of time to rake this entire site. Any ships they identify will be in flames before we can launch an attack."

"True, but if we can strike with my force, plus the Byotai, we can hit them from behind. Their escort is minimal, and we will be able to pursue them all the way to Micaya."

He licked his lip as he finished. The idea of surviving the battle had been his original intention, but the faintest possibility of getting the upper hand on one of these Arks was just too good a chance to let up.

"Communications, I need a priority directed narrow-range briefing with Admiral Anderson."

He looked back to his tactical officer and then to Captain Marcus.

"Anderson can hold the rest of their forces, especially with ANS Warlord entering the fray. If we can do this, we'll protect Micaya and destroy their fleet in a single action. It's going require the greatest of resolve. Can we do it?"

* * *

ANS Warlord, near Micaya Shipyards, Helios Sector
Admiral Anderson watched the mainscreen as though his very soul depended on it. The crew managed their approach toward the shipyards, and for this short moment he found a few seconds of calm. The ship shuddered continually from the rain of gunfire, yet nothing seemed to harm her. Particle beams ripped off chunks of the ablative armor on her bow, and entire sections of plate tore from her flanks, yet on went the massive vessel.

"What's their status?" he asked.

"Sir, we count thirty Biomantas destroyed plus eight Ravagers. That still leaves them with one hundred and fifty-three ships, plus the Ark."

"Yes, so our forces look equal. With Admiral Lewis and the Byotai, we will have twice their numbers. Good."

"Admiral, the Biomechs are redeploying."

"Show me."

The layout of the shipyards was a mess. The vast central structure was relatively uninvolved in the fight right now. Instead, there were two large spokes surrounded by ships, many of which were now damaged. Half of the Biomechs moved about at will, to attack whatever they could find. At the same time, the rest was heading to the outer limits to head off the Alliance reinforcements.

"I see, so what exactly is in front of me?"

"A single Cephalon, thirty Biomantas, and half of the Ravagers."

"Admiral, flash message from Admiral Lewis. For your eyes only."

He nodded and turned about in his chair to look at a smaller screen. A videostream appeared, along with a tactical plan. Before he spoke, he had already scanned through the schematic and the key points.

"Admiral Lewis, that's an interesting idea."

He shook his head as he continued.

"There's something I never did tell you though, about our little surprise."

The two Admirals looked at each other until finally the data arrived on Admiral Lewis' screen. The data transmission was a focused laser system that could only be identified or monitored by directly blocking the line of sight, something that was currently clear.

"Good God, will that really work?"

Admiral Anderson grinned.

"Why do you think I put her so far from everybody else? The Helions said this part of the station was defunct. I think it would be a fitting end to its service, don't you?"

Admiral Lewis looked at the imagery but found he was unable to even speak.

"That's exactly what I thought when Commander Erdeniz brought up the idea."

"Erdeniz? He's the man that had the great idea with Endurance. You trust his judgment?"

"That's why I put him in command of ANS Explorer. He assures me the timing sequence has been corrected. Apparently, the issue last time was the proximity of the entry and exit points. The Rift distortion overlapped and caused some kind of feedback loop."

Admiral Lewis didn't seem convinced.

"So it was like having a microphone too close to a speaker?"

He shook his head.

"All I know is that ship was lost and caused almost as much damage to my own ships as to the enemy. We estimate our crew losses were over five thousand following the blast."

"Yes, there is a great risk. But as in that tragedy there was still good. You won that fight, one that looked far from possible."

"And if he's wrong, Admiral?"

Admiral Anderson breathed in slowly through his nose.

"Nothing is certain, but if this works, we'll cripple them in ways they have never even considered. It is my intention to develop this system into a major weapon, if it works."

Even Admiral Lewis shook his head as he tried to imagine the power of this weapon.

"This will make the weapons on the planets seem inconsequential. This an apocalyptical weapon."

Anderson smiled.

"I like that."

CHAPTER FOURTEEN

What if the Alliance had never built that fated Spacebridge to T'Karan? Some postulate that humanity would have expanded as a natural phase of its development. There are many more that consider humanity would have fallen apart, due to the hidden enemies waiting on Hades and Mars. The Biomechs might have shattered the backbone of the Alliance but not invaded for perhaps another century. In the meantime, the machines would have smashed the Helions and become vastly more powerful. Instead, the Alliance was able to stand shoulder-to-shoulder with the other races in time for this epic war.

The Unforeseen Consequences

Battleship Retribution, Taxxu, Uncharted Space

There was nothing but blackness and a slight feeling of a cool, slightly chilled atmosphere. Spartan could sense the stillness around him, but he refused to open his eyes just yet. His body was upright, and he was able to stand without moving a single muscle; the feeling it gave him was almost of a weightless sleep.

You will strike, and you will kill. Cut off the head, Spartan, and the body will die.

The voice was familiar but as distant as the many other times he'd heard it. With his eyes shut, he could still sense everything around him. The connection between the Thegn armor and the machine allowed him to sense warmth, moisture, and sound, as if his skin was actually exposed, even though he was encased inside the metal machine. He could hear and feel a slight scraping on his armor, like a nail being drawn slowly across a board.

Open your eyes.

He opened them, even though it wasn't what he had intended to do, and let out a long, shallow breath. The oxygen-rich feed inside the armor allowed him to exert himself to levels he could never have managed on his own. His pulse had slowed, and he felt calmer than he had been for a very long time. He looked upon the Rift in space and imagined what might be waiting on the other side. The Ghost Warriors waited patiently, with every one of them connected directly to the machinery of the ship. The shape to his right was Thayara, but he ignored her for now and concentrated on the view being projected in front of him.

"How much longer?" he asked rhetorically.

Another shape moved, and this was the form of One-Zero-One.

"Forty-five seconds."

Spartan looked at the machine and found himself surprised the time had finally reached that final minute. The procedure had been running for so long now, but even as the minutes ticked by, he had no doubt in his mind as to what would happen. He looked down at his right arm and the short but deadly cutting blades. The blade was marked, and flakes of colored material showed where he had been scratching at something. He looked to the left arm. He leaned in close, but the voice of the machine spoke again.

"The fleet is ready and awaits your recommendations."

Spartan looked to Thayara and back to the machine.

"We go through and assemble on the other side. I will make a proclamation, a challenge to their citizens. Yield before me, or face atomic destruction."

"Why would you do this?" Thayara asked.

Her tone was flat, but the words cut deep. Spartan knew she would try to undermine him, to prove her way was best. Spartan was having none of it, though.

"I will sow the seeds of doubt and terror in their hearts. Some will fight, others will argue, and the rest will cower. My proclamation will spread to every world and remind them that man and machine are now one. I know their dispositions, their strengths…"

He then looked back to Thayara.

"And their weaknesses."

The Rift flashed once and then changed into what looked like a reflective pool.

"Spartan, the Spacebridge is open and stable. Are you ready?" asked the machine.

Spartan crashed his fists together.

"Hell, yes. Send them through. The invasion begins now!"

Thayara turned to walk away, and Spartan reached for her shoulder. She avoided him and twisted around in a position that would have made a normal person fall onto their back.

""What is it, Spartan?"

"Prepare the assault team."

One-Zero-One looked to the projection of the Rift and then to Spartan.

"Assault? I thought you intended on striking their ships and then making for the Helion homeworld. Have you changed your mind already?"

Spartan sighed.

"My plan will change as I see fit. Will you be second-guessing me at every stage? My skills and knowledge will win this fight, but not if you doubt me."

The machine waited and then spoke.

"You have proven yourself in the trials. It is time for

you to face your kin. We are ready."

"Then take us in."

Spartan could see no officers to direct, just the great projection showing all of the space around the ship. There was no way to tell through touch, but he could already see they were making their way to the Black Rift. One of the massive Rift Engines pushed deep inside the entrance, and half of the vessels immediately vanished. Two-dozen Biomantas followed next, and then it was their turn. The mighty battleship Retribution pushed through the Rift, and then with a single flash, they were in a completely different part of space.

Now fight! said the voice.

The view of the Helios System was anything but impressive. At this distance from the star, they would take weeks to get anywhere. Spartan moved his eyes and watched as ship after ship appeared on the model. There was a modest number of Helion and Alliance ships, but nothing close to a fleet. One-Zero-One highlighted them all before speaking.

"The enemy has deployed a small group of ships to defend the Great Seal. What are your orders?"

Spartan took a step closer to the ledge and looked down at his warriors.

"Spartan?"

Again he closed his eyes and blocked out every sound and sensation. Inside the armor he could choose what he wanted to feel, and right now that was nothing at all. He had the image of the Black Rift on both sides in his mind, as well as the massive fleet of almost inconceivable numbers. Hundreds upon hundreds of ships, thousands of warriors and battleships that were more than the equal of anything the Alliance could muster. He could visualize the six battleships, each bristling with nearly a hundred Ghost Warriors, and every one of them under his command.

I can send them anywhere, or send them nowhere.

His previous simulations shifted behind his eyes, battles with the Helions, Khreenk, and the Alliance. Space battles, land battles, sieges, and raids. He had tried them all, but there was just one thing he knew had to be done here.

I have to fight with such terror that the war will stop before it starts. I will protect lives on all sides by making this painless.

His mouth curved into a cruel smile as images of those that had wronged him sprung to mind. It wasn't something he'd intended, and yet they came to him, one at a time. Finally, he opened his eyes and looked at Thayara and One-Zero-One who had both moved in front of him.

"What wrong with him?" Thayara asked, "Should I take command?"

Spartan reached out and grabbed her arm.

"No. Rejoin the warriors and prepare a boarding party."

She tried to struggle free, but Spartan kept a firm grasp of her armored limb.

"Look at the ships. This is not the fleet we need to

defeat. It is not even a fleet that should concern us."

One-Zero-One extended one of his mechanical limbs to the projection.

"Yours orders, Spartan?"

"Bring in the rest of the fleet and assemble in battle array right here. I want three hundred ships and our assault force deployed out in front of the Rift. We are not scared of any of these enemies. We are not even concerned. Deploy ready, but do not open gun ports or any other action that looks like we are waiting to attack."

He nodded to himself with amusement.

"Let them sweat and debate. Are we here to negotiate, surrender, or fight? Trust me, very soon they will know."

Spartan pointed at the area of open space nearly fifty thousand kilometers from the Black Rift. He could sense the machine already doubted him, and now his own impatience was beginning to rise.

"Put me on an open channel. It is time for my announcement."

* * *

ANS Warlord, Micaya Shipyards, Helios Sector
Admiral Anderson watched the slowly moving formations of ships inching closer the closer. His own battleship was now directly in front of a Cephalon command ship, and they exchanged gunfire like two great warships of old.

The great battle wasn't what concerned him; instead his attention was on the vast shape of the Ark. Even his own ship would be no match for its power.

Not much longer.

The counter to the right showed the number of seconds until he could begin the next phase of the battle. The timing was critical for so many reasons. Admiral Lewis' ships would require enough time to power up, and the engineering vessel would need its own window to be able to power its systems. At the same time, the enemy fleet needed to be fully committed to battle with the ships already invested in the fight. Lastly, the Ark had to be on a course that was irreversible.

I wait too long, and they could reach our hidden ships. Too early, and the Ark will change course and head for the heart of the shipyards. This must be done to the damned second!

The numbers were moving slowly, but no matter what was happening out in space, he could see there was less than a minute to go. The nearer it came to that final moment, the faster time seemed to move.

"Sir, two more Cephalons are closing in on our position," said Captain Decker.

"Good, that's what we need."

He moved his hands about the tactical display and selected two squadrons of Crusaders and a pair of battlecruisers. The Cephalons were escorted by a similar number of their own heavy warships.

"Focus fire from all allocated squadrons."

The Alliance ships were already close by and quickly moved into the requested formations. There was a large amount of space between each vessel, and they presented their bows toward the approaching ships.

"Sir, shouldn't we hit the Cephalons first?" asked the Captain.

Admiral Anderson shook his head.

"No. We will deal with this situation using good old ratios and mathematics. I want their numbers reduced to increase out combat potential. The Biomantas go first, then the Ravagers."

"And the Cephalons?"

Admiral Anderson smiled at the question.

"If we've destroyed everything else, then I'm sure we can deal with the last of them."

A buzzing sound reminded him that the timer had run down. He reached for the ancient looking intercom and pulled it to his mouth.

"Phoenix is a go! Light the fires."

He replaced the device and looked to his crew.

"Give me every ounce of firepower we have remaining, and let's burn some ships!"

The formation of ships moved straight at the Cephalons, but when they opened fire, it was the two nearest Biomantas that took the brunt. Particle beams exploded entire sections of the ships, but it was the massed volleys of railguns that tore them to shreds. No sooner had one been destroyed, and another would start getting pummeled by projectiles.

Beautiful, he thought.

Both fleets moved close enough; they effectively merged into a single massive group with ships at different positions and angles. Even in such chaos, the Alliance ships continued to focus their fire on one ship at a time. It was a technique he'd seen the enemy use before, and in such messy situations it made tactical choices much easier. It wasn't perfect, however, and the Biomechs were already changing their positions to aim at different targets. He watched as multiple groups split off and made for different sections of his fleet.

"ANS Samson is gone!" said Captain Decker, "And Agincourt has lost main power."

The images on the mainscreen showed three Ravagers moving about the Crusader class ship and hitting the vessel from different sides. The firepower from the much larger enemy ships was superior, and between them they made short work of the vessel. The bow had been torn off, and flames licked through her hull from the innumerable mortal wounds. Anderson looked to the tactical display and how the enemy was changing their attack pattern.

They are working in groups of three, each of them targeting one of our own. This is going to get bloody.

"Sir, shall we assist them?"

Admiral Anderson swallowed. This was the part of combat he hated the most, where he was forced to make decisions that left his own people, damned good people to die. He could split his fire to help the wounded escape, but that would effectively create more deaths by giving the Biomechs more ships and time to fight.

"No. They will have to manage for now. Get a squadron of Hammerheads out there to assist. Keep hitting the selected targets. This is a war of attrition. Keep at it, and one by one we'll wipe out this damned fleet."

The great ship shuddered, and for the first time the breach alerts sounded. Admiral Anderson looked at the damage display. An entire section the size of a Mauler had vanished from the port stern.

"What happened?"

Captain Decker barked orders to the engineering team before turning to him.

"Triple volley of atomics, Admiral. They must have entered through a breach in the space armor. It could have been a lot worse."

* * *

ANS Conqueror, Micaya Shipyards, Helios Sector
A grinding sound reverberated throughout the entire ship as they pushed themselves out from their hiding place. At the same time, the rest of Admiral Lewis' fleet activated

their engines and advanced from where they had been waiting. Dozens and dozens of Alliance warships emerged like ghosts from the very heart of a graveyard.

"All ships focus your fire on any Biomech ship targeting friendlies. Hit them hard, and don't stop till they are all burning."

He looked over his own tactical display, just as so many Alliance commanders were doing at that very moment.

Where is he?

His hand moved and then stopped at the gray shapes.

General Makos. You had better be ready for this.

There was no need for him to micromanage the alien and his own retinue. The plan was prearranged, and already his force of beautiful looking Dragonfly vessels were extending their solar sails and opening their gun ports. Three of them flashed green, and a volley of spheres blasted out and into the path of an unsuspecting Biomanta. The impacts tore through the hull and left a burned out husk spinning uselessly.

And the others?

There were contingents from the Helions under the command of T'Kron, as well as the small force from the Klithi. Just as intended, the aliens were staying together and moving back to the burning shipyards to engage the scattered Biomech ships not currently involved in the colossal capital ship battle with Admiral Anderson and ANS Warlord.

His first view of a pair of Klithi traveler ships reminded him of deep-sea creatures from Earth. Like the Byotai, their craft looked heavily inspired by vessels of the deep ocean, though whereas the Byotai were large and complex with great wings and masts, the Klithi were more like whales. The alien ships moved much faster from their hiding places and were quickly beset by large numbers of fighters. At the same time, the gantries throughout the shipyards continued to break apart and burn. Two Biomantas trapped a single Crusader, and as they tried to eliminate the vessel, the Dragonflies too struck them. Energy blasts ripped them apart, leaving multiple sections crackling with energy.

"Sir, we have a Ravager bearing down on us. Our capacitors have failed. The main guns are…"

He scratched at his head while yelling.

"What the hell do you mean our primary guns are offline?"

The ship vibrated heavily as a double burst of gunfire clattered amongst the wreckage. The Battlecruiser had been safely nestling between two defunct Helion cruisers, but even that extra layer of protection was proving useless against the swarm of Biomech fighters and the single Ravager moving in on them. The ship moved out of the wreckage one meter at a time, and with a great, painful grinding sound that could be felt through the hard material of the ship.

"Sir, the capacitors are refusing to take the charge. I need to purge the system and do a full restart sequence. It must be the long exposure to the cold."

Admiral Lewis couldn't believe what he was hearing. The system should work in a near sub-zero environment, but now wasn't the time to argue about the science of the problem.

"And how long will that take?"

"Six minutes, maybe seven."

"Then do it, and get my guns online fast or we'll be dead."

He then looked to his XO.

"Get us into the fight. I don't care if we have to ram them. We need to hit them and hit them hard. If we don't, we'll be leaving Anderson to do all the heavy lifting."

"Yes, Sir," said Captain Marcus.

The engines detonated with a rumble, and they were out of the debris and moving toward the enemy ships. Five Liberty destroyers joined them, and more and more of his fleet emerged from their slumber.

"Sir!" said Lieutenant Vitelli, "The Ravager is changing course. It's General Makos."

He nodded, and the mainscreen changed to show the battle around the Ravager. It wasn't just that ship; there were eleven capital ships and hundreds of fighters, all of which had been heading directly toward him. Now they were changing course to meet the General head on.

"What are those?"

He pointed at spherical objects hurtling toward the Biomech fleet. There were hundreds of them, and they were moving at incredible speeds in a straight line. Every few seconds one would vanish, but plenty made it within range of the enemy.

Lieutenant Vitelli smiled when six of them changed course at the last moment and accelerated right into the engine vent of an already damaged Ravager. The right-hand side of the ship tore off in a massive blast and was quickly followed by many more.

"Klithi mines, Sir. They are self-homing and very powerful."

The expression of excitement on the tactical officer's face quickly faded; the very blood seemed to run from his skin to leave him pale and nervous.

"No. No way, they can't be."

"What is it?" asked the Admiral.

"The ships, they are all changing course, every single one of them. Even the Ark is using its engines to make a course correction."

"To where?"

The young officer simply pointed at the single most important ship in the entire fleet.

"ANS Explorer, Sir, they must have detected her energy signature."

He looked for and then grabbed his intercom.

"All ships, they're making for Explorer. The protection of this ship is the only consideration. Protect the ship! All other assets are expendable. Put up a screen around her."

The next four minutes were the most tense and violent minutes in Admiral Lewis' life. All the Alliance ships were on an intercept course; the majority forming up in a layer defensive wall less than a hundred kilometers from the ship. Hundreds and hundreds of fighters, Maulers, and drones plugged the gaps, and more arrived by the minute. At the same time, the engineering vessel continued its mighty energy buildup.

* * *

ANS Tempest, Micaya Shipyards, Helios Sector

They flew along the length of the Alliance engineering vessel and checked for signs of the enemy. Five more Maulers followed in a wide wedge formation; all that remained of the original eight. Every one of them now bore new scars from the fighting, from small bullet holes created by point-defense turrets through to the meter-wide hole in the flank of ANS Tornado caused by a thermite missile.

"Turn to my vector and begin tracking," said Captain Garcia.

The small group twisted about and faced in the direction of the massive skirmish screen. Out ahead were hundreds of flashes from the Alliance and Biomech fleets fighting at close range. It was impossible to tell who was winning; both sides had now moved from a tactical approach to the battle and on to a high-scale dogfight, with the ships fighting whomever was closest. All Captain Garcia cared about was his new mission.

"Okay, all units form up on the bow of the Liberty ships."

There was a squadron of nine fleet defense ships, and they had positioned themselves with their flanks toward the ongoing battle. Their gun and missile systems were optimized for tracking objects from the size of fighters right down to individual bullets. The Maulers went ahead of them and formed up. From the cockpit, it was possible to make out three more groups of Maulers, plus twice as many Lightning fighters, and a smattering of Hammerheads.

"Sir, I'm going to have to take engine number three offline. The shrapnel is causing the cooling system to fail."

He nodded in answer. A message arrived from the lead Liberty destroyer, ANS Citadel. It was an automated message and contained targeting data and information for scores of targets on the way.

"Sir, what are we facing?" Lieutenant Takeda asked.

"Uh…not much. Maybe ninety missiles, a dozen torpedoes, and a few hundred projectiles."

The computer tracked the identified targets and then

began plotting firing solutions. Both of them watched as more and more appeared. What was much more disconcerting was the time it was taking for them to reach their targets. Captain Garcia reached out and activated the firing computer.

"All ships, open fire."

Scores of turrets opened fire with deadly flechette flak rounds. Each was designed to split apart just before reaching their target and then showering the incoming weapon with chunks of razor sharp metal. The computer tracked the incoming fire, and the Mauler shuddered as the corner and nose mounted turrets emptied their ammunition bins. As each one ran dry, the robotic loading system changed to another box, and the shaking continued.

"Just look at that," said Lieutenant Takeda.

Even a few minutes earlier they had been involved in the massed ducking and spinning through the debris. That great and deadly dogfight had changed into nothing more than a static shooting gallery. They formed part of the last line of defense, and right behind them sat the big fat target of ANS Explorer.

Captain Garcia hadn't even noticed his officer was pointing to the massive Ark off to the right. It was only a bright dot this far away, but the very fact it was visible showed how much of a threat it was. At the same time, two of the nearby gantries from the shipyard vanished in a dull flash to leave only dust.

"Goddamned particle beams."

The guns continued firing into the wide flak corridor, making a direct approach to the Alliance ship almost impossible. Even so, every few seconds a hardened penetrator round or missile would make it through and explode against the modest armor of the vessel.

"Sir, look," said Lieutenant Takeda.

Captain Garcia looked to the overlay and the imagery of the fighter squadron. The computer had already tagged more than twenty, and the numbers were increasing.

"Great, they're moving along that pylon to the right for cover. We need to stop them before they can reach the ship."

With a quick nod of agreement, Lieutenant Takeda took over manual control and spun the vessel around. At the same time, Captain Garcia ordered six nearby Lightning fighters and a single Hammerhead to join them. The Mauler was slightly slower than before, due to the lost of the fourth primary engine. Even so, it was only a few seconds before they were moving along the pylon at the close distance of just a hundred meters. Captain Garcia sent an order to the rest of his squadron to stay and guard the approach.

"Here they come!" said Takeda.

With a quick tug, she spun the vessel about so that they slipped between two hulks and vanished from view while the other fighter spread out to fly over. Right above them moved a long column of small Biomech fighters. Captain Garcia tagged them and opened up with the turrets. Five vanished in as many seconds, and then they pulled up and went into a pursuit formation. The Lightning fighters were faster and moved in right behind them, quickly dispatching three more before they began to spin about to return fire. Two Alliance fighters were quickly torn apart, and then the Hammerhead was amongst them. Apart from its primary weapons, it was also equipped with turrets that fired continually in multiple directions.

"What the hell was that?" Captain Garcia asked.

A pair of Biomech fighters ripped apart and metal-limbed machines flew past them. He spotted one crash onto the Hammerhead where it proceeded to hack and smash into the outer skin.

"Help them!"

Lieutenant Takeda moved carefully behind the crippled Hammerhead and took as careful aim as she could manage. Though there was no atmosphere to shake them, there was the problem of the constantly jinking form of the Hammerhead. Each impact from the machine forced the maneuvering thrusters to move the craft off into the wrong direction. The Mauler was vastly bigger than the Hammerhead, and as they came in behind, their path was blocked by a Biomech fighter. This was a different design to the normal type. Instead of weapons, it carried four more of the Decurion machines.

"This is new," said Lieutenant Takeda.

She pulled the trigger, and the entire rear section tore off and vanished from view. She didn't hesitate and fired again, finally destroying the machine with a one-second burst. The debris scattered off to the sides but continued on in the same direction.

"This is Captain Garcia of ANS Tempest; I have multiple fighters on an attack vector to the prize. I repeat; we have another fighter wave coming on an attack vector. Triangulate a flank corridor on my position."

He looked to Takeda, but she was far too busy trying to aim at the Decurion still smashing and tearing at the Hammerhead. Finally, it was in her sights, and she pulled the trigger. Two turrets had line of sight, and both poured armor piercing rounds into the target. Her first shots went wide, but the second burst struck the thing in one of its limbs. Something caught her eye. A chunk of plating just behind the cockpit ripped off and metal limbs appeared.

"Seal the ship and spin!" he yelled.

Lieutenant Takeda didn't even have to check for herself. With a single button press, an extra layer of seals activated. Gas pumped into the open sections that would seal any small cracks or holes. Then came the spin. This was far greater than the movement normally reserved for dogfighting. This was a desperate measure designed to force incredibly high g-forces. By the time of the sixth full revolution, the ship had almost driven them unconscious.

"Re…recover," muttered Captain Garcia.

The pressure suit, including his naval PDS armor pushed down on his body, and the oxygen system struggled to keep them both conscious. Neither was able to initiate the recovery though, and it fell to the computer to take over. They made another four revolutions before slowing down and continuing on their previous course.

"That was…" started Lieutenant Takeda.

A single metal prong punched up through her chest and out in front of her face. She choked and a spray of blood burst from her mouth.

"Takeda!"

Captain Garcia automatically reached for the thermal shotgun fitted to the left wall. The point vanished from his pilot's chest, and she stopped moving, her lifeless body held in tightly against her seat. Captain Garcia activated his open distress channel.

"Mayday, mayday, this is ANS Tempest. We have been boarded. Requesting…"

The area of metal plating behind Takeda ripped apart, and a hole big enough to climb through appeared. He flicked off the safety on the shotgun and took aim. Something moved, and he pulled the trigger. A flash of flame from the shotgun punched a hole into the torso of a Decurion as it came forward. The wrecked remains were then ripped out of the way, and he could see back into the empty cargo hold. With there being no torpedoes left, it was just a big storage area. He fired two more shots and had the satisfaction of spotting another of the machines take a blast straight to the center.

Got to get out of here.

He looked ahead and toward the Liberty destroyers. The flak corridor had increased, and there were multiple fighters weaving in and out. Behind them an odd blue hue was increasing around ANS Explorer. An urgent flashcom sounded in his ears, surprising him for a brief moment.

"This is Admiral Lewis. All ships must leave sector Three Alpha immediately. Get out of there!"

Something moved, and he glanced over his shoulder to see two more of the machines pulling themselves over wreckage. The only reason they hadn't made it through already was because of the smashed Decurions and shattered loading racks for the now spent torpedoes.

"You have ten seconds. Get out of the blast zone."

Captain Garcia looked about for the zone markers, but the next machine was through. He twisted about and caught his arm on the control column. The Mauler started to twist.

"Dammit!"

He leaned forward to alter the controls, just as a metal arm swung overhead. The sharp metal scraped across his helmet and cut a deep gouge. Even though it was little more than a glancing strike, it was enough to make him turn back around. Captain Garcia lifted the shotgun while the Mauler continued to spin out of control.

"Two seconds!" came back the voice from the Admiral.

Captain Garcia fired once, twice, and then a third and final time. Each blast tore chunks from the machine, but as he fired, another chunk of metal tore away to reveal another of the things. Then came a blue flash that filled the cockpit and everything outside. He looked back and spotted the approaching gantries and metal structures of the vast shipyard complex. At the same time, the machines scrambled forward to reach him. He extended out his arm and struck the emergency autopilot. The Mauler immediately righted itself and pulled up from the shipyards. Even as Captain Garcia breathed in a sigh of relief, an arm punched past his shoulder and embedded sharp metal into the control panel. The electronics sparked and flashed, and then everything outside vanished in the blue orb.

Great, death by shipyard, Decurion or blue orb.

The blue vanished and right in front of him was the massive section of shipyard, along with several dozen scuttled ships. The flashing blue faded as quickly as it had arrived, and now his course had been completely reversed. A glance at the navicomputer showed they had moved to the opposite orbit of the shipyards, and all of the debris was heading toward a closing target.

"What?"

Captain Garcia was completely stunned, not by what

surrounded him, but by the massive shape of the Biomech Ark that grew larger by the second. Their total closing speed was in the hundreds of thousands of kilometers.

He didn't even feel the puncturing of the spikes from the machines as the Mauler and a massive section of the orbital facility crashed into the Ark at impossible speeds.

CHAPTER FIFTEEN

Olik, Khan, Gun, and Osk are some of the famous names that rose to prominence during the Great Uprising. Each of them was an experienced warrior by the end of the conflict and would go on to great significance in the period of the Alliance. Like all of their kin, they proved loyal even when harassed and persecuted. Some of their comrades were killed in the interwar years, yet even when provoked, the Jötnar refused to turn to their more primitive sides. In many respects, they made better soldiers than conventional humans, and some speculate that if the Echidna Union had been more careful it might have been able to use their skills to destroy the Confederacy.

Heroes of the Great Uprising

ANS Warlord, Micaya Shipyards, Helios Sector

The cheering inside the CIC was deafening as each of the officers watched in awe at the new development. The sight of the Rift opening up in the middle of battle was a rarity, but this was beyond what any of them had expected. The plan for the engineering ship had been kept secret, though most assumed it would be used in the same way as at Helios Prime.

"Watch and pray," said Admiral Anderson.

None of them had really known what to expect when ANS Explorer had activated its Rift generator hardware. The blue pulse appeared not in front of the ship, but more than a hundred kilometres away and in the middle of the orbiting shipyard complex. It engulfed dozens of scrapped ships, gantries, walkways, and most of one shipyard spoke. With a flicker, they vanished and then appeared on an opposite orbital path in front of the Ark.

"Incredible, have you seen the closing speed?"

The vast horde of space debris, wreckage, and junk smashed into the Ark before anymore of them could speak. The large spoke that had been connected to the central shipyard hub was almost as large as the Ark, and it tore through the front of the vessel like it was wet tissue paper. On and on went the wreckage until it reached the center of the vast vessel. Then came another blue pulse, and half of the Ark disintegrated.

"Yes!" Captain Decker yelled.

Hundreds of secondary explosions ripped through the vessel as it tore itself apart from the inside. Three more bright flashes tore at the bow, and then the innards of the thing spread in all directions, leaving nothing but a dark, dead husk. Admiral Anderson sighed with pleasure at the great level of destruction wrought from the Rift.

"That, my friends, is how you bring down a big beast. You create a Spacebridge with objects in opposite directions and cause an almighty collision."

He leaned toward the tactical display and lifted the intercom. With a lick of his lips, he glanced at the unit once more. With the Ark gone, the Biomech fleet was now heavily outnumbered and surrounded by the different allies. The Byotai were hunting down the remaining Cephalon command ship, along with their escort of Klithi and the remaining Helion ships. Admiral Lewis was busy defending ANS Explorer from a final big push at the center of the shipyards. His own ships were spread out and busy engaging the scattered Biomechs that appeared to have lost any focused battle plan.

"This is the Admiral. All vessels break and attack. Run these bastards down, all of them."

ANS Warlord was already turning about on the spot and firing up its primary engines. A small group of Biomantas and two Ravagers twisted away from the wrecked Ark to escape, but they were too slow. Railguns fired first, each sending a mixture of armor piercing and Sanlav rounds. Explosions ripped through the first Biomanta, and then the primary weapons opened fire. There was no light, not even a sign of a weapon firing. Just the massive explosion as half of the second Biomanta vanished in a cloud of broken metal and flesh.

"Good work, keep it up," said Captain Decker.

The experienced Captain moved about the CIC, encouraging her officers and keeping their guns on track. As the most powerful ship in the fleet, it came down to Warlord to inflict much damage in as little time as possible.

"That makes thirteen," said the tactical officer.

"There are plenty more targets out there," reminded the Captain.

Admiral Anderson left the management of the ship-to-ship battle to Captain Decker and focused his attention on what remained. He checked their dispositions and allowed a small smile to form on his face.

Perfect, this might actually work.

The Alliance forces around Admiral Lewis were increasing in numbers and had created an impenetrable wall around ANS Explorer. It left him free to move away to engage other targets that were trying to escape the shipyards.

Lewis can hold for now. This is an opportunity to end their fleet before they can escape.

"Admiral, there's a distress call coming from the Black Rift," said Captain Decker.

He looked to the ship's Captain and noted she was busily talking to the communications officer.

What now?

"Put it on the mainscreen."

She said a few more words and then walked back to him.

"Admiral, this is a problem."

The display showed the empty region of space that had been guarded for so long. Instead of black nothingness, there was now the mirrored shape with one of the hated Biomech Rift Engines protruding out of it.

"So they are trying to open it again, just as expected."

Captain Decker shook her head and pointed at the hundreds of ships moving themselves into battle array. They both looked at the dispositions for a few seconds before Anderson looked to her.

"Odd. The dispositions are standard for Alliance deployment. Look at the location of the flagships and the escorts."

He pointed to the mainscreen.

"Tactical, isolate and enlarge that one."

The group of ships blurred as the telescopes tracked and zoomed in on the larger vessel. As it stabilized, the size became apparent.

"That's new, looks like a battleship or heavy carrier of some size."

The shape of the ship had much in common with the normal Biomech ships. The engines, armored sections, and overall shape were like a super-sized Ravager class vessel. He moved his attention to the other vessels alongside it, especially those that looked like the Biomantas they were now all so familiar with. Although similar, there were noticeable changes. Every one of the ships had been embellished with extra equipment, more gun ports, and designs that covered their hulls. Many looked like ancient relics that had been modified dozens of times.

They've been waiting a long time for their return.

"Admiral, energy signatures building; there are more ships coming through."

Scores of massive vessels leapt into view and took up position behind the array of warships.

"Wait, they are opening up another Rift," said the tactical officer.

The tactical display showed Micaya and the other Helion worlds, but the Black Rift was a disconnected dot far off into the distance. A number of oval shapes appeared with one near to the planet of Micaya. More of the shapes flashed at different points around the Black Rift, the implication being that more Rifts were opening elsewhere.

"No, this can't be happening," said Admiral Anderson.

They all appeared in a circular pattern around the entrance to the Biomechs' domain. In total there were six new Rifts opening, and it didn't take the crew long to work out where they might be. Admiral Anderson looked to the display and shook his head as the data appeared from Micaya. Another Rift signature flashed by, and then an entrance appeared less than a thousand kilometers away, not far from the wreckage of three Ravagers and right in the middle of the shipyards.

"My instruments show that Rift leads right back to that battleship. The others are probably the same, Sir."

It was only then he noticed the battle seemed to have slowed. The data from the other ships showed the manned vessels such as the Ravagers had stopped their attacks and were deploying to a position not far from where Admiral Lewis was waiting. He reached for the intercom and selected the fleet-wide channel.

"This is the Admiral. The enemy fleet is withdrawing and quite frankly, I do not care why. Do not take that as a signal for us to do the same. Rally your ships, reload your guns, and finish them fast. I want every Biomech vessel to be nothing more than an empty shell before these reinforcements can come to their aid."

Even Captain Decker appeared taken aback by the order.

"Admiral, how can we attack them if they refuse to fight? What if they are going to the shipyards to prepare for a full withdrawal?"

Admiral Anderson walked two paces and pointed to the shapes gathering around the Black Rift.

"They are not withdrawing. This is a redeployment to hit Admiral Lewis. I am certain of it."

He wiped his brow, the tension and stress beginning to

show on his face.

"We might be minutes or hours from the total destruction of the entire Helios System. We have a chance to end this current battle in one swift action. Target the nearest ships and open fire. I want to see them burning. The rest of our ships need to get there fast."

There was a moment of indecision, perhaps a struggle of ethics behind her eyes. It didn't take long before a pair of Biomantas burned through the hull of a damaged Helion cruiser for her to make up her mind.

"Affirmative, Admiral, we will continue the fight."

Seconds later, the primary particle beams released an incredible barrage of energy that struck a retreating Biomanta in the stern. The impact of such energy and at such speed quickly disintegrated the warship and scattered its ruined hull in a dozen directions.

"Sir, the rest of their forces are rallying at point six-two. They are facing off toward our ships around ANS Explorer."

Anderson was busy checking the nearby enemy positions and giving orders to each of the squadrons. He could see the battle had turned, but also how spread-out his forces were. His eyes darted back and forth and then stopped as he watched the formation of ships around Admiral Lewis. Seventeen ships were now in a wide oval dispersion pattern, with the Battlecruiser ANS Conqueror in the center.

They are throwing themselves at Lewis, one last-ditch assault.

Even as he considered it, he came to another conclusion.

Or they are trying to force me to react? What if they want to force me to decide?

"Incoming signal, Sir. It's on the open channel. Actually, Sir, it's on all channels, using Alliance friendly IFF."

He looked to Captain Decker at the same time as she turned to face him.

"On screen."

The shape of two machines appeared. Both were bipedal and completely stationary. Behind them was a holographic representation of a star system with shapes moving about. The machine lifted up one hand and then pointed to the holographic map behind it. Admiral Anderson watched it for a moment and then nodded to his tactical officer.

"Scan and log all of that. Scrape any intelligence you can from it."

As he watched the videostream, he moved his hands about the tactical display to send another group of Liberty destroyers to help those trapped in the middle of the ruined shipyard.

"Warriors of the Alliance," were the first words he heard.

He looked back, and the machine continued to speak. There was no translator, and the voice sounded eerily familiar. It took just a few words before his throat felt dry, and he almost choked.

"I have been chosen to lead the people of Taxxu. I give you thirty minutes for your unconditional surrender, or you will face complete atomic devastation."

Admiral Anderson shook his head.

"I know that voice."

The officers continued to manage the space battle while moving the vessels into two large groups around each of the Admirals. The odd vibration rattled through the ship, but with the Biomech forces heavily reduced there was little immediate danger to ANS Warlord.

"You knew me as Spartan. Now I am warlord for the Machine Gods."

Just the mention of one of the most famous warriors in the entire Alliance military sent a shudder through the ship. Even Admiral Anderson felt something akin to pain in his chest at hearing the words. He shook his head and spoke quietly.

"There's no chance. Spartan is a hero of the Alliance. He has fought and sacrificed for most of his adult life."

"He's MIA, Sir," said Captain Decker, "He could have been captured, indoctrinated or brainwashed, somehow? Wasn't he a prisoner of the machines for months before appearing near Sol?"

The machine moved much more than the one alongside him, assuming the machine was the one actually speaking. Captain Decker spotted shapes on the tactical display, and two of her more junior officers ran over to point out additional forces creeping through the shipyard.

"Sir, the rest of their forces are coordinating a massive strike on our forces here."

She pointed directly to Admiral Lewis' ship.

"He's outnumbered. Should I change course?"

The videostream demanded his attention, but there was little chance he would simply abandon his comrades to watch it. A quick glance at the display showed him that Captain Decker was indeed correct. He grabbed the intercom, looking back at the videostream.

"This is the Admiral. All ships will converge at point six-two to assist ANS Conqueror. Maintain a defensive perimeter and look after our people. All attack squadrons will continue the pursuit of any stray Biomech forces."

He lowered the device and squinted as he watched the videostream. By merging his forces, he would create a single block in case they tried anything unexpected. It would slow down the pursuit, but it would preserve his force.

"Why is he not showing his face? Is that really him? It could be a recording."

Not knowing what was coming next was the part that unnerved him. Until the Rift had opened, he would have thrown his ships at the enemy with little concern given to damage or position. Now there was a chance they could do something, and that was something he didn't like.

"I know all of your strengths and weaknesses. That is

why I was chosen from hundreds of prominent humans. Just as Typhon, Pontus, and the others have served the machines, so now do I."

The machine twisted a fraction.

"I beat each of them in turn, and I am still undefeated in battle. You know me, and you know what I can do."

It was simple but obvious. Spartan was known for many of his great battles and struggles, but one stood out amongst them all. The assault on Terra Nova had ended the Uprising, but it had also seen untold destruction in the capital, a place unprepared for a violent ground battle.

"My orders are simple, and I will carry them out in whichever way I see fit."

Those words hit Anderson like icy daggers. The previous characters played a vital part in the civil war that had torn the Confederacy apart, decades earlier. The very idea that Spartan would work for the same enemy was the worst possible news. The machine looked back at the holographic model and made no attempt to hide a thing. It pointed at the shapes of worlds whose position suggested they were Helios Prime and Spascia.

"Reports from our ground troops confirm they are engaged in attritional warfare on Spascia and Helios Prime, just as planned. Our last ships are preparing to hurl themselves at your fleet in one glorious showdown to show me their loyalty. These are the outcasts, the remnants of those that remained following our exile."

MICHAEL G. THOMAS

Admiral Anderson swallowed uncomfortably at the mention of the word 'our'.

"It is their job to sacrifice themselves prior to our return."

Anderson looked to Captain Decker and then to the mainscreen. The number of enemy ships was vast, far more than he could ever hope to defeat. On top of that, the remainder of the Biomech fleet was assembling close to Admiral Lewis at the shipyards.

How many ships do they have facing Lewis?

He ran his eyes across the unit and checked the numbers. The remaining Cephalon was under heavy attack by the Byotai, but the Ravagers and Biomantas still numbered nearly sixty plus the numerous fighters.

Lewis can't take them on alone. If we don't assist, he, Explorer, and his entire force will be wiped out.

"Admiral Anderson, you will be commanding the fleet, of course, and it is to you I speak. You have one chance to end this war and save billions of lives."

There was no face, but even Admiral Anderson felt he could recognize something about the way the thing moved. The machine was moving continually as it spoke, far more than was necessary. He looked to Captain Decker.

"Get me Khan, and fast."

She nodded and moved to a nearby terminal.

"Order your ships to surrender, or suffer the unrelenting vengeance of the Machine Gods. Only together can we

405

save lives, not destroy them."

* * *

Khan walked back and forth in front of his personal bodyguard. Each of the other three sat or leaned on whatever piece of equipment they could find in the port hangar. A short distance away was a single Mauler. The hull was covered in dents, and an entire squad of engineers was busy patching it up. Khan stopped and looked back to the men and women.

"How much longer? I need to get back to my ship."

A young captain, who could not have been more than twenty-two, twisted around to look to him. His overalls were filthy and his face covered in a thick greasy smear that ran from his ear down to his shoulder.

"Another ten minutes, Sir. Like I said, the last volley breached the outer walls. You're lucky the round didn't hit the engines."

He went back to his work, and Khan found himself waiting again.

"What's the rush, Khan?" Olik asked.

"It's not like we even have a mission, right now," grumbled Knaprig.

Their leader looked to each of them.

"The rest of the Black Ships are still out there, waiting at the Black Rift. We need to get back there, ready to go and find Spartan. I'm tired of waiting on this ship, and for what?"

Olik sighed.

"Khan, you've tried how many times now? The Admiral won't allow the Rift to be opened under any circumstances, not even for Spartan."

Tajt, who had been silent until now, decided to chip in.

"My great friend is right, Khan. They should have landed us on Spascia where we could do some good. Instead, we've left the warriors Spartan gifted us to sit out there with nobody but Olik and Terson to command them."

Khan didn't seem very impressed by this.

"With Z'Kanthu gone, the others were considering continuing the war alone. On'Sarax was able to persuade them to hold back and to wait. Major Terson has orders to keep them away from the Rift unless they hear directly from us. I just wish I knew what we were waiting for."

He scratched at his cheek through his open visor.

"At least if we get back on Devastation we can prepare the bandon there for the next attack. We still have plenty of warriors."

"Don't forget our friends from Prometheus and Hyperion," reminded Tajt.

Khan nodded.

"True. How their transports have survived this fleet battle, I'll never know."

A light blinked inside his armor, and a poor quality image of Admiral Anderson appeared.

"Admiral, good to see you. Are we winning?"

The man's face was stern, and he simply ignored Khan's words.

"The Black Rift has opened, and Spartan is with them."

Khan was stunned, and his two comrades could see that something had happened by the expression on their friend's face.

"What's happened?" Tajt asked.

The conversation continued until finally Khan licked his lips and looked to his comrades. He moved close to them and crashed his arms down on Olik's shoulders.

"The Black Rift is open, and Spartan has come through, at the head of the Biomech army."

They were all stunned into silence. Khan took a step away and then looked back at them.

"Anderson needs me in the CIC. Keep on eye on them. I reckon we'll be needing that Mauler very soon.

With that, he was gone and running from the hangar and toward the wide passageway that led deep inside the ship. As he moved, he accessed the latest video logs and the live stream sent by the Admiral. An image popped up of machines with Spartan's voice in the background.

What have you done, Spartan, you crazy bastard?

* * *

Admiral Anderson watched the videostream from the Biomech ships. At the same time a number of urgent messages were coming in from craft throughout the Helios Sector. It was the one being rerouted via the Black Rift control station that he was most concerned about. The entire facility had been abandoned weeks earlier, but the exterior cameras were still active and showing the massed Biomech force that continued to grow by the minute. He looked at the machines, taking in every detail. The leader kept opening and closing its hand, as though nervous or trying to grab something. At the same time, the other arm scratched at the metalwork of the forearm.

Wait, that was Spartan's missing arm. Wasn't it?

The rest of Spartan's announcement continued, but he found himself drawn to the body language rather than the words. It went on for almost half a minute, and by the time the machine had stopped speaking, the entire CIC was silent. Each of the officers watched the shape but said nothing.

"Thirty minutes or watch the atomic destruction of Helios Prime. I will rain fire down upon this world with radiological weapons. When I am finished, the entire planet will be rendered barren. My shock troops will then arrive in the millions to annihilate any survivors."

He paused, letting the dreadful consequences sink in.

"Terra Nova will follow, then Centauri Prime, Earth,

and onwards."

Admiral Anderson looked to Captain Decker once more.

"Where is he?"

"On the way. Admiral. He says he needs to see the video feed."

The ship vibrated, and one of the displays flashed white and then stopped working. A number of sparks rippled off to the right, and a pipe tore from a bulkhead and struck a young Marine guard.

"Three Biomantas have worked around the wreckage and are hitting our flank," said Captain Decker, "They are trying to keep is away from ANS Conqueror."

"You know what to do, Captain. I need the fleet together and fast. How long until we can help Admiral Lewis?"

"Eleven minutes to clear the third shipyard spoke and the wreckage."

Admiral Anderson's mind was far from the few remaining Biomech ships, though. The Rifts that had been forming were of much greater importance. Worse than either was the fact that a great warrior, and a personal friend, appeared to have sided with the enemy in the most desperate of hours. He glanced at the Captain who was busily arranging for fighter cover as they headed toward Admiral Lewis. Confident all was taking place as he had planned, he returned to the dreaded mainscreen where Spartan was still speaking.

"I have four hundred advanced ships filled with warriors, and hundreds more just waiting for their orders to join us. You have no chance here, Admiral. Your forces are weakened and separated. Even now, our ships have isolated a fraction of your fleet and will soon destroy it. With one word, I can order them back."

The image of the machines vanished and changed to one of the transports. Inside waited legions and legions of warriors. Thousands per ship and each crammed in tightly. The footage quickly flashed back to Spartan.

"I have twice your number and over a million fresh warriors. Make your choice. Will it be genocide or peace? You have thirty minutes."

It looked as though the transmission would end, but instead it stayed with the three machines. Admiral Anderson began to move away when Spartan spoke one last time.

"I have sent you a small gift, something to help you understand the gravity of this situation."

The videostream cut off, and the view changed back to a wide view of the Biomech fleet. A barrage of objects rushed out from the largest and most prominently positioned ship in the fleet. The objects moved at increasingly fast speeds toward the Rift. Captain Decker didn't check with anybody else and went to issue orders.

"Forget it," said Admiral Anderson.

"We don't have a ship anywhere in range of the Helios

Prime Rift."

She looked to him.

"How do you know that's where it's going?"

He nodded to the tactical display just as the objects vanished from the forces waiting at the Black Rift. The delay from Helios Prime was a matter of minutes, but the local Rift allowed much quicker communications. In seconds, the revised data arrived to show the missiles dropping down to the southern hemisphere of the planet, well away from the Alliance strongpoint.

"Just pray those missile strikes are random."

Even as the space battle around the Micaya Shipyards continued, the eyes of the senior officers aboard ANS Warlord were on the satellite feeds from Helios Prime. The missiles were already through the atmosphere and heading for an already devastated part of an industrial facility and habitation zone.

"Population prior to the invasion was upwards of nine million," said Captain Decker as she read the figures showing on the nearest screen.

She then turned to look at Admiral Anderson with eyes that seemed to be almost blaming him for whatever was about to happen.

"Current estimates are five to ten thousand, the rest are deep underground. The surface was eradicated during the orbital bombardment."

"Sir, five seconds," said the tactical officer.

The video feed was very poor quality and shook continually before a bright white light completely blew out the color. Finally, the image returned with a vast cloud where the city ruins had once been. Khan entered the CIC at a jog. He knocked over a Marine guard before stopping directly in front of Admiral Anderson and looked at the atomic impact on Helios Prime.

"Khan, have you seen the footage?"

Khan nodded slowly.

"Well?"

"It's Spartan all right."

Both of them looked to the display.

"What is he telling us? There's something about his body language. Is this threat serious?"

Khan's expression moved from disappointment to almost glee.

"Oh, the threat is definitely real, but so is the invitation."

Even though the warrior was a giant compared to the Admiral, that didn't stopping him from grabbing his arm and pulling him back to face him.

"What do you mean?"

Khan lifted the right of his lip in a weird expression.

"Spartan will come here if he has to. That is what his mouth is saying. His body is saying we need to go to him. He wants us at the Black Rift, and before he uses the atomics."

"Khan, he's a prisoner. They've brainwashed him,

turned him against us. If he wants us to attack him, then why the hell would we listen?"

The tactical officer hit a button, and the mainscreen shifted to show a group of thirty warships moving in front of one of the newly opened Rifts. As they waited, their gun ports opened and out came dozens and dozens of missiles. Each pushed out into plain sight and pointed at the Rift.

"Admiral, they have ships doing the same at all five of them."

Anderson wiped his forehead, instantly understanding the threat. Captain Decker was a little slower, but then the horrible realization almost made her wretch.

"They have nukes pointing at every planet, and they can hit them at will by using the Rifts."

Captain Decker nodded in agreement.

"What can we do?"

Khan spoke first.

"Simple. We mount up and meet them at the Black Rift, all of us versus all of them. If we are quick, we can hit them."

Anderson licked his lower lip.

"And what about Spartan?"

Kahn's eyes flickered slightly at the question.

"Get us to the Rift, Admiral. We will find which ship he is on, and I will deal with him myself. With Spartan gone, we can beat them. We've beaten them here, we'll go and do the same at the Black Rift."

Admiral Anderson looked to the tactical display and the widely spaced out formation of ships. He counted just under two hundred vessels close enough that they would be able to come through and assist, but only by leaving Admiral Lewis on his own. That included the Byotai and Klithi contingents that were still mainly intact plus a handful of Helion cruisers. Admiral Anderson continued sending assembly orders throughout the fleet. At the same time, videostreams of General Makos and Admiral Lewis appeared on the mainscreen. General Makos was first to speak.

"The Cephalon is gone. What is next?"

His voice was gruff and emotionless as always, with the translator doing little to curb the way he sounded. Admiral Lewis joined in.

"The Biomechs have ANS Explorer surrounded. I've deployed all of my forces in a defensive screen, but we can't holds them back forever. If they attack, we will be…"

His face flashed three times as a computer screen out of view lit up his face.

"Dammit, they are coming for us."

He moved closer to the screen.

"Admiral, I'm outnumbered three to one. I need help and fast!"

The imagery crackled and then vanished for a second before returning. The expression on the Admiral's face was grim but determined. Flashes in the background indicated each time something exploded nearby and was reflected back to the camera. General Makos grunted as his translator kicked in.

"I will be there soon."

Admiral Anderson felt a pain in his stomach, like a knife stabbing deep into his flesh. He knew what was happening, and he could already see the Biomech plan had been changed in a matter of minutes. The CIC was dark, but even through the red lighting and the long shadows he could see the grim expression on Khan's face.

"You have to make a choice, Admiral. The fleet or the System?"

He already knew this, and that was what was killing him. He could save Admiral Lewis and the seventeen Alliance ships, but only if he sent in the bulk of his remaining forces.

If I do that, I'll leave every planet at the mercy of these damned weapons.

"Damn you, Spartan. You've signed these people's death warrants."

He looked into the face of General Makos and the blinking display with Admiral Lewis.

"I am going to take the fight to them. It was always the plan, now I have no choice. I'm sorry, Admiral."

"What?" snapped back General Makos, "My ships will be there in minutes."

Anderson pointed to the tactical display and the markers for all the ships and astronomical objects in the Micaya System. He isolated the Rift that led to the Black Rift.

"They will use this Rift, along with the others to unleash their atomic strikes. Every world will suffer unimaginable losses; the shipyards and any of our ships will vanish in nuclear fireballs."

He looked back to General Makos.

"No, in the time it would take you to get to Admiral Lewis, you could be half way to the Rift with me. Even at full-speed, we will reach the gate with two, perhaps three minutes to spare."

Without checking with them, he lifted the intercom and selected all friendly forces.

"This is the Admiral. All fully functional ships are to make for the enemy Rift. Assemble at the designated point and wait for my arrival. If you are unable to reach the directions within the timeframe, you will move to assist Admiral Lewis. Make haste, people. Lives hang in the balance."

The video feed cut completely to Admiral Lewis as the Biomechs intercepted, scrambled, or blocked the transmission. Instead, Admiral Anderson took in a long breath and nodded.

"What if the enemy collapses the Rift and destroys our ships?" Khan asked.

Admiral Anderson only needed a few seconds to

consider the argument.

"We send the ships through in groups of no more than six at a time. That will be the limit of our exposure. There's no time to redeploy once we get through. I want the capital ships brought down first. Then we destroy the Rift machines as quickly as possible."

There was silence, but already the forward view had changed as ANS Warlord amended its course to make for the Rift. There was a barely perceivable shift in gravity; the inertial system compensated for the increasing thrust.

"Khan, General Makos, Captain Decker. You heard my orders. Get everybody ready, and meet me at the rendezvous. Hurry!"

They saluted, or nodded in the case of the General, and then moved to their posts. Only Khan remained.

"What about your Black Ships?" Anderson asked.

Khan smiled.

"They've been waiting in their moorings at the Rift control station. Their life-support systems are offline, and they are leaking radiation from their engine coils."

"What? You lost the ships and the warriors?"

Khan smiled.

"It was a precaution. Major Terson and I agreed that until the fleet returned they would wait in silence. The machines have powered down, and the Thegns are back in hibernation. All it will take is a few minutes, and they will be back in the fight."

Admiral Anderson walked to Khan and placed his hand on his shoulder.

"Khan. Send the signal; we're going to need every warrior you can muster. The last of The Twelve is the one trick we have remaining."

Khan nodded, but he had somebody else in mind.

CHAPTER SIXTEEN

The SAAR project created a whole array of machines, of which only one made it into combat in time for the events of the Black Rift. Other projects that required further investigation were space-based assault robots. These machines, nicknamed crabs, were modified construction vehicles fitted with shuttle components. They would be launched in battle and attached to enemy vessels. The robots would then tear apart whatever they were attached to. Crabs would ultimately have been modified for launching directly from warships via low-velocity railgun sleds.

Robots in Space

Battleship Retribution, Black Rift, Helios Sector
The vast glowing sphere rotated just meters in front of Spartan. Now that they had traveled through the Rift and entered the Helios System, the data had been updated by

the second. He could see formations of Biomech ships and bandon of warriors in scores of locations, some of which he'd never even realized. He lifted his hands and examined the short but deadly blades he'd fitted. The empty forearms had been annoying him, and these new, brutal weapons were just the thing.

There is a Thegn cell still operating on Hades, in the T'Karan sector. Fascinating.

The enemy vessels were spread out, but he could see the primary threat was the fleet under the command of Admiral Anderson. He counted at least two hundred ships, and each was making its way toward the Rift he'd instructed his forces to open.

"The fleet is ready, Spartan. The Rift Engines are in position and stabilizing the bridges," said One-Zero-One.

The large structures had half entered each of the Rifts within seconds of them opening. Now that they were correctly positioned, they could stop any of the Helion or T'Kari weapons from collapsing them.

"What about their planetary defense weapons?"

"What about them? They can do little more than be a distraction. At short ranges the disruption is just seconds long. Our engines can keep the Rifts safe, providing the engines themselves are protected."

Spartan turned his attention back to the shapes marking out his own newly arrived forces. The vast horde of warships, including the six battleships and the hundred

Despoiler transports that lay alongside his monstrous army. Spartan looked at the forces arrayed before him, and his mind ran wild with possibilities. With these numbers, and the technology at his disposal, he could mold and shape the star systems into a strong and stable society. His very blood seemed to pump harder as he envisaged scores of star systems with his Biomech allies managing the entire thing. Something moved in his mind, a memory, almost a voice, and then vanished to the back of his mind.

"What now?" asked the machine.

Spartan turned to the machine and hissed his words back to him.

"I am in charge of this attack, am I not? So wait and listen. When I have orders, I will give them. Understood?"

The machine was silent and then finally spoke in a hushed tone.

"Yes."

Spartan lifted his arms and looked out at his warriors still waiting in long lines. His raised position was the perfect platform from which to give his orders. There were other similar platforms throughout the ships structure, but all of them were empty. He did notice the large number of Decurions and other much larger and more advanced looking war machines. Many of them appeared to be looking at him. He looked down at his armor and smiled.

"I'm quite liking this new body."

He lifted his eyes and watched as shapes appeared

through one of the many Rifts he'd ordered to be activated.

"Should we close the Rifts, Spartan? They could destroy our machines, just as happened in the last attack."

He closed his eyes and took in a breath.

"No, unlike your last effort, we will not fail."

One-Zero-One tilted a few degrees to the right.

"Fail? No, we achieved our objectives. We sowed terror in the hearts of the creatures of Helios, and we allowed the greatest of their warriors to reveal themselves to us. We had no idea you were one of our secrets. The hidden warriors found and prepared by our outcasts."

The machine pointed again to the Rift.

"Now, what about them?"

Spartan sighed.

"No. Trust me. The only chance they have is to strike hard and strike now. Why do you think I gave the order for our forces to finish them off at Micaya?"

The machine made calculations, and then faced the ethereal figures of the other Biomech leaders that were watching the events in silence. The glowing figures hovered around like a circle of demi-gods, and not one of them spoke in such a way that Spartan would understand. One-Zero-One turned back to Spartan.

"We do not understand. We can cripple their forces as they come through."

Spartan shook his head and pointed toward the machine.

"Don't you dare! Defeating their ships is just one part

MICHAEL G. THOMAS

of the strategy. They must feel they have a chance, no matter how slight. We will not defeat them while they sleep or when they are unprepared. When they are defeated, it must be when they feel they can win. This will make them throw all that they have at us, and their pain will be that much stronger upon their defeat."

"It is too late. They are through."

In small groups the ships of the enemy vanished from points at the Spascia shipyards and then reappeared just twenty thousand kilometers away from the Black Rift. Their numbers were small, but every few seconds more arrived. One-Zero-One pointed at the Rifts connecting to Spascia and Helios Prime. Nearly thirty more shapes came in via those Rifts and accelerated to join the others.

"They are sending in every warship they can find against us."

Spartan watched with interest as more and more came in.

"Good. How many are left?"

One-Zero-One scanned the Rift points on the holographic model in seconds.

"Three more ships."

"As soon as they are through, you will pull back the Rift Engines and deactivate the Spacebridges."

"I see," said the machine.

Spartan wasn't sure if that was true, but it didn't really matter.

"That is it, all of their forces are here."

A flashing series of icons at the dormant control station off to the right caught his eye. With a quick movement of his right arm, the model shifted about and zoomed in to show multiple vessels pulling away and powering their weapons.

The Black Ships.

He smiled to himself as he remembered being inside them, seeing the lines of warriors waiting, much as inside this battleship. The fleet under Admiral Anderson closed the distance with surprising speed, and after only a few more minutes, the Black Ships drifted into the rest of the formation. One-Zero-One was engaged in a lengthy discussion with his kin when Spartan tapped his shoulder.

"I have news for you."

He pointed to the center of the fleet.

"I had no idea they were still here. Those ships, they house the last of The Twelve, plus their own warbands of warriors."

There was no need for translation when each of the ethereal beings heard the words. The very mention of their hated former brothers sent a chill through the ship. Spartan could sense the change, even deep inside his suit of robotic armor. The one taller creature at the center spoke directly to him for the first time.

"Spartan. Bring us the heads of our lost brothers, and your place among us will be confirmed."

Spartan nodded happily.

"Very well. I will offer them the prize they seek. They will put out their necks, and when they are too exposed, I will personally cut them off."

With a series of gestures, he selected the squadrons of ships and transports as he had been taught in the training scenarios. They responded instantly to his commands, no matter how unexpected.

"Put me on the videostream. I want to speak to everybody."

"It is done," said the machine.

Spartan flexed his muscles and moved to the edge of the precipice.

"As leader of this host, I gave you a guarantee of peace. Surrender your fleet, and lay down your arms. Or suffer our eternal vengeance. The Helios Sector is ours."

There was no reply, no audio message, not even a flash of light from a signaling system. Instead, the gun ports of two hundred ships from the Alliance of different races opened up. Energy signatures from the Byotai and Alliance indicated they were preparing to fire their direct-energy weapons. Even the great ships of the Klithi were there, each waiting with their bows facing the Biomech fleet. One-Zero-One looked to Spartan.

"They have given their answer. What are your orders?"

There was no way to see it, but Spartan's smile had widened.

"Reply to them. Let the Helios Sector burn!"

* * *

ANS Conqueror, Micaya Shipyards, Helion Sector

The Alliance fleet at the Micaya Shipyards burned like the French fleet had done on the Nile. Each had been holed in a hundred places, yet this time the Biomechs were not destroying the crippled vessels. With each of them knocked out, the victorious enemy moved in around them and launched wave after wave of shuttlecraft.

"Why are they not just finishing us off?" Captain Marcus asked.

Alarms sounded in every direction as the Battlecruiser sustained a massive assault upon its left flank. Blast after blast marked where missiles and gunfire had penetrated the spaced armor and now crashed deep inside the hull. Another missile struck, and Admiral Lewis was knocked to his knees by the impact. Captain Marcus rushed to help him and lifted the man up as a series of flashes knocked out five displays.

"It's as Anderson predicted. The machines think they have already won. We are not just an enemy to beat; we are a resource. They can melt down or cannibalize our ships."

"And us?"

The grim expression from Admiral Lewis should have been enough for him to understand.

"You've seen what they do to the dead and dying. They are experts at recycling."

Another explosion rumbled; this time much deeper inside the Battlecruiser.

"Admiral, they've made it past the barricades," said Lieutenant Vitelli.

Captain Marcus looked at his commander as a trickle of blood ran down from his mouth.

"The escorts are gone. Explorer is abandoning ship, and the last of the reinforcements are holding on as long as they can."

"I know," said Admiral Lewis.

"It's our turn to make the hard decision. We will not surrender, and we will not give ground. We will fight them in every part of the ship."

Another flash at the doorway marked the use of grenades, and the Marine guards rushed outside to do battle with whatever monsters were heading their way. Admiral Lewis went to the nearest wall, hit the arms lock, and removed a cut down L52 carbine. Captain Marcus did the same.

"All of you; prepare yourselves. They are coming."

The emergency doors hissed into position to barricade off the CIC to the rest of the ship.

"Take cover!" Captain Marcus called out.

There were almost twenty officers in the CIC, and each wore the latest issue PDS Navy armor. Half carried L52 carbines, and the rest a mixture of sidearms and thermal shotguns. One by one, they moved behind the broken screens and the tactical display, training their weapons on the two entrances into the room. Admiral Lewis and Captain Marcus knelt down behind the corner of the tactical display and took aim.

"Is this how you thought it would end?"

Admiral Lewis smiled.

"I always knew I would go down with my ship. No matter what happens, there's no way they are keeping her."

It was only then that Captain Marcus noticed he'd been busily entering in security data into his personal secpad. He tapped it one last time and then passed it to his XO.

"I need your codes to finish the sequence."

Captain Marcus looked at the timed autodestruct sequence and shook his head.

"Admiral Anderson could have stayed back with us."

"Yes he could, but for what? We win here, but lose the war. He's looking at the big picture, and for us to have a chance to win, we will face death."

With that, Captain Marcus entered in his codes and activated the routine.

"There, we're on a ten minute destruct sequence. Either of us can stop it at any security point."

A bright flash was all that marked the destruction of the first door. Chunks of broken metal scattered about, and then in came the Thegns. Admiral Lewis opened fire first, putting four rounds into a creature before it staggered and fell to the ground. Another clambered over the body and succumbed to gunfire, but not before it dropped a small sphere to the floor. The device rumbled along the floor and then exploded. The blast sent hot fragments of metal in all directions, hitting computers, Thegns, and Alliance officers indiscriminately.

"Hold them back!" Captain Marcus yelled.

He lifted his head just a fraction to take aim and was immediately struck by a blast from two Thegns. His lifeless body spun back and fell to the ground just centimeters from Admiral Lewis. More Thegns streamed in, and then came the Decurions, their monstrous limbs hacking and stabbing. Screams echoed through the CIC, and then the artificial gravity failed. Admiral Lewis lost his footing and drifted up from where he'd been hiding.

What a way to go.

The Admiral took aim with his carbine but with nothing to hold onto, he drifted about. A Thegn moved into view, and he pulled the trigger. The first shot was on target, but the recoil sent him spiraling through the CIC and right back against the wall. The Decurions were in their element and tore through the defenders with ease. He lost count as dozens ripped through displays and human flesh, butchering any that they found. He lifted the carbine and locked his left arm against the bulkhead, holding him into place two meters off the ground.

"Go back to hell!" he cried out.

Holding down the trigger, he fired until every round had been expended. There were bodies everywhere, but nowhere could he find the sign of his comrades still alive. Three Decurions pulled themselves along the walls and moved in from each direction. He pushed the carbine away and grabbed for his pistol. They were only three meters away now. The gun seemed puny against such things, and he counted the rounds as he fired. Eventually he hit nineteen.

Time to go.

There was no hesitation as he flipped the weapon to his temple and squeezed the trigger.

* * *

ANS Warlord, The Black Rift, Helios Sector

The sound of battle filled the CIC. It was a song they were now all too familiar with. Engineers managed the power systems for the engines, life support, and weapons while the tactical officers targeted enemy vessels and took the fight to them. Every few seconds the ship shuddered as the secondary railguns fired. The recoil from the massed expulsion of energy and matter could be felt even through the vastness of the mighty battleship.

Come on, we don't have time," Admiral Anderson muttered.

He paced back and forth impatiently. His boots hit the metallic surface with a cracking sound from every step. The rest of the CIC was a hive of activity, few having even a fraction of a moment to look to their Admiral.

"Have you located the source yet?"

He looked up hopefully and found his eyes drawn to the massive mainscreen. The images were enough to make even the strongest man balk. Even the enemy Biomantas were enough to match his fleet, yet still the Allies moved forward and directly at them.

They outnumber us two to one, and I have no reserve. Is this it?

The chief science officer, a temporary transfer from one of the lost T'Kari scout vessels looked back to him. Her translator was up-to-date and responded in a fraction of a second after she spoke. Her technical skill was beyond anything anybody on the ship had seen before.

"The probes, Admiral. One of the six made it through the Rift. We have only six hundred kilobytes of data. The probe then stopped transmitting."

"What did we get?"

Two of the senior engineers looked at the screen, along with a third science officer. The data was mangled and lacking in detail, but with careful use of filters they were able to access at least part of it. The T'Kari officer waved frantically to the Admiral.

"I have over seventy targets, all large vessels. There is a planet in close proximity to the Rift exit point, several orbital structures that match the layout of the invasion Arks, and these."

She pointed to the graphs that presented the composition data in as simple a form as possible. Admiral Anderson looked carefully, but only parts of it made sense.

"I don't understand. I see partial data for more ships around the orbital structures. What about them?"

"The ships contain biological signatures, millions of them."

Admiral Anderson straightened his back and looked ahead. The return fire from the enemy ships reminded him of looking up at the sky when it rained. But this time it was missiles, torpedoes, guns, and particle beams that were coming toward him.

"Sir, reports from Micaya," said Captain Decker, "It's Conqueror."

Admiral Anderson swallowed and almost choked. He looked to the Captain and could see from her expression that it was the worst possible news.

"She just detonated. Long-range cameras show the remnants of Admiral Lewis' forces are falling back to the orbit of the planet. The Biomech force is in pursuit."

He closed his eyes but only for a second. The man was a good friend of his, and if his ship was gone, then so was he.

"How many ships are lost?"

"Seven, the rest are engaged in a fighting withdrawal.

Other ships are moving in to the area to help. Some might make it out of there safely."

He wiped his brow and looked back to the mainscreen. Three Liberty destroyers were already burning, and yet they pressed on. The tactical display showed his force was deployed in a large formation, almost triangular in shape, and with the most powerful ships at the tip of the formation. He slowed his breathing, calmed himself, and began issuing new orders to the ship squadrons. He also gave the emergency dispersal order to all squadrons.

They can't do any good waiting inside the hull, can they? If they were going to die, it would be better in the cockpit than in the hangar.

That reminded him; Khan and his comrades were still on board. He located their position and made contact.

"Khan, get ready. Are you sure about this?"

"Admiral. As soon as you have his location, you can just point a finger. I'll do the rest."

The communications officer tried to catch his attention.

"Admiral, their commander is transmitting again."

"Can you track it?"

The officer nodded.

"Yes, Admiral, it's the large battleship two rows inside their formation."

He scrolled through the enemy dispositions and then found the group right in the center of the fleet. There were twenty Biomantas in a very loose position, and behind them sat the squat haunches of a massive capital ship. The computer had already identified another five of the same configuration.

"Are you positive? According to me, they have others with the same specification."

Captain Decker pointed to the shape.

"Only one of them has twice as many escorts around it as the rest. Where would you be?"

Anderson wasn't quite sure if that was a complement or a subtle snipe at him.

I have to be certain.

"Is Spartan still transmitting, as in, right now?"

His communications officer nodded and pointed to the image of the talking machines off to the side of the mainscreen.

"Good."

He went back to the tactical display and selected every single squadron, no matter their designation, weapons, or capabilities.

"Everything, fire on him now!"

The speed and efficiency shown by the men and women of the Alliance Navy could have choked up the strongest of officers. It took just seconds before the first ships opened fire, then every gun in the fleet was firing at that single target. As the first projectiles arrived, he watched the footage of Spartan. At first nothing happened, then the feed began to shake, and he spotted vibrations and a few flashes in the background.

It's him.

He pulled the intercom from its mount.

"All ships; proceed with attack plan Alpha. Clear me a path to their General!"

He deliberately avoided using Spartan's name. There were so many, including him that regarded him as something of a living legend. Even now, as he fought against his friends, he found it hard to believe it was really him.

"Captain Decker. Lead in the assault ships. I want boarding parties ready. If we can't destroy her with gunfire, then by hell we'll take her man-to-man."

Ignoring the other battleships and escorts, the combined forces of the Allies focused their efforts on the vessels in close proximity to the flagship of the Biomech fleet. That was the point at which the six battleships opened fire, and both sides joined in the battle. Every Biomech ship opened fired with the weapons available to them.

So it begins.

Admiral Anderson watched the mainscreen with horror as ships exploded every few seconds. The first to go was a Ravager, one of the mightiest of the enemy warships. Combined fire from more than twenty ships of the Grand Alliance tore it apart. Immediately after came three flashes; a Crusader and two of its escorts were vaporized in a similar volley of concentrated fire.

His hands changed the view, and he watched the flagship

as hundreds of fighters moved around the bow, creating a living shield of biomechanical fighters. More and more Biomantas pulled in close and fired on ships from each of the contingents.

Makos, where is he?

A quick glance on the tactical display showed the additional force of ships. Off to the right, and behind the cover created by the destruction of four Ravager warships moved a large force. He counted fifteen Liberty destroyers, all of the Black Ships, and the warships of General Makos. They advanced under a continuous flak corridor from the Alliance ships while hundreds of fighters circled around the ships to fight off their Biomech opposite numbers or to protect against missiles.

Excellent, Makos is the spearpoint, and I'll use it to ram right down Spartan's throat.

With a quick gesture and order, the communications officer opened a secure videostream to the alien commander.

"General."

"Admiral Anderson. What can I do for you?"

"You've found a breach in their flank."

"That's right," he replied in his usual gruff tone, "I've lost six ships getting past their frontline. We're through, and I'm moving back to…"

He considered his words.

"…roll their flank. We'll meet you in the middle."

"Good. Is Khan with you?"

The alien nodded, a custom he had learned quite recently.

"I have all of the remaining Biomech warriors, bandon, Jötnar, and three companies of marines."

"Excellent. Just make one revision to the strategy."

"Yes?"

"Send in the Black Ships, plus all ground forces at your disposal."

"Where to?"

Admiral Anderson selected the ship on his tactical display and sent the data to his opposite number.

"The battleship?" General Makos asked.

"Yes. Send them against the enemy flagship, General. We're having a hard time getting through her screen of escorts. Get your troops on board, find Spartan, and bring him down. Dead or alive, I need him out of the picture. Once you have the ship, we'll finish off the rest of the fleet."

The General gave his customary salute and signed off. Admiral Anderson looked to the scene of the bloody battle at the Rift and shook his head ever so slightly.

Who am I kidding? We'll finish off the rest of their fleet.

He laughed.

With what? We don't have the numbers to win this fight.

* * *

Battleship Retribution, Black Rift, Helios Sector

Spartan watched the battle without making a sound. Both fleets were now committed, and it was obvious to him that in two, perhaps three hours the battle for Helios and the galaxy would be decided. Numbers flashed by inside his armor, but it was the columns of ships on the massive holographic display that interested him the most. As well as showing his dispositions, it toted up the number of active, damaged, and destroyed ships. One-Zero-One watched eagerly as ship after ship was crippled or boarded.

"Ten percent of their fleet has been neutralized," said the machine.

"I know," answered Spartan.

His voice was emotionless. He had already lost thirty ships, and that was half as many ships again as those commanded by Anderson. The losses surprised him, especially with the much-improved Biomanta ships. He could only put it down to the advanced weaponry used by the Byotai that had also joined battle. Not that any of this really mattered. He had numbers on his side.

"What about the reserve?" he asked.

The machine looked at the numbers for several seconds.

"We do not need them. At this rate, their fleet will be gone well before ours. Then we can bring in the rest to begin the conquest of their worlds."

Spartan laughed at the machine's simplistic plan.

"There will be no conquest after this battle. With the fleet smashed, they will have little option but to surrender."

He turned from the hologram and to the machine.

"Did I not promise to win this war within twenty-four hours? They are not interested in the destruction of our ships. Or even the machinery to enter the Rifts. Their eyes are on me, and as long as I live, they will fight to stop me."

"How do you know this?"

Spartan licked his dry lips and found the taste odd.

"Because If I was out there, this is exactly what I would do. Cut off the head, and the animal will die. They are outnumbered. Their only chance of victory is to get to me before they lose all their ships."

"And what if they do?" One-Zero-One asked.

Spartan laughed at the suggestion.

"I have never been beaten in battle before, and this ship is too strong and well protected to be destroyed in time. They can fight for as long as their fleet remains. The numbers are simple; they will have to come here and board this ship, and we will all be waiting for them."

The machine seemed nervous.

"You want to bring them here?"

Again Spartan laughed.

"Of course, I am counting on it.

* * *

ANS Hyperion, The Black Rift, Helios Sector

Khan twisted about and struck his head against the bulkhead inside the Mauler. He was fully armored, and there was no chance of his sustaining even a bruise. Even so, it reminded him that while the battle raged, the only danger he'd faced so far was his own vessel. He straightened himself up and growled.

"What the hell is going on? We have a battle to win. Come on."

He had been waiting since their arrival at the Black Rift for a worthy target, and still they held back behind the protective screen put up by the Liberty escort. The videostreams on his visor showed him the mighty battle, and even he could feel it was the fight to end all fights. He just wanted to be a part of it. Finally, an image popped up. This time it was the Byotai general.

"What do you want?" Khan asked.

The General hissed words back to him while Khan waited for the translation.

"Anderson has given us a new target. We're losing ships too fast. We need something to change."

Khan crashed his fists together.

"Then let me fight. Give me a target."

"Don't worry, Khan, you have one. You're to lead the assault on their flagship. You have command of all my ground forces at your disposal. I am releasing them to you now. Spartan has destroyed more than twenty of our ships already. He must be stopped."

The reptilian alien almost seemed saddened at what was happening. Khan, on the other hand, was nothing but frustrated.

"End this battle, Khan. Bring me his head."

Khan lifted his arms high to the air.

"Yes!"

The image of General Makos vanished, and he found himself almost alone, with just his small entourage of two comrades nearby.

"We have a target, my friends, and it will be glorious."

"What is the plan?" asked Olik.

Knaprig remained silent, but he did lean in a little to listen.

"The flagship. We are to lead the assault. Are you ready?"

Both of them roared approval.

"Good. We will stand alongside Spartan once more."

Both of his friends seemed overjoyed at the chance for battle. Even as they continued their celebration, he found himself remembering the last fight on the Rift Engine. The great battle where he'd been unable to reach his old friend in time.

I failed you, Spartan. I promise we will meet one last time, but one of us will not return alive from the fight.

Olik noticed the glum expression on Khan's face. He must have been all too aware of his feelings about what they had to do.

"Brother, do not worry about such things. We'll probably be dead before we reach him!"

Khan barely heard him, though. All he could do was think back to that last meeting before the battle. Where he, Z'Kanthu, and Spartan had spoken of the plan, and of what was to come. It was then that Spartan had asked him to promise to carry out his wishes, no matter what he saw. It had meant little to him at the time, and he'd easily agreed. Even Z'Kanthu had been eager for him to agree.

Look where that got the old machine? He's just as lost to us as Spartan is.

He shook his head and then moved into his old routine. One at a time he checked his armor, seals, power levels, and weapons, then the high-speed communications between each of the units under his command. He sent status requests, and each of them came back. The first was from Major Terson and Tajt.

It simply read, 'We are ready.'

CHAPTER SEVENTEEN

The worlds of Sol rose to greater importance at the same time as the arrival of Comet C34. Earth and Mars had become backwaters, yet the discovery of hidden machines in the asteroid belts turned the attention of the Alliance military back to these old colonies. Never again would the old worlds of humanity be forgotten. With renewed interest came tougher Alliance control. It would not be long before Earthsec itself would be consigned to the history books.

A Brief History of the Alliance

The Bastion, Old Spascia City, Helion Sector

The column of Alliance Bulldogs moved quickly over the rough terrain. They had been working their way along the narrow trail marking the end of the chasm. The powerful vehicles left a trail of dust behind them that both provided cover and also warned the enemy they were coming.

Right above them hovered two reconnaissance drones. Gunfire from nearby Eques walkers landed around them. The rearguard Bulldog took a heavy hit that blasted away one of its wheels. Incredibly, the tough armored vehicle kept going, its other five wheels maintaining balance and traction. A familiar voice popped into her head.

"Teresa, we've just had word from Anderson. They've smashed the Biomechs at Micaya."

Teresa smiled at the news, but even with all the noise going on, she could tell there was more to it.

"That's good news. We might have a chance."

"Yes. Don't waste time. Get them out of here, and meet me at the mountain. We need to talk."

He disconnected before she could ask any more.

Typical Gun, mysterious to the last.

Jet engines screamed overhead, and a pair of Alliance fighters rushed past the column and strafed at a line of approaching Thegns. The Bulldogs ignored the threat and climbed the last ridge. Finally, the Bastion defenses came into view.

"Okay, Marines, this is it. I want this done and fast, no heroics. Just grab them and get back in."

She checked her own carbine and looked back to the view from the front of the vehicle. The Bastion was an impressive name for what amounted to little more than additional piles of debris. They hit another bump, and then they were just meters away from the temporary barrier that served as a gate.

"Here we go!"

They crashed through just as it pulled apart and raced inside. Teresa's Bulldog was second to go in and skidded to a halt. The door swung out, and then she was on the ground. Shots rushed in from two directions, and the constant chatter of machine guns and carbines told her they were under heavy attack.

"Everybody inside. We're leaving!"

Handfuls of marines and Navy officers pulled wounded comrades and carried them to the vehicles. A female officer helped a Navy Commodore who lifted his hand to make her stop.

"Colonel Morato, good to see you."

"Commodore. We don't have much time."

The man nodded.

"Tell me about it. There is a convoy of machines coming from the south. I have SAAR robots in a rearguard three hundred meters back. They won't last long."

Teresa tagged the location and sent the two Bulldog Mobile Guns into position. They crashed into what remained of the Southern wall and turned their heavy gun turrets on the distant targets. Each of them was equipped with a heavy 60mm Bulldog railgun. They concentrated fire on the heavy walkers and blasted them with repeated volleys of fire. Almost immediately, they were answered with fire from the Thegn skirmish screen and the remaining

Eques walkers.

"In here!" called out a lieutenant from the fourth Bulldog.

More of the survivors came out from their defenses and to the waiting transports. Overhead the screaming sounds of Biomech fighters were joined by newly arrived Hammerheads. The heavy Alliance fighters were well equipped to deal with the lighter enemy craft and showered them with turret fire.

"All done," confirmed the officer.

Teresa was already at the door of her Bulldog and waved the Commodore and three more marines inside. After what felt like an age, she jumped in and hit the button for the door.

"Marines, get out of here!"

The armored personnel vehicles were out first, leaving just a single SAAR robot to defend the bastion. The mobile gun variants began to pull back, but a triple burst of fire from the quickly approaching Eques walkers hit one of them. It caught fire and then spun out of control before tipping over. Teresa watched in horror as another walker clambered over the Southern wall and fired at point blank range.

They had no chance.

She didn't even know the names of the crew inside that vehicle, and now they were dead; all volunteers for the rescue mission. She breathed slowly and looked across to the Commodore.

"Looks like you had a hard fight back there."

The man nodded, but his face showed he was in a great deal of pain.

"Colonel, your status?" Gun asked over the communications channel.

"We're heading for the bridges. ETA three minutes."

"Good, don't hang around. We've got trouble on the way."

Teresa shook her head, more of annoyance than surprise. She activated the external feeds and connected to them via her helmet interface. The old city of Spascia was ablaze and surrounded by smoke. Apart from that she could see little had changed.

"What is it?"

The audio crackled before Gun spoke.

"They are bringing in the last of their ships, and I mean, everything. Their course will bring them directly to our current position."

"You think this is the big one?"

"Based on what's happening everywhere else, yes. This is the Biomechs' big push. Get over the bridges fast, Colonel. I am blowing them the second you cross."

"Understood."

The remaining Bulldogs made the trip in substantially less time than it had taken to get there. As they streamed across the bridges, it was clear that Gun was taking no chances. All Allied forces had moved back, leaving nothing but sentry units and SAAR robots to provide a modicum of defense. As they reached the halfway point, a massive barrage began. The entire side of the chasm nearest the mountain was filled with flashes, as everything from railguns, mortars, and the Helion mountain guns and the exotic weapons of the Khreenk joined machine guns.

"What's happening?" asked the Commodore.

Teresa shook her head in astonishment. She tapped a button, and a large display unit activated toward the front of the vehicle. The footage was grainy but gave a good view from exactly three hundred meters above their current position.

"It's a defensive bombardment. The Biomechs have the city, and they are almost at the bridges."

One of the marines gasped as the narrow, most northern bridge vanished in a series of blasts. The other bridges quickly followed, and the man looked back to Teresa, his face white with nerves.

"What about us?"

Teresa nodded.

"Don't worry. Gun won't kill us."

The man seemed far from reassured. Even so, they reached the last section of the bridge and skidded past the landing pads that were already being abandoned. No sooner had the final mobile gun variant crossed than the first three Decurions reached the opposite side.

"Look," said Teresa.

She pointed at the shapes moving onto the bridge. At the same time, a pattern of flashes started at the strong points and mountings. Then one by one the long span sections tore away and dropped down into the chasm. The small number of wounded cheered inside the Bulldog. It was half-hearted, but the relief was clear. They continued up the trail to the blast walls the marines had been constructing. Each line was at least five meters tall, thick, and topped with razor wire. Metal towers were spaced apart at regular intervals and fitted with standard heavy weapons. The videoscreen changed as it was overridden by Gun. The imagery showed him inside the mountain, surrounded by his personal guard.

"We have detected incoming radiation signatures. This may be an atomic strike. All forces are to withdraw to secure locations in the mountain or in your vehicles. The first impacts will take place in...sixty seconds."

"No way, man," moaned the pale-faced marine.

Teresa disconnected her harness and pulled open the hatch leading to the driver's compartment. The two marines at the front were chattering nervously while maneuvering around the scores of personnel running for the mountain.

"How much further?"

The second marine, who had been waving his arms to the front, looked back at her and answered, "Colonel, uh…just a few more seconds. The Helion blast doors are right there."

He turned back around and pointed to the vast doors. They were meters thick and big enough to drive multiple vehicles through in one go. The space off into the distance was completely black, in stark contrast to the muted light outside.

"Hold on," said the driver.

They hit a bump where the corrugated road laid down by the marines joined up with the ancient Helion surface. It was a minor surface change, but it still threw the occupants about. Then they were inside the mountain, and the exterior lamps on the vehicle activated. That, combined with the lights inside tunnel, showed the mass of refugees from the outer districts of the city. They moved on another fifty meters and into a vast underground parking pool. Ramps went both up and down, and dozens more military vehicles were ferrying people about. They moved onto the lower ramp and to the level that ran alongside a vast parade or assembly ground. Hundreds of marines were scattered about in clumps, while dozens of Vanguards moved about among them.

"Everybody out."

The Bulldog skidded to a halt, and Teresa jumped out. As her feet hit the ground, she felt the rumble of guns. These were not the artillery strikes from before; these were the smaller turrets and gun mounts firing.

Air defense, they are here.

She looked to her right and found the massive armored form of Gun and six of his bodyguards approaching. Behind them came another platoon of marines with the odd Khreenk straggler staying with them.

"Colonel, good work," said Gun.

A loud thump made her turn around. She could just about see the entrance to the tunnel that they had recently entered. The light faded and then vanished.

"We're sealed in?" she asked.

Gun nodded, moving closer.

"I've positioned units on every level. This is the lowest central complex. The tunnels on this level move out to the armories, medical bays, and vehicle pools."

A great rumble shook the ground, and handfuls of dust fell from the high ceilings. Teresa looked back at the vast open space and the waiting warriors. Looking up the chamber seemed more like the inside of a volcano. Ramps led off at the flank, and right above them was a ceiling made from solid rock.

"Six levels up; that's where the weapon is fitted. We've got it working again, and it's operating in a schedule. Orders from Anderson are to hit the Black Rift, whether it's open or not."

Teresa grabbed his arm.

"What did you want to tell me? Have you had news about Spartan?"

The wizened warrior's expression changed at the mention of the name. He looked at her, his expression suggesting he was thinking, perhaps deciding what to say.

"Come on, tell me."

A triple blast echoed from below, and the ground shook as though an earthquake had just occurred. Gun ignored her question and pointed up into the hollowed out mountain.

"Teresa, I need response teams to cover their assault. Drone scans show they are coming here with a purpose. There are ships heading this way, and I think they intend on ending this today."

He pointed at Teresa.

"I want you to take a team to the top. If they try and burn their way through, they will be bastards to dig out."

"And you?"

Gun beamed at her.

"I will be three levels down with the siege guns. Captain Tycho is with the Vanguards. He will operate our rapid reserve. Anything we need, he can send up the mountain through the shafts."

Teresa nodded in agreement.

"What's this place like?"

"Complicated. Our engineers counted over sixty kilometers of tunnels."

Teresa looked at him and found herself surprised at how far he'd come. On Prometheus he'd been a monster, but one with a conscience. Now he was an articulate leader of men, a warrior that millions would follow into battle. Even her.

"And my son? Where is he?"

Gun indicated to the entrance near the ramps leading to the next levels up. He's in the medical bay, along with the other wounded. He's on the grid. You can monitor his progress."

Teresa did just that. With a few levels of authorization, she had the real-time information. She shuddered at seeing his prognosis. It wasn't good.

"He's still in a coma," she said quietly, shaking her head.

"Wait," said Gun.

His expression changed to a frown. He spoke a few words and then looked to her. He clearly wanted to say something. A red flash lit up his visor, and he moved quickly to his right.

"Take cover, now!"

The mountain shuddered, and then came impact after impact. Teresa ran along with dozens of marines, as they made for the protection of arches, tunnels, doorways, and shafts. More dust broke free from the ceiling, and then gaps appeared. Teresa reached a ramp leading down to a storage facility. She made it halfway down when the first massive impact occurred. The strike was so great that she was lifted from her feet. Gun was thrown to the nearest wall and fell backwards. His bodyguards rushed to help, and then more impacts came in.

"Stay down!" he yelled.

Cracks popped up throughout the ceiling, and then entire sections of masonry ripped off. The ceiling was so far up in the air that it took sometime for the chunks to hit the ground. Another impact quickly followed, and a huge chunk of wall near the motor pool vanished. A rock splintered and tore apart and was replaced by the bow of a crippled Ravager warship. The wreckage pushed on until it reached halfway into the facility. Teresa tried to stand, but the impact continued.

"Jack!"

She looked around and then spotted the entrance to the medical bay. Dozens of people were rushing inside. More masonry above the site broke apart, and another chunk of shattered ship tore through, vaporizing the entire area in an instant. The ruined section spun about and crashed into the crippled Ravager.

"No!" she yelled.

Hands pulled her back, but she pushed them away. The dull rumble of short-range atomics continued to echo through the mountain. Dust and explosions filled the air, and still the impacts continued. She glanced at the real-time data from Jack, but all contact had been lost. Hatches and doors opened throughout the Ravager, and hundreds of Biomech warriors streamed out. The first to hit the ground were Thegns, and right behind them came the entire range of war machines.

"Stay down!" hollered a nearby marine.

Teresa ignored the man and walked out into the open. She pulled up her carbine and blasted the first two Thegns. One spotted her and returned fire. A single round deflected from her leg, and she dropped down to one knee. More shots whisked overhead, and she put rounds into another creature. Small groups of marines emerged from their hiding places to surround the crashed ships.

"Protect the Colonel!" someone shouted.

Five marines ran past her and right into the path of an Eques walker. The machine crashed down from the Ravager, along with a large group of Decurions. Vanguard Marines advanced from the left, but the Biomechs had numbers on their side. Teresa aimed at the machine, but it turned its attention on the nearest marines. Its turrets spun about and opened fire. Two were torn apart, and the third took a round in the face. A small proximity bomb rolled along the floor, and Teresa scrambled to get out of the way. It exploded, and sent her flying nearly ten meters through the air.

* * *

The first thing Teresa felt was a sharp pain in her leg. She looked down and spotted the piece of metal embedded just below the knee. It looked like the arm of a Decurion that had been snapped off half a meter from her. Blood ran down the wound, and when she tried to move, there was nothing but numbness from the knee down.

It's the armor, painkillers and suppressors.

"Colonel, we have to move."

She looked to her right and found Gun holding the broken body of a Decurion. He lifted it to the side and then hurled it at two approaching Thegns. One raised its arms to protect itself, and Gun used the opportunity to open fire with his shoulder-mounted gun. He looked back to her and nodded. A pair of his bodyguards helped her to her feet, and she immediately groaned.

"You have to walk. The facility has been breached. They hit us with atomics and then crashed the last of their ships all around the mountain. First to go was the landing pads, then the air defense sites."

Gun grunted as a bullet struck his armor. He turned around and blasted a Thegn emerging from the blackness.

"The armory medical center, vehicle pool. It's all gone. We've got no air cover left, and the fleet left to help Anderson and his plan. We're falling back."

The mention of the medical center wasn't a shock, but it still dulled her thoughts even more. She looked about but didn't recognize the place. The ceiling was much lower, and the lighting was only provided by the armor worn by the defenders. There was barely enough room for Gun to move.

"Where are we?"

Gun looked back, fired a single shot, and then kept on moving.

"The machines have taken the upper levels. Our engineers set thermite charges before we left. The mountain is gone. We're heading for the west and the secondary lines. Captain Tycho is preparing them right now."

Teresa took a step, and the pain almost threw her down. The ground shook, and part of the tunnel behind them lowered with a grinding sound. Chunks of rubble dropped down and struck those nearby. Teresa tried to move to help, but Gun grabbed her, pulling her toward the direction the rest of the marines were heading in. She hopped and groaned as they moved meter-by-meter from the devastation wrought through the mountain.

"No, they need our help!"

She pushed back at him, but his armored limbs were impervious to her touch.

"Behind us!" shouted a marine.

The man turned back and pulled himself low. He lifted his carbine and fired a long burst before looking to Gun.

"General, we've got more back there. They're pinned down at the junction."

Gun tried to move back, but the partial collapse of the tunnel made it impossible for him to get through. He bent down and shone his lamp deep into the ruins of the mountain. Further back was the wide-open intersection where the tunnels from all four directions joined. The center space was large enough for half a dozen Bulldogs. In the middle were thirty or more marines, with a sprinkling of Helion militiamen.

"He's right. I need a squad to go back."

Part of the ceiling cracked, and then another chunk dropped down to open a hole to the level above them. A Decurion dropped through and embedded its blades into the nearest marine. One of Gun's bodyguards smashed its fist into the machine and then forced it against the sidewall. Two marines blasted it apart with close range carbine fire. More limbs appeared in the hole, and three more machines dropped in to attack them. Gun swung his fists at any that dared to come near him. As he released his grip, Teresa took that as an opportunity to get away. She staggered from Gun and looked to the marine next to her.

"Pull it out, now."

She nodded to the embedded chunk of metal. The Private turned to check with Gun, but Teresa struck him across the helmet with the butt of her carbine.

"Now!"

The men knelt down and placed his knee against her armored leg. He grabbed the chunk of metal and then yanked. The severed and razor sharp piece pulled out and clattered to the ground. Blood oozed from behind the hole and ran down her leg. Teresa cried out but punched at the ground, making sure she stayed conscious. With two commands, she sent the drugs through her body, as well as the sealant mist to stem the bleeding, cauterize the wound, and keep her in the fight.

"Are you insane? You cannot go back," said Gun.

Other marines were still moving out of the tunnel, with only two standing their ground with their commanding officers. A single Jötnar in the color of Gun's personal guard was also there. Teresa shook her head.

"Spartan's lost somewhere up there, and Jack is probably dead inside this mountain. I have to do something."

Teresa nodded to the direction they were retreating to.

"You need to hold this side of the tunnel. Watch our backs. We'll be back."

She didn't even wait for his answer. Gun watched as the wounded Colonel crawled back through the rubble, along with two marines. In seconds they were gone, and Gun was left in the tunnel with just the last two marines and the single Jötnar.

"Typical Teresa," he said with a chuckle.

"General, get back."

He moved, not even thinking of what it might be. The Thegn landed a meter to his side and swung a pair of razor sharp blades. Gun blasted it to shreds with his shoulder-mounted gun while laughing.

"Come on, you can do better than this."

He could hear movement above and used the moment

of calm to shuffle back a few more meters, still keeping his lamps and weapons trained on the hole. A quick movement of his eyes gave him a glimpse of the small gap in the tunnel that Teresa had gone through. He could hear gunfire coming from that side.

Spartan, you old fool, it's best she never knows.

Teresa reached the other side and activated her vision modes. The thermal imaging allowed her to see through the smoke and dust. At the end of the shaft were the intersection and the pinned down marines. Thegns and Decurions hit them repeatedly from three directions, and more climbed out of a breach in the floor just the other side of the rubble. One jumped out and turned around to rush the trapped marines.

"Hey!" Teresa shouted.

The Thegn looked back, surprised to find anybody at the partially collapsed tunnel. A single high-power round tore through its body. The two marines added their own fire and shredded the unfortunate creature. Two more climbed from the hole and fired toward the intersection.

"With me."

Teresa limped closer and closer to the Thegns and embedded her bayonet in the back of the nearest one's skull. The second saw the attack and twisted around, but it was too slow. The pair of marines shot at point-blank range, killing the thing instantly. The bodies fell to the ground, and they moved on past them.

"Don't shoot," said Teresa, moving out of the darkness.

"Where the hell did you come from?" asked a tall Marine sergeant.

Teresa glanced at the man, recognizing him from somewhere.

"Sergeant…Stone."

"Yes, Sir," said the man.

Teresa looked down and found the reason for them staying where they were. The badly mangled shape of a wounded lieutenant lay there. He was missing a leg, and there were two deep wounds in his chest. Even so, the man still lived.

"Lieutenant Elvidge," said the young officer, "You need to get out of here. This entire place is falling apart."

"Colonel Morato, and we're getting out of here, all of us," Teresa snapped back.

"Morato?" Sergeant Stone asked.

A howl came from the shaft off to the left.

"Come on," said Teresa.

The group moved back along the debris-filled shaft; each taking care to protect the route back. No sooner had they left the intersection when more than a dozen Decurions with Thegn support moved in from two of the tunnels. They merged at the intersection and looked about aimlessly, lost now that their prize had vanished.

"Keep going," said Sergeant Stone.

The first of the group were already at the section with

the collapsed rubble. Several new chunks had broken down, and it was now only big enough to squeeze through one at a time. Teresa and Sergeant Stone brought up the rearguard while the others helped each other through the narrow space.

"Hold them back," said Teresa.

The enemy had spotted their attempt to escape and opened fire. Two rounds struck nearby, and a third hit the Sergeant in the chest. The round deflected and embedded itself deep into the tunnel walls.

* * *

Gun watched the survivors crawl from the hole with widening eyes. First came a pair of privates, then a badly wounded officer with a missing leg. By the time the sixth came through, they were hit again. More holes had opened up on the sidewalls right next to the partially collapsed ceiling. Thegns appeared almost continually now, and for a moment the evacuation stopped.

"Get them out of here!" growled Gun.

He moved closer to the damage and blocked the path. Each time a Thegn appeared, he would stab or shoot instantly sending them back. After the fourth attempt, they backed off.

"Now, send more through."

Another marine climbed through the gap and squeezed

past Gun and out into the tunnel. More followed, but Gun could hear the sound of further enemy forces closing the distance. He took a step back and crouched down, but the gap was too low and too small for him to see through. Another marine came through and then an entire group of them. He was forced to stand back as each of them struggled to get past his armored form.

"More artillery!" shouted one as he rushed away.

Gun checked his helmet display, but he'd lost all contact with friendly forces. In any case, it didn't matter. The shells struck in a bombardment that occurred one after the other. Sections of the ceiling tore apart, and he was forced to keep moving back or risk being trapped inside.

"Colonel, get out of there...now!"

He spotted movement in the gap and reached out to help. It wasn't friendly though, and instead the arm was metallic and sharp. It flailed about and tore a chunk of plating from Gun's arm. He took aim, but another clambered out of a breach in the ceiling and ripped at his main gun.

"Gun!" yelled his guards.

All of them opened fired, and the shaft filled with muzzle flashes and bullets. Thegns squeezed through and began to overwhelm the rearguard. Gun became enraged and swung and smashed his legs and fists into anything he could find. Blood, metal, and flesh filled the tunnel. One Thegn stopped as it emerged from the hole and then a blade pushed out through its mouth. A marine pulled himself past the body and then looked back to help pull Teresa through.

"Good, follow me."

Gun turned around and moved back nearly ten meters. Another massed bombardment shook the tunnel, and a piece of masonry dropped down and struck his neck. He stumbled and fell to one knee. He looked back and saw dozens of Thegns swarming in after him. One hacked and stabbed at Sergeant Stone, but he struck back with his bayoneted carbine. Something grabbed at Gun, and he looked up. A Decurion had worked its way along the ceiling and then dropped down onto a bodyguard's torso. It punched blades into his armor before moving to the marines. More of them swarmed in from a dozen breaches, and Gun and his escort were quickly surrounded.

"Kill them all!" he yelled, and in a berserk fury he struck at all and any that dared to come close. After the third kill, he could just make out the hole where Teresa and the Sergeant had been. There were dozens of Thegns there now, and he could only imagine what horrors lay on the other side. Then he spotted an arm, then a face.

"Teresa!"

The battered marine pulled herself through the hole and dropped down alongside Sergeant Stone. Her armor had been penetrated in a dozen places, and her helmet ripped off. Even as she lay there, a Decurion advanced and threw itself at the two marines. Sergeant Stone forced himself to his feet and lifted his carbine. He was still firing as the thing hit him and pinned his body against the Colonel's. More of them rushed in to block the tunnel, and that was when Gun spotted Teresa's hand. She clenched her fist tight around a thermite detonation charge. Gun swung his fists again and crunched a Thegn against the wall. Another Decurion punched a limb through his shoulder, and then the end of the tunnel vanished in a bright flash that collapsed the entire section furthest from Gun. Whole chunks of stone dropped down around him, but as the dust cleared, he could see nothing of the two marines, or even the foes that had assaulted them.

"General, can you move?" asked a voice from behind.

With great effort, he twisted around and looked at the faces of three young marines. He pushed hard, but his legs were trapped.

"Kind of, give me a moment."

With all of his strength, he pushed the ground hard and forced his battered body from the rubble. Pain seared through his shoulder, as half of the broken Decurion slid off to leave two deep puncture wounds in his torso. His left leg was still trapped, and he was tempted to tear the limb off to escape.

"Captain Tycho sent us and the rest of the 35th to secure the breaches."

The man turned around and waved to a distant shape. It

stomped closer until Gun could see it was a bullet ridden CES engineer.

"Hold on, Sir. I'll get you out of there in a second," said the operator.

The CES unit smashed and dug away to clear the debris. As it worked, Gun looked back at where he'd last seen Teresa and the Sergeant, and sighed.

It was a good death.

CHAPTER EIGHTEEN

Hyperion was a thriving world, filled with vegetation and wildlife. The colonization by the Jötnar might have been the end for this way of life, but unlike most Alliance worlds, Hyperion flourished. Wildlife continued to thrive, and the Jötnar took to the lush planet with relish. Even when captured Biomech creatures were released, they turned large swathes of forest into great hunting reserves. Over time, the Jötnar would prove some of the least destructive custodians in the history of man.

The Downfall of Hyperion

ANS Hyperion, The Black Rift, Helios Sector

Khan growled as a burst of gunfire raked his Mauler and tore off one of its engines. The Alliance Navy pilot pulled off an impressive spin to avoid further shots and then fell in alongside the scores of other similar craft.

"How much longer?" Khan asked.

"Sixty seconds," replied the pilot over the intercom.

The craft shuddered again with such large numbers of Maulers and fighters streaming in to the battleship. Capital ships moved in with them so that the distance between the vessels of both sides dropped down to just a few kilometers. Explosions followed one another, as ships and fighters were ripped apart in a vicious maelstrom. One Liberty destroyer was cut clean in half from a Ravager ramming it at high speed.

"Thirty seconds."

They were past the escort now, and Khan could see the forward view from the Mauler directly inside his visor. The battleship completely filled the view, and the levels of gunfire were like nothing he'd ever seen. As they swept down to the shattered hangar on the port bow, he found himself shaking his head in amazement.

"How the hell did we survive that?"

Olik laughed.

"Plenty didn't. What about the Black Ships? They are still closing, and we're running low on Maulers."

"Ten seconds."

Khan felt his muscles tense up.

"Ram her. They can disembark through the breaches."

Olik and Knaprig were amazed at what they heard, but neither made a protest. Khan sent the orders, and then the Mauler shook violently. The display went dark, and Khan was forced to revert to his own eyes and sensor.

"To me, my brothers."

The doors hissed open on both sides, and the ramps dropped down. To Khan's surprise there was normal, if slightly heavier gravity than was standard on Alliance ships. He took three steps and leapt out to land hard onto the hangar floor. The other two followed right behind him, along with a dozen marines. The Mauler groaned and then lifted itself up and twisted around. With a short burst from its engines, it pushed away, and its place was taken by the next. Khan watched it move back into space and then shook his head.

Weird.

He looked back deep inside the enemy warship. It was a large, but poorly lit space. He'd counted multiple similar entrances on the way in, and each of them joined two passageways through doors at the far end. The walls curved up to meet above them in what looked like a long, spinal central section. Khan turned his eyes a little to the right and checked on the arrival patterns of his forces. They were taking lots of fire coming in, but already he could see he had troops at three more hangars just a few hundred meters away.

"Secure the hangars, establish a perimeter."

His orders were simple and direct. More marines were already in his hangar, and they rushed ahead in a loose skirmish line. Two SAAR robots trundled after them, continually scanning left and right with their built-in turrets. Khan followed ten meters behind them. They traveled at a fast walk, all checking the shadows for signs of the enemy. There were no spacecraft in the open space but plenty of racks for machine parts, as well as two dismantled transports that filled the right-hand side. The doorways at the far end were big and shaped in much the same way as the walls and ceilings. Each was sealed with a thick metallic like blast door.

Keep moving, Khan told himself.

He looked up and only now noticed the single gantry running directly under the spine on the ceiling. He tracked along it and found it vanished into a hole near the back wall. An alert sounded, and he turned his head to watch a fourth Mauler unload its precious cargo. This time is was Major Terson and his entourage of marines and Thegns. They stormed out in equal numbers and made for the sidewalls. The Major, however, just marched in a direct line toward Khan. Behind him came three CES engineers and a handful of Vanguards. They moved with little grace as they stomped through the cavernous ship.

"That man is either brave or stupid as hell."

Olik laughed.

"Like he's doing anything different to us."

"Major Terson. There's another way in to the ship, along the ceiling gantry up there," he said over the internal network.

The Major was a hundred meters away and stopped to check the structure.

"I see it, sending scouts in now."

The officer gave several hand gestures, and then two-dozen Thegns armed with Marine Corps carbines split off and began climbing the walls. They were quick and reached the gantry in less than a minute. Major Terson reached Khan, and both watched the rest of the Thegns pour inside from newly arrived Maulers.

"We're ready, Khan. What's the plan?"

The huge warrior extended his right arm to the doorways ahead.

"We breach the doors and then swarm the place. The layout is new to us, so we sweep the entire ship."

"Spartan?"

Khan nodded grimly. "Anderson wants his head. Dead or alive."

"Fair enough," said the Marine, with a little too much relish for Khan's liking.

"Let's do this," Khan gave the signal, and the engineers moved forward. The three of them advanced past the lines of warriors and right up to the massive reinforced doorway.

"Will they get through?" Olik asked.

Major Terson looked up to him. Next to each other the marine looked puny, with the Jötnar well over two and half meters tall and encased in armor. Like all of those that had left Prometheus, he now wore the crimson of the Red Watch. It was an honorific gift from Osk to all of those that took part on the battle for Prometheus. She was the Jötnar garrison's commander of the Alliance outpost.

"They are Alliance engineers. There's nothing they can't build or pull down. Just watch."

Khan did, but he also sent the same orders to all Alliance forces landing on the battleship. As sparks began to fly, he checked the status of the space battle and felt his heart lurch. A crusader had just been destroyed, and lifeboats were swarming around it.

Time is not with us. When that comes down, we're going to have to hurry.

He looked to the Major.

"The SAAR robots go in first, then the reconnaissance drones. We need to find the CIC or throne room. Whatever it is they have, we need to be in there in minutes."

"Agreed."

More flashes came from the great doorway, and then came bright white blasts. An urgent fleet-wide flashcom scrolled along the bottom of the visor. It was short and simple.

'One Planetary defense system is active. Impact due to arrive in ten minutes.'

"Not much longer," said the Major.

Khan cracked his joints and activated his arm blades. Short but cruel looking weapons slid out to the sides of his arms. The shoulder-mounted Gatling gun spun three revolutions and then stopped. Then the engineers tore the doorway apart, and a great gust of cool air washed out into the hangar.

"Attack!" was the only word Khan needed to say.

The SAAR robots went through, and the rest of the warriors surged in behind. Khan spotted the shapes of his own Thegns on the gantries above them. He held his breath, leapt through the breached doorway, and emerged into a massive facility that must have run almost half the entire length of the ship. There were shielded compartments in all directions, and multi-level gantries disappeared up high into the vessel's superstructure. Right in front of the door there were at least a dozen curved ramps that led up into the ship.

"Incoming!" yelled a marine.

Unlike the hangars, this large section of the ship was a hive of activity. Flickers of light rippled off into the distance and up the ramps, gantries, and platforms. A dozen marines were cut down where they stood before the Vanguards, Jötnar, and CES engineers could push past. With their thick armor, they deflected most of the fire and pushed ahead into a wide crescent. Khan took the center and did his best to ignore the warnings from the computer as dozens of projectiles struck him.

"Send in the Thegns. Spread out and attack. Swarm them!"

It was a cruel tactic, but Khan saw the Thegns as expendable meat shields, and they did their job well. More than a hundred rushed out in front of the line of armor, while a similar number pulled their bodies on top of the metal walkways and moved like spiders up through the compartments. Marines followed them, but they were more cautious.

"Advance."

The line of armored warriors took a step at a time behind the skirmishing Thegns. Gunfire flashed down to meet them, but the return fire had now increased. Additional SAAR robots had rushed in and were sending long bursts high up into the superstructure. Every few seconds, the body of an armored Thegn would tumble down and crash to the ground.

"Keep going. Get close and past their guns."

Khan would have ideally kept them back so they could take their time to work through the vessel. Time was a luxury he lacked, and there was a good chance that if they were slow, the enemy would simply abandon the ship. On they moved and did their best to ignore the fire. Blue pulses crashed down at them from hidden Biomech soldiers, but each shot was responded to by a flurry of gunfire.

"Sir, look," said a marine.

Khan glanced to the right and tried to forget about the bullet that had just managed to pierce his thigh armor. To the right he could see a ramp running down a level and leading to a wide-open space. The doorway was tall, and inside were lines of suits of armor.

"Looks like an armory. Well found, Marine."

A quick check on his visor showed him where the squad commanders were. He tagged the nearest.

"Lieutenant, take a demolition team into these locations and destroy anything you find."

"Yes, Sir."

Khan couldn't even see the man from where he was, but that didn't matter right now. He took another four steps and passed under a low-hanging bridge. The section connected the sides of the hull together and also doubled as a point to reach the next two levels up.

"Time for the machines."

Major Terson was a short distance behind him and sheltered behind Khan's leg. A rocket whistled down and was destroyed by the built-in interceptors on Khan's armor.

"Decurions?" asked the Major.

Khan nodded.

"They can easily take these levels. Bring the Eques walkers to this point and establish a bridgehead. They might try to work around our flanks."

Major Terson looked confused.

"A bridgehead. You planning on staying here for long?"

Khan laughed.

"If Spartan is here, you know what the fight is going to

be like. We can take no chances. If this thing falls apart, then the machines will have to be our rearguard while we get everybody else out."

"Understood."

* * *

Battleship Retribution, Black Rift, Helios Sector

The rotating holographic model was a complete mess. Biomech ships and their foes intermingled in a vast battle that now covered thousands of kilometers in every direction. Fighter squadrons fought continuous battles against each other while capital ships lined up to exchange broadsides. The modified Biomantas operated in hunting packs to pick off damaged or stray ships while avoiding the box formations of Liberty ships.

"This is a bloodbath," he agreed, more to himself than anybody else.

One-Zero-One kept looking down from their high position deep inside the warship. The machine gave the impression it was fearful, always on the lookout for something dangerous. It looked back to Spartan.

"Why have you let them board us?"

Spartan sighed.

"Have you not listened to a word I have said? They are throwing their best at us. When their commanders and elite troops are gone, who will remain?"

Thayara approached from the darkness and to alongside Spartan. There were marks on her armor and fresh cuts to her right leg.

"The weak will remain. Spartan is right. They have sent their best. The only question is can they be beaten?"

All three machines turned to face each other, an unholy triumvirate of metal and flesh.

"How many?" One-Zero-One asked.

Thayara laughed.

"Thousands. They have warriors, machines, and even your own Thegns."

Spartan turned away and pointed to the battle raging throughout the Helios Sector.

"We have drawn them all here. Some of The Twelve will be here, on this ship to command the bandon."

The machine shuddered and approached him. It extended one of its limbs to touch him.

"And the others?"

"If we make this the focus of the battle, then they will come. They cannot afford to ignore our other ships. The new Biomantas are picking off any ship firing on us. It will take too long to destroy us, and time is a luxury only we have."

"What do you suggest?"

Spartan looked at Thayara and then to the machine.

"You take command of the ship. Stay here and direct the battle. I will join Thayara and lead the Ghost Warriors into the heart of their boarding party."

He then pointed to the machine.

"Send in Biorays from the Ravagers. Hit their capital ships with assault teams. That will stop them sending in more help. Keep them busy and their attention away from what is happening."

"And what of The Twelve?"

Spartan laughed at the question.

"Trust me, when they know I am here and killing their allies, they will come. Don't forget, I slew their leader in front of you."

Spartan turned away and made it a few meters before Thayara stopped him. She looked back to One-Zero-One.

"Do you have footage of the death of the heretic?"

A blue sphere appeared alongside the machine and then a slightly grainy model of Spartan and the machines popped up. The death of the noble leader of the rebels could be clearly seen, as could Spartan.

"Good. Send that out on all channels. It should be enough to motivate them."

Spartan pushed her away and continued toward the edge of the exposed plinth. He balanced right on the edge before turning his gaze to them.

"Do what you want. It is actions that will end this, not words."

With those bitter words, he leapt from the raised position and sailed down. It took several seconds before he crashed feet first to the ground. The pistons groaned under the weight of the impact, and then he was upright and in the middle of the columns of Ghost Warriors.

"Thayara, with me. Let's end this, today!"

The lithe female warrior leapt from the same tall balcony and twisted about in a balletic fashion before landing just five meters from him. Her feet struck the ground with enough force to leave deep gouges in its surface.

"Warriors!" she cried out.

A loud screaming sound of ancient metal moving on tortured cogs marked the release of the bars holding the armor in place. As each rod of metal slid back, another Ghost Warrior stepped out from its resting place. Dozens and dozens of them were freed until after less than a minute the entire complement of seventy-five were ready. Hundreds more of the heavily armed Thegns moved out from a myriad of passageways and secret walkways throughout the ship.

"Spartan!" called out One-Zero-One from his position up high, "Our ships are being pressed. The Byotai have destroyed one of our ancient battleships. Seventy-five of my kin are lost forever."

Spartan looked to Thayara and to the machine.

"I thought you could to send in another Ghost warrior?"

One-Zero-One said something unintelligible, clearly an insult.

"No. Only those with a place among our ancestors are

safe from death. The others, the Defeated, they must earn their place by defeating the enemy before being granted such an honor."

Spartan moved two steps and looked back.

"Like you?"

"The three of us have been granted this honor. Do not waste it."

Spartan wasn't quite sure what this meant, but the vibrations for multiple hits to the ship pulled his attention back to the fight. He left at a quick pace while One-Zero-one called after him.

"The enemy are causing heavier than expected causalities. There is a chance they could match us and fight to a draw."

Spartan looked up at the machine.

"Just keep us in the fight. Bring in the reinforcements and smash them. You deal with the fleet; I'll deal with the intruders."

He didn't bother checking to see if the machine had heard, let alone acknowledged his orders. Instead, Spartan marched out, with Thayara beside him, and a long column of biomechanical warriors following right behind. He'd never paid much attention to the internal layout of the ship, yet as they walked the details popped up like newly loaded software. The schematic inside his armor showed all of his warriors, as well as the known positions for the enemy.

"So, we get a mystical free pass to live with the ancestors. Mean anything to you?"

Thayara sighed.

"Spartan, I really do not care. We have a battle to win. I say we head for their landing sites at the bow. Cut them off and then work our way back. They will be trapped and easily overrun."

Spartan nodded in agreement.

"Good plan. Take half with you and hit them hard."

Thayara stopped and turned back to him.

"And what about you?"

"Two-thirds of their troops are coming down the central spine and making their way to the battle deck. I'm going to meet them right in the middle."

He tagged the location in the center of the ship, and Thayara instantly recognized it. The shape was a vast dome, surrounded by high viewing platforms and entry points to a hundred different tunnels through the vessel.

"The training arena?" she asked.

"Yeah, we'll end this the way it started."

She split away from him, and three files of Ghost Warriors followed her. There was little, if any way to tell them apart, but for now they operated under their joint command. Spartan imagined it wouldn't take much for them to revert to their normal programming.

"With me," he snarled.

Spartan left at such a pace, only the Thegns could

initially keep up with him. They passed two separate sets of ammunition stores and the secondary weapon deck before moving to a massive ramp. It was wide enough to land an escort warship on, and the ceiling must have been at least fifty meters from the ground.

* * *

Kha'Dri, Taxxu, Uncharted Space

The Biomech commander watched the stable Rift without flinching. Hundreds more ships waited patiently for their orders. The Rift flickered, and flashes and sparks rippled along the Rift Engine positioned inside the bridge in space and time.

The fools, they think they can control our Spacebridges. At this point, all they can do is be a nuisance. They are too late.

The Rift Engines, the mightiest vessels in their entire arsenal, dwarfed even the battleships. Groups of ancient Biomantas circled them as though they expected trouble.

The Defeated, ever watchful of themselves.

The machine looked to the cocoon and felt a wave of resentment, tinged with responsibility. As the youngest, he was expected to do more than their kin had managed in the past. He was no different to any of the other so-called Ghost Warriors. Even the one called One-Zero-One was little different, but to him only their history mattered. Along with the other five, he was the most sacred of

484

less than a thousand remaining Kybernetes, the ancient steersmen of old.

What would they say? he wondered.

He wanted to speak with them, to seek their advice. But to do so would be to consign his race to the present age. Encased in machines they could live for centuries, and inside the confines of an ancient Ark like Kha'Dri, they could rest their immortal remains for several thousand years. After that, they could only ever expect to live inside the confines of the ancient Core. Even thinking about the Core, that ancient tomb that sat deep inside Kha'Dri, sent a chill through his own ancient body.

I must seek their wisdom.

He was tempted to contact them, to explain his plan for their victory and salvation. But a nagging doubt, a fear that the Defeated might fail stayed his hand. The honor of joining them in the Core was a gift granted to few, and there was nothing he wanted more than to live alongside his ancient comrades once more.

I will wait until I have news. I must show myself as worthy.

That wasn't a problem, but there was always a chance the invasion might fail, in which case he would have marked his entire species for extinction.

No, it is enough to risk one of us to end this. I have to succeed.

The interior of Kha'Dri, the last remaining operational World Ship of his race was a vessel of awe, even to him. His ancestors had used such vessels to travel vast distances and to colonize worlds, while maintaining the wisdom of those that had passed on long before. Now just two remained and the other, known by its sacred name of Du'Li had been abandoned followed the murder of its occupants in the uprising with The Twelve. Now its hulk drifted around Taxxu, a constant reminder of the betrayal and the war that had split their race apart. Even its Core lay shattered, the memories and thoughts of a billion Ancients lost to war.

We are the last six of the living Ancients. The last that retain mortal flesh and remember the days before the colonization of these worlds. We will use their flesh to rebuild our people, to create a new generation of flesh and metal. The enemy will be destroyed, and their very essence used to breathe life into our people. We will return, and I will be remembered for it.

A blue sphere flickered in front of him with the shape of a machine.

"One-Zero-One. Have you completed your mission? Have the Defeated redeemed themselves?"

"Soon," said the machine.

Even though they were separated by thousands of light years, the machine still felt a need to cow down before him.

Good, the Defeated still know their place.

"The enemy is strong. Our forces are evenly matched. I need…"

The imagery broke up at just the same time as energy

from the Helion weapon struck the Rift. It didn't last long, but its affect annoyed the machine disproportionately.

"Fools!" snapped back the ancient machine, "Their ships are broken, their crew exhausted, and they are outnumbered. Yet still you bleat for help?"

He turned his back on the imagery and instead looked to the rest of the Defeated, the remnants of the last war that wait for their orders. He despised them, those that had fled instead of fight. They were no different to him, other than being younger and more importantly, the survivors of the great defeat.

The Exiles have done their part without question, but the Defeated always want more. They can never succeed without bleating for help.

He looked back to One-Zero-One and noticed that the machine had fallen dormant for a second.

The Rift, he is unable to communicate with his Ghost Warrior. He should have kept his soul aboard the ship instead of with us. He has no place among us on Kha'Dri.

The machine began to move and then spoke.

"They have an active defense weapon on Helios Prime. Our ground forces will renew their assault within the hour."

"This is irrelevant. They cannot fire continually. Keep fighting. I will send in the rest of the Defeated. You will end this…today, or die in the attempt."

"What of the Great Seal, my lord? If they can collapse

it, I will be unable to control this battle. Spartan and the others will also be unable to…"

"Your whining offends me. You have no place here on Kha'Dri. Your fate will rest with the other Defeated. I am sending for your mortal remains to be sent across the Great Seal to join you on your ship. See this as an incentive. Now go!"

He disconnected the communication channel and waited for the ships to begin their journey. It took some time, but finally the second wave of ships was making its way through the Rift. He then accessed the ancient computing Core and checked the location of the newly added flesh. He moved through them and isolated One-Zero-One.

There you are.

With a simple order, the machinery began the process of transferring the machine's ancient remains to an automated transport.

Now, what of the others?

He began to look for the other souls as they called them. Before he could get much further, a report arrived from One-Zero-One's battleship. He staggered back at what he had seen.

The traitors, they have joined battle.

The memory of the destruction of Du'Li still felt fresh. The loss of the machinery and Ghost Warrior bodies was one thing, but it was the destruction of the mortal remains of hundreds of his kin that still stunned him. The rebels had vaporized even the ancient Core in a final bloody action before they had escaped.

They must be destroyed.

With that thought, he cancelled the transfer of One-Zero-One.

Perhaps I will grant you a final chance for salvation. Destroy the traitors, and your position on Kha'Dri and of immortality will be yours. You remains will stay with us, and when your time comes, we will consider your transfer to the last great Core.

He turned his attention back to the rest of the Defeated. The motley collection of warships and transports slipped through until none remained but the two ancient Arks and the myriad of Tomb Ships.

That's better. No, I shall wait and prepare for the next phase. The end will come soon enough, and we must be ready.

* * *

Battleship Retribution, Black Rift, Helios Sector

The first squads of Alliance marines had already broken through the port hangar bays. Spartan took two hits to his leg, but nothing was going to stop him from reaching the largest and most significant part of the ship's interior. Two groups of Thegns split off to cover their approach as well as five Ghost Warriors. Ahead of Spartan was the vast curved shape of the arena and its intricate sculptures and markings.

Different entrance to last time.

This was something far grander than the way he'd entered the place before. As they ran up its length, he wondered if all the battleships were fitted out in this way, or it was just something for his own ship. He kept moving and noted that the boarding parties had now pushed a third their way into the ship. They were spread out and meeting resistance at every point. As he had predicted, their heavy infantry had taken the most direct route. It was the only point where his defending troops had been completely routed.

That's where they will be.

Spartan reached the top of the ramp and entered the structure. The mist was no longer there, and this time he could see halfway into the blackness. He glanced back to watch the crowd of hundreds of Thegns plus half of the seventy-five Ghost Warriors. For the briefest of moments, he suspected they might have held back to let him go at it alone. Two of the mechanical Ghost Warriors stopped alongside him as though about to question what he was doing. One was completely black, save for the scratched paintwork and armor. The second was shorter, with thick legs and two arms on one side. The other side was taken up by an odd gun arrangement that merged back into the armor.

"What?" he asked.

The machines said something in their own tongue that Spartan couldn't quite understand. The suit's sensors detected something, and he looked inside the arena to see multiple shapes ahead. At first he thought it was his Thegns, but then he spotted the larger shapes moving with them.

Jötnar!

Wheeled robots raced to the flanks, and even more Thegns were already taking high positions throughout the arena. Spartan took a step forward and then another. In seconds, he was moving at a fast walk to the center of the open space. The Ghost Warriors fanned out to create a thin wall just two warriors deep. There were gaps between them so that the Thegns could move freely. Gunfire licked down at them, but Spartan had already sent in eight squads of Thegns to attack those on the high ground. The taller, black armored machine spoke to Spartan.

"Do not betray us, Spartan. We are all watching you."

Spartan could feel the blood pumping, and the mere suggestion that he would betray anybody was too much. He swung his right arm low and smashed the blade into the center of the machine's torso. It grunted but that was enough. Spartan pointed both of his arms at the thing and thought the command to attack. Two blue pulses flashed out, and the machine disintegrated, sending chunks of metal and flesh across the ramp. He looked at the other Ghost Warriors that watched on in silence. Even the

Thegns had stopped.

"Never, ever question my loyalty!"

He turned; presenting his back to them, and then pointed his bloodied right arm toward the enemy forces.

"Now...attack!"

The shapes ahead of them were becoming clearer as a skirmish line of Thegns charged ahead. Both sides reached a hundred meters when Spartan spotted their Thegns drops to the ground. At first he thought they had all been hit, and then one by one they opened fire. Massed railguns ripped into his own forces, and dozens of his Thegns were killed or wounded. Spartan kept on moving and aimed his arms at the targets. He could see all manner of foes, from the Jötnar encased in armor to the Vanguards, Marines, and the Thegns.

"There!"

Right behind them was the shape of a Biomech commander.

One of The Twelve.

"That is one of the traitors, the rebel Twelve. We will take their heads. Follow me!"

The hundred meters between the two sides was like no battle scene Spartan could ever have imagined. There was no cover, just a great open space with warriors on both sides trying to get to grips with the other. He made it to the first groups of Thegns and butchered three with a single cut. At a similar height to a Jötnar, he felt like a giant.

Each time he swung his mechanical arms, he killed more of them. Marines scattered to avoid his attacks, but then he was amongst them. A SAAR robot tried to avoid him, but it was too late. With a quick step, he smashed his foot into the turret and yanked the front apart with his right arm. Pieces of metal flew in all directions. Two Vanguards followed next, and they opened fire at close range. The internal warnings flashed as impacts were registered.

"No, not today!"

Spartan took three steps to the right, ducked under the arms of one of the Vanguards, and then punched upward. The advanced Marine armor lifted off the ground and flew back to land flat on the ground. Spartan jumped after it and stabbed his blades at its chest. Another arm blocked his path, and he twisted about to strike again and found himself face to face with a trio of Jötnar, each resplendent in crimson armor. Something akin to a powerful drug pumped through his veins as the suit pushed him on to greater feats. He recognized the face inside the armor, and it set his veins alight with anger.

"Khan!" he hissed through his teeth.

He stabbed once, then twice, but one of the other Jötnar knocked him aside. Two more Thegns tried to grab at him; one even managed to put three rounds into his left arm, shattering the inbuilt guns.

"Fool."

A quick swipe cut the warrior down.

"Spartan?" Khan asked.

The Jötnar circled him warily. Attached to both of his arms were retractable blades, each one as big as a man and gleaming. The other two Jötnar were busy as the Ghost Warriors arrived and drove back the marines with a mixture of heavy weapons fire and brutal close combat attacks.

"Yes, it's me...old friend."

Spartan struck once, twice, and then underneath the Jötnar's arms. A marine ran between them before being cut down by a pair of Thegns. Spartan ignored them and stepped around Khan, directly at the Biomech rebel. From his position, Spartan could see three of them, each a different color and specification. They had much in common with the Ghost Warriors, but their lack of uniformity marked them out as different.

I'm coming for you.

He made it three paces before Khan grabbed him around his shoulder and snapped him back. Hundreds of gunshots moved back and forth, but there was no way to find a frontline. The Thegns from both forces were intermingled and hacking away. Marines sheltered behind the dead and wounded, while Jötnar and Vanguards provided small clumps of armor, each group like a miniature bastion.

"Not yet, first you deal with me!" Khan growled.

Spartan staggered and then tipped over. The heavy

weight of his armor pulled him down and straight to the ground. A Thegn and a marine ran to hold him down while an entire platoon of marines streamed past to engage the rest of his troops.

Yeah, that's not good.

He struck out wildly and hit the marine, sending the poor man staggering about before he struck the ground. A Thegn leapt on him, and then the two vanished from view. The other Thegn was raising a carbine to shoot into his armor. Incredibly, the foot soldier managed to loose off a round before Spartan could shake himself free. He lifted to one knee and then came a powerful strike from below. Khan hit him hard in the torso, and Spartan was soon flying through the air. As he spun about, he could see the shapes of the Jötnar tearing through his Thegns with ease. Then he hit the ground with a crash.

"Spartan!" Khan shouted.

He charged him down like a wild rhinoceros. Spartan was up and braced himself.

Here he comes.

Spartan had just seconds, but it was enough to adopt a strong fighting stance. He remembered his friendly bouts with Khan in the past, and also that for some reason his foe would not shoot him.

He wants a prisoner. That is his weakness.

He flung down his arms and laughed.

"Come on, Khan, is that all you have to offer?"

The charging Jötnar missed by just a few centimeters as Spartan spun about and cut into the warrior's flank. The short but razor sharp blades cut deep into the metal. Spartan howled at the sight of the trickle of blood that ran down from the gash. As Spartan laughed, he felt a dull pain in his lower body. He looked down and found a curved blade pushing out of his stomach. With a hiss it retracted, and another Jötnar moved around to face him. Blood dripped from the weapon as it took aim with its shoulder-mounted Gatling gun.

"Olik?"

There was a glimmer of recognition, perhaps even pity as the weapon opened fire. Spartan's armor was resilient, but at a range of just three meters, the rounds easily penetrated the plating. Round after round ripped inside and damaged systems until one by one the internal modules failed. Spartan found himself almost immobile, with just one leg and his upper torso still able to move. He staggered back and tripped over a fallen Thegn. He dropped down, and only the intervention of his right arm stopped him crashing down face first.

"Protect him!" yelled a Ghost Warrior.

Four of them, each resplendent in their individual colors jumped past him and opened fire with their deadly weapons. Marines and Thegns were cut down, but the Jötnar simply ran straight at them. One vanished in a bright blue fireball, and then the Jötnar were on them. They stab, tore, and fired at close range until all four were nothing but shattered hulks, dripping flesh and blood.

Get up, you fool!

Spartan rose slowly, but Khan was there once more. They faced off against each other, a man encased in armor and a Jötnar in the same.

"I'm sorry," said Khan.

He swung his right arm and embedded his weapon deep into the machine's torso. The he took aim with his shoulder-mounted cannon. The gunfire ripped the armor apart until the wrecked machine dropped to the ground and fell to its side. Khan knelt down alongside the ruined form of his friend and yanked open the petals of armor around the torso. Blood and fluids flowed out to the ground, but there was little flesh, just the shattered remnants of an AI Core and the associated biological nervous system that was hardwired into the armor.

"What is this?" demanded Olik.

Khan smiled.

"It's a flesh suit."

A Thegn fired a burst, and two rounds struck Khan in the leg. He turned his gun around and blasted the creature without even looking at it.

"So where is Spartan?" asked Olik.

"Where he always is," muttered Khan, "In the most dangerous place."

CHAPTER NINETEEN

Particle beam weaponry proved itself on the killing fields of the Black Rift. The explosive energy released by such weapons was capable of destroying fighters and small escorts in one shot. Later developments saw modifications that would allow repeated bursts of energy that could ripple through ship from bow to stern. None of these second-generation weapons would be ready for use against the Biomechs. If they had, there are some that postulate the outcome for worlds like Helios Prime might have been very different.

Direct Energy Weapons – An Introduction

Kha'Dri, Taxxu, Uncharted Space

Spartan shuddered at the shock of the gunfire. He could feel the hits where the armor registered the impacts. Each round shattered his body, yet the pain was more a notification than something that would affect him physically. By the time he lay on his back, the images and sounds had vanished, to be replaced by blackness. He opened his eyes but found nothing more.

So this is it? You die and there's blackness?

Something pulled at him, like a giant magnet that wanted to suck him to another place. He could see shapes off into the distance and the pull of the armor.

Of course, the Ghost Warriors never truly die.

The armor moved closer and closer until he could feel the sensors and the connection. Then came another flash and the blackness returned.

Is it time?

Spartan knew the sound. It was the ancient machine, the leader of the rebels. He shook his head and tried to open his eyes wider. Still there was nothing but the blackness. He thought back to that last intimate discussion between the rebel, him, and Khan. They had discussed the plan for victory, the plan for the sacrifice.

The plan.

He closed his eyes and concentrated on the machine's voice. It was emotionless, yet somehow it felt warm, almost comforting, a reminder of a time before the most recent battles and bloodshed. There was another flash, and he was there, back on the ship with the two of them.

* * *

Spartan looked at them as though floating in the room. The figures had a misty look about them and the temperature was cool. He was inside an empty briefing room aboard an Alliance warship, empty other than for the three of them. There were no emergency alarms, alerts, or any signs of the urgent battle currently taking place at the Black Rift.

"General Rivers will never go for this," said Khan.

The Jötnar marched back and forth, impatient and a little angry. He stopped and pointed at Z'Kanthu. Neither he nor Spartan wore their armor, but the machine, as always, was encased in its thick plating.

"You're telling me that they did something to us when we were prisoners?"

Z'Kanthu remained motionless.

"Yes. Both of you have been prepared, ready for their call. I have seen this before. It is how we used to force others to fight with us."

Spartan shook his head and walked up to his friend.

"I didn't believe it either, but it makes sense. Remember the escape? We tried for weeks, months to get out. And then somehow we got out. Why?"

Khan rubbed his chin.

"But what if they just kill us? How will that help us?"

Z'Kanthu, that ancient machine, raised one of his battered looking limbs and directed it right at Spartan.

"We will have to show them we are of more value alive. No matter what, they will sacrifice thousands to take The

Twelve prisoner. If they succeed, they will activate you, and you will be their puppet. Their hatred for the last of The Twelve will outweigh they suspicions of you."

The three were silent for a short moment.

"If you will trust me, I can use your mind as a temporary repository, a place to hide away my essence. I know the technology, and I know the ships. Destroying their troops or ships will not end this war. It will be won by destroying their heart and mind. When the time is right, I will…"

Wake up!

The sound of the machine pounded in his head.

Wake up, now!

* * *

Kha'Dri, Taxxu, Uncharted Space

Spartan opened his eyes and found himself trapped, encased in metal, and floating in fluid. A soft pipe ran to his mouth and throat. He tried to speak, but instead of words there was just a dull echo. He twisted, pushed, and then he was falling. The view was blurred, but then the impact with the ground made him retch. He began to choke, his vision blurred, and then he clawed at his face. The pipe and mask easily pulled away, and he was immediately blinded by light.

"What's going on?" he yelled through his burning throat.

Spartan rolled about on the floor, the fluid still dripping from his chest and face. He lifted his arms to wipe it away from his eyes.

My arm, so the bastards did do at least one good thing.

The stump was still there, but the modified limb he'd received on Earth was nowhere to be seen. Instead, he found the mechanical limb that seemed to have much in common with the flesh and skin of the Thegns. He looked down to his middle section and limbs; he was covered from neck to toe in the flesh armor. For a horrible moment he thought he might even be a Thegn; that was until he saw a reflection of himself in the pools of fluid on the ground.

Okay, what now?

His memories, especially those that had been suppressed were rushing back; visions of battles, people, and events that he'd forgotten about for weeks. Each moved back with a vengeance. It was those of his family and friends that were most prominent. Khan and the other Jötnar, the marines he'd fought alongside, but Teresa and Jack were the greatest of them all. He felt a pang of loss and separation. He was a long way from them, and it felt an impossible distance to overcome.

Spartan, are you ready?

The words from Z'Kanthu sounded little different to as if he had been standing alongside him. The words were so real that he even looked around to find him.

"Where are you?"

His eyes burned from the fluid, but he ignored it and looked around at his surroundings. The empty capsule he'd been inside was torn open and shattered; its embryonic sack flaccid and useless. Pipes hung down, and more fluid continued to drip out. The room was not large, hexagonal in shape, and with more of the objects concealed behind the thick, semi-translucent skin. He moved to the nearest and pushed at it. Something inside moved about.

What is it?

The voice of his machine friend returned.

The connection to the machine network, you need to access it. Get me access, and I will do the rest.

Spartan looked around and back to the shattered sack he had occupied.

No, the other one.

Spartan's eyes returned to the previous sack. He moved close and then ripped at it with his hands. The material was taut and easily broke under his fingers. Fluid poured out, and then came the shaking, panicked figure of a creature. It stumbled about on the ground and then tried to lift itself up. It was taller than Spartan, but much thinner and similar in many ways to Thayara.

"Spartan," it hissed.

The sound wasn't familiar. It said more, but the words meant nothing to him. He looked about for a weapon and found little of use, so he stepped in front of the creature and pulled his arm back to strike. The creature lifted its arms defensively.

"One-Zero…"

Spartan ignored and struck it hard in the throat. It dropped to the ground choking, and Spartan stepped inside the small cubicle area. The floor was slick with fluid and undamaged pipes and cables hung down. The voice of Z'Kanthu returned.

My guess was correct. Their command structure is not based on the homeworld anymore. I am detecting the source is somewhere deep inside this ship. I will release you and move into their computer system.

Spartan laughed as he listened to the machine.

"Are you kidding? How are you going to do that?"

Yes, Spartan, I am. I will move into their system and locate their Core. But first I need you to listen very carefully.

* * *

Battleship Retribution, Black Rift, Helios Sector
Khan lifted a Thegn and tossed its broken body directly at the cowering Ghost Warrior. The body struck the machine in the torso, and it staggered back two paces. It tried to right itself as dozens of Thegns swarmed over and stabbed and shot at it. Chunks of metal tore off as they dragged it down like stone-age men bringing down a mammoth.

"Khan, are you there?" asked a familiar voice on the

secure channel.

"Who is this?"

He swallowed, almost fearful to believe.

"You know who it is, you fool. Z'Kanthu survived the trip. I'm out and on one of their ships. I'm sending coordinates to you now."

The audio vanished and was replaced by a howling sound. Then it returned.

"Spartan?"

"Yes, of course it's me."

Khan shook his head in amazement.

"The plan worked? You are inside their command structure?"

The howling returned, and Spartan's voice reduced substantially in volume.

"Get a message to Anderson; the large orbital facility, at these coordinates. This is where their leaders' bodies are located. Everything they hold dear lives inside this ship. The commanders of the battleships, their bodies are all located here, just like I was."

A Thegn wearing the colors chosen before the battle was knocked to the side by a Ghost Warrior. Khan grabbed the machine, tore a limb off, and then cut a gouge through its torso with his gun. He forced his arm inside and ripped it open. Fluid and loose flesh dropped out, but no body.

"What about these soldiers? Where are their bodies?"

Spartan sounded as though he was laughing, but it

could easily have been interference.

"They are called the Defeated. Their flesh bodies are on the battleships. They are not allowed a place on the command ship until they are victorious."

"But they gave you a place?"

This time there was a pause.

"I killed their greatest traitor. That bought me a lot of credit. Look, Khan, get a message to Anderson and fast. I don't have much time. They will know I am out. Tell him this is where we can end this. Call off the battle and get through the Rift."

Khan took aim at the next two Ghost Warriors while Olik moved to his flank to add his own fire. Dozens more crimson armored Jötnar moved ahead and out of the bloodied arena.

"What about Z'Kanthu? We've seen the footage, you really killed him?"

Again the audio crackled.

"Another time, Khan. His mind is intact and exactly where we hid it. Right now, I'm looking for a body for him. Get them here, fast!"

It had taken his built-in computer system that long to identify the area of space that Spartan was referring to. It was nowhere near their current position but thousands of light years away. He almost discounted it when realizing the location matched the data they already had on the enemy domain. It was one of the unknown enemy orbital facilities.

He's at their homeworld, the crazy fool. Z'Kanthu was right. We hit their heart and war is won.

"I'll do what I can. Are you safe?"

"Not even close, Khan. I'm unarmed, and I've got no idea where I am. Just bring them through the Rift and get to this location."

"Bring who?"

The laughter coming back put a smile on Khan's face.

"Everybody!"

Three clicks followed, and then the channel died. He looked to his left; half expecting to see someone telling him it was a joke. Instead it was a single Vanguard. The machine stomped on by and then disappeared out of the area and toward the enemy. He moved on ahead and to the top of the ramp. From there he could see down into the vastness of the ship. The multiple levels, gantries, and walkways gave the vessel the impression of a vast power complex or work site.

This ship is almost ours.

He tried not to think of how many warriors they'd already lost in the assault. There were hundreds of bodies on the ground, with many more inside the arena. Streaks of gunfire blasted in all directions from warriors fighting desperate small battles throughout the ship.

"Khan, we have troops in their CIC, or whatever they call it," said Major Terson.

Khan took aim at a Biomech Ghost Warrior and put a burst into its torso as it struggled to escape. The Major continued to speak even as Khan kept shooting.

"As soon as we arrived, their commander dropped dead, not a mark on him. I've never seen anything like it. There are no bodies inside the suits, just the bare minimum of flesh."

Khan stopped and checked for signs of the enemy. All around him his own forces were cutting down any remaining Thegns near him, and he could feel the tide already turning.

"Can you take control of the ship from there?"

"No, but On'Sarax is working on it. She believes she can control their systems soon, why?"

Three Eques walkers turned around to face back in the direction they had arrived from. A single SAAR robot deployed its primary weapons and then exploded in a single bright explosion.

"Incoming!" yelled a marine private.

He too was cut down by hundreds of rounds fired from the next level up. Shapes moved through the arena and poured out to strike Khan's position from behind.

"It's a trap. To the rearguard!"

A pair of Ghost Warriors dropped down from the next level up and faced off against Olik and Khan. Behind them came more Thegns and six more Ghost Warriors. More and more streamed out from the arena, and for a fraction of a moment, Khan felt doubt. He glanced to Olik and Knaprig. The latter held his one good arm up, with its blade extended out in front of him. His lost arm had been replaced with a secondary gun mount slaved to the computer. It gave him an odd, slightly robotic look.

"Major Terson has what he needs. We need to buy him time."

The other two grunted in agreement and separated, increasing the gap between them. Dozens more marines moved back while others took position in cover to provide help. Two Vanguards rushed back, both firing at the Ghost Warriors as they skidded alongside Khan.

"Need help, Sir?" asked the first.

"Yeah, follow me."

He took a step forward and then increased in speed. Fire from both sides ripped marine and Thegn apart with ease, but it was the Ghost Warriors, Vanguards, and Jötnar that proved more difficult to kill. The Gatling guns of the Vanguards ripped chunks of armor from the Biomechs, while blue pulses from their weapons quickly dispatched a Vanguard and disabled Knaprig so that he fell to the ground. Olik spotted his friend fall, but Khan called him off.

"Hit the bastards, Olik. Remember what they did on Prometheus!"

Olik barely needed the reminder. The most recent battle was enough to ferment an almost religious zeal amongst the Jötnar. Their origin on Prometheus was an even darker chapter, and one the Jötnar always looked to avenge.

They moved quickly, each tracking the enemy machines. One of them barked orders in some odd alien tongue, immediately drawing Khan's attention. This one's armor was different, embellished, and marked and narrower than the others. The machine also moved with great athleticism. Khan was convinced he could make out Anicinàbe markings along its torso.

Odd.

"Die!" it hissed.

Khan was so surprised by its speed that he didn't even notice he'd understood it, or of the venom in the machine's tone. It leapt passed the other two and extended two short reflective blades. He'd already seen their configuration, just like those carried by the enemy's Thegn and Biomech warriors.

"Try it, monster!"

They reached the Biomechs out in the open. There were now six of them, and just a single Vanguard and two Jötnar still able to fight. Olik ducked past the first of the machines and moved toward the more agile of the group.

This is going to be interesting, thought Khan.

He pushed down hard and jumped a meter in the air. He came down with a crash while slamming both of his arms into the first Biomech's chest. Two plates ripped off, and Khan continued to cut and strike until he'd ripped the thing to shreds. Two more came at him, but he sidestepped and let gunfire from the Vanguards slow them down. A missile fired from the next level up, screamed down, and struck one in the arm. The warhead fizzled and hissed; a small flash blew a hole the size of a man into the shell.

Not bad.

The machine twisted about, but a fusillade of carbine fire punched a hundred holes into it. It dropped down to join the other shattered husks. Now the odds were a little fairer. Four against three, and Khan was just beginning to feel his blood begin to boil. Thegns were running past them in all directions, but he ignored them, only striking out if they came too close. He extended his arm and pointed at the most agile of them all.

"You!"

The machine spotted him and called out an order. The three remaining machines formed a defensive wall in front of it, a shield of metal and flesh. Khan didn't care; his rage was at its peak, and he charged. A blue flash slammed into his shoulder and tore off the weapon as well as all the plating. He howled in pain but kept on. Another blast struck the ground beneath his feet, but he was already airborne. Khan crashed into the line and toppled it, landing directly on the lithe warrior at the rear.

The other three were trying to stand as Olik and the Vanguard arrived. They blasted them mercilessly, tearing armor, weapons, and limbs off with brutal efficiency.

Khan held down his foe with both arms.

"Who are you?"

A long, slow sigh came from the machine as though it was releasing its last breath.

"Thayara."

* * *

Military Outpost, Rintau, Eos.

The wall was gone, holes taking up more space than actual rock and stone. A smashed Eques walker lay straddled across one of the many breaches, and dozens of dead Thegns filled the breaches. The rockets had stopped, but the fusillade of small arms fire had reached a crescendo. A single NHA body lay among the fallen Thegns, a testament to the brutal assault that had almost seen the base fall.

"Corporal, take three marines and cover the south wall. More of them are coming in."

Wictred nodded and ducked low, doing his best to hide his large form from the Thegn sniper's position that was less than a hundred meters from the outpost. With quick hand gestures, he signaled the marines to join him. With every step, another bullet struck nearby. He ran past the heavily damaged Mauler and on to the partially damaged wall. The Bulldog waited patiently, it's turret turned and guns pointing off into the distance. Four Helion soldiers manned the position, and they seemed to relax as the

Alliance giant arrived alongside them. Three marines joined him and placed their carbines and a single L48 rifle onto the low wall.

"How much longer, Corporal?" asked the pale looking private.

Wictred checked the figures on his visor. They had already lost contact with those ships still in orbit over Eos, but he had the projection for the arrival of the relief party.

"They should be here is eleven minutes, maybe twelve."

He looked over the top and felt his heart stop. A wall of warriors filled his view. They were partially obscured in the cloud of dust they'd kicked up, but the sight of hundred of warriors was a sight not mistaken for something else. There were even Eques walkers amongst the hordes of Thegns.

"This is gonna hurt."

He placed his looted Biomech cannon onto the wall and then looked to the other marines. Each was experienced in battle and had seen the enemy on multiple occasions. Even so, he could see the fear and the nerves on their faces.

"Just hold them back for eleven minutes. That's all we have to do."

He looked back at the enemy and took aim. Two rounds glanced off his helmet, and he ignored them, as if they were nothing more than chunks of ice.

"Fire!"

* * *

Kha'Dri, Taxxu, Uncharted Space

Spartan detached the cables from the access points in the flesh armor he still wore. As he removed the last flat cable, he could sense a calm, something akin to relief as his last contact with the machines was severed. Even the sound of Z'Kanthu had vanished, leaving him with just his thoughts.

What did he say? Three on the left and down under the floor?

The words were strange, but he followed them. So far, the wizened machine had been correct at every point. He moved carefully through the ship. It was unlike any vessel he'd ever seen before. The corridors looked organic, with rib like bones making up the walls and thick piping filled with colored fluid running in all directions. The air was very dry, to a level that almost hurt his throat. Spartan followed the direction until reached the small passageway. There were pipes on almost every surface, but in the middle was an access point. He bent down and grasped the lever. It pulled with a groan and then detached. He cast it aside and lowered himself into the new space.

Just drop.

He released his grip and fell for the briefest of minutes. His eyes shut as he hit the ground, and his legs flexed, taking the strain from the landing. The adrenalin felt good, and each second that it pumped through his body, the more alive he felt. His eyes opened, and he almost staggered back at what he saw. The room was long like a barracks, and along the walls were dozens of Ghost Warrior armored suits. Each of them was open at the front to reveal they were empty.

"Just what I need," he said aloud, forgetting for a second that he was trying to be discreet.

"Exactly," said a familiar voice.

He spun about and found one of the suits waiting in the open. The armor was sealed, yet it moved with purpose.

"How did you do that?" he asked suspiciously.

"As agreed, I told you I would keep part of my essence with you, now it is inside their Core. They will find me eventually, but until then I can control a machine body. I have chosen this one."

Spartan shook his head.

"Z'Kanthu, you're full of surprises."

"There is more," he said, "You must prepare yourself. Take one of them, and finish this. Do it for your people, and for mine."

* * *

Kha'Dri, Taxxu, Uncharted Space

The ancient machine watched the Rift with growing impatience. He began to pace, waiting for news of the

Defeated and their final victory over the enemy. The ship felt empty, even though it was filled with thousands of his own dormant Ghost Warrior suits, all ready to be controlled by the ancient Core deep inside the ship. Then came a single flash, an indicator that something was coming through.

"What is this?"

The shape transformed into the massive hulk of the battleship Retribution. The machine hissed to itself.

So, the Defeated prove their name is well deserved, once more.

Then more shapes came through, first a just a handful, and then scores of ships from multiple races. For a moment the machine was confused, then it recognized the shapes of the Alliance warships. Biomantas came through with them, and the space battle continued just as it had on the other side of the Rift. He sent the command to One-Zero-One, but nothing came back, just the silence brought on only by the true death.

"I have been betrayed!"

With a single thought, he screamed a warning through the entire ship. The shockwave rippled through every section of the vast behemoth. One by one, the machines of the ship were accessed and taken control of by those souls drifting inside the ancient Core. He watched as hundreds, and then thousands of machines activated around him.

It is time for them all to fight.

One more order sent the same activation signal to

every vessel in Taxxu. Even the dormant Tomb Ships activated their defense routines and woke their biological warriors, summoning them all to the fight. He looked at the indicators and began to calm. There were limitless ships and millions of warriors, all of them expendable. He looked back to the capsules that kept his five kin in their ancient slumber. For a second, he considered leaving them, waiting to see what might happen. But then came the warnings from his ship commanders, and the news sent a shudder through his soul.

They are coming here?

He turned to face his five equals, and with a heavy heart began the procedure to waken them, just as One-Zero-One had done for him.

Very well, their end will take place here, and not in their own domain. It makes little difference to me.

* * *

ANS Warlord, Taxxu, Uncharted Space

Admiral Anderson looked upon the new region of space with calculating eyes. All round the battleship were the survivors of the battle at the Rift. Even now, the Spacebridge was shuddering, doing its best to collapse. On the mainscreen were videostreams from General Makos and now from Major Terson and Khan. Dozens of impacts registered along the warship, as those vessels near the enemy flagship turned on the new arrivals.

"Admiral, the coordinates sent to Khan are for that ship, the one that is similar in configuration to the Arks, just massively bigger. It will take days to destroy it, assuming we could even get through in one piece."

"It's true," explained Khan, "The plan is working, sort of."

He looked to his tactical officer.

"What can you tell me?"

The man breathed in deeply. On the mainscreen a Crusader was ripped apart by the combined fire from twenty different Biomech ships. Admiral Anderson watched the destruction and shook his head bitterly. It was only then that he understood Khan's words.

"Plan, what plan?"

The tactical officer interrupted his question before Khan had time to respond.

"It's big, Sir, very big. Approximately five times larger than the Arks we've seen before. There are hundreds, perhaps thousands of ships moving in to protect it."

Admiral Anderson licked the corner of his mouth.

What have I just done? We've entered the Lion's den.

The communications officer looked back at him.

"Admiral, contact from the enemy ship. It is Spartan."

The very mention of the man's name sent a chill through the CIC. The ambient noise levels dropped substantially.

"Put him on."

The image appeared, but rather than the external feed that showed him and other machines, this one was dark and from the interior of some sort of armor.

"Admiral, it's true. I've infiltrated their command ship. We have identified their weakness."

His face vanished, but it wasn't through jamming. It was a change in the lighting, and it took a moment for the computer to match the brightness levels.

"Z'Kanthu came with me. He transferred a part of him to me, to wake me when the time was right."

The Admiral shook his head and lifted his hand.

"Uh...wait. What?"

Spartan frowned.

"He is inside their Core and trying to get me a physical location, but his time is short. If we want to end this, we have to strike now. Hard and fast, right to their heart."

Instead of answering Spartan, he turned to Khan.

"We've lost hundreds of ships, thousands of lives, and the enemy are being advised by Spartan. Now you tell me this is a plan?"

Khan look unsurprised at his response.

"They had to believe they had turned him. He killed the rebel leader and has been grinding down our last fleet. All of this is to bring us to this one point, one where the machines feel they have brought us to the brink of destruction. At our point of weakness, we will be able to strike."

Anderson did not seem very impressed.

"Z'Kanthu promised he could protect us from their influence. We should act before we lose the fleet."

Admiral Anderson could see the logic, but his mind was overwhelmed with a sense of betrayal and loss of control. He needed information to win battles, and right now he felt the outsider. He scratched at his head and looked back to Spartan.

"I cannot win this space battle, and if I try and come through, I will lose most of what's left. Tell me you can do something?"

Spartan smiled.

"This ship, it is called Kha'Dri, and it is the last of what they call their World Ships. Z'Kanthu says there is a Core inside, similar in design to the one we found on Terra Nova. When their people reach the end of their lives, they transfer their minds to the system. It is their most prized possession. There are also the mortal bodies of their commanders, including their six leaders and the commanders of each of their battleships."

"So?"

"There's more. The soldiers on the battleships, they have not been given a place on this station. First they must be victorious; that means they can operate outside of the influence of the command structure."

Admiral Anderson watched as his tactical officer tagged those ships as they talked. Four of them were already showing as making it back to this part of space. One had been captured, and that meant the other six must be on the other side, probably ready to come through.

"Admiral," said Spartan, his voice beginning to sound desperate, "This ship contains thousands of machines, their Biomech Soldiers they call Ghost Warriors. Each time they are destroyed, the Core can simply activate more, and control it with the mind of one of those encased. It is their last and strongest line of defense. They have me here because there is nowhere more secure."

"And you want us to assault this fortress, with the small numbers we have left?"

Spartan nodded.

"Yes, because we have the trump card. We have a man on the inside, and I don't mean me. You need to hit this place and fast. They are already calling in biologicals to defend it, millions of warriors, each constructed from their fallen kin and captured enemies. We've seen these enemies before, Sir, back on Prime in the war."

Spartan blinked and then whispered.

"Z'Kanthu has found it. He has just sent me the coordinates for their Core. Meet me there, Admiral, and bring everything. We cannot hold back on this one. He says he will initiate a general disconnection from the Core. As soon as this happens, all of their commanders and any warriors on this ship will lose control of their machine bodies. They can transfer back in seconds, but it will buy us a small window."

His image vanished and then came with a crackle.

"Ten minutes, Admiral. Start the clock…now."

With that, Admiral Anderson was left alone, with nothing but his junior officers and the images of Major Terson, Khan, and General Makos.

"Well?"

General Makos spoke first.

"I was suspicious of this change with Spartan. My people have faith in him. We will attack."

Major Terson nodded in agreement.

"We will die out here whatever happens. At least this is a chance to end the war. I say we hit them, and with everything we have left."

The last word came to Khan.

"Spartan has made himself the villain, our greatest enemy, so that we can win this war. We cannot let him down. I will not allow it. I and all my kin pledge to fight with him, or we will die in the effort."

It was unanimous, and for the first time in days, even as starships continued to explode around him, he actually felt calm. He looked to Captain Decker.

"Prepare for boarding operations. Take us there. I want the guns of the fleet locked onto their battleships. When the counter hits zero, we will open up everything we have on them."

He pointed on the tactical display and at the large shape

in the heart of the growing enemy fleet that orbited the dead husk of a world, known only as Taxxu.

The doom of our people will be decided there, around a dead world and on a fortress filled with the dead.

* * *

Kha'Dri, Taxxu, Uncharted Space

Spartan had already chosen his weapons from the massive metal racks on the one wall. All it had taken was to press the stumps of his Ghost Warrior into the unit and to select the required weapons. He chose the short blades he'd used so successfully already. The guns were a temptation, but in his experience, the armor in the machines took too long to eliminate with simple gunfire. He did select the blades with attached cannon though, even if they were little more than secondary weapons.

More like it.

He was at the doorway and leaving the armory when the first of the suits began to close. He watched as one by one the armored shells hissed shut. In seconds, the first that had moved took a step out of its enclosure. Like all of the Ghost Warriors, it was little different to Z'Kanthu or any of the other great machines. They were all large, thickly armored, and yet subtly different. Two more stepped out, moving and shuddering as though getting used to their bodies.

Oh, this is good. Are you kidding me?

The machine controlled by Z'Kanthu faced toward him.

"I will hold them back."

Spartan reached out to what he considered his friend, even if it were little more than a virtual presence.

"You will be destroyed."

"No, this is just a machine. I can reactivate other machines, until they find me. Hurry, Spartan, I will do what I can both inside and out of here."

Spartan struck the machine and then left the room. He rushed off in the direction given to him by Z'Kanthu. As he made it to the end of the next passageway, he looked back for one last glimpse and immediately regretted it. Z'Kanthu had blocked the doorway with his body, and the machines were busily ripping his limbs apart. The sound of an energy blast rippled through the ship, and he stumbled. There was nothing left of the machine or those fighting to move past him. He took a step away and then spotted more of them dragging away the wreckage. He knew he should keep moving, but the sight of them sent pangs of hate through his very bones.

I had to work for them, to kill for them.

He lifted his arms and sent the command to fire. Pulses of blue energy flashed out from both limbs and struck the nearest of them. He continued shooting until the machine was a shattered, half melted wreck.

Move! Z'Kanthu said.

He went deeper into the ship, avoiding the growing numbers of sentries and defense systems. Passages ran into rooms, and then into massive compartments full of powerplants, manufacturing equipment, and even half assembled ships. On he moved and toward the image in his mind, the great chapel in the heart of the ship.

Not much further.

He reached a long hallway; dozens of machines flanked it on both sides. The vaulted ceiling was again build from a half-biological looking spine. Ribs ran down and connected to the sculptures in a sickening fusion of metal and flesh. Off into the distance was a semi-translucent entrance to a cathedral like structure.

That has to be it.

Spartan turned and ran past the first of the sculptures. Shapes moved, and he quickly spotted hatches on the high levels opening up. Machine emerged. Some were Ghost Warriors, but many more were variations of the horrific Decurions. Hundreds of machines scuttled out from their hiding places or detached from the very walls. Intricate sculptures and artworks moved and came to life. As before, Z'Kanthu spoke to him from inside the machine he sought to defeat.

It is the Core. They are taking control of their machines. We are running out of time. They are looking for me, Spartan.

He moved as quickly as his metal body would allow.

Directly above him was a beautifully intricate dome that gave a view of the Rift, presumably the one back home. Black shapes were silhouetted against its colors. Lines and streaks from hundreds of ships jumped about as a vast battle lit up this sector of space.

The fleet, they came.

Something struck him, and he found himself on his back. He shook his head and looked up at the ancient forms of a group of six machines. They were Ghost Warriors that much was certain, but the armor was different, embellished in ways far beyond his experience. Dozens more Ghost Warriors moved around them, each armed and equipped in a similar fashion to Spartan.

"Who the hell are you?" he asked, angrily.

"Spartan, the traitor. You will suffer an eternity of agony for this," said one of them.

CHAPTER TWENTY

The last stand of Captain Carter on the world of Eos is one of those events that few known of. The details were hidden and the involvement of all but the Captain. Few details are known, apart from the fact that this one small stronghold held off an entire army until the enemy ceased their assault. The losses on both sides were heavy, but the resulting battle saw the Biomechs isolated and almost entirely destroyed. Less than ten percent of the attackers left Eos under close guard, and Captain Carter and his polyglot unit moved on to even greater and more famous engagements.

Accounts of the Prophecy of Fire

Battleship Retribution, Taxxu, Uncharted Space

Khan remained motionless as the ship buffeted about on its approach. He wasn't sure which part had been worse, the fighting on the enemy battleship, or this approach to the enemy fortress. The ship had already sustained heavy damage, but with On'Sarax and three of her kin, they had managed to take control of the vessel. Major Terson waited next to him and watched the massive holographic representation of where they were in space. The sound of small arms fire continued to echo throughout the ship.

"How will we get inside?" Major Terson asked.

Khan turned his head a few degrees to look at the man.

"Oh, this one is simple. We'll make a hole and step inside."

For a few seconds the Major was confused. Then he realized exactly what Khan was saying. He shook his head in amazement.

"Really, that's your plan?"

Khan began to laugh, and soon Olik was doing the same.

* * *

Kha'Dri, Taxxu, Uncharted Space

Spartan was trapped inside the armor, his limbs attached via thick magclamps that pinned him to the wall. There was still power to his secondary functions, but only so that he could see, no more. He was far from the ground, suspended directly above a great holographic orb that showed the battle. Around this great sphere stood the six machines, each resplendent in their armor. They spoke, but none of their words made any sense to him. Further away, he could see hundreds more in their machine bodies moving about and managing the ship. Decurions marched in formations, some even carrying firearms attached to their bodies. It was like a wasps' nest, filled with dangers. And here he hung, incapable of doing a thing.

A few hours ago and I understood it all; things change fast around here.

"Hey, you!" he yelled.

One of the machines, the one that had struck him, looked up and said something. The others made odd sounds, and they looked back to the orb. Spartan shifted.

The remnants of the Alliance fleet and their allies were nearing the Kha'Dri. The heavy warships took the lead positions, with ANS Warlord and the captured battleship Retribution taking the van. Crusader and Conqueror class vessels followed right behind, and squadrons of Liberty destroyers hugged their flanks. All friendly fighters had been pulled in close to provide a tight escort for the final assault of the war. Biomech ships moved in around them, but for a few minutes at least, they had been granted a relatively clear run to the enemy vessel.

As the fleet reached a range of a hundred kilometers, the fortress' defensive system activated. Thousands of turrets opened fired with a mixture of missiles, shells, and particle beams. Spartan watched impotently as the weapons blasted the fleet apart with more firepower than he had seen in his entire life. A different machine looked up to him.

"Traitor, you have failed. Watch the end of your people."

One of the Byotai ships, a beautiful, organic looking craft moved to the flank of the fleet. A line of shells chased it and tore off a wing in a colorful flash of materials. They were close now, so close that some of the ships were big enough to make out the windows or gun ports. Another vanished in a flash.

"Just a few more minutes, and your fleet is gone."

Thirty seconds, Spartan.

Flames and streaks rippled across the two nearest vessels. Both were massive, at least battleship class, and they approached like a pair of oxen pulling a cart. Spartan tugged and struggled, but no matter how hard he tried, he could not move.

Spartan, are you ready?

Spartan almost cried out at hearing the machine.

"Bet your ass I am. We have to do something, anything."

They have nearly found me. Prepare yourself. I must throw them off my scent, and yours. I have one last gift to give you. Call to me when it is time.

His voice faded as he finished the final words, and Spartan knew this might be the last time he would hear from the old machine. The onboard systems in his armor activated, and he could feel the augmented limbs straining at the magclamp.

Okay, that kind of helps.

There was a sound from the machines below him. It was a panic, as though something terrible had happened. Spartan looked down to them and noticed the six machines were in something of a daze. A crackle of energy ripped through the ship, and the lights dimmed.

Odd.

He looked off into the distance and found the same with the large numbers of Ghost Warriors. Some continued to move, but many had stopped, with quite a few toppling over. Then every single machine stopped, apart from the six leaders. That was the moment he noticed the guns were offline.

You crazy fool, you've bought us a window.

Spartan wasn't sure how, but it was obvious the ancient warrior had managed to temporarily sever the connection between the minds in the Core and the machines in the ship. Spartan's mind raced ahead as he realized that would also include the leaders on all of the battleships, the command vessels for the Biomech fleet.

Thank you, Z'Kanthu, that's the window we need. Leave the rest to us.

Explosions filled outer space, and he was convinced he could see two of the mighty Biomech battleships exploding from long volleys of gunfire. Light caught his eye, and he looked to the great wall of curved glass. It was shaking, and then the shapes outside struck it. The material shuddered, then shattered. Blast panels rushed down to seal them in, but the top superstructure of a Biomech warship crashed through, and Spartan found himself flying through the air uncontrollably.

Great, here we go again.

* * *

Spartan opened his eyes. He was alive, that much was clear, but what else was happening he had no idea. He shook his head and lifted himself up. There was still gravity, but the armor showed the atmosphere had been vented into space. He realized he was on the ground and between the six machines. All of them were functional, and each was pointing weapons at him. Hundreds more of their warriors were scurrying about.

Great, they are back in control.

"Spartan, the betrayer. We offered you immortality and you destroyed Z'Kanthu, for what? Tell us what did you do? How did you breach the Core?" demanded the nearest.

Spartan ignored it and looked from side to side. The interior of the ship was a mess, with huge chunks of the ceiling missing. Blocks of metal and masonry littered the place, and the sparks and flashes of yet more damage showed in all directions.

"Forget him, now, he dies," said the second of the

ancient machines.

It took a step toward Spartan, lifted its arm, and then flew sideways and crashed to the ground. Hundreds of shots from Gatling guns ripped around them and struck into the machines. The other five separated, leaving Spartan out in the open. Dozens of the normal, and expendable Ghost Warriors formed up in a shield wall to protect the five ancient warriors.

Yeah, you protect them. I know their little secret, though. Just like The Twelve, these Ancients are still inside their armor. That makes them mortal, and that means I can kill them.

He pulled himself to his feet and found a whole column of Decurions scuttling in to join battle. Spartan lifted his arms and fired, blue flashes of energy ripping into them.

"Spartan!" yelled a familiar voice.

Further back and atop of the wreckage of part of a ship came dozens of marines. At their head was Major Terson, dressed in battered PDS armor and carrying an L52 carbine. He stopped as he reached the top of the rubble and fired off into the distance. More of them poured in like troops landing on a beach from landing craft. They went from a few dozen to hundreds in seconds. From upper levels, hatches blew open and Helion and Byotai soldiers entered the vast complex.

"A hand, Spartan?" asked a familiar voice.

He looked about and then spotted the Jötnar on the ground, pinned under the heavy form of one of the commanders. He pulled back his arms and stabbed at the thing repeatedly.

"Khan."

Spartan staggered over to his friend and yanked away the metal machine. Khan extended an arm, and Spartan pulled hard. The Jötnar steadied himself and then struck Spartan hard.

"That's for giving us a hard fight."

Spartan shrugged, not that Khan could tell through the armor.

"What's the plan?"

Khan pointed to the increasing number of troops.

"We crashed the first three ships into the upper structure of this fortified ship, or whatever it is. Olik is taking the Thegns to hit them from below. Terson and I brought the heavies right here. Where is this damned Core?"

Spartan turned around and pointed to the shadows that led further into the ship.

"The transmissions are coming from back there, inside the area they call the Reliquary."

"Good," said Khan, "Then let's crack the walls of this place and get us some payback."

They began to move, but Spartan reached out to his friend.

"Helios, what's happened back there? When I was a prisoner I could see their plans, their dispositions. Spascia looks like it's in trouble. Jack and Teresa are both there, aren't they?"

Khan closed his eyes and tried to think of the best way to tell him.

"Spartan, I'm sorry. They were forced to the mountain. Last we heard from Gun was that Teresa died in the last stand. Gun is still fighting them tunnel by tunnel, but he can't last much longer."

"And Jack?"

Khan shook his head. Spartan looked to him but found no solace in his friend's eyes, only the bitter truth of what had happened.

"We couldn't help them and be here at the same time. It was them or the war."

Spartan knew he was right. It was a decision they had all made, but that made it no less bitter to him. He clenched his fists together tightly.

"I want them dead, every single one of their machines."

They both left the crash site and went into the darker regions of the ship. The space became narrower, and the resistance tougher the further they went. Finally, the passageway shrank to just ten meters wide, with a tall ceiling made from the foul biological bones matter. Off into the distance a great statue of a half creature, half machine filled the wall. It was fifty meters tall and surrounded by a blue glow. Black flooring ran at multiple levels around the sculpture. They walked a little further and into the massive inner sanctum. Dozens more passageways ran into the same place, with a mixture of friend and foe streaming into the site.

"So, their reliquary contains a statue of some stupid beast?" Khan muttered.

Spartan took aim and blasted a Decurion as it emerged from one of the entrances. Khan did the same as hundreds of marines and friendly Thegns swarmed past them. Gunfire licked at them from different heights, and Ghost Warriors dropped down amongst them, hacking and shooting at anything they got in their way.

"There!" Khan said.

He pointed to the space around the base of the mighty statue. A glowing blue sphere ran at ground level and then extended up into the creature itself.

"Is that it?"

Spartan shrugged.

"No idea, shoot it anyway."

Both opened fire, along with many of the marines and Vanguards. The rounds chipped away at the stone and metalwork but had little, if any impact on the blue matter. Major Terson came in through another of the passageways three levels up. Three of his marines were cut down, and he was forced back to the entrance, using its sides as cover. On'Sarax stepped out and gazed upon the sculpture.

"Spartan, Khan. On'Sarax says the top level is the source of the signal. It is built into the head of that thing," said the Major.

Shouts from above came from the enemy, and then a pair of the ancient warriors threw themselves down from the top level.

They hit the ground with such incredible force that marines were scattered in all directions. On'Sarax stepped out to face them, along with three more of her rebel kin. The machines hissed and spoke in their ancient tongue, words that meant little other than by their tone.

"With me!"

Spartan ran across the open ground, ignoring the gunfire that seemed to come from every direction. Khan chased after him, as well as a handful of marines. Three were cut apart before they reached the curved black ramp that wound all around the sculpture. Decurions rushed down to meet them, but Spartan hacked and smashed his way through them as if they were nothing. Not even Khan could match his pace or ferocity.

"Slow down, Spartan!" he yelled.

Down below, the lowest levels had turned into a scene from hell itself. Bodies from both sides littered the floor while the great machines battled it out. On'Sarax had already lost an arm, yet still she fought on against her hated enemies. Most of the ground troops from both sides had now pulled back, doing their best to avoid the bloodbath around the titanic creatures. On they went while Spartan, Khan, and two marines reached the top of the ramp. Waiting before them were the last two ancient machines.

They waited, shoulder-to-shoulder with the face of the demonic entity directly behind them. Spartan lifted an arm and blasted the face, but as before, nothing happened.

"You cannot win, traitor!"

One of the machines emitted a hissing sound, and from several hidden access points came Thegns. These were the new models, each with the thick hide and reflective blades. The first five were easily blasted, but the numbers kept on coming. A marine was butchered before Spartan's eyes, and even as he killed the Thegn, two more took its place. Khan took a step back and opened fire with his gun taken from a fallen Vanguard. Dozens of the creatures fell, and then came the Decurions. Three fell from the ceiling, directly onto Khan. One stabbed at his damaged shoulder; the other wrenched the firearm from his very hands.

"This is the end, for both of you!" said the machine with a cackle.

Spartan was knocked back, and Khan pinned to the wall with two blades from the machines. More rushed in to surround them and then began to move down the ramp, heading for the battling machines on the ground. A dozen more Ghost Warriors entered and formed up in a line behind their master.

"Our Tomb Ships are here, and so are our legions. You have no more reinforcements. It is over."

It lifted its arm and pointed to Spartan.

"You have done well, my friend. Now kneel and ready

yourself. We promised you immortality."

Khan forced his way from where the Decurions had pinned him, cast one aside, and then swung at the enemy commander. His blades curved perfectly and made it to within a meter when Spartan lifted his own weapon arm and parried the blow. He stepped out in front of his friend and waved him off.

"No, not today."

More Decurions advanced around Khan and forced him back to the wall. He lifted his arms to strike, but multiple weapons from the Ghost Warriors turned to point right at his head.

"Good," said Spartan.

He then turned back around to face the machines and without hesitation, dropped to one knee.

"The plan was costly, the sacrifice of the Ancients was a heavy price to pay. I am sorry it took longer than expected. Now you have all of their greatest warriors and the entire Allied fleet in one place. You can end this war."

"Yes," said the machine with a groaning sigh.

"We are the custodians of the Core. We were never its masters. My kin have already transferred into its heart. You have done all that we asked of you, Spartan. You destroyed the traitor, devastated their fleet, and then brought their survivors here for their execution. You truly are our greatest creation, Spartan, warlord of our people."

The machine moved close to Spartan and looked down

at the kneeling Ghost Warrior armor.

"It is time for you to carry out your last orders, and then we will move you to join us, for eternity, as promised."

The machine extended its arm and pointed at Khan.

"You're right," said Spartan in a cool, calm voice.

The machine let out a long, slow hiss, but Spartan continued talking.

"They are sending troops to the rear decks. They want the Core. Their last troops are looking for it."

The machine let out a clicking sound.

"Good, then they will die like the rest. Even if they find it, they will have to fight past three hundred of our most experienced Ghost Warriors. Excellent work, Spartan."

Spartan's eyes flickered inside his armor as he watched the new orders being sent throughout the ships. Legions of warriors were moving about to protect various subsystems. It was the newly activated group of three hundred that caught his eye. They had been given a single location, and it was nowhere near where he would have expected. He sent the signal and waited for the acknowledgement. It took nearly ten seconds, but the ID codes matched Admiral Anderson.

"Thank you." He said quietly. "This is over...for you."

He lifted himself to his feet so that he was upright and tall before the enemy machine. The Biomech machine took a step back in surprise.

"Z'Kanthu lives, and you never controlled me, not

once. We played you, and like arrogant fools, you fell for it, just as we knew you would."

"It's over," said Spartan, almost repeating their words, "End the battle and surrender, or suffer obliteration."

One of the machines emitted a noise, and the Decurions nearby slowed and then stopped, though they kept their limbs poised to continue the fight right alongside the Ghost Warriors. Gunfire continued elsewhere in the ship, but for now, this one section was free of violence. The machine looked around, as though stunned it had been surrounded so quickly. The second machine appeared less patient. It began moving, and the first tried to stop it. With a shake and a cut with its blade, it pushed away to face Spartan.

"No, you are lost. Our souls live on forever."

The machine hissed and then swung at him. They were evenly matched in height and mass, crashing into each other like a pair of wrestlers. Both swung their reflective blades and cut chunks of armor off with each strike. Khan tried to help, but the Decurions kept him pinned down.

"No, leave him be."

The machine swung low and embedded its arm deep into Spartan's flank. The blade penetrated the armor but missed his flesh by millimeters. He placed both of his arms against its torso and opened fire at point blank range. The first two shots burned through carapace, but the next six turned its innards into melted goo. It dropped to the ground, a messy ruin.

"Another one down."

He lifted his arms up high into the air and howled, but the enemy was already on him. Thegns leapt at him while Decurions hacked at his limbs. Spartan swung his left arm, and another Thegn died. A bright blue flash cleared the Thegns around him. One Decurion lifted a limb, and two massive bursts of fire tore it apart. Spartan shook his head and looked to the doorways to the left. He expected to see more of the enemy horde, but it was Olik and a Byotai warrior, covered from head to toe in thick armor.

"Spartan, need a hand?" said Olik, laughing.

The Jötnar swung his arms and cleared the open space right in front of the two remaining Biomech commanders. The machines stepped back, but more marines moved in around them. The Ghost Warriors held back, waiting to defend their kin with their infinite machine bodies. Only one of the Biomech commanders remained, and it stepped back behind its wall of defenders. Spartan lifted his head to look at the remaining machine. It tried to step back, but the thick metal and stone of the demonic sculpture pressed into its armor. He moved closer until he was just a meter away. The machine looked almost identical, apart from the fact that Spartan's armor was shredded and covered in blood.

"The war is over," it said. "My troops have blocked off your escape, the breaches are sealed, and the Core is surrounded. Your forces will never get close to it."

Spartan extended one of his blades and held it to the throat of the machine. The nearby Ghost Warriors all pointed their weapons at him, but he merely laughed and shook his head.

"You are wrong."

The machine hissed and said no more. The sound of fighting had died down to nothing, and Khan took the opportunity to walk to the end of the high level. He looked down to see the bodies on both sides. Machines, Thegns, and Decurions had pulled back and eyed each other cautiously.

Spartan sighed.

"You ancient fool. Z'Kanthu managed one last trick before your people erased him from your Core."

He noticed the shudder from the machine.

"Yes, you know where he was, and you know what he could do. Now, you have sixty seconds before your racial heritage is nothing but a bad memory. Right now our entire fleet has its arsenal pointing right at your Core."

He pointed to the sacred sculpture and hoped against hope that his ruse would work. "This is merely the antenna, the communication mast for your kin. Falling back here was a good ruse to draw us away from the prize while your reinforcements arrived. Now, accept my terms, or face the genocide of your race, as you have tried with mine."

The machine hissed again. It bent down and extended

its arms in submission. There was no pause this time.

"What do you want?"

Spartan nodded.

"I want your unconditional surrender, and I want it now. Stop the fighting."

Spartan's nostrils twitched as he said that last word. He wanted to strike the machine. The sculpture itself flashed and pulsed, and then a great blast of energy ripped outward, engulfing everything there. Apart from the shock, it had no effect on Spartan and his allies, but one by one the Thegns and newly arrival Biomech creatures turned to face him. Spartan approached the two Thegns waiting alongside the machine.

"Who do you serve?"

They looked to each other and then back to him; neither said a thing. He looked back to Khan and then to Major Terson who had just finished climbing the long curved ramp.

"They've all stopped. Anderson says the ships have closed their gun ports. What's going on?"

"The Biomechs have surrendered their forces on this ship."

"Why?"

Spartan looked to him.

"That was the price."

He looked back to the machine.

"My son, my wife. They have all suffered for your wars.

Do you think this is over with an agreement? Can you ever be trusted?"

The machine lifted itself tall. It held its arms out to protect itself. Several of the Decurions moved close to its body, each of them watching him carefully.

"You sent the signal to all warriors on this ship? All of your forces have received their final order to lower their weapons?"

The machine replied in the affirmative.

Spartan turned back and pulled himself back into his armor. The petals of plate clamped down tightly. He took a step back and then accessed the myriad of digital channels to communicate with.

"What's he doing?" Major Terson asked.

Khan checked his weapons were active but shook his head.

"Major, I really don't know."

"The last thing Z'Kanthu did was to send me this."

Spartan closed his eyes and recalled the information Z'Kanthu had given him in their last moments. He concentrated and then spoke the words directly to the Core.

Still be alive, you crazed fool.

He waited, desperately hoping that the mind of Z'Kanthu was still there, drifting throughout the artificial intelligence Core that housed almost infinite data.

Come on.

Deep inside the ship, the Core sent out its wail, a shockwave that severed connections between warrior and Core. One by one, the Ghost Warriors lost contact with the Core and leaned or tilted, their systems now devoid of control. It was temporary, but more than enough for Spartan to see they were offline.

"You have a thirty-second window at most, destroy it!"

* * *

Captain Darryl Wilks hid behind the line of generators and looked to the lines of machines in front of them as they continued to march off to the right. The walls to the Citadel, as his men had nicknamed the structure were impressive.

"Sir, there's no way the charges will blow that thing," said Corporal Sherril.

He looked back at his squad of engineers. He'd lost almost half of his number to injuries getting this far, and now they were directly between the hull of the ship and the location of the Core.

"Son, we're not here for that. All we do it create an opening. The Admiral will do the rest."

He watched as the unarmed SAAR robot moved into position nearly two hundred meters away and right behind a series of bulkheads.

"Captain, it's ready," said Tech Sergeant Gardiner.

"Good. Get in there, now!"

The entire unit climbed through the blast door and turned back to look at their handiwork. No sooner had the last marine moved through when the signal finally arrived.

"Do it!"

The SAAR robot vanished in a localized atomic blast that tore a section fifty meters in diameter through the side of the ship. Armored plating, gun turrets, and bulkheads were torn apart to expose the Citadel to the void of space. Captain Wilks hung to the nearby bulkhead with all of his strength and sent the signal he'd been waiting to send for what seemed like an eternity.

"Admiral, she's breached."

At the same time, Tech Sergeant Gardiner activated the blast door and brought it down to protect them.

"Get back to the rendezvous!"

The marines ran as fast as their legs would carry them, far away from the sight of the horrendous bombardment. Like the mighty dragon of ancient myth with its single weak spot, the combined firepower of the fleet hammered the wounded ship. Railguns did the work for a change, as round after round smashed through the weakened structure and right into the housing of the Citadel. Kinetic rounds tore holes into the plating, but it was the volley of siege atomics that did the final work. With nothing to impede their progress, they struck the plating of the Citadel and exploded with the heat of a small star.

* * *

Kha'Dri, Taxxu, Uncharted Space

The ship shuddered as a mighty blast ripped through the innards of the vessel. More and more blasts continued, and Spartan turned his attention to the last of the Biomech commanders. He walked close and then stopped directly in front of it. Three Ghost Warriors toppled to the ground right next to his feet as he waited there.

"Traitor," hissed the Biomech.

Spartan's first blow stuck the armored shell, but he kept at it like a wild man attacking a punch bag. The machine struggled to defend itself, but Spartan had already shattered the shell of its torso. It cradled its limbs around the body to protect itself, but Spartan had become a beast. He yanked it to the ground.

"Finish him!"

Two of the marines ran over and emptied their clips into it without a moment's hesitation. Spartan turned to call for Khan, but his friend was already there. The Ghost Warriors began to reactivate one at a time and threw themselves at their aggressors. The battle was savage and evenly matched, but Spartan knew they had the edge now; there was a chance. As he thought that, a pair of the enemy crashed into him and forced him over the ledge.

"No!"

He flailed, desperately trying to grab the edge. One hand missed, and as he slipped away, he embedded the reflective blade deep into the obsidian material. As he hung there, the two machines looked over and down at him, one took careful aim.

This is not how it was supposed to end.

The guns began to heat up, and then both tipped over and fell down past him. He looked down to watch them crash to the ground, and then spotted the other Ghost Warriors dropping around him like flies. He looked back up, and the armored arm of Khan extended out to pull him up. With a firm yank, his friend pulled him back to the ledge and away from certain death.

"The Core is gone, and with it, all of their race."

Spartan shook his head. "No, there are some on board their battleships."

Khan shook his head.

"No. They were all brought aboard this fortress to protect the Core and their masters. Their last warriors are leaderless. They are just carrying out whatever their last orders were."

Major Terson walked close to the two of them.

"What have you done, Spartan? You are committing us to genocide. With the Core and their ancestors gone, the war will never end. They are aimless and leaderless. What of the legions back in the Helios Sector?"

Spartan walked to the ledge and looked down to the

blood-covered shapes of On'Sarax and her comrades. They waited in a circle and chanted something in an odd, alien sequence. Even as they spoke, the Thegns and Decurions around them stopped fighting and lowered themselves as though in the presence of gods.

"No. This is their domain. On'Sarax and the others are their Machine Gods now, the last of the Ancients. They will send out the word to every corner of our territories. This war is over. It is time for their warriors to come home. Z'Kanthu paid the ultimate price to end this war, and to free the last of his people."

The interior of the ship had already changed from the short burst of violence and death to one of celebratory gunfire. Olik and Khan moved up to Spartan as he opened up his armor. He began to step out and then changed his mind.

"What now?" Khan asked.

"You can't go home, not yet," said Olik.

Major Terson heard them talking and moved to his left, then right to survey the vast numbers of dead.

"Victor or not, you're not too popular back home. If you ask me, I'd stay away from Alliance jurisdiction for now. Last thing you want is to go home a war criminal."

Spartan nodded in grim agreement.

"I've got nothing to go back for."

Khan looked confused.

"So where then?"

Finally, Spartan smiled. He closed the armor up so that he was once again encased in metal, and then slapped his friend on the back.

"That, my friend, is a damned good question."

On'Sarax and one of her yellow painted kin finished their long climb to the top to meet with the survivors of the battle. She stood in front of Spartan and gave him a short, slightly uncomfortable bow. She then went to the sculpture and placed an armored hand onto the object. It immediately glowed brightly.

"I am giving the call to return. You have our word. The machines will be deactivated, the ships scrapped, and the biologicals..."

"Yes?" Khan asked, "What about them?"

"They will be freed."

Khan looked to Spartan with hopeful eyes. Spartan shook his head in amazement.

"What the hell do you want to do with legions of Thegns and other...creatures?"

Khan laughed.

"They helped us win this damned war."

Spartan nodded in complete agreement.

"Very true, my friend."

He looked at the bodies of the smashed machines, torn bodies, and thousands of rounds of discarded ammunition. He couldn't imagine how many had now been killed in the war, but he was certain it was finally over. He looked back to Olik and Khan.

"You know what? I'm sure we can find them something to do."

* * *

Grand Palace, Terra Nova

Senator Yatsenyuk and her committee members looked at the images coming in from each of the war zones on the military tactical display. The unit had only recently been installed, and around it stood the virtual images of the primary commanders on the ground. Admiral Churchill was the only member of the military actually physically present in the room.

"So, Spascia and Eos are clear of Biomechs. How about Helios Prime?"

General Rivers looked as grim as ever.

"They have been marching back to their ships for the last three days. We've retaken ground they took and taken control of their fortifications. Even if they changed their minds now, they would be lost. It's the same everywhere."

General Gun grunted at this.

"They have left Spascia, not that there's much left of it."

Admiral Anderson then spoke.

"Senator. Our forces have suffered terrible losses. Over a hundred ships, if we include the transports. Infantry has taken a beating, and our allies are not much better. The Byotai have their own problems, and the Helions, well, they don't even know where to start."

"I understand, Admiral. We have arranged for aid convoys to begin immediately. They asked for our help, and they will get it. As a provisional member of the Alliance family, they will be treated like any of our own worlds."

She moved the back of her hand nervously across her chin.

"That brings us to the Black Rift and that can of worms."

Admiral Anderson lifted his hand and answered without waiting any further.

"The Black Rift is secure, and the Spacebridge, against our better efforts is permanent. We have seven of the so called Rift Engines, and the rebels are prepared to show us how to use this new technology to create permanent Spacebridges between planets and stars."

Another of the senators started to speak, but Senator Yatsenyuk talked the man down.

"What of the Biomechs?"

The man would no longer be silenced, and he called out from the back of the small group.

"What of Spartan? Because of him we were unable to relieve Spascia in time. Thousands more died in the atomic strikes. His hands are bloody with the..."

"Senator, I was not aware that you were personally

involved in the relief effort. I did not see you there," Gun snapped back.

"Spartan had a choice, to end the war or send our last chance for peace to protect his son. He made the only choice, and it worked. The enemy is defeated; every one of them is dead. Their Core is gone, as are their memories and their history. For that, he paid a price in blood, both strangers and his own family. Be careful before you judge him."

"It is true," said Admiral Churchill.

He turned to face Senator Yatsenyuk.

"Their legacy of the Biomechs remains. We have their technology, and we have what is left of their military forces. Their machinery is being scrapped, but the Thegn foot soldiers and their other biological warriors are a problem."

"Yes," said Gun, "and it is not a problem we can wish away. They were created for war, just as my own people were. We must find a way for them to integrate. I will not stand for their extermination."

Senator Yatsenyuk smiled as best she could.

"General, this regime has changed. We understand and appreciate your long commitment to the Alliance. We will find a way for the war victims on all sides to co-exist."

She then looked to the tactical display and pressed a button. The maps vanished and were replaced by the model of Spartan, resplendent in his armor.

"What of Spartan? Has he gone off the reservation?"

Gun laughed at the question.

"We won't be seeing him for quite some time. He needs to be left alone. His losses are great, and his remaining friends are few."

Senator Yatsenyuk nodded slowly.

"We understand. The decision amongst the emergency committee was not unanimous, but we have still decided to grant Spartan, and any that worked with him, full amnesty. His actions were from the very beginning in the interests of the Alliance, and to end this war."

Admiral Churchill walked in front of the group and next to the Senator.

"It is a minor thing, but in recognition of the supreme sacrifices of so many in this war, Alliance High Command has requested, and been granted the privilege of creating a new honor."

He looked back and a young Marine captain, dressed impeccably in her dress uniform walked into the room. She marched to the Admiral and saluted crisply. Admiral Churchill removed the small medal in the shape of the Helion Nexus, the image first seen on Biomech technology back before the first Rift was created to the Orion Nebula.

"The Order of the Nexus War is to be granted to all forces, regular, militia, human, and alien that fought for peace."

He replaced the object and then pulled out another.

"From the metal taken from the destruction of CCS

Crusader in the Uprising, we have created the Order of Victory. This honor is specifically to those that performed actions of supreme courage in times of great adversity."

He paused for a moment and looked to those present.

"Colonel Teresa Morato is to be the first to receive the Order of Victory, for her supreme courage in the Nexus War, and for her selfless sacrifice in the Battle of Spascia."

He looked to Senator Yatsenyuk who gave him the nod.

"The second recipient is Spartan, former Marine, troublemaker, rule breaker, and the greatest hero of not one, but two wars. As legate of the Alliance, he is a man that has done more for the races of this sector of space than perhaps any other soul."

He raised his hand in a quick salute.

"We salute their courage, and their deeds will never be forgotten."

"Never forgotten," said each of them, but none louder than by Gun.

As the sound died down, one of the senators made to move. Even from his position far away, Gun could spot the movement.

"Admiral Churchill. How many more names are there?"

The officer smiled as he answered.

"Another two hundred and seventy-three."

"I would like to hear them all."

"As would I," added General Rivers.

Senator Yatsenyuk looked to the other senators, the

majority of whom appeared to agree with the General.

"Of course. It is the least any of us can do."

Admiral Churchill lifted his secpad and held up the medal once more.

"For conspicuous gallantry in thirteen major star ship engagements, Admiral Lewis. Hero of Helios Prime and the scourge of the Micaya Shipyards."

Each of them, military and civilian remained on their feet.

"Never forgotten."

EPILOGUE

Who were the victors of the Great Biomech War? Many worlds were left in ruins, and the armed forces of the Helions were smashed beyond recognition. Alliance forces were heavily eroded, yet the core infrastructure had been ramped up to a war footing. Higher employment and greater productivity had resulted in even the average Carthago citizen having the chance for a decent life. Expectations following the crisis were higher than they had been for generations. For the Helions it would be a time for austerity, but for the Alliance it was the beginning of a golden age.

The Price of War

Spascia City, Helios Prime

Spartan reached the top of the mountain and looked back to gaze upon the ancient, smashed remains of the Helion world. Like most places visited by the Biomechs, little remained worth protecting. It was over a month since the fighting had stopped and still the fires burned.

"So this is where it all happened?" he said quietly.

At his side stood the figures of Khan and Olik, both scarred veterans of the war. For the first time in months, all of them waited on the peak without their armor. Spartan had reverted to militaryesque clothing, with a layer tunic, loose pants, and a tight cut leather jacket. He wore a bandolier across his chest and slung down low on his thigh sat a Khreenk pistol. The sound of loose rocks caught their attention, and one by one they looked back at the shape of a lone Jötnar coming up behind them.

"Thought I'd find you up here," said Gun.

He made the last few steps and hobbled as he moved. Finally, he reached the other three and stopped to look upon the battlefield.

"We could have done with you all on this battlefield. I've never seen anything like it."

Spartan swallowed painfully, and Gun immediately realized he'd said the wrong thing. He began to speak, to explain himself, but Spartan reached out and placed his hands on the Jötnar's arm.

"I know. I could have done a lot differently. Teresa and I made a deal, and it cost us. She would come here to protect our family. I would stay with the fleet and end the war."

Gun looked to Olik, Khan, and back to Spartan.

"You both succeeded, then."

Spartan looked to the mountain that was now partially collapsed. The wreckage from the multiple Biomech ships still lay all over the site, with another five ships jammed into the chasm. Part of the mountain had given way into a great fissure, and deep inside it burned the heart of one of the enemy starships. The reactor had gone critical during the battle, and it still burned like the inside of a volcano.

"We both paid one hell of a price. Jack and Teresa dead, half our friends gone in the fighting, and this."

He extended his two arms out to encompass the burned husk of a planet. None of the others had anything else to say, so they watched as dozens of civilian ships continued the long process of dropping off aid supplies and taking away the wounded. Above them, as always, sat the squat shapes of Alliance ships. Gun reached into a pouch and pulled out six shapes. They were the medals he had been sent from Terra Nova. He held out his hand for the other three to take them.

"What's that?" Olik asked.

"Medals, from Alliance High Command for all of us."

Spartan turned to spit on the ground.

"It was Admiral Churchill's idea. It isn't for me, or you. They are to remind everybody else of what we all had to do to end this."

Spartan looked at him and then slowly nodded in agreement. None of them took the medals.

"The extra two?" Spartan asked, though he already knew the answer.

"Teresa and Jack. Teresa was the first to be awarded for the entire campaign."

Again he raised an eyebrow and extended his hand further. Spartan shook his head.

"No."

He then twisted his head about and nodded in the direction of the superheated fissure off to the side of the mountain.

"Are you sure?" asked Gun.

Spartan nodded but Olik spoke.

"Hand them over."

Each of them took random medals until only three remained. Spartan looked at them, but they might easily have been each other's as his, Teresa's, or Jack's. He took them and then turned to the fissure. One by one they dropped the small trinkets down, and they vanished into the fire. Spartan's face glowed red in the heat coming up, but he refused to look away until he lost sight of them. Khan shook his head and looked off to a Byotai transport as it landed in a temporary landing bay. Its long, elegant wings were almost transparent at the center, and it positioned itself nearby to an Alliance Mauler. Vanguard Marines used their heavy augmented armor to help unload supplies to load onto the scores of wheeled vehicles.

"So, what now?"

He looked to the other three but stopped upon seeing Spartan. His face was hard, stern, and drained of emotion.

"I have a few ideas."

They moved in close to listen to what he had to say. Finally, he stopped, and the three Jötnar joined him to watch from the ridge. The ruined city seemed an apt place to think for such people. Warriors in the center of a warzone, with no war to fight.

"Are you in?" Spartan asked.

Khan was the first to look to his friend.

"Did you need to ask?"

THE BLACK RIFT